MR. SEDUCTIVE

by

SERENITY WOODS

DEDICATION

To Tony & Chris, my Kiwi boys.

CONTENTS

Chapter One

All day long, the ground had rumbled beneath his feet.

Toby thought he'd grown used to the sensation of living atop some monstrous beast that stirred restlessly in its sleep, but even so, as he placed his groceries on the supermarket conveyor belt, he couldn't help looking at the checkout assistant with alarm when the tiled floor trembled again.

She swiped an item across the scanner and smirked. "I'm guessing you're new to Christchurch."

He retrieved his wallet from his back pocket, not missing the amused glance from the young lad packing the carrier bags. "Actually, I've been here six weeks. I thought I'd got used to the shocks."

"Don't worry." She met his gaze with a flirtatious bat of her eyelashes. "If there's an earthquake, I'll protect you."

He grinned. She couldn't have been older than eighteen, and her tiny frame wouldn't have protected a mouse. "I might hold you to that. I scream like a girl when I'm scared, though, I have to warn you."

She giggled and gestured to the keypad. "When you're ready."

He swiped his debit card. About ten feet away, a toddler yelled, echoing loud through the afternoon quiet of the supermarket, and he glanced around. The boy sat in a shopping trolley and clearly wanted to be somewhere else. His mother had fastened his safety belt. The boy did *not* want it fastened.

Toby's lips twisted. His own mother had told him how he used to show her up in supermarkets. She'd said people staring made it worse, so he was about to turn away when something about the woman caught his eye.

Average height and slender, she had sleek brown hair pulled off her face in a clip. She wore long brown pants and an orange top so bright it made him want to don his sunglasses. But the bag resting on her hip was what caught his attention. The slogan on the chocolate-brown material read *Life is Short, Read Shakespeare* and bore an illustration of the English bard.

There was more than one bag like that in the world, surely. It wasn't her.

Having finally fastened the belt, she glanced over her shoulder.

Their eyes met. Toby inhaled sharply, his heart giving a gigantic thump as adrenalin surged through him. A vivid image of the woman lying naked, eyes closed in sublime pleasure as he thrust inside her, shot through his mind. Whoa. That was the quickest he'd achieved an erection since he was fourteen.

She stared at his face, and then her eyes widened as she obviously realized she wasn't dreaming.

He couldn't think what to do or say. The toddler squawked, but the woman remained staring at Toby, shock apparently freezing her feet to the floor. Even from across the aisle, he could see the flush fill her cheeks. So she remembered the holiday in Fiji too, then. She'd been so hot in bed, she'd almost set the covers alight.

He opened his mouth to say something—anything, conscious of the checkout assistant watching them both with amusement.

And then a huge bang shook the supermarket, and the world fell apart around him.

He ducked instinctively, swearing as the ground heaved. Crash after crash echoed through the building, shelves tipping and tins falling to the floor.

The checkout girl squealed and dropped to her knees, crawling under her till, and the packing lad ran around to join her. Toby froze, unable to believe his eyes as the tiled floor at the other end of the supermarket rose. *The monster's awake.* The thought shot through his head crazily, and he ducked again as a nearby display of boxes exploded into the air as if it weighed no more than polystyrene.

A wail brought his attention back to the woman and the trolley, and with alarm he saw she was having trouble getting the toddler's belt undone. Stepping over fallen bottles of bleach, he ran toward her and skidded to a halt by the trolley.

"I can't get it undone." She tugged with panic at the plastic clip, trying to keep the wailing boy's hands out of the way. "First I couldn't fasten it, and now it won't come apart."

Toby took the two sides of the belt in his hands and wrenched it open with brute force. He lifted the boy out of the trolley, tucked him under one arm, ignoring his squeals, and pushed her toward the exit. "Quick!"

They'd taken two steps when the ground split under the nearest shelving. The metal racks crashed down on top of the trolley, crumpling it as if it were made of tinfoil.

His heart in his mouth and the boy tight under his arm, Toby ran toward the exit. Even before they were halfway there, he realized they weren't going to make it. The ground buckled ahead of them, spilling tins and packets across their path, and she stumbled and fell.

She pushed herself to her feet and then fell again as the ground heaved, throwing her off balance. Under his arm, the child cried out, clamping his arms and legs around Toby, and Toby tightened his grip, determined nothing was going to wrench the boy out of his arms.

He bent and put an arm around the woman's waist and heaved her up, half-lifting and half-dragging her across to a table against the far wall. Pushing her underneath, he passed the child to her and then followed them under, covering them with his body as a horrendous bang echoed through the building.

Clouds of dust filled the aisles, and he put his hand over the boy's nose and mouth as it blew over them. For a moment, he couldn't catch his breath. Grit filled his mouth, and his lungs burned as he tried to inhale. A huge crack split the air, and something came crashing down onto the table. For a brief, scary moment, he thought the three of them were going to be squashed into a pancake. But the table held.

He'd tried to tuck his legs under and only realized he hadn't been completely successful when something fell on his feet. Swearing loudly, he curled around the woman, pushing the boy between them, and held them both tightly as the world continued to wrench itself apart.

In all, it could only have lasted about forty seconds, but it felt like a lifetime. Toby had never been so scared. The noise was deafening, crashes and screams and hideous screeching sounds that must have been the twisting of metal beams, but made him think once again that somewhere beneath the earth's surface medieval monsters were battling it out and ripping each other apart with giant teeth.

And then, all of a sudden, it stopped. In the distance, glass continued to shatter and displays crumbled. The ground trembled, but it stopped heaving and throwing them up in the air. For a moment, though, he stayed where he was, too frightened to move. He'd been in an earthquake. He couldn't believe it.

Then, finally, he turned onto his back and pushed up onto his elbows. He had a vision of looking at the bottom half of his body and seeing his legs missing, but to his relief they were intact. He wiggled both feet, relieved when the worst he felt was a stinging where falling debris had bounced and grazed him.

Next to him the boy shifted, and Toby looked down, thankful to see both the toddler and his mother still in the land of the living. She pulled back and lifted the boy with urgent hands, presumably checking for blood and making sure he was breathing. He coughed and rubbed his grit-filled eyes with his tiny fists, but he didn't cry.

"Thank God," she whispered, clutching him to her.

Her eyes, huge in her dust-streaked face, met Toby's over the boy's head. It couldn't have been a less romantic setting. Toby knew he must look a sight, covered in gray dust and probably blood too, judging from the throbbing behind his left ear. But at that moment, all he could think was *I found her*, and in spite of their predicament, his heart swelled.

"Hey, Esther," he said.

She blinked. "Hey, Toby."

"We're alive," he observed. "Result!"

She laughed with relief. "Yeah."

He couldn't help himself. Slipping a hand behind her head, he leaned forward and pressed his lips to hers. He'd only meant to snatch a quick peck, but to his surprise, she opened her mouth, her tongue searching for his. He moved his arm around her, drawing her to him, and they exchanged a deep, dusty, heartfelt kiss.

A sneeze brought them apart.

The boy coughed. "When the ground went bang, you said fuck," he accused Toby.

Her eyes widened. "Charlie!"

"I did," Toby said, still feeling the press of her lips on his. "Sorry about that, but the situation kind of called for it." Charlie had a round, plump face, curly blond hair—now covered with dust—and big brown eyes.

Eyes the mirror image of his own.

Toby's gaze slid to Esther's. He calculated rapidly. The boy looked about two and a half years old. He'd met her on holiday in December. Three years and two months ago.

No. Surely not.

She met his gaze calmly. Then, without saying anything, she rolled over and crawled out from under the table, bending to pull Charlie with her.

Toby pushed himself backward and got to his feet. Only then did he comprehend the extent of the devastation. The whole west wall of the supermarket had collapsed, and sunlight poured through the open roof, highlighting the rubble. All around, the cries of hurt or trapped people echoed through the building.

"Jesus." Horror filled him. How long would it be before the emergency services arrived?

Esther had picked up her son, who'd started to cry. She tried to soothe him, stroking his back, whispering in his ear.

"Is he okay?" Toby took a step toward them, but she moved backward, tightening her arms around the boy, and he stopped. She didn't want him near the kid. The exultant feeling that had swelled inside him died down.

She stroked Charlie's hair. "He lost Bear."

"Bear?"

"His Pooh Bear. It's okay—it could have been a lot worse." She looked around. "Damn it. I dropped my bag somewhere under all that rubble too."

Behind them, a hanging beam fell to the floor with a crash, and they all jumped.

"We've got to get out of here in case the place collapses," Toby said. There would be time later to talk to her about the boy. For now, he had to get them to safety. Debris had blocked the exit, but the window nearby had broken, giving access onto the street. "Come on, and mind the glass."

He led the way over to the window. Shards of broken glass still jutted from the frame, so he removed them carefully before climbing over. "Pass him to me," he instructed her, holding out his arms.

She hesitated for a moment, then handed the boy across. Toby held him in one arm and offered a hand to help her, but she ignored it and climbed over on her own. Letting his arm drop, he turned his attention instead to the child.

Charlie snuffled against his dust-streaked shirt. "Bear," he mumbled. "I want Bear."

"Shh, it's okay." Toby stroked his hair. His heart pounded. "I'll find him for you."

Esther took Charlie from his arms. "Don't make promises you can't keep," she said sharply. "I've never lied to him, and I'm not about to start now."

He put his hands in his jeans pockets, unsettled by her defensiveness. "I'm not lying. I'm going back in there. I'll keep an eye open for the toy."

Her eyes widened. "You can't! It's dangerous—it could collapse at any minute."

"There are people trapped in there."

"The emergency services will be here soon. It's their job. They always say never to go back into a building after an earthquake."

He shrugged. "I've got to do it. I can't stand here while people are in there, in trouble."

She crushed Charlie to her. Her large eyes met his, hard as emeralds. "You're not being brave—you're being an idiot."

The comment stung. He wasn't doing it to be a hero. The thought of going back made his stomach clench. But there had been other children in the shop and housewives buying the family shopping. The young checkout girl and the teenage boy who did the packing. How could he live with himself if he went home without knowing if they'd made it?

He glanced over at the building, then back at her. "How will I find you again?"

"I'll find you," she said. She must have seen the wariness in his face, because her expression softened. "I promise."

His gaze fell to Charlie. "Is…is he mine?"

She swallowed. Then she gave a small nod.

His eyes came back to her cool, emotionless ones. How could she be so calm? A hundred different emotions roiled inside him, and he clenched his fists in an attempt to keep them in.

What a day to find out he'd fathered a child. He was going home at the weekend. He'd booked the flights, and his best mate was getting married in a week's time—he had to be there. And after that, he had plans for his life. Things he wanted to do.

Bringing up a child wasn't one of them.

He couldn't think how to put his emotion into words. One day, he would have liked to have had a family. But not yet. His friends and family teased him constantly for being a Peter Pan. What would they say when they found out he had a son? Not that it appeared he had any choice in the matter. He was a father, whether he wanted to be one or not.

Nobody would blame him if he left the scene now to work things through with her. He hesitated. Then, behind him, someone screamed.

"Be careful." He ran back to the window and climbed over the ledge into the building.

Chapter Two

Esther walked the short distance home to find her apartment devastated, sat there for a while looking up at it, and then wandered back to the tent that the firefighters and aid workers had set up as a central rescue point. She accepted a cup of coffee more out of politeness than anything, and fed Charlie bits of a ham sandwich as firefighters brought survivors out of the rubble and secured the area as much as they could.

Someone tried to get her to go with them to their house, but she refused politely and continued to sit on one of the fold-up chairs a volunteer had kindly donated. Charlie was unusually content to sit still, eyes wide at the sight of the firefighters and army personnel rushing around rescuing people.

She saw Toby from time to time over the next few hours, clearing piles of debris and helping injured people to safety. When they first turned up, the fire service had tried to get him to stay outside. He'd ignored them, though, and continued to help move beams and bricks to release those trapped. She guessed that eventually they must have decided they'd only be able to keep him out by restraining him, and that seemed pointless when he was obviously doing some good.

She rocked Charlie in her arms as he dozed, and accepted a blanket from one of the ambulance men and a drink from another as she waited for Toby to tire. It proved to be a long wait. She'd forgotten how tall, how strong he was. He must be six three or four, she thought as he emerged from the wreckage carrying a woman as if she weighed no more than a pile of blankets. He'd liked to lift Esther up to kiss her, wrapping her legs around his waist as he lowered his lips to hers. The memory made her shiver.

He'd been big three years ago, but he'd broadened even more since then, his muscles filling out the T-shirt that had been white when she'd first seen him standing at the checkout, although it was now almost completely black. His dark curly hair fell across his forehead in the same wild mop. The boyish good looks she remembered had matured into a rugged, bristled face, which nevertheless was still handsome enough to make her catch her breath. He tripped over bricks occasionally, proving to her that he'd gained no more coordination over his large feet than he'd had in Fiji. But that didn't detract from the fact that he was movie-star gorgeous.

He was a carpenter and had lived in the Northland. What was he doing here? Probably helping rebuild Christchurch after the earthquake the previous September, she thought sadly. The city had just started to get back on its feet. And now look what had happened.

A firefighter caught Toby's arm and gestured toward the tent. He put his hands on his hips and nodded wearily before making his way over.

Pushing herself to her feet, she lifted Charlie higher in her arms. He stirred and woke, looking around blearily. Toby ducked under the flap at the top of the tent, stopping as he saw her. Pleasure and relief lit his tired face. "You're here." He walked over to them.

"You have the stamina of a steam engine." She handed him a bottle of water. "Don't you ever get tired?"

"When I get going, there's no stopping me." He winked, confirming he'd totally meant the double entendre, and laughed as she rolled her eyes. Taking a mouthful of water, he walked outside, swirled and spat, then drank half the bottle in one go. "Jeez. That's the best drink I've had in, like, ever."

"Do you want something to eat? There are sandwiches over there."

"In a minute." He wiped his mouth and came back to stand before them. "How are you two doing?"

"Okay." She kissed Charlie's curly hair where he nuzzled up against her. "We're in one piece anyway." She cleared her throat and met Toby's big brown eyes, so like Charlie's. "Thanks to you."

Admitting she was in his debt wasn't easy, but she was honest enough to accept that if he hadn't helped her to get Charlie out of the trolley, the falling rubble would have buried them.

He said nothing for a moment. Her cheeks grew warm as his lips gradually curved. Was he thinking about Fiji? That moment when they'd met on the beach? The memory still made her heart pound, the attraction that had shot between them, sharp and powerful as an electric shock. She'd never felt anything like it before, or since. One-night stands had never been her thing, but she'd gone to bed with him willingly, and the sex had been so great that she'd returned to his room the next night, and the next. In fact they'd barely left the complex the entire fortnight.

His gaze moved to her lips. He wanted to kiss her again. She remembered the way he'd pressed his lips to hers in the supermarket, under the table. Both of them had been covered in dust, grit in their mouths and their hearts still racing from the way the ground had ripped itself apart, and yet he'd managed to ignite something within her that had remained dormant for a long, long time.

"Bear," Charlie said. He raised his head. "Did you find him?"

"Oh, sweetheart." She kissed his forehead. "Toby's been far too busy to look for Bear. People have to come first, honey. I'm sorry." She bit her lip as Charlie's eyes went glassy. He'd had Bear since he was born. Losing him somehow symbolized the whole futile situation and everything else they'd lost.

"Ah," Toby said. "But I never go back on a promise." He fumbled behind his back and pulled something out from the waistband of his jeans.

"Bear!" Charlie screamed, snatched the soft toy, and buried his face in the grimy fur.

"Oh my God, how did you…" Her voice failed her.

"I knew he'd probably dropped him when I lifted him out of the trolley. Luckily there wasn't too much debris in that part of the room." Toby stroked Bear's head. "I saw his paw sticking out from under a brick. I think he was trying to crawl to safety."

Emotion washed over her, and she pressed shaking fingers to her lips. But she couldn't stop the sob that escaped them.

Charlie raised his head, puzzled. "What's up, Mummy?"

Toby smiled at him. "You want to come with me with for a sec? I'm starving and I think I can see chocolate bars over there."

"Buttons?" Charlie asked, reaching out his arms as Toby took him from her.

"I don't know—let's go and find out." He walked off, still talking to the boy, to investigate the food they had to offer.

Esther sank onto a nearby chair and buried her face in her hands, taking long, shaky breaths. How had he known the last thing she would have wanted was platitudes or attempts at physical comfort? If he'd tried to put his arms around her, she would have pushed him away.

She smoothed her hands over her cheeks, wiping away her tears, probably smearing black dust across her face. Across the tent, Toby and Charlie talked to one of the volunteers, discussing which chocolate bar was their favorite. He was going to be hyper all night if he ate that. She smiled wryly. She could have been talking about either of them.

She watched them, a hand across her mouth as she tried to control her emotions. Charlie rarely went to strangers, and yet there he was, not even glancing around to see if she was nearby, happily taking chocolate from the giant whose white teeth shone in his filthy face. Had her son recognized on some subconscious level that Toby was his father?

Even if he hadn't, why wouldn't he trust Toby? Not only had the guy saved his life, he'd also gone on to rescue Bear. He was an old-fashioned hero, a white knight on a charger. The thought warmed her right through.

It also filled her with panic.

She stood as they came back, and took Charlie from Toby's arms, even though both of them looked quite comfortable together. Charlie squirmed, but she tightened her arm around him, and he sagged against her. "Thank you," she said formally to Toby.

He nodded. "Are you going home now?"

"That might be difficult."

"Why?"

She hesitated, wishing she hadn't said anything. "Don't worry about it. It's not your concern."

He frowned. "What's happened?"

"There was some damage," she said reluctantly.

"Some?"

She said nothing.

He walked out into the early evening sunshine, stopped, and beckoned with his head. "Show me."

She went because she didn't have the energy to argue with him, and because she didn't know what she was going to do. They walked silently along the road, weaving amongst the bricks and piles of rubble. Charlie sucked quietly on chocolate buttons as they walked, his hands soon a mess of melted chocolate and dust, but she was too tired to say anything and let him grab her top with his sticky fingers.

As they walked, Toby took out his mobile phone. "I'd better let my mother know I'm okay," he said, pressing buttons. But after a moment or two he sighed and tucked it back into his pocket. "I guess the system's overloaded with everyone trying to call—I can't get through."

"Maybe give it half an hour."

"Yeah." They turned the corner, and Toby gasped. "Jeez."

She pointed along the road, past where a huge crack had appeared, to a collapsed building at the end. "That's my apartment."

It looked like a doll's house, as if someone had come along and lifted off the front panel to look inside it. The wall facing the street had disintegrated into a pile of wood and bricks in the middle of the road. Broken pipes and cables moved in the breeze, as if the body of a creature had been slit open to expose its innards.

"That was mine," she said, indicating the top right room. She could just see Charlie's broken bed, and a heap of matchsticks that had been her wardrobe.

"Jesus."

"Yeah." She shivered, feeling like crying, but refusing to give in to it.

He shook his head. "So what are you going to do tonight?"

"Don't know. I lost my purse in the supermarket. But last year lots of people opened their houses to the homeless. I guess I'll go back to the tent and see if someone can place us somewhere."

"Don't you have family nearby?"

"No." She straightened her son's soiled top. "Dad died while I was pregnant. It's just me and Charlie now."

For a moment, Toby said nothing. He stared at the panes of glass and broken wood in the streets. Then he said, "Come and stay with me. I have a small apartment—if it's still there."

She shook her head. "We'll be okay. There'll be somewhere we can—"

For the first time, he frowned. "If you really want, I'll find somewhere else to sleep. But you and Charlie need a shower and a bed, and I have both."

Charlie complained. She'd squeezed him too tightly. She loosened her grip, so tired she was almost asleep on her feet, but still protested, "I couldn't. You've worked so hard. You need to rest and—"

"Esther." He put his hands on his hips. "Don't be so bloody ridiculous. I'm not having my son sleeping on the street. You're coming with me."

My son. She bristled at Toby's words, wanting to tell him that Charlie had had nobody but her since he was born—he didn't need a father waltzing in and trying to shoehorn his way into their lives. She'd managed perfectly well for two and a half years and she could cope with this on her own.

But she bit her lip. Charlie *was* his son. There was no denying it. Maybe if she'd lied outright from the beginning and told him he wasn't the father, she would have been able to tell him to get lost. But she hadn't, so for better or for worse, Charlie's father was now in the picture, and legally he had a say in her son's welfare.

Part of her was nervous about the inevitable conversation they would have, about why she hadn't told him he had a child. When he'd asked if Charlie was his and she'd said yes, she'd waited for some sign of emotion—bad or good—but none had been forthcoming. Was he angry? She didn't know him well enough to tell. In the two weeks they'd spent together, he'd come across as placid and playful, and she'd seen no sign of anything approaching a temper, but then there hadn't been a situation that had called for it.

Either way, he deserved to know the truth and to spend some time with his son. She sighed. "All right." It came out grudgingly, and she winced as he frowned again. "I'm sorry. I'm exhausted and that wasn't fair. Thank you for offering."

"No worries." He gave her a half smile. "I'm glad you waited for me."

She couldn't think of anything to say to that. Her insides tangled with varying emotions. She suspected she was in shock. A strong cup of coffee, something to eat, a shower, and a good night's sleep would help set her right. Then, maybe, she'd be able to deal with the physical and emotional upheavals she'd had that day.

Chapter Three

Relief swept through Toby that Esther had finally agreed to stay at his place. While helping survivors in the supermarket, he'd wondered whether she would decide not to wait for him. He still wasn't sure how to deal with the unexpected news he'd received that day, but either way, he had to face up to it rather than look the other way. "Come on then," he instructed her, turning to walk along the street.

She fell into step beside him. "Where do you live?"

"Not too far." He noticed she was limping. "Are you okay to walk? Did you hurt your leg?"

"I fell awkwardly and bruised my hip. I'm fine, don't worry about me."

She didn't look fine. She looked in pain, but he knew she wouldn't accept any help. He'd learned in the small amount of time they'd spent together three years before that she was fiercely independent.

Unless they were in the bedroom. Where sex was concerned, she'd shown a surprising penchant for being dominated. His lips curved at the memory of the first time he'd realized that in spite of her feisty nature in everyday life, nothing turned her on more than when he took control in bed.

They'd returned to his room one evening, slightly drunk after sharing a bottle of champagne, and had gone out onto the balcony to look at the view of the ocean. He'd only had eyes for her, though, and had stood behind her, kissing her neck, his hands wandering over her body. She'd laughed as he unbuttoned her shirt, and although she'd protested somebody might see them, her protests hadn't been vehement enough to make him think she'd minded that much.

Until a couple out on an evening walk had appeared on the beach.

Esther had exclaimed and, still giggling, tried to push him away, but she'd been braless beneath the shirt. The sight of the moonlight on her skin had fired his blood, and lust had swept over him. They hadn't yet turned on any lights in the bedroom, and he'd known they would be difficult to see from the beach.

He'd caught her shirt and tugged it down her back, locking her arms by her sides and baring her breasts to the moonlight. She'd gasped as he'd pinned her from behind against the balcony and slid a hand between them to push up her skirt and slide down his zipper. "Toby!" Her eyes had been wide as she'd looked at him over their shoulder.

He'd hesitated, not wanting to misread the signs. "You want me to stop?" He'd wrapped an arm around her breasts and kissed her shoulder. The last thing he'd wanted was to take it too far.

She'd moistened her lips and met his gaze for a moment. To his surprise and delight, her eyes had lit with excitement, and she'd given a little shake of her head. Heart racing, he'd dropped his arm and had gone on to take her there and then, in full view of anyone who might have cared to look up at them, although luckily there had been no more walkers on the beach. And she'd loved it, so much so that they'd spent the remainder of their holiday exploring variations on that theme. It had been the most fun he'd had in years.

He risked a glance at her. Almost every day since they'd parted, he'd thought about her and wondered what she was doing. He knew some of it now. Having his son, alone. She was aware roughly what area he lived in, what job he did. Had she tried to find him at all?

Although darkness was falling, the streets heaved with people, from emergency services trying to keep everyone safe to volunteers handing out blankets and food and finding places for the homeless to stay. Twice someone offered them a room in their house, but each time Toby turned them down kindly, and they plodded on, growing more tired with each step. Thank God it was late February, the height of summer. Going through all this in the depths of winter would have made everything twice as hard.

Her pace grew slower, and once she stumbled and Charlie cried at being jolted out of his doze. Without another word, Toby took a blanket from an aid worker and lifted Charlie out of Esther's arms. She protested, but he ignored her, wrapping the boy up and keeping him tight to his chest. Ignoring his outstretched hand, she walked on, but she didn't argue any further. Taking that as a victory, he led the way, trying not to notice that his son's hair smelled of baby shampoo, in spite of the dust that had settled on it in a thick layer.

When they reached the line of apartments, he sighed with relief to find them still standing. The place heaved, most people opening their rooms to others who had nowhere to stay.

He led her up the stairs to his apartment and opened the door. She walked into the living room and stood in the center, looking around in a daze. He locked the door behind them, still holding Charlie, who'd now roused.

"Quick shower," he instructed, "just to get the worst off." He went into the bedroom, and Esther followed him and sat on the bed. After walking through to the adjoining bathroom, he turned on the shower. "We're going to clean you up, boyo," he told Charlie.

"I stink," Charlie said. "Pooh!"

Toby smiled. "Just like your Bear."

"Yes." Charlie giggled. "You stink too."

"I do, thank you for pointing that out."

"What's your name?" The boy looked up at him with wide, innocent eyes.

Toby swallowed. Too early to admit to Daddy. Besides which, he wasn't sure what Esther would say about him telling Charlie the truth before she got a chance to.

"Toby," he said.

Charlie's face lit up. "Like in Thomas Tank!"

"That's right." Toby tested the water. It was supposed to be cool for kids, wasn't it? Something about sticking your elbow in it, he seemed to recall. He bent his arm and let the water run over it, surprised to find it warmer there than on his hand, and turned the dial to make it cooler. "He's number seven, if I remember correctly."

"Yes." Charlie seemed delighted that Toby knew what he was talking about. "And he has two coaches, Henr'etta and Victor'a."

"You've got a good memory."

"I can count up to umpteen," Charlie stated.

"Wow, that's ten more than me. You are clever." Toby carried him back into the bedroom, saying, "Shower's ready," only to stop at the sight of Esther lying on the bed, fast asleep.

They both stared at her thoughtfully. Toby's gaze lingered for a moment on her small form. Her beauty was obvious even beneath the dust, her curves evident beneath her grimy clothes. Her pants emphasized her tight butt and slender thighs. He could remember those legs wrapped around him, her back arching as he plunged into her.

He sighed and returned to the bathroom.

"Mummy's asleep," Charlie observed.

"Yep. She's tired," Toby said, wondering why he'd been left with the baby when he was the one who'd spent hours rescuing people out of the supermarket.

He studied the shower. Would it be weird if he got in with the boy? Would Esther report him to child services for being a pervert?

"Fuck it," he said out loud. "You're filthy, and if you get in by yourself you'll probably fall over."

"You said fuck."

"Yes, thank you Mr. Observant. Clothes off." He stripped and then tried to remove Charlie's tiny T-shirt.

"Ow. My ear's stuck."

"Sorry." It wasn't as easy as it looked. He'd had remarkably little practice at dealing with kids. Oh, he'd played cars and trains and chased his niece and nephew around the garden, watched children's TV shows with them and read them bedtime stories, but he'd always managed to hand them back to their parents when feeding or clothing issues arose.

Finally, however, they were both naked. Leaving Bear watching them on the sink, Toby got in, sat on the floor of the shower cabinet, and helped the boy in. Charlie sat in front, facing him. "Here." He gave Charlie the sponge to play with and squirted some shower gel onto it. "Scrub, scrub."

"You scrub too. You're filthy." Clearly, his mother used the word to describe him a lot.

"You're filthier than me." He put a small amount of shampoo onto the boy's curly hair and massaged it in.

"No, I'm not."

"Are too."

"Am not!" Charlie beamed, delighted at the argument.

Toby smiled and rinsed the shampoo carefully, keeping it out of the boy's eyes as much as he could. He suddenly realized the curly hair—like the brown eyes—matched his own, although the blond locks hadn't yet darkened. This was his son. He caught his breath. He and Esther had made this little person. How amazing was that?

"You've got a big willy," Charlie observed. "It's bigger than mine." He studied his own offering.

"Size isn't everything, dude, or so they'd have us believe." Toby took the sponge and cleaned the rest of the dust and grime from him. Had Esther dated many men since she'd had Charlie? Somehow, he thought not. And her dad had died. She'd told him in Fiji that her mother had died a few years before, and her father had taken it hard. It must have been difficult for her, bringing up the kid on her own.

"Mummy hasn't got one."

Toby chuckled. "No, that's true."

"Why not?"

"Oh, good grief." He'd known the kid half a day and he was giving him the facts of life. "Can you wash my hair for me?" He squirted shampoo onto it and offered it to his son.

Charlie spent a few minutes clutching his fingers in and tugging at Toby's hair, and then Toby rinsed them both and turned the shower off. He got out, dried himself quickly and pulled on his bathrobe, then got the boy out and toweled him off. Only then did he realize he didn't have anything for Charlie to wear. "I don't have any boy's clothes," he admitted. "Can you go to sleep like that?"

"In my birthday suit," Charlie said.

Toby laughed. He had a vivid image of Esther prancing around his room in Fiji, suggesting that when they went out that night, she wear her birthday suit. "Okay. What about a nappy, do you wear one at night?"

Charlie blew a raspberry. "Nappies suck."

"They do, you're absolutely right."

"You suck."

"No, you suck." Shushing the boy's giggles, he maneuvered him over to the toilet. "Can you pee standing up?"

"I need my step."

"Ah." Toby fetched a box from the bedroom and placed it under the toilet for Charlie to climb onto.

"Do you like Lego?" Charlie asked as he stared into the toilet.

"I love Lego." It wasn't a lie. Jeez, how long since he'd played with Lego? Did his mother still have all his old blocks in the garage?

That made him think about his parents. What would they say when they heard he had a son? What would the rest of his family say, and Dan and Rusty, his best mates? He wished he didn't have to tell them. They'd make fun of him for not being careful, even though he'd never had sex without a condom—how had it happened, come to think of it? One of them must have split. Or they'd tease him about being a terrible father. He didn't need to be teased—he already knew how crap he was going to be.

What a shame he couldn't stay a few more weeks in Christchurch and keep the news to himself for a while longer, until he'd got to know the boy better and had grown used to the idea. But he'd booked the flights back, and Dan was getting married Saturday week. He and Rusty were joint best men, and he had to be there.

"I can make a huge car," Charlie said.

"I'd love to see that."

"Huger than this house." Charlie spread his arms wide.

"Wow. That would take a lot of blocks."

Charlie turned to look at him. "Huger than the moon!"

Toby moved the boy's shoulders to face forward. "Rule number one, boy—watch what you're doing or it'll go everywhere."

When Charlie had finished, he helped him down and took him over to the sink to wash his hands.

"Bear's still filthy." Charlie pouted at the black toy.

"We'll wash him tomorrow." He held Bear over the shower tray and shook off the worst of the dust. He could remember protesting to his mother there was no way he could sleep without his toy. It would be pointless to make Charlie wait until Bear was clean. "Here you go."

He led the boy into the bedroom and lifted him onto the bed. His muscles ached, but it was a good ache, and he didn't regret the work he'd done that afternoon.

Charlie snuggled under the covers, talking softly to Bear. Toby hesitated. Should he wake Esther? Get her to move under the duvet? She looked very young lying there, her face relaxed in sleep. She could only be—what—twenty-three? Twenty-four? Women had children a lot younger than that. And yet she seemed too young for the responsibility she'd had to bear alone.

Nearly every day, he'd cursed himself for letting her go. But he'd been young too, only twenty-four himself when they'd met, cocky and self-assured. At the end of the fortnight's holiday, she'd tentatively asked whether they'd see each other again.

She'd lived in Christchurch, over eight hundred miles and a whole island away, and the thought of carrying out a long-distance relationship had filled him with horror. He'd had no desire to move away from his family, and he hadn't been able to envisage a way to make it work without costing a fortune and spending hours flying back and forth.

And also, although he hadn't wanted to admit it to himself at the time, his feelings for her had scared him. He'd been extremely fond of her, and he hadn't liked the way it made him feel. Making sure the woman enjoyed herself in bed was important to him, and the general consensus seemed to be that he was good in bed. But for the first time, lovemaking had involved his emotions, and he'd been aware the fantastic time they'd had together had partly been because he'd felt a greater need than usual to ensure she enjoyed it. But he wasn't ready for monogamy. He didn't like the idea of being tied to one person. The very words "settling down" had made him shudder.

So he'd brushed her off, thanked her for a great time, and left her in the airport lounge without looking back.

As soon as he'd boarded the plane, he'd regretted it. He should have asked for her number. All the way back to Auckland, he'd cursed himself for his stupidity. But by then the deed was done.

He'd contacted Canterbury University, where he knew she worked, but although he'd left messages, she hadn't returned them. Either she'd decided as well that the idea of a long-distance relationship wouldn't work, or he'd hurt her feelings and she just didn't want to see him again.

Was that why she'd never contacted him to tell him about Charlie? Had she done it as a punishment for leaving her? His stomach churned uneasily. He'd made a mistake, but did it warrant missing the first two years of his son's life?

Chapter Four

Esther roused when Charlie bounced on the bed. For a brief second, she had no idea where she was, and then she saw Toby standing watching her, hands in the pockets of a white toweling robe.

"Oh," she said. "Sorry, I fell asleep." Charlie sat naked in the bed, clean and smelling of men's shower gel. "Gosh, you're clean."

"I hope you don't mind," Toby said. "It seemed the easiest way."

She ran her fingers through Charlie's hair, and the boy pushed her hand away. It took all her self-control not to yell at Toby and tell him she didn't want him interfering—didn't want him anywhere near her son. But instead she nodded. "No, that's okay. Thanks." She got up. "I'd better rinse off some of this dust."

"I'll look after him while you're in there, if you like."

She hesitated for a moment. Normally, Charlie would have sat on the floor of the bathroom and played while she showered. But she had no toys to entertain him. Everything had gone. She'd been sensible enough to have contents insurance, but right now, at this moment, they had no clothing, toys, food, indeed no belongings at all. What was she going to do?

Her throat tightened, so she cleared it. It went against the grain, but she was going to have to accept his help. "Okay. Um… Do you have something I could borrow to wear for bed?"

"Oh, yes, of course." He fetched her a T-shirt.

She took it and went into the bathroom. As she shut the door, she could hear them discussing whether Optimus Prime or Bumblebee was the best Transformer.

She showered quickly, trying not to think about anything but removing the grit from her hair and the stains from her arms and face. After she'd dried herself, she put on the T-shirt. The sleeves came down to her elbows, and the bottom just covered her butt. She slipped her panties back on, deciding the first thing she needed to do the next day was buy some new underwear. If she could get the bank to give her some money. If the bank was still there.

When she came out, Toby lay stretched on the bed and Charlie was talking animatedly, explaining how his Bear didn't like honey but preferred chocolate spread on his toast. "Bear thinks honey's yuck," Charlie said.

"I agree. Chocolate spread rules." Toby pushed himself up as Esther walked in. "Hey. Feel better?"

"Yeah."

"How's the hip?"

"Sore."

"Would you like some Panadol?"

She hesitated. "Yes, please." Crossing her arms over her chest, she waited as he found them and brought them over with a glass of water.

"Is there anything you need?" he asked as she took them. "For Charlie, I mean?"

She swallowed the pills and thought. "Do you have any milk?"

"Yes."

"He normally has a bottle in bed—only the one a day, he drinks from a cup now. But it helps him get to sleep." Why was she being so defensive? She didn't have to explain herself to him.

Toby just nodded, though. "Hold on, I'll be right back."

"No, it's…" Too late, he'd gone out, still in his bathrobe.

Charlie stood up. "Where's Toby gone?"

"Not sure, honey. He'll be back soon." She climbed onto the bed and slid under the covers.

He cuddled up to her with Bear. "Toby's funny."

"Is he?" She swallowed as her throat tightened. "Do you like him?"

"Yes. He's Charlie's friend."

"My friend," she corrected. He'd yet to master the pronoun.

"My friend." His arm tightened around the soft toy. "Toby found Bear."

"Yes, he did." She kissed his curls. For that, she was thankful.

In less than a minute, the door opened and Toby reappeared, a bottle in his hand. "The couple two doors down have a baby," he told her, bringing it over to her. "She was happy to loan us one. She said it's been sterilized. Is it okay? I can always see if I can find a shop that's still open and—"

"It's fine," she said gently. "Thank you."

He nodded and met her gaze for a moment. Then he walked out into the kitchen to the fridge. She could just see him at the worktop, filling the bottle with milk. "How long?" he called as he put it in the microwave.

"Oh, thirty seconds? Just to take the chill off."

He pressed the buttons, flexing his arms and arching his back as he waited.

After all that physical work, he must ache, she thought. All those people he'd rescued. She'd told him he wasn't brave—that he was being an idiot. The memory of the words made her cringe. He'd spent hours rescuing those trapped in the rubble and clearing the way to make it easier for the emergency services to move around. He'd found Bear, and then he'd offered them his home. She still wasn't sure how he felt toward her, but clearly he wasn't going to turn his back on them.

He waited until the milk was done and brought it over. She handed it to Charlie, who examined it thoughtfully. "Not Charlie's," he stated.

"It's all we've got," she told him. "You remember what our apartment looked like? I can't get the old one, sweetie."

He stared up at her with his big brown eyes for a moment. Then he stuck the teat in his mouth. He sucked a few times, obviously found it acceptable, and curled up next to her, propping the bottle on Bear. She yawned. It was only about seven o'clock, but her eyelids were already drooping

"You want anything to eat?" Toby asked.

"Nah. Too tired."

"Okay. I'll take the couch." He smiled at them. "Sleep well."

"Wait... Toby..." She sighed, filled with guilt. "Look, it's a big bed and you can't sleep on the sofa after all the hard work you've done today. Come on. There's plenty of room."

He hesitated. Charlie looked up at him as he sucked, his eyes wide. Toby frowned. "Are you sure?"

"It's been a crazy day. And I'm far too tired to care."

His lips twisted. "Yeah. Okay. I wonder if the phone's working yet? I'd better call my parents again." He found his mobile and dialed. "It's ringing," he announced and walked into the kitchen.

Esther helped prop up Charlie's bottle, finding it strangely comforting to watch the milk level slowly fall. She could just hear

Toby talking on the phone, reassuring his parents he was in one piece, asking them to inform the rest of his family and friends. Would he tell them about her and Charlie? She listened carefully, but he didn't mention them, talking instead about how it had felt to be in the middle of an earthquake, and the state of the city.

Sadness swept over her. There was nobody for her to call. Her parents were dead. She was an only child, and although she had other more distant relatives, she couldn't imagine they'd given her a second thought. Maybe there were people at the university who wondered if she was okay, but she couldn't imagine them lying awake worrying about her. Nobody cared whether she lived or died.

She bit her lip as emotion welled inside her. Wasn't this how she'd wanted it? She'd kept her distance, isolated herself on purpose, wanting it to be just her and Charlie. Life had shown her she couldn't rely on anyone, and she'd been determined to prove she could cope on her own. She wiped her tears away. This was good—she didn't have to answer to a single soul. Her life was her own—she had Charlie, and that was all that mattered.

She tried not to think how close she'd come to losing him. If it hadn't been for Toby... Briefly, she pictured the way he'd broken the strap in the trolley as if it were made of paper. He'd thrown himself on top of them under the table without a thought for his own safety. She wanted to resent him for not thinking she could take care of her son herself, but lying there, eyes drooping, she could only remember his strong arms around her, and the way he'd protected Charlie's mouth with his big hand.

Toby came back in then, flipping his phone shut.

"Everything okay?" she asked sleepily.

"Yeah. Mum had me buried at the bottom of a pile of rubble. Funny how mums always think the worst."

She could understand that. "True."

"Apparently, there are over a hundred missing people so far. And the cathedral's damaged—half of it has gone."

"Oh no." Her heart sank. That poor, beautiful building.

"And the Canterbury Television Building collapsed and caught fire."

"Jeez."

"The earthquake was a 6.3."

"That's smaller than the September one," she recalled. That one had awoken her but hadn't caused damage in the area.

"Yeah—I guess this one was closer to the town center." He held the phone out to her. "Do you want to call anyone?"

She shook her head.

"Come on." He waggled the phone at her. "There must be someone who's wondering how you are."

She shook her head again, her throat tightening, and looked down at Charlie, lifting the bottle so he could get the last few ounces of milk. Toby said nothing, and after a moment placed the phone on the bedside table.

She looked back up as he went over to the chest of drawers and extracted a pair of boxers. He pulled them on, facing away from them. Then he untied the robe and let it fall. She'd meant to look away, but her gaze was drawn to his body as he climbed underneath the covers. He was even more magnificent than he had been three years ago, and he hadn't been bad then. But he'd filled out, his limbs muscular and toned, his chest broad and the muscles well defined.

It had been a long time since she'd looked at a man with anything approaching desire—three years in fact, and the surge of lust that swept through her took her breath away. She concentrated on holding Charlie's bottle, waiting for her racing heart to slow down. The last thing she wanted was to rekindle any feelings she might have had for Toby Wilkinson.

Charlie popped the bottle out of his mouth. "Are you sleeping here?" he asked Toby.

"Yes. This is my bed."

"We're in your bed?" Charlie queried.

"Yep. I hope you don't snore."

Charlie giggled. "Mummy does."

"I do not," she protested.

"Yes, you do." A hint of amusement glimmered in Toby's eyes. "Very delicately."

Her cheeks warmed, and his lips curved even more.

"Will you be my friend?" Charlie asked him.

"Of course. We're best buds." Toby ruffled his hair.

Esther caught her breath. Charlie had never asked why some of the kids in the daycare center had daddies but he didn't, so she'd never discussed his absent father. She wished things had been different, and that she didn't have to tell him. But it wasn't fair, with Toby lying next to them in the bed.

She stroked his cheek. "Charlie?" He looked up at her as he continued to suck at the bottle. "You know Robert, at daycare?" He nodded. "You know how sometimes his mummy comes and picks him up, and sometimes his daddy does?" He nodded again. She could feel Toby's gaze on her, but she kept her eyes on her son. "You've never asked me where your daddy was," she said softly.

He pulled the bottle out. "I haven't got one."

"Yes, you have." She reached out and rested a hand on Toby's arm. "Toby's your daddy."

Finally, she raised her gaze to meet his, surprised to see his eyes shining. They both looked down at their son.

His brow had furrowed. He blinked a few times as he looked up at Toby. "You're my daddy?"

"Yep. 'Fraid so." Toby's voice was husky.

Charlie returned to the bottle and sucked for a while. He didn't say anything—he just lay there and studied Toby thoughtfully. But eventually he picked up Bear and offered him to his father.

Toby inhaled, then swallowed as he reached out and accepted the offering. "Thanks." He looked at Bear, brushed some more dust off his nose and kissed one of his little round ears before handing him back. "You look after him for me, though."

Charlie pushed Bear back under his arm. His gaze moved to his mother, and she bent and kissed his forehead again, more touched by his reaction than she could say.

Charlie's eyelids drooped as he pulled the bottle out of his mouth and murmured, "Daddy's willy is bigger than mine."

They both laughed. "Yes, it is," she said, unable to stop a smile stealing onto her lips. She sent Toby an apologetic look. "Sorry. He has a fixation with his penis at the moment."

"Like father, like son," Toby grunted, settling down. "Don't expect that to change any time soon."

She chuckled and curled around Charlie as his eyes finally closed. She'd lost her home, all her belongings—it had been a terrible day.

And yet as she dozed off, her heart was filled with smiles.

Chapter Five

When Toby awoke, it was still dark. His eyes were blurry with sleep, but he blinked them clear as he realized the bed was empty.

The voices in the room convinced him Esther and Charlie hadn't left, though. He raised his head and saw them on the floor with his torch, looking at a magazine.

Moving to the end of the bed, he looked down, relieved to find it was only a copy of GQ and not a Playboy. "Hey, you two. It's the middle of the night."

"Sorry," Esther said. "Charlie doesn't do quiet."

"What's the time?"

"Five thirty. That's a lie in, for him."

"Jeez." Toby sighed. "What are you doing down there?"

"Trying not to wake you."

"And failing." He held out a hand. "Come on, get up here, both of you."

"We're perfectly fine…" Her voice trailed off as Charlie scampered to his feet and tried to climb onto the bed. Toby switched on the bedside light and helped him up. She mumbled something he couldn't hear and passed them the magazine.

Toby leaned back on the pillows, and Charlie sat upright next to him, turning the pages and giving him a running commentary. Esther got to her feet and wandered around the room, examining his belongings. Toby let her, wondering what she was looking for, content to watch her move around and gain the occasional glimpse of her pink panties beneath the T-shirt.

"Red car," Charlie said, pointing to the vehicle in the picture.

"Yes, that's right. It's a Ferrari."

"It's red."

"Yes, it's a red Ferrari."

"'Rari," said Charlie. "'Raris are good cars?"

"Ferraris are fantastic cars. They'll get you a great girlfriend."

Charlie blew a raspberry. "Girls suck."

"Only the good ones."

Esther gave him a glance, half-amused, half-exasperated. He grinned back. "What are you looking for?"

She shrugged. "Nothing. Just seeing what you've got here."

"Not much. I've only been here six weeks and I'm going back Saturday." He thought it best to tell her, get it out of the way. "One of my mates is getting married. I'm best man."

"Crikey. He wants the church in one piece, does he?" She obviously remembered how clumsy he was. Two left feet and fingers too large to press the buttons on most phones didn't make for elegant maneuvering.

"Ha ha." He pointed to the rugby player in the magazine. "Who's this?"

"Don't know," Charlie said.

"Don't know? Esther, what have you been teaching the boy? Charlie, this is Dan Carter, king of the All Blacks."

"Dan?"

"Yes. He's a superhero."

"Like Superman?"

"Just like Superman."

"Does he fly?"

"He's a fly-half, that's almost as good."

"Jeez." Esther didn't look around. "I can see what effect you're going to have on his education."

"Listen, knowing who Dan Carter is will be more of a life skill for him than knowing who Shakespeare is, believe me."

"You're probably right." She sighed.

He rolled onto his back and put his hands behind his head. "Do you still work at the university?"

"Yes. At least I did. I presume it's still standing. I lecture there three days a week. Charlie goes to daycare." She looked through the half a dozen books resting on the shelf and picked one up. When she turned, the pleasure on her face made him smile. "To Kill a Mockingbird?"

"So it is."

"I suggested you read that."

"I know. Hence the book."

She looked puzzled. "You're reading it because of me?"

"Yes. I've already read it twice. I thought I'd bring it with me, for something to do."

Her lips twitched. "Along with the Playboys under the bed."

"Ah…"

She laughed. "It's all right. I put them in your suitcase, by the way. I'd be the same if I didn't have Mr. Nosey around asking questions."

That didn't surprise him. She'd read an erotic literary story to him in bed in Fiji. It had led to a particularly raunchy lovemaking session, if his memory served him correctly.

He shifted away from Charlie, who seemed content to continue his quiet commentary as he flicked through the magazine. The last thing he wanted was his son remarking on any changes happening to his body under the covers.

Esther rubbed her thumb over the cover of the book, studying the picture. What was she thinking?

"Are you considering that maybe Charlie already knows more about classical literature than I do?" he asked her.

"He could probably give me more quotes from Macbeth than you."

He smiled. "I am unsurprisingly dense about Chaucer's work." It was a joke, and her wry glance told him she'd guessed that.

"You're not dense. You're uneducated. There's a difference. It's not your fault you went to a crap school."

"I guess."

She frowned at him. "You were like this three years ago—I thought you might have moved on since then. Why do you insist you're stupid?"

He shrugged, unoffended. "It's difficult to think otherwise when I'm surrounded by clever people."

"Like…"

"My brothers. We went to the same high school, but they somehow managed to rise above the mediocre teaching we were offered. One's a doctor and one's a lawyer. I guess I was at the back of the queue when the smart genes were handed out."

She turned to face him and leaned against the wall, arms crossed. "That's rubbish. You're intelligent. You just don't like to show it. I bet you have no trouble using math when you're at work."

It was true—he found it easy to calculate measurements and quantities that some of the other builders struggled with. That didn't convince him he was clever, though.

He turned a page for Charlie and held the magazine up for him to investigate the advert for aftershave as he continued, "Look, I can talk about wall frames, exterior claddings, and timber weatherboards until the cows come home. But it sounds surprisingly unimpressive when one of your best mates is a history teacher and the other is manager of a large computer firm. I'm not complaining. I like my job. And anyway, I have plans. I'm going to university next year."

Her eyes widened. "To study what?"

"Architecture. Soon I'll have a degree along with the rest of them."

He'd thought she'd be impressed by that. Instead, however, she frowned. "Is that really what you want to do?"

He blinked, confused. When he'd told his family and friends, everyone had praised him for his ambition, pleased he'd finally committed himself to a real and impressive career. "Don't you think it's a good idea?" he asked, hurt she hadn't reacted the same way.

"It doesn't matter what I think." She turned away and continued brushing her fingers along the bits and pieces he'd left on the shelf. "What's this?"

He glanced over. She'd picked up a small box from the corner of his suitcase labelled *Naughty Nights* in fancy red script. The picture on the front was a stylized version of a couple engaged in an interesting sexual act. Alarm shot through him and he glanced at Charlie, who luckily was fascinated by an article about different kinds of wristwatches. "Oh Christ, it's not what you think." What with this and the magazines she'd found, he wasn't coming across well.

Chapter Six

"It's not a sex game?" Esther was teasing him, but Toby looked horrified that she'd found the box.

He winced. "Okay... So it is what you think. It's not mine, is what I meant."

"One of your girls left it here?" She made her voice innocent, trying not to laugh at his pained expression as she took off the lid and pulled out a handful of the cards.

"One of my... Jeez, Esther, I haven't had any girls up here. Hence the Playboys."

That she found hard to believe. "You haven't had sex for six weeks?"

"I haven't had sex for six months, but that's another story. No, Faith gave it to me. She's Rusty's wife."

He'd told her about Rusty and Dan—his best mates—in Fiji. "Your best mate's wife gave you a sex game?"

"No. I mean yes. Look, she writes for a women's magazine. She writes this blog about sex, about ways to spice up your love life. It's how she and Rusty became an item—he offered to help her investigate the sins and they ended up staying together."

Esther stared at him, surprised. "The Seven Sexy Sins?"

"That's the one."

"I read that column." It had been fun, based on the seven deadly sins, with each one relating to a "sexy sin" like stripping or oral sex to encourage couples whose love lives had grown staid. Faith Hillman was a well-known columnist and adviser on women's matters, and the magazine's large following had watched with avid interest as she gradually fell in love with the secret partner with whom she'd explored the sins. "Oh, I read she married him, in November, wasn't it? Your Rusty was Mr. Sinful?"

"Yeah. Her brother wasn't best pleased, but he came around when he saw how right they are for each other."

It was a lovely romantic story. Esther had read about the sins each week, envious she didn't have someone to try them out on. She sighed and turned her attention to the cards in her hand. "So... What's with the Naughty Nights?"

"Faith's researching for another article on sex games. They've been teasing me because I haven't had a date in ages, so she gave me the game and told me to find someone to try it out on—for research purposes."

"But you haven't found anyone?"

"Not yet." He met her gaze. Something in his expression gave her the feeling he was thinking about Fiji, and she had a vivid image of him lying back, arms behind his head like he was now as she straddled him and welcomed him inside her.

Charlie plopped the magazine onto his chest, making him jump, and she hid a smile as he turned his attention to the "Top 10 Action Movies" list Charlie had found and began to discuss them.

She looked back at the cards. They were small and glossy and came in two sections—one with red lettering and the Venus symbol, one with black and the Mars icon. One lot for men, one for women, presumably. Each card bore a scenario, either a role-play suggestion or something to try in the bedroom.

She read the top one. "Goodness." Her heart raced. She'd never taken part in role-play. The most exciting time she'd ever had in bed was with Toby, when he'd tied her to the bedpost. That had been a night to remember. The thought of playing out a scenario like the one on the card made her dizzy with lust.

Toby glanced up. "What?"

She swallowed. "Have you read these?"

"Not really. Seemed like pointless torture. Why? What does it say?" His big brown eyes met hers, his expression curious.

Warmth crept into her cheeks, and her lips curved. She glanced at Charlie, but he was busy labelling the various types of dinosaur in the number five action movie, and besides, there weren't any words in the text as such that he shouldn't hear.

She cleared her throat. "This is a guy's one. 'As Roman emperor, you have the pick of all of the slaves in the Empire. Go to the market, choose yourself a girl, and take her back to your villa. She is yours for the night, and must do anything you tell her.'" She looked up. "It gives some suggestions."

Toby blinked. "Huh."

She bit her lip. No way could she read those out. For example, *tell her to pleasure you using only her mouth*. Or *describe how you want her to touch herself while you watch*. Jeez.

She lifted her gaze to his again. The first time they'd gone down on each other had been on a quiet beach of white sand, tucked out of sight behind a cluster of palm trees. Did he remember? Yes, was the answer, judging by his raised eyebrow and the curve of his lips.

She put the card back and pulled out another one—this one red. "Ooh."

"What?"

"It's a girl's one. 'You're a very expensive, high-class hooker, looking for customers in a bar. You see a businessman ordering a drink. Go up to him and ask him if he would like a companion for the evening. Get him to buy you a drink, and then let him take you back to his place. Ask what he wants, and tell him what it will cost. And if he wants anything extra, well, that's up to you.'" She looked up at him.

"Nice." Toby's eyes glittered in the light.

"What's a hooker?" Charlie asked.

Shit. She'd forgotten Charlie had ears. She opened her mouth to tell him not to be so nosey.

"A hooker's a rugby position," Toby interjected without hesitating.

"Like Dan Carter?" Charlie asked brightly.

"Well, I wouldn't call him that to his face."

Esther gave a wry smile and put the cards back into the box reluctantly as Toby proceeded to tell their son about Keven Mealamu and what role the hooker played on the rugby field. How were you supposed to have a love life when you had a two-year-old? Even if she had met someone she'd been attracted to, with nobody to babysit there was no way she could ever go on a date.

Weariness overtaking her, she came back to the bed and stretched out next to Charlie. She ran her fingers through his curls, and he pushed her away and moved to the end of the bed, climbing down. "I'm going to sit on the sofa," he announced, clear as anything, and ran through into the living room with his magazine.

She sighed and lay back, unable to summon the energy to go after him. Looking up at the ceiling, she thought about the Naughty

Nights game and wondered who would get to play it with Toby. Would he tell the lucky girl he had a son? Would Charlie feature in his life at all from now on?

Toby hadn't said anything for a while, so she turned her head to look at him, only to find him watching her, head propped on his hand. Charlie had pushed the duvet to Toby's waist, and she could just see the line of dark brown hair heading down from his stomach, disappearing into his boxers. She swallowed and raised her gaze to his in time to see he'd been looking at her legs, bare and exposed right up to the hem of the T-shirt. She smiled, but he didn't return it. His gaze lingered on her mouth before coming back to hers.

"Why didn't you try to find me?" His tone wasn't accusatory, just puzzled. "When you found out you were pregnant, I mean?"

Heat flooded her cheeks. She swallowed. "I did. But the Northland is a pretty big place."

It was a lie. First, she hadn't tried to find him because she hadn't thought he'd be interested. And besides which, he'd already turned her down once. If she'd contacted him to inform him he was going to be a father and he'd reacted by telling her to get lost, how would that have felt? For herself? For Charlie?

Second, she hadn't told him because she'd wanted to punish him for walking away from her. In the beginning, anyway. She didn't like what that said about her, but was honest enough to admit it. After her father had died and Charlie was born, she'd thought often about trying to track Toby down. Half of her wanted to keep the boy to herself, half of her wanted to share the experience of having a child with someone, plus Charlie deserved to know his father. But something had always made her hold back from contacting Toby. He'd hurt her terribly, and she hadn't been able to move on from that.

"But I left you messages," he said. "At the university."

Crap. She'd forgotten that. The receptionist had put them in her pigeonhole every day for weeks, but she'd torn them into pieces and thrown them away.

She couldn't admit to him that she'd refused to contact him on purpose. Not now. "Messages?" she said. "I didn't get any messages."

Relief washed over his features. "I assumed you didn't want to contact me. I didn't realize you never got them."

She looked at her hands, her gut twisting with guilt. She was terrible at lying, and she wondered if he'd be able to read the truth on her face. If he did, how would he react? He had every right to be angry with her. She'd denied him the first two years of Charlie's life. It wasn't as if he'd made the decision to be an absent father. Maybe he would've liked to change nappies and do the two a.m. shift. Hard as it had been, the thought of missing out on that quiet time with her baby snuffling at her breast, of not seeing his first smile, first mouthful of food, first step, made her catch her breath. Toby hadn't had any of that.

He didn't say anything, and she couldn't read what he was thinking. How did he feel about having a son? Was he pleased or annoyed she'd upset his plans for the future? What would he do after he went back to the Bay of Islands? Would he stay in contact with her or turn his back on her again?

By law, she could demand he pay toward Charlie's upkeep, but that seemed unfair when she'd denied him access these past years. Shame and defensiveness twisted inside her at the same time. Part of her hated him for finding her, for seeing her in that supermarket, for saving her. She'd been happy in her own little world, just Charlie and her.

Hadn't she?

Chapter Seven

"Tell me about your dad," he said.

She looked up at the ceiling. "Not much to say."

"What did he die from?"

Her throat tightened, and she cleared it. "Officially, a heart attack. Unofficially, I think he died of a broken heart."

"He missed your mum?"

"Yeah."

"When did she die again?"

"Five years ago. Cancer. He struggled on for a while, but it felt like he faded away, you know?" Sadness overwhelmed her, and she fell silent.

Toby didn't reply. He remained quiet for a moment while she fought with herself to keep her emotions in check.

Then, to her surprise, he inched closer to her.

She looked at him in alarm. "What are you doing?"

"Moving closer."

"I got that much. I meant why are you doing it?"

In answer, he lifted a hand to touch her face and brushed her cheek with his thumb. She stiffened automatically, little shivers shooting down her spine at the contact. Her instincts told her to move away, but his touch was so gentle, she couldn't help but linger.

She'd put aside her physical desires since having Charlie, had given every ounce of her affection and energy to him. She'd forgotten what it was like to be Esther, to have someone talk to her, touch her as something other than a mother.

He slid his hand into her hair and cupped the back of her head. His warm eyes searched her face, resting on her mouth. Her lips parted. He was going to kiss her, and that was a step too far. She froze, moving back, but she'd forgotten how strong he was. Holding her in place easily, he smiled, clearly amused at her struggle.

Damn the man. He was remembering their time in Fiji too clearly. She'd never considered herself submissive before—she usually hated being told what to do and thought herself a modern, independent woman who enjoyed being in control of her life. If someone had suggested before she met Toby that she'd enjoy being dominated, she'd have laughed in their face.

But there'd been that incident on the balcony, and she'd been shocked by how much it had aroused her. Afterward they'd talked about it, and she admitted that him being a little... coercive... turned her on. Not being forced obviously, she'd added hastily—she wasn't into rape fantasies or anything like that. Toby had just grinned and had apparently understood exactly what she meant, because the following night when they were walking along the beach, he pulled her onto the sand behind a large group of rocks and proceeded to make love to her there and then. Shocked and slightly panicky—again—at the thought of being discovered, but extremely turned on by his persistence, she'd half-protested that this wasn't what she'd meant until he found ways to shut her up. It had been some of the best sex they'd had, and she warmed right through as she remembered it.

But that was before, and this was hardly the time. Indignation swept through her, and she put both hands on his chest and pushed. He caught one wrist in his hand, however, and then the other, and before she knew it she was on her back, pinned in place by the strength of his arms and the weight of him on top of her.

"Toby!" Her chest heaved with resentful breaths. He was so much bigger than her, all brown skin and rippling muscles and hot breath. And she wasn't turned on by it at all. *At all*, she scolded herself, trying to ignore her pounding heart. "Let me go."

He looked up and tipped his head as if he was thinking about it, and then his gaze came back to hers, hot and taunting. "No."

Their eyes met. Fury blazed through her at his arrogance, his smug smile. "Let me go or I'll—"

He cut her off by crushing his lips to hers. She squirmed beneath him and tried to give a muffled complaint, but as she opened her mouth he took the opportunity to sweep his tongue inside, and that brought her world crashing down as much as the earthquake had the day before.

Her complaint turned into a low moan as he kissed her thoroughly. The tension melted, and his lips became gentler as her resistance faded. She closed her eyes and gave herself over to the moment, to the feel of his young, strong body pressing against hers, to the power of his passion and need for her.

There was something about him that was so full of life. He was like a comet blazing through her cool, quiet solar system, awakening every nerve ending in her body that had slept for so long. Her nipples tightened against his chest and a dull throbbing began between her thighs. He pressed his erection against her, and she sighed at the thought of him sliding inside her, filling her to the brim.

She loved the way he gave a low murmur of approval when she moved beneath him, how he took such delight in just kissing her. He'd done this to her in Fiji, coaxed her out of her shell, seduced her, brought her alive with his enthusiasm and ardor and his expert touch. She'd had such little experience in the bedroom, just a couple of partners at university, and sex for her had been awkward and polite, not at all like it was in the movies. Before, she'd felt self-conscious the whole time in case she did something wrong, wanting to let go and experience the passion she knew was inside her but too awkward with her partners to give in to it.

With Toby, though, it had been exciting and fevered, right from the beginning. He'd lit her up like a lantern, and he hadn't cared if she got her hair caught in her top or bumped noses—in fact he'd told her at the time, "Sex isn't about being polite, honey. Give me everything you've got." She'd done so nervously at first, slightly overawed by this huge, enthusiastic, passionate man who certainly knew his way around the bedroom and seemed keen to show her a thing or two. But the more she'd let go, the more it had turned him on, and in the end she'd held nothing back.

Maybe that was why it had hurt so much when he left her.

The thought of him walking away killed her passion. She'd never be able to forget the pain that had knifed through her. All the nights she'd lain awake, thinking about him, aching for the touch of his hands on her skin. The times she'd awoken with a gasp from a nightmare of drowning or falling, and him turning away. How could she ever get over that?

Toby obviously felt her passion ebb because he lifted his head to look at her.

She pressed her lips together. "I can't," she whispered.

A frown appeared on his forehead, and for a moment she thought she'd made him angry. To her surprise, however, he just kissed her nose. "I know." He released her hands.

She rolled over and sat up, fighting to keep back tears, only then realizing that Charlie stood in the doorway, watching them. Alarm shot through her. He was sucking his thumb, but now removed it to say, "Daddy kissed you, Mummy."

"Yes." Flustered, she couldn't think what to say. "It's okay, it's…" Her words trailed off as she noticed his face bore several black marks. Her gaze dropped to the item in his hand. "Oh shit."

"You said shit," Charlie announced.

She ran up to him and dropped to her knees to remove the marker pen. "Oh, Charlie, where did you get this?"

"It was on the worktop." Toby walked past them into the kitchen. He stopped in his tracks. "Ah."

She pushed herself to her feet and followed him out.

The previously pristine white cupboards were covered with drawings.

"Oh my God." Blood drained from her face and left her dizzy. "Toby, I'm so sorry."

He put his hands on his hips. "Well, I guess that's my deposit gone."

Cold filtered through her. If he hadn't been there she would have scolded her son and given him an appropriate punishment—no television for the day, or no chocolate—something he would have understood. But she wasn't sure how Toby was going to react, and she couldn't suppress the instinct to defend Charlie, even though he'd done wrong. Would Toby get angry, yell at the boy? Tell them to leave?

To her complete shock, he burst out laughing.

Flooded with relief, nevertheless she gave him an admonishing look. "It's not a laughing matter."

"No, it's not," he said, laughing anyway. He picked his son up, carried him back into the bedroom, and dumped him on the bed, where he proceeded to tickle him relentlessly. "Repeat after me," he instructed Charlie, who was contorted with giggles. "I will not write graffiti all over Daddy's kitchen units."

"I'll not write feet on Daddy's units," Charlie yelled, delighted. "Stop it, Daddy!"

Esther put her hand over her mouth and watched them. She'd honestly never expected to see Toby again. The thought that he was here, now, and her son was calling him Daddy, filled her with a warmth she had never expected to feel. But it was a dangerous warmth, and fire could consume you. He hadn't changed—he was still the same man who'd left her without a second thought.

And it wasn't only herself she had to worry about. Charlie's heart would be as vulnerable as hers. He was excited to find out he had a daddy—but what if that daddy then turned his back on him and walked away? How could either of them recover from that?

And what on earth had she been doing, kissing Toby? Her body— so long flooded with oxytocin and other breastfeeding and caring hormones, had been overtaken by pheromones. She'd been unable to resist his sheer masculinity, the size and weight of him, the heavenly smell of aftershave and healthy sweat and musky male she'd forgotten existed. But that had to stop, right now.

It had taken her a long time to recover from Fiji. In fact, she probably was still recovering from it. She didn't need or want to start all over again.

She walked to the bed. Giving Toby a brisk, businesslike smile, she picked Charlie up. He struggled, but she held him firmly. "Come on," she told him, "let's find you something to do." He pulled her hair, but she welcomed the pain. Anything to distract her from the deep ache inside at the memory of what she'd lost.

*

Later, when the rest of the world awoke, Esther rang the university campus to find it was closed indefinitely. "Great. Now I'm homeless and jobless," she said as they ate up at the breakfast bar, Charlie smearing peanut butter across the table.

"I guess I'll be busy." Toby made them coffee. "There'll be a lot of areas that need to be made safe today, I'm thinking." He sat beside her. "What are you going to do?"

"I'll go back to my apartment and see if I can salvage anything. My guess is there won't be much, but I might be lucky and get a few bits. Unfortunately, I lost my purse in the supermarket, so I guess I'll have to see if the bank's open and if they'll let me have any money without my cards." She cursed her bad luck—she needed clothes and food and the hundred other items a child couldn't seem to live without, and her bank balance wasn't exactly overflowing.

Toby pulled his wallet from his back pocket. He took out a credit card and pushed it across to her.

She stared at it as she sipped her coffee. "What's that?"

"A credit card."

"I know it's a credit card. Why are you giving it to me?"

"You need stuff, right? I don't know what shops will be open, but if you find what you need, put it on there."

Shock and resentment flooded her. "I can't take your credit card. I don't need it."

"You just told me you lost your purse."

"Yes, but—"

"Esther." He spoke patiently, as if he was speaking to Charlie. "You've managed two and a bit years without any handouts from me. I've never given Charlie anything before. I've got plenty of money— I've been saving up for university, and I haven't had a lot else to spend it on. Take it and use it to get what you need."

"You don't even know me," she said, heart pounding. "You don't really know the first thing about me. How can you just invite me into your house and give me your credit card—hell, you don't even know for sure Charlie's yours—how can you?"

"I've got eyes," Toby said.

"Brown eyes and curly hair? Come on, you can't be a hundred percent sure. Why are you so trusting? I could be out to take you for a ride."

He crunched his toast and eyed her thoughtfully. "True. But you didn't expect to see me in that supermarket—I could tell by the look on your face. Charlie would have been conceived just over three years ago, which would make him the perfect age to be my son. When we slept together in Fiji, it became very clear to me that you hadn't had a lot of sexual experience. Considering the fact that you are obviously pissed I walked away that day, it tells me you took a while to get over what we'd had. That also tells me you probably didn't fall into bed with someone else immediately after you got back. Which leads me to conclude the likelihood is that Charlie's mine." He took another bite of toast.

She stared at him, stunned by his insightfulness. "Who do you think you are, Sherlock Holmes?"

He gave a short laugh. "Look, even if Charlie wasn't mine, you're a single mum who's been through a traumatic experience, and even though you're stubborn and defensive and you won't admit it, you need help. I'd do the same even if I'd never met you before."

Her eyes filled with tears at his kind, generous nature, but she bit her lip to stop them falling. She looked at the credit card. It was an extremely generous thing to do, and it would be rude to say no. She reached out and took it. "I'll do it for Charlie."

"Sure." He sipped his coffee, although she was sure he did it to hide a smile.

He told her his PIN and gave her one of his keys, telling her she was welcome to stay there for the next few days. Then he went to work, giving Charlie a final ruffle on his curly hair before he left.

She didn't kiss him goodbye, though.

Chapter Eight

Toby spent the day with the building firm helping to make the city safe for its inhabitants. When he finally got back to his apartment, tired and aching from a day's heavy labor, it was to find Esther and Charlie curled up on the sofa reading a book, dressed in pajamas, smelling of baby shampoo and talcum powder.

The apartment also smelled of warm food. She'd placed some kind of baked pasta dish in the oven.

"I hope you don't mind," she said as Charlie ran up to him. "I thought you might be hungry." She glared at his raised eyebrows. "Don't go getting used to it. It's a one-off."

"I wouldn't dream of it." He bent and lifted his son up as the boy hugged his knees. "Hey, buster."

"Hey, Daddy." Charlie threw his arms around Toby's neck and planted a wet kiss on his cheek.

Toby's throat tightened with unexpected emotion. Over Charlie's shoulder, his eyes met Esther's, which reflected the same surprise, pleasure, and concern he himself felt. She dropped her gaze and he turned away, covering his unease with the pretense of getting a drink from the fridge.

All day, as his body had settled into the regular rhythm of work, his mind had mulled over the implications of getting involved in Esther and Charlie's life. Not that there was anything he could do about it now. He couldn't turn back time and change their meeting, and neither did he want to—after all, he was certain he'd saved their lives in the supermarket, and he didn't want that fact to alter any time soon. But the closer he and the boy got, the more Charlie would miss him when they had to part.

Because of course, part they would have to. He was returning to the Northland, and Esther had made it clear that although she was willing to accept him as the father and allow him to play a role in Charlie's life, there was no way she'd allow him back in her life romantically.

True, just like in Fiji, her resistance had faded rapidly once he got his lips on hers, and he was sure the kiss had fired her up as much as it had fired him. He'd been unable to resist touching her when she lay beside him, all soft and sweet smelling from the shower. And when she'd melted against him, desire had thundered through his veins.

But he'd felt the moment when she'd decided she wanted him to stop. And as much as she'd loved to play the "I say no but I mean yes" game, he'd been able to detect the subtle difference. She couldn't forgive him for walking away, and that was fair enough. But he couldn't escape the fact that he had some obligation toward them now. And he wasn't sure how to fulfil it.

"Hey, buster, I nearly forgot—I got you a present." He went back to his workbag and extracted the item he'd hunted for during his lunch break.

Charlie's eyes lit up at the sight of the Thomas the Tank Engine plastic train, and he positively exploded when Toby pressed the button on the top and it made a noise.

Toby set him on the floor with the toy, smiling. Esther walked into the kitchen and started dishing up the pasta. "What do you say, Charlie?"

"Thank you, Daddy," Charlie said, beaming.

"You're welcome," Toby replied awkwardly, aware of Esther's flushed cheeks.

"Thank you," she said while Charlie steered the train around the sofa, talking away to himself. "You'll be his best friend forever now."

"I hope so," he said sincerely. She didn't look at him, so he added, "I didn't buy it to win his favor."

"I know." She brought the pasta over to the breakfast bar, and they hopped onto the stools.

Toby tucked in—he'd only had a sandwich at lunchtime, and he was ravenous. "I had a great time in the toy shop. I was like Tom Hanks in *Big*."

She laughed. "Yeah, I can see that. I think you'll be eternally eight years old." He said nothing, and she frowned. "I'm sorry. I've upset you."

He was taken aback that she'd picked up on his feelings. Most people didn't realize how sensitive he was. He smiled though. "You've not said anything my friends and family haven't said to me many times before."

"And you don't agree with that observation."

He shrugged. "A year ago, I would have said absolutely. It was very true for the guy you met in Fiji, and I don't mind admitting that. I just wanted to have a fun time, and I didn't care that everyone thought I'd never amount to anything."

"So what changed?"

As he ate, he watched Charlie crash the train and make up a story about the passengers escaping from the wreckage. "I think part of it was when Rusty and Faith announced they were getting married. Six months before that, Rusty, Dan, and I had all been single, and it seemed like it would remain like that forever. Then Dan and Eve hooked up, even though for a while it wasn't serious. But I never thought Rusty would settle down. I thought he'd be an eternal bachelor—we always used to laugh about growing old together like the guys in the Muppets."

She smiled. "You were surprised he fell for Faith?"

"Oh God no, he's been crazy about her for years, and vice versa. But he had issues to do with his father and I didn't think he'd ever let his heart get involved, you know?"

"So why did what happened to them change how you felt about yourself?"

He hesitated, the fork halfway to his mouth. How could he explain how he'd felt? "Well, suddenly it was just me. Peter Pan, refusing to grow old. And while I'd ignored all the comments people had made about me before, about being a drifter, not being serious, never amounting to anything, suddenly I didn't want to be that person. But the talents I have aren't valued by society, by my friends and family, as much as if I were a doctor or lawyer."

"And what talents do you have, Toby?" Her eyes gleamed as she placed a forkful of pasta delicately into her mouth.

Trying to tear his eyes away from her soft lips, he said, "I don't want to say. You'll laugh." She was ten times cleverer than he was, with a mountain of knowledge compared to the anthill-high pile of information in his head. He couldn't bear it if she poured scorn on him too.

She put her fork down with a frown. "I'm many things, but one thing I'm not is a snob. God gives us all gifts, and I believe it's our role in life to discover what they are and to use those to help our fellow man. Let's face it, what does being able to quote most of King Lear line by line really add to humanity?"

"I suppose," he said doubtfully.

"So what's your gift, Toby?"

"Buildings talk to me," he said, sitting back.

Her eyebrows rose. "Okay."

"Not literally, I hasten to add. I mean the materials, especially wood. When I hold a piece of wood, I can almost feel the tree talking to me. I love wood, I love holding it, working with it." He smiled as she giggled. "Yes, all carpenters are used to erection jokes. But the thing is, different woods have different patterns and textures and smells. I can tell by touch which part of the tree it comes from, and I have to take that into account when I carve it or the shape won't look right."

He stopped talking, embarrassed. He'd never tried to explain himself before. When he put it into words, it sounded stupid.

But she just said, "Go on."

He cleared his throat. "Look, I know this is probably a terrible thing to admit, but Christchurch has held a strange fascination for me since the earthquake last year. Collapsed walls reveal old, sealed doorways and intricate timber ceilings. The marks of craftsmen, long forgotten. I like to think about them while I seal that history in with plywood. I don't know much about history, but I feel connected with the past, when I work on buildings like that. I'd love to help rebuild the cathedral."

Her expression had softened, and her eyes looked at him with something like wonder. "Why on earth would you think you don't have a gift?"

"Dunno. Nobody else seems to think so. It's not written on a piece of paper anywhere. You can't grade something like that, or get a certificate for it. And that's all that seems to matter, to most people."

"So that's why you're going to university."

He nodded, tucking into his pasta again. "I figure if I get a qualification, maybe people will take me more seriously. And then I can take myself more seriously."

"I understand why you would think that. But to be honest, I think you've got it the wrong way around. If you were to take yourself more seriously and accept you don't have to have a piece of paper to prove you're special, everyone else would follow suit."

They said nothing for a while, watching Charlie pushing the train around the carpet while he related stories. Toby thought about what she'd said. Was she right? His parents loved him, his friends and family adored him, but nobody had ever told him he was special before. Was that because he didn't believe it himself?

His gaze fell on Esther. The buttons of her new blue pajamas strained slightly across her breasts—they'd grown since he last saw her, changed no doubt by motherhood. How else would her body have changed? He was surprised that the thought of stretch marks and the loosening of her previously tight, fit body didn't put him off. Quite the opposite, in fact. She'd carried Charlie for nine months before giving birth in the fascinating, scary way women did. He'd put the baby inside her. He still couldn't get his head around that. It truly was a miracle.

She'd had his baby, and now they were linked for life in a way he'd never considered before, never expected. And in spite of the fact that she'd kept Charlie from him, and obviously still bore him resentment, suddenly, as he studied her slight form and remembered the smell and taste of her, he wanted her.

Chapter Nine

Esther saw him studying her pajamas and remembered the receipts she'd meant to give him. She pulled them out from under the bowl on the counter. "Here. This is what I bought today."

He looked at them without taking them. "I don't need those."

"Of course you do. You need to know what I spent."

"No, I don't."

"Toby." Exasperation flooded her. "I bought some clothes for both of us, a couple of toys, bathroom stuff, bottles…" She told him how much she'd spent, wondering if he'd exclaim that she'd cleaned him out.

His eyebrows rose. "Is that all?"

"Well…" She couldn't think what to say to that.

He finished his pasta and pushed his plate away. "That was lovely, thanks." He stood, went over to the fridge, and extracted two beers, then held one out to Esther inquiringly.

She blinked. "I haven't had a drink for three years. It never seemed right, when I was the only person Charlie had."

"Way overdue then." He popped the top, passed it to her, and sat back on the stool.

She studied it doubtfully. "I don't know if I should."

He waved it in front of her nose. "Drink me. Driiiink meeeee…"

Giving a small laugh, she took the bottle. "You like tempting me, don't you?"

"Oh yeah." His eyes gleamed.

Realizing as soon as she'd said it how it could be misconstrued, she sent him a remonstrative glance and sipped the beer, sighing as the cool liquid slid down her throat. "Oh, that's nice."

"It certainly is." There was a hint of heat in his expression, and she wasn't entirely sure he was talking about the beer as his gaze ran briefly down her. But he didn't say anything else. Instead, he stretched out his legs and took a long swig from the bottle before continuing. "So I guess we should talk about where we go from here."

"Literally, spiritually, or metaphorically?"

"All three, probably."

She picked at the label on the bottle, unsure whether she was ready for this discussion, but there were only a couple of days until he left, and she was just putting off the inevitable. "I'm not sure what to say," she admitted.

He took another mouthful of beer as he watched Charlie playing. Her gaze lingered on the impressive width of his biceps as he lifted the bottle, and the defined muscles under his tight T-shirt. He swallowed the lager. "I suppose the main question is, do you want me to play a part in Charlie's life?" His eyes came back to hers, gentle and calm.

His generous query tied her tongue in knots. He could easily have demanded his rights to see Charlie. Accused her of denying him the years he'd missed. Told her he didn't want anything to do with her. But instead he'd asked her what she wanted. That didn't mean he wasn't going to argue with her answer, but she appreciated he was thoughtful enough to ask.

She cleared her throat. "I can't say I'm not nervous about this. It's only been Charlie and me—since Dad died anyway, and I'm honest enough to admit I feel uneasy about sharing him with anyone else."

She looked down at her hands, not wanting him to see the rawness she felt inside at the thought of someone taking Charlie away from her. What if Charlie loved Toby more than her? It was a stupid thing to worry about, but all boys wanted to be like their fathers, didn't they? What would happen if Toby visited them and then Charlie wanted to go with him when he left?

"I would think that was perfectly normal," Toby said. "And honey, there's no way I'd want to come between you and the boy."

The tears came in a rush, surprising and embarrassing her. Jeez, this was the second time she'd cried in front of him in as many days. She pressed her fingers to her lips and struggled to control the emotion that flooded through her.

Toby put down his beer. "Time for chocolate," he said. He walked over to the fridge and retrieved the bar he'd put in there when he first came in, as well as a packet of buttons. Waiting until she nodded her assent, he opened the packet and gave them to Charlie before taking his seat and opening the chocolate bar. He broke it into pieces, popped one into his mouth and pushed the rest over to her.

She blew her nose, then took a cube of the chocolate and sucked it. "Why does chocolate always make things better?"

"Dunno, but it does." He turned the bottle in his fingers. "Look, why don't we be honest with each other? This isn't the easiest situation. Basically, if we hadn't met in the supermarket, I'd be none the wiser and you'd still be on your own. But we did, and everything's changed. I'm not quite sure how it's going to work, and my gut feeling is to give it a little while for us to come to terms with what's happened and to think about what we want from the relationship."

She nodded, wiping away the remains of her tears. "That sounds sensible."

"With that in mind, I have a proposal for you." Her eyes must have widened, because he gave her a wry look. "Don't look so alarmed—it's not that sort of proposal. I know you well enough to guess what the answer to that would be. Look, I've already told you I've booked flights for this weekend. Dan gets married next Saturday, and I have to go."

"Of course."

"But here's an idea... Why don't you come with me?"

She stared at him.

"With Charlie," he added. "Obviously."

Her mouth fell open. "You mean...to the Northland?"

"Yeah. It doesn't sound like the university's going to be open any time soon, so you probably won't be working for the next couple of weeks at least. You don't have a place to stay, and it will take a while to sort out your insurance. It will be a break for you to get away, especially after the earthquake."

"I...I couldn't."

"Because..."

She couldn't think of an answer.

"It would give us time," he said. "For Charlie and I to get to know each other."

"We'd stay with you?"

"If you wanted, or I can arrange somewhere else. You can decide when you get there, if you like."

"But I'd have to meet your friends and family..."

His eyes were calm but firm. "Don't you think it would be nice for Charlie to meet his grandparents? And for them to meet him?"

Fear made her words dry up. He had every right to want to take his son to meet his family. But the thought filled her with panic. She glanced at her son, who was feeding buttons to Thomas Tank while he gave a running commentary about them being bad for Thomas's teeth. She didn't want to share him with anyone. But she had to think about what was best for Charlie, and surely having an extended family was a good thing?

To her surprise, Toby reached out and took her hand. "I'm not going to take him away from you."

His sincere words brought a lump to her throat. She'd never be able to forgive or forget the fact that he'd walked away from her, but he'd said to her, *I was very young, Esther.* Perhaps he'd changed. And even if he hadn't, he was still Charlie's father.

She went to say something, but Charlie interrupted her with a complaint that a chocolate button had somehow "got stuck" in Thomas's wheel. She spent a minute levering it out with a spoon, sighing as he returned to the floor. She'd forgotten what she was saying.

"Having an extended family does have its benefits," Toby said. "Like babysitting."

She gave a short laugh. "I can't remember the last time I had an hour to myself when I wasn't working."

"There you go. Perhaps we can go out for a meal or two, to talk things over."

She met his gaze. His warm brown eyes held a very small hint of mischievousness. "Don't even think about it," she warned. "This morning's kiss was a mistake. It won't be happening again."

"Of course not." But the twinkle didn't disappear.

For some reason, the box of cards he had in his bedroom jumped into her mind. Naughty Nights. Even the name gave her goose bumps. How exciting it would be to play that game with him. But it had been a long, long time since she'd had sex. Would she remember how to do it if she ever got back in the saddle?

"What are you smiling about?" he asked.

The beer was starting to have an effect, and some of her reservations died away. This man was the father of her child. He was hardly a stranger. She leaned her head on her hand and sighed. "I was thinking that the last time anyone touched me intimately was to put stitches in."

He winched. "Ouch!"

"Yeah. It would be nice to have a memory of being touched down there that didn't include rubber gloves and forceps."

He chuckled. "Well, if I can help, you only have to say."

She took another swallow of the beer and studied him dreamily. He'd been so good in bed. Considerate and gentle, and yet also a delicious mixture of commanding and the right amount of forceful. The memory made her shiver.

One night in Fiji, a few nights after their almost-exhibitionism on the beach, they'd had a drink on the balcony and got talking about women's rights. He'd purposefully adopted a misogynistic attitude to wind her up, which had worked to the extent that she'd eventually thrown her wine in his face and risen to leave. In reply, he'd picked her up and carried her into the bedroom, ignoring her complaints. He'd thrown her onto the bed, pinned her there, and kissed her, refusing to let her go, and eventually he'd taken her with a luscious roughness, in spite of the fact that she'd already given in.

His gaze fell to her lips, and she couldn't stop herself moistening them with her tongue. He noticed, and his eyes grew a few degrees hotter.

"Don't look at me like that," she whispered.

He said nothing, but his lips curved.

Her heart thumped wildly. "You'd be disappointed in me. I've had a baby—I'm all stretch marks and saggy boobs and belly."

His gaze dipped to her breasts. "They still look pretty good to me."

Warmth flooded her cheeks. "Toby!"

"What?" he asked innocently.

"I'm an old mother now. I should be knitting and making flans."

He gave a short laugh. "You don't look bad for a pensioner."

"I mean it. You're all young and...vibrant. I'm—"

"Twenty-three?"

"-four," she said lamely. "But I feel seventy most days." She sighed and studied the beer. "I've grown so weak. One bottle and I'm practically comatose."

"Cheap date," he said.

"I guess." Self-pity washed over her. "I don't want to feel old. I mean, I don't regret having Charlie at all, he's the best thing that ever happened to me, but my whole world revolves around him and daycare and feeding times and what's on TV, and sometimes I just wish…"

He leaned closer to her. "What do you wish?"

She moistened her lips again. "When we were in Fiji, you made me feel so…"

"So…?"

"Alive. You're like the sun." She was almost asleep.

He reached out a hand and tucked a lock of hair behind her ear. "And you're like the moon."

"Cold and distant?"

"Breathtakingly beautiful." He slipped his hand into her hair and cupped the back of her head as if he was afraid she might pull away, but the warmth of his compliment spread through her, and as he lowered his lips to hers, she gladly moved the last inch to meet him.

He tasted of chocolate and beer, summer and happiness. She let him kiss her slowly, closing her eyes, and enjoyed the movement of his lips across hers, the stroke of his tongue into her mouth. *What are you doing?* yelled her brain, but he was such a good kisser that her body refused to move.

"Kissing's yuck," said Charlie.

She pulled back, wondering if Toby would look exasperated, but he only seemed amused. He turned to face his son, who stood before them, Thomas Tank in his hand. "Hey, buster." Toby lifted him up and sat him on the breakfast bar, placing the engine beside him. "Kissing's not yuck. Not when you like the girl."

Her cheeks grew warm, and she stood to clean away their dishes, letting her hair fall forward to hide her face.

"I'm never going to kiss anyone," Charlie stated as she started to run the hot water.

"Fair enough," Toby said.

"I'm not going to sex anyone neither," Charlie announced.

Esther stared at him, startled, as Toby burst out laughing. "Charlie!" she exclaimed. Where had that come from? She'd never heard that on Thomas Tank.

"That's very wise," Toby told the boy. "You'll save a fortune in condoms."

"What's a conbom?"

Toby lifted him down from the breakfast bar. "It's kind of like when Thomas enters a blocked tunnel," he said. "And about as reliable, apparently. Now look, you've missed two chocolate buttons. If you don't eat them, I'll have to eat them, and I'll end up looking like the Fat Controller. You wouldn't want that, would you?"

Charlie giggled and ran off to get the buttons. Trying not to laugh, Esther glared at Toby. "For God's sake, stop leading him astray."

"Okay," he said. "I'll keep that for his mother." He winked at her before turning away, giving her a splendid view of his tight ass as he bent to fight Charlie for the last button.

She sighed and went back to cleaning the dishes, smiling as Charlie tripped over the carpet, followed two seconds later by Toby. Going to the Northland with him would be a huge mistake. Because Toby himself was like a packet of Cadbury's Buttons, and it was as if she hadn't had a taste of chocolate for three years. Once she opened the packaging, how was she going to stop herself eating the whole lot?

Chapter Ten

Esther had only been to the Northland once, and that was fifteen years ago. She'd forgotten how different the climate was compared to Christchurch.

As soon as they stepped down from the small plane at Kerikeri's tiny airport, the warm air wafted over her. She slipped off her jacket and hung it over her arm as she helped Charlie down the steps. "Wow, that's warm."

"I'd forgotten," Toby said. "Jeez, I love it up here. I don't know how you guys get off calling it summer down there."

Certainly, it was never so humid in the South Island. The sweat was already trickling between her breasts. "How are we getting to Kerikeri from the airport? By taxi?"

"Nah, someone's picking us up."

The first twinges of alarm shot through her. She hadn't expected to meet strangers as soon as she set foot on the runway. "Oh."

He reached out and squeezed her hand briefly. "Don't worry. They'll love you." They watched as Charlie missed the last step and fell flat on his face. "I don't know about him though."

"Like father, like son."

"I can't argue with that." She could remember Toby walking into doors and stubbing his toe in Fiji.

He took her travel bag from her so she could pick Charlie up, and she followed him across the tarmac. Her heart hammered. Why had she agreed to this? All her instincts had told her not to go, but she kept telling herself it would be best for Charlie—that he deserved to get to know his family, and vice versa, and so eventually she'd agreed.

Toby turned to wait for her to catch up, and for a moment hesitancy flickered across his face. He was nervous too. This was as scary for him as it was for her. Somehow, it made her feel better, as if they were in it together.

Inside the gate, several people were waiting to welcome the arrivals, and a couple waved to Toby as he approached.

"Hey." He walked up to them with a smile.

Esther slowed as the young woman ran up to him and threw her arms around him. "I've missed you!" She gave him a big hug. Of average height and with a slim but curvy figure, she had long, brown, wavy hair and a pleasant, girl-next-door face. Esther recognized her from her picture in the women's magazine—this was Faith, author of the Seven Sexy Sins articles.

So the guy standing with her must be Mr. Sinful himself. Around six feet tall, Rusty was a good-looking man, slim but muscular, with reddish-brown hair that curled around his ears. When Faith finally released Toby, Rusty shook his hand, and then Toby pulled him closer for a manly bearhug.

"Good to see you," Rusty said. "It feels like you've been gone ages."

"I know. It's good to be back." Toby hesitated. "Um, guys, I've brought someone with me. A friend." He turned toward Esther and smiled.

Heart in her mouth, she walked forward to stand next to him, conscious of their curious looks. Balancing Charlie on her left hip, she held out her hand to shake Faith's and then Rusty's as Toby introduced them.

"This is Esther," Toby told them.

Recognition dawned on their faces. "Oh…" Faith said. "So *this* is Esther."

Esther glanced at Toby. What did that mean? He'd said he'd only told his parents about her and Charlie coming up north with him.

They looked at the boy in her arms, and Toby cleared his throat. "And this is Charlie."

They stared at him. There was a moment of silence.

"No…" Rusty said.

Faith's eyes widened, and she turned her stunned gaze onto Toby. He nodded in answer and said sheepishly, "He's my son."

Esther's cheeks burned as she waited for their reaction. She'd expected a thousand questions, denials, shock, even accusations.

She didn't expect the look of pure delight that spread across Faith's face as she said, "Oh my God, Toby, you're a daddy?"

He grinned then. "Yeah."

Faith squealed and threw her arms around him, kissing him on the cheek, then broke away and came over to Esther. "I can't believe it!"

Her eyes danced. "He told us all about you ages ago—I'm so glad you're here." She held her hand out to Charlie. "And you! You are so like your daddy. Look at your gorgeous curly hair! Hello, young man. I'm very pleased to meet you. I'm Faith."

Charlie curled up to Esther shyly, but held out a hand and let Faith clasp it.

Rusty shook Toby's hand again, smiling. "Congratulations, mate, that's wonderful news."

Esther nearly cried at the relief that swept over her. Faith obviously spotted her reaction and rubbed her arm. "Are you okay? Has it been a long flight?"

She shook her head. "No. It's just... I'm a bit overwhelmed, that's all."

"Of course you are. How nerve-racking for you. Come on, let's grab your bags and we'll take you home for a cup of coffee, and you can tell us as much or as little as you want."

"Thanks." Esther concentrated on straightening Charlie's T-shirt as she tried to hide her emotion. Although she got on well with her colleagues at the university, and the other mothers at Charlie's daycare center were always friendly, she hadn't had any close friends since school. True, she'd purposely kept herself to herself and she'd coped remarkably well on her own, but, still, she envied Toby his close circle of friends and family. How different it would have been to know she had other people to rely on during the difficult times. She couldn't imagine it.

They collected their bags and walked to the car. It was only then that Faith said, "Oh, I just realized, we don't have a car seat for Charlie."

"We've got that old one at home Cole gave us." Rusty smiled. "I'll nip home and get it."

"No, no." Esther flushed with embarrassment at their friendliness. "He can sit on my lap and I'll clip us both in, providing it isn't far."

"No, it's only five minutes. If you're sure?"

"Of course. It's no problem."

They piled into the car, and Rusty drove them into Kerikeri to his and Faith's house. Once inside, Faith made them all a coffee, and they took the cups outside to sit on the decking under the shade of a large umbrella, while Charlie scribbled on a plastic doodle pad that Faith kept in a cupboard for visiting kids.

Esther sipped her drink, finally beginning to relax. She hadn't realized until then how tense she'd been.

"You'll have to tell us all about the earthquake," Faith said to Toby. "We were so frightened for you when we heard about it, especially when we couldn't contact you. Was it scary?"

"Terrifying," Toby said. "I screamed like a girl."

Esther smiled as they laughed, but said, "He did not. He saved my life. And Charlie's."

"Wow," Faith said. "A real superhero."

"Like Dan Carter," Charlie announced, making them all laugh.

"I can tell he's your son," Rusty said to Toby wryly.

Toby ruffled the boy's hair. "His rugby education is sadly lacking, but I'm attempting to rectify that."

Faith met Esther's gaze and smiled. Esther studied her coffee cup. Faith's eyes seemed to see right through her, to her most vulnerable spots. She supposed that the other girl had some inkling of how she felt. Faith had been open in her articles with the way her relationship with Rusty had progressed, and she'd obviously been through the mill before the two of them gad finally settled down.

They talked for a while about the earthquake, and Toby explained how he and Esther had miraculously met up again. To Esther's relief, neither Faith nor Rusty enquired why she hadn't told Toby he had a son for two and a half years.

Eventually, though, Faith said, "Where are you staying, Esther?"

Esther recognized the unspoken question beneath Faith's query— were she and Toby back together? She couldn't look at Toby. They hadn't finalized details, although she knew he would let her stay at his house. But she wasn't sure that would be a wise idea.

The night after she'd had the beer and he'd kissed her, he'd told her he was sleeping on the sofa, and she hadn't contradicted him. Since then, he'd made no further move on her. He could probably sense her confusion, she thought. She was still attracted to him, but the last thing they should do was get involved again. She had to keep their relationship platonic and concentrate on what was best for Charlie.

She cleared her throat. "I'm not sure. I hadn't actually decided..."

Faith smiled. "Then why don't you stay with us? We have a spare room, and I can borrow any bits and pieces you need from Toby's sister-in-law—her boy's four now, but she's kept most of his clothes and toys and stuff, and I know she'll be happy to loan them out."

Esther bit her lip and finally glanced at Toby, wondering if he'd be annoyed that she wouldn't be staying with him, but he just smiled. She sighed with relief. It would give her the space to work things out and would remove the temptation of being in his company at night time. "Well, if you're sure…" She wondered if Rusty would be alarmed, but he was just watching his wife with a smile. "Charlie can be a bit loud," she told them.

"It'll do him good." Faith's eyes twinkled. "Give him some practice." She exchanged an amused glance with her husband.

"I thought so," Toby said. "Congratulations, you two—when's it due?"

Chapter Eleven

They both stared at him, shocked. "What do you mean, 'I thought so'?" Faith demanded.

"I'm a father now. I know these things. I'm very sensitive, you know."

Faith blew a raspberry. "Give over. You probably saw my pregnancy magazine on the table." But she laughed as he gave her a hug.

Esther smiled, but she couldn't help but study Toby as he shook Rusty's hand. He *was* sensitive, surprisingly so, but clearly his friends had no idea. How strange that she should recognize it and they didn't have a clue.

"Congratulations," she told them. "When's it due?"

"August," Faith said. "I'm only just three months. Hopefully you'll be able to give me some tips!"

Esther pulled a face. "Jeez, I made it up as I went along. I was so clueless."

"But look what a lovely boy you have. You must have done something right."

Esther was unable to stop a flush of pride spreading warmth into her cheeks. "Thank you."

Charlie brought the doodle pad up to Toby and tried to climb onto his lap. Toby lifted him up. "Draw a 'rari, Daddy," Charlie instructed.

"A Ferrari? Jeez, mate, start with something easy, why don't you?" But Toby began sketching, and Esther noticed that whereas her cars consisted of a box with two circles for wheels, Toby's looked like a sports car, to Charlie's delight.

She looked up. Faith was observing her watching Toby. Faith now smiled, a mischievous twinkle in her eyes. "Perhaps you'd like us to babysit tonight for you? I'm sure the two of you have a lot to catch up on. You could go out for a drink this evening."

Toby glanced up at Faith and pointed the stylus at her briefly before returning to his drawing. "Stop interfering."

"What?" she asked innocently.

He didn't look up again. "You know perfectly well what."

"I'm still waiting to write that article, Toby."

Esther couldn't help but smile at that. "Are you talking about the Naughty Nights?"

Faith grinned in delight. "Did he show you the game?"

"She found it by mistake." Toby added headlights to the car. "Don't go getting any ideas."

"It looks fun though, doesn't it?" Faith's eyes challenged Esther to deny it.

Two can play at that game, Esther thought, enjoying the exchange. "I'm surprised you two didn't give it a go," she said, indicating Faith and her husband. "It would seem like your kind of thing."

"Ah." To her delight, Faith's cheeks turned pink.

"Yes," Esther teased, "I read all about the Seven Sins. Mars Bars, eh, Rusty?"

He gave her a look, half-amused, half-exasperated. "Why does everyone pick on that?"

"I'm just glad it wasn't a Curly Wurly," Toby said.

They all laughed. Esther realized she was enjoying herself. It had been so long since she'd spent time relaxing in the company of people her own age.

"Anyway," Faith said, "moving swiftly on, are you going around your parents' house now, Toby?"

"Yes, I think so." He smiled at Esther. "Are you ready for that?"

"Um…"

"Don't worry." He reached over and squeezed her hand briefly. "They'll be great."

Faith started collecting the cups. "And don't forget—we'll look after Charlie tonight if you'd like to go out."

"Thanks." Esther took Charlie from Toby's lap, deciding she wasn't going to think about it for now. "We'd better get you washed and brushed up if you're going to meet your grandparents, eh?" Grandparents. Oh dear God. Things had gone well up until now, but explaining to Charlie's grandparents exactly why she'd never contacted their son to tell him about his child wasn't high on her list of ways to spend a pleasant weekend.

*

In the end, though, it all went surprisingly well. Luckily, Toby had spoken to his parents at length the previous night, telling them what had happened, so it wasn't a shock as such when they turned up at their house.

Still, initially Esther sensed a coolness from the efficient, organized Martha Wilkinson, who had clearly wondered what sort of person would keep such information to herself. But merely five minutes after meeting her grandson, who behaved impeccably, right down to his pleases and thankyous when she offered him a biscuit and a drink, she warmed to Esther. By the time they left, both Martha and the reticent Graham Wilkinson expressed great delight at having met her, and told her they'd love to have Charlie for the day if she'd like to go shopping or spend some time exploring the Northland.

"That went well," she said when they finally got back in the car. Rusty had previously dropped them at Toby's house, and they'd picked up his car before driving to his parents.

He smiled, heading off back into town. "I told you they'd be great."

"Your mum was wary at first though."

"Meh. I knew you'd win her over."

"Charlie was the one who won her over. You were such a good boy!" She reached over to the back seat and patted her son's leg. Faith had lent them a booster seat for him, and he sat there now, thumb in mouth, eyes drooping. "You're ready for your snooze, aren't you?"

"He can doze on my bed," Toby said, "if you want to come in for a coffee."

"Okay." She was interested to see inside his house. They hadn't gone in when he picked up his car, although she'd noted that the long, low wooden house that lay tucked amongst the mandarin trees looked neat and tidy—not quite what she would have expected a single guy's place to look like.

It was only a short drive to the road that led to the Kerikeri inlet. He pulled up in front of the house, and she lifted out a half-dozing Charlie. Toby led her over to the front door, unlocked it, and stepped back to let her enter first.

She walked into a light and airy living room overlooking the Waitangi Forest. It housed only a cream sofa and chairs and a huge television in terms of furniture, but scattered around the room were numerous wooden sculptures ranging from small koru leaf shapes on the walls to huge Maori fish hook carvings inlaid with paua shell.

"Toby, did you make all these?"

He placed his suitcase and carry bag on the floor and stuffed his hands in his pockets. "Yeah. A little hobby of mine."

"Oh my God, they're beautiful."

He shrugged, but she could see her words had pleased him.

Charlie toddled over to one and went to pick it up, and she stopped him hurriedly. "No, honey, these are Daddy's special carvings—they're not toys."

"Oh Christ, Esther, they're only made of wood. I can make a dozen a week. He can do whatever he wants with them." He dropped to his haunches in front of a carving that curled like a silver fern. "Look, Charlie. See how smooth it is?"

Charlie ran his grubby paw around the polished kauri wood. "Daddy made this?"

"Yes. I'll show you how one day, if you like."

Esther's breath caught in her throat as he continued to talk to his son about how he'd carved the wood in the right shape and then sanded it to make it smooth. His words indicated that he planned to stay in Charlie's life for a while. Of course it didn't mean anything—they were just words, and as soon as he got caught up in university life, any good intentions he'd had would probably go out of the window. But the words spread warmth through her, all the same.

Charlie yawned, so Toby picked him up and carried him along the corridor and into his room. Esther followed, hovering in the doorway until he beckoned her in.

She held back the covers for Charlie and covered him up, watching his eyes close. Then she kissed him and returned to the living room.

Toby had just boiled the kettle, and he came in carrying a couple of cups of coffee. He opened the sliding doors, and they went outside and sat on the swing seat together, close, but not touching.

Esther sank into the cushions and sighed. "It's so beautiful here."

He sipped his coffee and turned in the seat to face her, smiling. "It certainly is."

She gave him a wry look. "I was talking about the view."

"So was I." His eyes twinkled.

His T-shirt stretched across his muscular chest, and his legs were tanned under the swim shorts. He was a wonderful specimen of masculinity, and once again something stirred inside her, long forgotten, like the Loch Ness Monster swimming at the bottom of the lake.

"What?" He tipped his head at her silent observation, amused at her introspection.

It was so warm, she thought—sweat trickled between her breasts, and her hair clung to the back of her neck. Toby's skin glistened damply. If she touched her tongue to the hollow at the base of his throat, it would taste salty.

The weather had been like this in Fiji, and even though they'd made love under the slowly turning ceiling fan, they'd still stuck together, skin sliding against slippery skin. In the beginning, she'd worried about it and had wanted to keep showering, but he'd soon put an end to that. And after he'd licked and sucked her everywhere a woman could be licked and sucked, she'd given in and let him worship her warm body as often as they could both manage it.

What was it about the warm weather that made a person feel so sexy? Conscious of the way the humor in his eyes was gradually turning to desire, she closed her eyes and leaned her head on the back of the cushion.

Don't do it! Her brain tried to warn her, but her libido gagged it and yelled *Go for it!*

Would it be a terrible mistake, to sleep with him? Not if she kept her heart separate. To fall in love with him would be a disaster greater than the Christchurch earthquake. But it had been so long since she'd had sex. If they just kept it physical, if she held it in her mind all along that eventually she'd go back to Christchurch, what could go wrong? It was the twenty-first century after all—people had sex for fun all the time. Many people were likely to have had thirteen partners, not three. She'd been sensible and cautious for so long— didn't she deserve to have a little fun? And it wasn't as if he was a stranger—he was Charlie's father, and although she didn't completely trust him, and the hurt he'd caused her still simmered beneath the surface, she couldn't deny that she wanted him, or that the sight of his strong body made her ache to take him inside her.

She opened her eyes, not surprised to find him watching her. He smiled as she looked up at him, and she let her gaze caress his face for a moment, enjoying the gentleness of his warm brown eyes, his wide nose, generous lips. She'd be a fool to pass up on this chance.

Lifting a hand, she slid it into his thick, dark hair, and pulled his head toward her.

Chapter Twelve

Toby closed his eyes as Esther's lips touched his, startled by her forwardness, but more than happy to comply. She kissed him calmly, unhurriedly, and when he brushed her lips with his tongue, she didn't complain but instead opened her mouth and welcomed him inside.

It was perhaps the laziest, most erotic kiss he'd ever had, with the only sounds the singing of cicadas in the bush and the buzz of someone's lawnmower way off in the distance. The smell of lemons and jasmine hung in the air, and Esther's lips tasted of strawberry lip balm. Her skin was warm under his fingertips as he rested his hand on her knee.

She showed no signs of wanting to stop, either, clearly enjoying this quiet, gentle afternoon, the peace and heat of the summer day after the cool frenzy of her home in the South Island. Affection washed over him for this girl, who'd brought up their son alone, struggled for years with no one to help her through the hard times. True, that had been her own choice, and he still wished she'd tried harder to find him, but it didn't change the fact that she'd coped alone. He wished he could turn back time and make things right between them, but that was impossible. Instead, all he could give her was here and now.

Kissing her was heavenly, but an urge to pleasure her further flooded through him. He couldn't suggest anything too advanced with Charlie asleep in the next room, but that didn't mean he couldn't give her ten minutes of summer-filled bliss.

Moving his hand beneath her loose skirt, he started to draw patterns languidly on her thighs. He continued to kiss her, making the circles wider and higher, until eventually he brushed her panties, and she gave a little gasp and opened her eyes. In reply, he moved closer to her and lifted her leg across his lap.

She gave a bigger gasp at that and tried to sit up. "We can't."

He tightened his arm around her, forcing her to sit still. "No, we can't, but you can."

She flushed at his smile. "I... I couldn't."

"Couldn't you?" He touched his lips to hers. "Come for me, honey. Make my day."

She blinked repeatedly as if shocked. "What about Charlie?"

"We'll hear his feet on the floorboards," he murmured. "And anyway, it just looks like we're having a cuddle."

She breathed heavily, stiff with tension. "I haven't been touched there since I gave birth." she whispered.

Understanding dawned, bringing with it a touch of pity—she was worried her body had changed, and he might not like the new her. Little did she know the thought that she'd harbored their son inside her was strangely alluring. Her body was so different from his own— he'd never really thought about it before, beyond the obvious attraction of female curves. But his newfound awareness of her femininity stirred something inside him he'd not explored before. She fascinated him. She'd given him a son. And for that, even though having Charlie brought its own problems, he wanted to crown her with flowers.

He continued to draw circles on her inner thighs. "What's a stretch mark or two between friends?" he teased. "I've got a few myself."

She gave a short, embarrassed laugh and pushed him. "Idiot."

He nuzzled her ear. "Why don't we see if everything still works? Nobody's watching." He kissed her jaw, brushed his lips against hers.

She lowered her lashes, but didn't push him away, so he took that as acquiescence.

He began to stroke her through the thin cotton of her panties. She met his gaze, and he smiled when more color flooded her cheeks. He loved her innocence—she'd been like this in Fiji, wide-eyed and half-shocked most of the time... *Toby, what do you think you're doing, we can't possibly...* until her passion had overtaken her, and then she'd met him thrust for thrust and sigh for sigh. He'd loved pushing her boundaries, encouraging her to explore her sexuality with him. It had turned him on, and the mere thought of what they'd gotten up to in the Pacific paradise now made him hard.

"Close your eyes," he said, kissing her cheeks, the heat there burning his lips. She did as he bid, although her body remained tense, her hands against his chest as if she might push him away at any moment.

He stroked her a little more firmly, pressing his fingers gently into her soft folds through the thin cotton. "Just relax," he whispered, and covered her mouth with his, sliding his tongue into her mouth. She made a little sound deep in her throat as she kissed him back, and then she obviously decided to give in, because she melted against him, her body turning soft and yielding in his arms.

"Good girl," he murmured, pleased she'd submitted to him. He lowered his lips to kiss her again, continuing to stroke, gentle but firm. Her panties quickly became soaked, and when he finally hooked his fingers around the cotton, she didn't complain.

She was already swollen and slick with desire, and he sighed as his fingers slid easily into her warm flesh. He moved them down inside her, and she moaned softly against his lips as he brought them back up, coated with her moisture, to start caressing her clit.

"You're so beautiful," he muttered, meaning it, loving the way her dark hair curled damply around her neck, the glisten of sweat in the V of her breasts, the dark desire in her striking green eyes. "I wish I could slide inside you now."

"God, don't..." She shuddered, arching against him, not objecting as he pushed her legs a little wider and continued to stroke her firmly beneath her skirt. "Toby..."

"Is that good?" He kissed her lips, her cheeks, her forehead, then back to her lips again, letting his mouth hover over hers, exchanging hot breaths.

"Oh... yes... You seem to know ...right where... the best spots are... Oh..."

Desire flooded through him, and his erection strained against his tight shorts. He crushed her mouth to his, holding her tight against him. She moaned deeply, and he kissed down to her throat, around to her ears. "I wish I could taste you," he said, grazing his teeth on her neck. "I want to lick every inch of your body and then plunge my tongue inside you, and suck this soft button of yours until it makes you moan." He circled her clit lightly, teasing her, enjoying her gasps of delight.

"Oh, fuck..." She tipped her head back as he laced his tongue across her throat.

"I want to do that too. I want to throw you onto the bed and thrust deeply inside you, and feel you tighten around me as you come."

"Toby…"

He pulled her onto his lap, dizzy with desire, wanting to feel her soft body. Turning her so she faced away from him, he pulled her back against his chest, groaning as she ground her buttocks against his erection. He slipped his hand back beneath her skirt, wishing he could strip off her clothes and see his fingers sliding inside her. She wore no bra, and her breasts were soft through the cotton vest.

There was something about Esther's body he loved. She was soft everywhere, so womanly. Childbirth had only emphasized this—her breasts were larger, her body slightly yielding to his fingers. How could she think it had made her less attractive?

"Tell me you don't want me," he said hoarsely, stroking her more firmly and rolling her nipple between the fingers of his other hand. "Tell me you don't want me inside you."

"Oh, God, I do," she whispered, rocking her hips against his hand as she leaned her head back on his shoulder. "I want you…" She turned her head to meet his lips, her kiss hungry and demanding.

Her body shuddered and stilled. He pressed his thumb against her clit and slid two fingers inside her as she came, smothering her soft cries with his mouth. She tightened around his fingers, and he sighed as her muscles pulsed, surprised at the intense feeling of satisfaction he got at the thought that he was responsible for her pleasure.

Then she went limp in his arms, and he withdrew his hand, turned her, and cradled her against him. Her heart raced under his hand where it rested on her ribcage.

Feeling strangely protective of her, he tightened his arms and kissed the top of her head.

"Thank you," she whispered.

He chuckled. "You're very welcome. Good to see everything is still in working order."

She gave a short laugh. "Yeah."

"What a pleasant way to spend a Saturday afternoon."

She lifted her head to look at him. Her cheeks were still flushed. "I half-expected to look up and see Charlie standing there."

He laughed at that. "That would probably put him into therapy for the rest of his life."

"Jeez. Don't even go there."

Their eyes met, and she reached up a hand to cup his face. He lowered his head and kissed her.

When he lifted his head, she pressed her lips together. "You know this can't go anywhere, right?"

His joy faded at her words. But she spoke the truth. They still lived at opposite ends of the country. And there were too many issues between them now—his leaving her in Fiji, her not finding him and telling him about Charlie. She said she'd tried, but how hard? A niggling doubt told him she'd wanted to punish him and, even if she had attempted to track him down, she'd probably given up easily. How could they ever move past those problems?

She stroked his cheek with her thumb, and a mischievous twinkle appeared in her eye. "However…"

He raised an eyebrow. "Yes…?"

"It would seem a shame to waste a golden opportunity."

What was going through her mind? "Oh?"

"You deserve a reward for being so generous today."

"I do," he said, warming up to the game.

"And for saving my life."

"That deserves an extra-special prize," he admitted.

She smiled. "I was thinking about the Naughty Nights game…"

His heart rate increased a little. "I see."

"Poor Faith's still waiting for her article."

"It seems a shame to disappoint her."

"My thoughts exactly." Keeping her eyes on his, she wiggled a little in his lap, pressing against his still-firm erection. "Fancy doing some research?"

"Oh yeah." His reply was so heartfelt, she giggled.

"You like that idea?" she asked, amusement lighting her eyes.

He grazed his hands over her, brushing her soft breasts. "I'd be a lunatic to turn down a chance to see you naked."

"Even with the stretch marks?" She looked suddenly vulnerable again.

"Especially with the stretch marks." He kissed her. "Your body's amazing, Esther. Soft and luscious. I can't fake this." He pressed his erection against her. "You drove me insane three years ago—and you've only gotten better with age."

"Like wine?" she suggested, letting him nibble her earlobe.

"I was going to say like vintage cheddar cheese, but it didn't seem very romantic." He lifted his head to look into her eyes as she laughed. Memories of their time in Fiji came flooding back—lying on the white sand, drinking cocktails; dancing on the beach as the sun went down; making love under the ceiling fan, skin sliding over damp skin, him moving slowly inside her, trying to make their time together last.

"What?" She looked self-conscious.

He felt an urge to be honest. "I know there's a whole world of reasons why we would never work. I know I hurt you badly, and I wish you'd found me when you discovered you were pregnant. And I don't know that I'm ready to be a father. But I just want to say, for going through it, for growing our child inside you, for giving birth alone when you must have been scared as hell, for bringing Charlie up into such a great boy... Well, thanks. That's all."

She bit her lip, and her eyes turned glassy.

"Have you turned soppy in your old age?" he teased.

She shook her head, lowering her lashes. "It's just... sometimes I wondered what you'd say if you ever found out. I thought you might be angry."

"Angry?" That puzzled him. He was hurt she hadn't found him. Nervous about being a father. Apprehensive about the future, about how to make it work so he played a part in Charlie's life emotionally, physically, and monetarily. But anger had never been a response he'd considered. "It wasn't your fault," he said. "We used a condom. For all the fucking good it did."

She touched his face again, brushing the slight stubble on his cheek. "You really don't know why I thought that, do you?"

"Er..."

"Do you ever get angry at anything?"

He said nothing, confused. Computer viruses made him angry. Cars when they wouldn't start. Missing a nail with a hammer and hitting his thumb instead. Not Esther. Why would she make him cross?

She laughed and pushed herself off his lap onto the seat. "Why don't you go and get the game, and we'll pick our first role-play?"

"Okay." He got up and walked into the living room to his suitcase. He wasn't sure why she'd asked to play when she obviously hadn't forgiven him for leaving her at the airport, but he wasn't going to argue when sex was on the table.

Chapter Thirteen

Esther watched Toby walk away and then lay back on the swing seat, arms above her head. The warm Northland sun beat down onto her, and although she knew she'd end up getting sunburned if she stayed out there much longer, for the moment she just reveled in its hot, healing rays.

Her muscles felt loose and relaxed after the mind-blowing orgasm he'd just given her. Warmth flooded her cheeks yet again as she thought of how easily he'd made her come, but she couldn't in all honesty say she regretted it. He was too good at it for her to bemoan his insistent attitude.

While they were on holiday, he'd brought her to the dizzy heights of ecstasy with embarrassing ease time and again. She'd thought about it often since, and had never been sure if it was because he was such a skillful lover, or if it was just because she'd been so lacking in sexual experience that the first guy willing to spend five minutes on her had seemed like an expert.

There was no doubt he was an unselfish and generous lover. He'd always made sure she achieved orgasm, usually more than once, before he gave in and relaxed his tight control. In fact, he'd always seemed to enjoy giving her pleasure almost as much as taking it himself, a fact she was sure not every guy could claim.

And yet now she knew that wasn't the only reason why she'd responded so well to him. It wasn't just because of the way he touched her—that he seemed to understand instinctively where her erogenous zones were, or that he pressed everything in the right order. Now she realized she responded to his generous spirit, to his warmth. She loved his sense of humor, his complete openness, as if he kept no secrets at all hidden in his heart. Back in Fiji, he'd been playful, sexy and, looking back, so, so young. Now he was quieter, more serious, but he was still as warm-hearted and generous as ever.

Good job she wasn't going to let her heart get involved in this, because she could get into some sticky trouble if that ever happened.

"Found it," he said, appearing back on the deck with the box. "I checked on Charlie too by the way—he's out for the count."

She glowed at the fact that he'd thought to check on their son. "Yeah, he normally has about an hour and a half."

"Oh to be two again," he sighed, gesturing for her to sit up, taking the seat beside her as she did. "I could easily sleep for a couple of hours in the afternoon." He put the box on her lap. "There you go."

She scooted to the end of the swing seat and opened the box. "How are we going to decide? Randomly?"

"I don't mind. You choose." While she flicked through some of the cards, he read the instructions in the accompanying pamphlet.

"What does it say?" she asked.

"It suggests trying to stay in character as much as possible, because it makes it easier to try new things if you're acting rather than being yourself."

"I suppose that makes sense." Certainly, some of the scenarios in her hand would be easier to carry out if she was someone else. Just reading them made her cheeks grow warm.

He glanced up at her and grinned. "You're blushing."

"Am not."

"Found a good one?"

She had, and it featured… well, suffice it to say there was no way she was reading that one out. "Actually, I think I might go for the one I read to you in Christchurch."

"The hooker one?"

"Yeah." She pulled out the card.

"Read it again."

"'You're a very expensive, high-class hooker, looking for customers in a bar. You see a businessman ordering a drink. Go up to him and ask him if he would like a companion for the evening. Get him to buy you a drink, and then let him take you back to his place. Ask what he wants, and tell him what it will cost. And if he wants anything extra, well, that's up to you.'"

Her heart beat a little faster at the thought of playing out the role. Could she really do it? Act like a prostitute and pretend he'd paid for her services for the night?

"Do we have to dress up?" she asked nervously.

"Of course."

"It's all right for you—you only have to dress up like a businessman."

"That doesn't come naturally, I assure you."

"I bet it comes a damn sight more naturally than dressing up like a hooker. I haven't got a clue what to wear. Actually, I don't have anything to wear at all."

"We'll find you something revealing." He grinned.

"I haven't worn anything revealing since I was about fifteen."

"You'll have to improvise. Ask Faith."

"I can't ask Faith!" She stared at him in horror. "What would she say?"

"I suspect she'll probably cheer. She's been desperate to get me fixed up with someone for ages." He rolled his eyes.

She frowned, leaning her head on her hand. "You said you hadn't dated for six months. Why not?"

He stared out across the Waitangi Forest. "Other things on my mind," he said.

Had a girl broken his heart? The jealousy that surged through her at that thought surprised her. Just because he was Charlie's father didn't mean he belonged to her. He'd probably slept with a dozen girls since Fiji, maybe more. Still, she couldn't stop her fists clenching at the thought of him touching them as he'd just touched her, pleasuring them, loving them. Had he been in love? Her chest tightened uncomfortably. She couldn't think about it—it was going to make her cry. Damn baby hormones still hanging around.

When she looked up, he was watching her. Why did he always make her feel as if he could see right through her, into her very thoughts?

"Nobody's matched up to you, Esther," he said.

He had read her mind. "Bullshit."

He chuckled. "It's the truth, but I know you'll never believe me. Okay. So it's a date? What time does Charlie go to bed?"

"I usually put him down around six thirty."

"Okay, shall we meet in town at, say, seven thirty—give you time to settle him?"

"Sure." She was glad he'd been considerate enough to think of Charlie's needs. "Whereabouts?"

"At the Five Palms."

"Where's that?"

"I'll ask Faith to take you."

"You'll do no such thing."

He put the lid on the box and handed her the card. "You can show her this. She'll help you get ready for tonight."

"Toby!"

He sighed. "She's nice, honey. She won't laugh—at least not at you, at me maybe. Open up a little. It might be nice not to have to do things on your own for once."

She said nothing, but his words played on her mind as they woke Charlie and got ready to go back to Faith and Rusty's place. She was an only child, and although she'd tried over the years to open up and share herself with people, it had always backfired on her. Eventually, she'd given up, tired of being hurt, and now she kept distant and withdrawn, hiding behind a protective shell. But for once, it might be nice to talk to a woman her own age, to have a friend. Even if she was only going to be there for a week.

Toby drove them back and came in with them. They walked around the house, onto the decking, and through the sliding doors to the living room.

"Hey, you two." Faith got up from the dining table at the far end of the room where she'd been sitting surrounded by a pile of papers. Rusty remained sitting there, also surrounded by papers, but he lifted a hand in welcome.

"Hey." Toby helped Charlie up the step and followed him in. "What are you guys up to?"

"Essays," Rusty grunted, pulling another paper toward him. "What exciting lives we lead."

"I'll brighten up your day then," Toby said. "We'd like to take you up on your offer of babysitting tonight if that's okay."

Faith's eyebrows rose, but she merely said, "Of course, that's why I asked. I popped around to a few friends today and picked up some bits and pieces, including a couple of boxes of toys for Charlie."

"That was… very kind." Esther spoke awkwardly, unused to people helping her out. Charlie had already found one of the boxes Faith had left in the living room for him, and he ran over with a squeal at the sight of the wooden trains.

"You've made a friend for life," Toby said wryly. He turned to Esther. "I'll see you at seven thirty." He bent and kissed her on the cheek.

"You two have a lot to talk about?" Faith's question sounded innocent, but her eyes sparkled with interest.

"Yeah," Toby said. "Lots to talk about." He winked at Esther, and her cheeks grew warm.

He walked over to Charlie and dropped to his haunches beside him. "Hey, buddy."

"Look, Daddy." Charlie showed him how two of the trains connected.

"I know—wasn't that nice of Faith to get those for you? Look, I'm going to pop home now. You and Mummy are staying here with Faith, okay?"

Charlie nodded without looking up.

"I'd like to take Mummy out for dinner later," Toby told him. "Once you've gone to bed. Faith and Rusty will still be here to look after you. Is that okay?"

Charlie looked up at Esther, suddenly wary, unused to being apart from her.

Faith sat on the floor next to him, however, and started putting together a train track for him. "Of course we'll be okay, won't we Charlie?" She winked at him. "I've got a special present for you."

He stared at her. "What is it?"

"It's a big red box full of Thomas Tank stories. I thought we could read them in bed."

Charlie's eyes widened. "A Cow on the Line?"

"I think so," Faith said. "All the stories are there. The one with the balloon, the one where he gets stuck in a tunnel."

"Like a conbom," Charlie said.

"Pardon?"

Toby cleared his throat. "That's my cue to leave." He ruffled Charlie's hair, then came over to kiss Esther on the cheek, grinning at her glare. "See you later." He waved goodbye to Faith and Rusty and made a quick exit.

Esther shook her head at Faith's questioning look. "Don't ask."

Chapter Fourteen

Trying not to think about what Toby was teaching her son, Esther indicated the toys on the floor. "Thank you so much for going to the effort of getting these."

"Oh, you're welcome—people are happy to clear out their playrooms, I think." Faith finished connecting the train tracks to make a loop and got to her feet. "Want a coffee?"

"Please."

Faith led her into the kitchen, and Esther perched on one of the stools at the breakfast bar. "I certainly don't think Rusty and I will be short of clothes or toys when the time comes," Faith said as she poured water into the kettle.

"That's good. It's such an expensive business, and kids grow out of their clothes so quickly." Esther watched the other woman bustle about putting coffee into cups. Faith positively glowed with happiness. Had she herself had that tell-tale glow when she was pregnant? She doubted it somehow. She'd been too worried about money and how she was going to cope to really enjoy her pregnancy, and then of course her father had died. The usual sadness filled her at the thought of her father dying, but she pushed the emotion away and smiled as the other woman hummed to herself. "How are you feeling?"

"Better now." Faith leaned on the breakfast bar. "I felt very queasy the first three months, but I wasn't actually sick. I think I'm coming out of it now."

"That's great. I threw up every morning for the first twenty weeks."

"That sucks."

"Yeah."

Faith smiled and leaned her chin on her hand. "So… You and Toby. Got a lot to talk about tonight?"

Heat crept into Esther's cheeks. Both girls started laughing. "You got me," Esther admitted. "We're going to do some research for you."

"The Naughty Nights game? Excellent!" Faith grinned. "Which scenario are you going for?" Esther glanced over her shoulder at Rusty, who still sat at the dining-room table, working. She felt too embarrassed to say with him listening. Faith waved a hand. "Don't mind him—he's used to this sort of thing."

"I remember," Esther said. "Handcuffs, wasn't it?"

Rusty gave them both an exasperated look and returned to his papers as they giggled.

"He loves being teased about it really," Faith said. "This is all an act." She walked over, stood behind him, and put her arms around his neck. "Isn't it, honey?"

"I can tell by the scowl," Esther said.

"I'm not listening." He continued to grade his papers as Faith kissed his jaw. "La-la-la-la."

She said something in his ear, and he laughed and reached up to capture her for a kiss. Esther looked away. She couldn't help but envy their relaxed and loving relationship. She'd never had that sort of intimacy—hadn't even lived with anyone before.

"You're embarrassing Esther," he scolded her when he finally let her go. "Go make me a drink, wife."

She stuck her tongue out at him before returning to the kitchen to make the coffee. "See what happens? Give them an inch, they take a mile."

Esther smiled. "And you love it."

Faith grinned. "Maybe."

She made the coffee and delivered Rusty his, then gestured for Esther to follow her past Charlie and out onto the deck. They put up the large umbrella over the table and sat out of the scorching February sun.

"Come on then," Faith said when they were both settled. "Spill the beans. What scenario?"

Esther sighed, pulled the card out of her pocket, and passed it to her.

Faith read it. "Ooh."

"Yeah."

"So you're meeting him in town?"

"Yep."

"What are you going to wear?"

"No idea. I only have the clothes I bought last week—two pairs of jeans, half a dozen T-shirts, and some practical undies."

Faith eyed her thoughtfully. "We're a similar size, I think. You're only a bit shorter than I am. But I'm sure I'll have something you can wear."

"You have clothing put aside in case you need to dress like a prostitute?"

"You never know when you might need it."

They laughed and sipped their coffee. Esther glanced over her shoulder. Charlie played happily with the trains, driving the engine and its carriage around and around.

"Toby adores him," Faith said.

Esther met her gaze. Faith smiled, and Esther smiled back. "I always feared he'd be angry, but he wasn't, not a bit."

"Toby doesn't do angry."

"I'm beginning to understand that." Esther nibbled her bottom lip as she studied the other girl thoughtfully. Should she ask Faith about Toby? The part of her she kept locked away from other people didn't want to open up and admit she was curious. But Faith was one of Toby's oldest friends, and she seemed a genuinely nice person. She gave in. "He told you about me then?"

Faith laughed. "God, yes."

"What did he say?"

"Well, first of all you have to understand what Toby's other girls have been like."

Jealousy flickered through Esther, but she clamped it down. "I'm guessing there have been plenty."

"The usual amount, I suppose. The majority with a bra size bigger than their IQ."

"Really?"

"Oh yeah. Toby's never been known for his subtlety. Big boobs, a pretty face... nothing else seemed to matter. I don't think he ever thought there *was* anything else."

Esther frowned. "That doesn't make sense. You're hardly a bimbo, and I'm assuming Eve isn't either."

"I meant that he wouldn't have thought smart women would find him attractive. You know what Toby's like—he has a very low opinion of himself."

Which his friends and family hadn't helped. She thought it, but she didn't say it. Faith obviously loved him, but from what he'd told Esther about everyone who knew him, their teasing hadn't helped his self-image over the years.

"And then he met you," Faith said, and smiled.

Esther's heart thumped hard. "What did he say about me?"

"Not an awful lot to begin with. He was oddly quiet when he came back from Fiji. He was supposed to go with Dan, my brother, but at the last minute Dan had something on at work and he couldn't go, so Toby went alone. We all presumed he hadn't enjoyed himself much because, well, you know what he's like—if he's got something to say, he doesn't normally keep it to himself."

"I suppose."

"But then one night when we were all having a drink, he suddenly announced he'd met this girl. We waited for him to joke about her chest size and how many times they'd had sex and that sort of thing, but when we pressed him for details, you know what he said? 'She was special.'"

Esther's cheeks burned. "Oh."

"Yeah. That made us all sit up. I'd never heard Toby say anything like that about a girl before."

"He's never been in love?"

Faith shrugged. "Not that I know of. We tried to get him to tell us more, but for the first time there were no gory details. In fact, in the end he walked off, wouldn't say anything. We knew this girl had gotten to him in some way, but we never found out what had happened." Faith studied her curiously. "What did happen?"

"I don't know. I mean, I don't know why he acted like that. We had a great fortnight. Barely got out of bed." She smiled wryly. "At the end, we went to the airport together, and I asked whether we could stay in touch, but he said there was no point. He walked off and didn't look back. I assumed he'd never given me another thought."

"Well, I can't say for certain what went through his head, but you definitely were not just another girl," Faith said firmly.

"What about since then?" She couldn't help asking. "Have there been lots of girlfriends?"

"Nobody for about six months after the holiday. He was very quiet, not himself at all. Then finally he seemed to move on, and went on a few dates with a few different girls. Nothing serious. But after Rusty and I got together, he changed again. I think he's only been out with two girls over the past year, both of them fleetingly. He decided he wanted to go to university and then he travelled a bit, working to make himself some money. We all felt that maybe he'd finally grown up."

Esther didn't know what to say. Why had their fleeting relationship affected him so much? She knew why it had affected her—she had physical evidence of her transformation, evidence that was currently moving an engine under the dining table beneath poor Rusty's legs. But why had Toby changed so much when he quite clearly hadn't been interested in prolonging their relationship or trying to find ways to make it work?

"So you got back home and found yourself pregnant," Faith said.

"Yes. A few weeks later. I couldn't believe it—we'd used a condom every time. I know they're not a hundred percent reliable, but I always thought the one percent failure rate was due to someone not using them right, you know? I never, ever considered I could get pregnant if I took precautions. It came as such a shock."

That was the understatement of the year. She'd nearly fainted when she took the test, and she'd had to hyperventilate into a paper bag in the doctor's surgery. "The doctor must have thought I was such an idiot. I mean, in this day and age, a woman not realizing that feeling sick in the morning could mean she was pregnant?"

"It was out of context, wasn't it? If you'd been trying to get pregnant, it would have been the first thing you'd have thought of."

"Yes, I suppose so."

"Did you try to track him down?" Faith asked the inevitable question that Esther had been dreading, but the other girl's eyes were un-judgmental, her expression relaxed.

"I did, briefly," she lied. "But four months into the pregnancy, my father died."

"Oh, Christ." Faith looked suitably horrified. "Esther, I'm sorry."

"Thank you. It was very difficult. My mother died years ago, so I had to make all the funeral arrangements on my own. And I just gave up looking for Toby after that."

"And then you had to cope with giving birth all alone." Pity settled on Faith's face. "How awful."

Esther looked at her hands. "It was hard. I made it harder on myself, I know. I withdrew from everyone—I wouldn't accept any help. I decided it was just going to be me and the baby. And we've done just fine." She couldn't help the edge of defensiveness that crept into her voice.

"Of course you have," Faith said smoothly. "Look at Charlie— what a wonderful little boy."

Esther bit her lip. "You're such a nice person."

Faith laughed. "I'm really not. Especially in the morning—ask Rusty."

"I mean it. Toby's your friend. You had every right to demand to know why I never told him he had a child."

"I wouldn't presume to ask you that." Faith looked puzzled. "You're a grown, educated woman, and I assumed you had your reasons. Toby's a great guy, but he's no angel."

"Ain't that the truth," Esther said. In the bedroom, he wouldn't look out of place in a pair of horns and a forked tail.

Faith grinned. "Come on, why don't we see if we can find you an outfit for tonight?" She stood and beckoned Esther to follow her into the living room. "Then I'll make some dinner. You like fish fingers, Charlie?" She bent to look under the dining-room table.

"With beans?"

"Of course! Got to have baked beans with fish fingers."

Charlie beamed happily as he ran the wooden engine over Rusty's feet.

"Sorry," Esther apologized to the patient teacher.

"It's okay. Kind of feels like a massage." He wiggled his toes, and Charlie giggled.

Faith leaned on the table next to her husband. "Hey, what kind of clothes should a hooker wear?"

He turned over a paper without batting an eyelid. "Why, are you thinking of earning some extra money?"

"Ha ha. Esther's dressing up for Toby for the Naughty Nights game."

He chuckled as Esther glared at Faith. "One thing you need to know if you stay with us is that there are no secrets where Faith's concerned."

"I'm beginning to get that," Esther said.

Faith grinned. "So? Outfit?" She took his pen away.

He paused then and glanced up at her with exasperation. She raised her eyebrows, waiting for a reply, so he sighed and moved his gaze to Esther. He studied her for a moment, starting to smile as her cheeks grew warm.

Then he dropped his gaze and picked up another essay. "The blue dress," he said, taking back his pen, and clicking it on. He started writing.

Faith straightened. "Of course!"

"Ankle length, up to the chin?" Esther asked hopefully.

"Some hooker you'd make. Come on, honey. Let's see if we can't make Toby's eyes pop out of his head."

Chapter Fifteen

Toby saw her as soon as she came into the bar.

Of course, it helped that he'd had his eyes glued to the door for the past ten minutes, but things had become more difficult when an old friend of his father's spotted him and came over for a chat.

As Esther walked in, however, Toby stood and picked up his glass. He tried to interrupt the old man, but he was currently in the middle of a story and hadn't taken a breath for the past five minutes.

Toby nodded politely, hoping the old boy would take a hint considering he was now standing, and his gaze slid over to the woman at the bar. She looked stunning. She wore a skin-tight sky-blue dress he'd seen Faith in once, although Faith had worn it with leggings and a baggy jacket. But Esther wore it on its own, along with high-heeled silver sandals that showed off her shapely legs to perfection. The dress came down to mid-thigh and clung to her curves. The top was low cut enough to show a great deal of cleavage. She obviously wore some kind of bra that propped everything up and out. If she wore any panties at all, they had to consist of hardly any material, because there was no sign of a VPL.

He'd never seen her in anything like this—in Fiji she'd worn shorts, and last week she'd bought herself two pairs of jeans. He'd forgotten what a great figure she had. There was no doubt she drew every eye in the bar.

Okay, two seconds into the evening and he already had a hard-on the size of the Eiffel Tower.

The old guy droned on without a pause, and Toby sighed silently, wondering how to excuse himself without being rude. He glanced back at the bar and then froze at the sight of a guy approaching Esther. Shit.

"Nineteen-thirty, I think it was," droned the old guy. "The shops weren't there then, you know."

"Fascinating," Toby said, watching the young guy lean on the bar next to Esther and start talking to her. "Well, it's been great talking to you, but my friend's here now so I've got to go, sorry."

The old guy looked over at the bar and grinned. "'Friend', eh?"

"Special friend," Toby said, winking.

The old guy laughed. "Say g'day to your dad for me, won't you?"

"Will do. See you, Ben."

He picked up his empty bottle and walked over to the bar. Leaning on the wooden surface, he smiled at the barman and ordered another beer.

"Thanks," he heard Esther say, "but I'm really not interested."

"Aw, come on," the guy pushed. "You're obviously out for a good time. Let me buy you a drink or three and then we'll go back to my place. You won't be disappointed—I've got a ten-inch dick." He rested a hand on her butt.

Aghast at the audacity of the male species, Toby bristled and opened his mouth to say something to the idiot, but Esther spoke before he could get a word out.

"Okay, as you obviously can't take a polite hint, I'll say this in the sort of language you'll understand. Fuck off."

Amused, Toby turned and leaned on the bar. As the guy opened his mouth to retort, he said, "Dude, take a hint. She's not interested."

The guy spun around, presumably intending to mouth off to whoever had interrupted him. When he found himself on a level with Toby's chin, he looked up with alarm. Toby raised an eyebrow. Picking up his beer, the man walked off without another word.

Toby met Esther's gaze and his lips curved. "Wow, that was subtle."

"He was being rude," she said defensively.

"Sweetheart, I meant his comment, not yours. I thought you were remarkably restrained."

"Oh."

"I'd lay my house on him not having a ten-inch dick."

"Thank the Lord I'll never have to find out," she said, clearly relieved.

The barman came back up with Toby's beer. Toby nodded at Esther. "And whatever the lady wants."

The barman raised his eyebrows as if wondering if Toby would get the same treatment as the previous guy.

Esther cleared her throat. "Glass of chardonnay, please."

He nodded. "Oyster Bay, ma'am?"

"Lovely, thanks."

As he went off to pour the glass, Toby sipped his beer and studied her. "So he wasn't the sort of customer you were looking for tonight?" he asked in a low voice.

She raised her lashes and met his gaze. He caught his breath. Something passed between them, sharp as static, and his heart rate increased, blood surging through his veins. From his high vantage point, he had a great view down her cleavage, and he noted that she'd made up her eyes with mascara and dark eyeliner and had highlighted her lips with red gloss. An image leapt into his head of those lips closing around the erection that had miraculously sprung to life, and he started to smile.

Her lips curved in response. "He didn't look the type who'd be prepared to pay the price." Her eyes danced. "I'm very expensive."

"I see."

The barman brought over her glass, and Toby paid. When the barman moved farther down the bar to serve another customer, Toby turned his attention back to her. "So you are open to offers tonight?"

"Why else would I come to a bar on my own?" She ran her gaze slowly down him, then back up. "You look the rich sort."

He chuckled. "I'm here on business."

"Oh? I thought businessmen wore suits."

He looked down at himself. The truth was that he didn't own a suit, and he hadn't yet picked up the one he'd hired for Dan's wedding the following weekend. Instead, he wore jeans and the smartest item in his wardrobe—a dark grey, long-sleeved dress shirt embroidered with black velvet thread. "Only to work," he clarified. "This is a businessman at leisure."

She giggled. "I wasn't complaining. You look..." She ran her gaze down him again, then slowly back up. "Nice." Her eyes twinkled.

He smiled. It looked as if she was enjoying herself. He was glad. Something told him that, apart from Charlie, she hadn't had an awful lot of fun in her life over the last few years.

"Would you like to share a table with me?" He indicated one over by the window that looked out at the palms outside the bar entrance. "Perhaps we could discuss an... arrangement for the evening."

She picked up her glass. "Sure."

He led the way over, held out the chair for her, moved it in as she sat, then took the seat opposite. It was a small, square table, and their knees touched underneath. Toby sat back and took a mouthful of beer, watching as she sipped her wine and tucked a strand of hair behind her ear.

She'd taken care over her appearance, with her skillfully applied makeup and curls pinned up to reveal her slim neck, and she'd borrowed a pair of Faith's hooped earrings. She must have confided in Faith. He knew Faith would have helped her out—she would have taken great delight in having a project. But he was taken aback that Esther had opened up to her. The warmth that flooded through him surprised him. He liked that the women in his life were friends.

She looked up and met his gaze. "So… Are you looking for company tonight?"

"Maybe."

"Because if you're not, I'd rather you tell me now. I don't want to waste my time—there are plenty more clients in here." She scouted the room airily.

"Like Mr. Ten-Inch Dick?" He grinned.

"Maybe not him. I wouldn't go with him if he were a millionaire. Well…" She thought about it, then shook her head. "No, not even then."

"I'm glad to hear it." He drank some of his beer. "Do you enjoy your job?"

"Getting paid for sex?" She shrugged. "Easy money. Just have to lie there and think about the housework while the client does his thing."

"That's nice to know. Now I'll be wondering if you're pondering on the vacuuming while I'm going at it."

They both laughed. She ran her finger around the rim of the glass. "I'm joking, of course. There's more to being a good hooker than just lying there and thinking of England."

"There is?"

"Oh yes." She dipped her finger into the glass, then placed it in her mouth and sucked the drip of wine off it.

He hardened again at the thought of those red lips around him. He'd not seen her act like this before. In Fiji, she'd followed his lead most of the time, like a country girl spirited to the city, staring up at the bright lights. Willing enough to do whatever he suggested, but rarely taking the initiative. Which he'd loved, enjoying giving her the guided tour. But this flirty, saucy wench made his heart race.

"Do elaborate," he said.

She moistened her lips with the tip of her tongue. "Well, maybe for some hookers it's just about lying there, but I'm different. You see, I was trained at an expensive establishment, where I learned the art of pleasing a man."

"Oh?" He loved that she'd thrown herself into playing the game. "And what sort of things does that involve?"

"You'll have to pay me to find out." She sipped her wine, her eyes dancing over the rim of the glass.

His lips twitched. "Okay, so tell me, what does an exclusive lady like yourself charge the average gentleman?"

She looked startled, as if she hadn't thought about it. "Oh, um, I calculate the rate on a case-by-case basis."

"Okay, let me put it like this." He leaned forward, his gaze resting on her lips, enjoying the anticipation of the pleasure that awaited them both. "How much is it going to cost me to fuck you senseless for the rest of the evening?"

Chapter Sixteen

Esther didn't have to fake her gasp at Toby's outrageous words. She stared at him, seeing by the curve of his lips that he'd meant to shock her. He'd loved doing this before, enjoying her reaction when he overstepped her previously narrow boundaries, saying things to make her exclaim and scold him, before eventually admitting he turned her on.

She sat back in her chair, giving herself a moment for her heart rate to slow down. Part of her still couldn't believe she was doing this. It had taken an immense amount of courage to walk into the bar dressed in such a revealing outfit. Even now, she had to fight to stop covering herself up as Toby's gaze dropped to her breasts, barely covered by the skimpy material.

She forced herself not to, though, instead taking the glass of wine and sipping it slowly. The alcohol had started to thread through her, giving her the courage to play him at his own game.

Letting her gaze roam over him, she appraised him properly. He sat back and accepted her perusal, content to wait until she'd drunk her fill. He'd taken time over his appearance—he'd showered, shaved, and used product in his usually unruly hair. He smelled delicious, of freshly washed, warm man tinged with a subtle aftershave.

It was the first time she'd seen him in a dress shirt, and the effect blew her away. She'd thought him handsome in his well-worn tees and scruffy jeans, but in the dark shirt, neatly groomed and with that naughty twinkle in his eye, she was lost.

She was going to have sex. Very soon. With this gorgeous man. Possibly more than once and, knowing Toby, in a variety of different positions. Probably with numerous orgasms each time.

When had she died and gone to heaven? Had it happened and she'd missed it?

He signaled the barman and ordered another round of drinks— wine for her, Coke for himself as he was driving. He continued to wait patiently for her to speak, obviously enjoying the effect he'd had on her, his dark eyes challenging her to react to his provocative statement.

She cleared her throat. "It depends."

He tipped his head. "On what?"

"Positions. What other requests the client has."

"I'd like some details if I'm going to part with my hard-earned cash."

"Fair enough." She should have thought about this. How much did a classy prostitute charge? She had no idea. In *Pretty Woman*, Richard Gere had paid Julia Roberts three thousand dollars to stay with him for the week. What was that, about four hundred a day? But that was over twenty years ago—she had to account for inflation.

Inflation? She started to giggle.

"What?" He smiled as she tried to smother her laughter.

"Nothing. I'll tell you later." For God's sake, she told herself, this was make-believe. It didn't have to be accurate.

The barman brought over their drinks, and she sipped her wine. When the barman left, she said, "There's a flat rate of five hundred dollars for my time."

"Okay."

Well, at least he hadn't burst out laughing. That gave her the courage to continue. Time to tease him.

She leaned forward, knowing the way she rested her breasts on her arms was probably forcing them almost out of the dress. To his credit, he didn't stare at them, but his smile increased. "That includes missionary," she told him. "Everything else is additional."

"Okay."

"Me on top—two hundred dollars."

"Of course."

She was beginning to enjoy herself now. "From behind—three hundred dollars."

He chuckled. "Right."

"Oral sex—five hundred."

"Giving or receiving?" His eyes gleamed.

"Well, you receiving of course." She sipped her wine and grinned. "I'll pay you for giving it."

He laughed and leaned forward again. Just another six inches or so, and he'd be able to kiss her. He looked into her eyes, obviously enjoying himself. "And what extras do you offer?"

She thought about it. "Mild BDSM, five hundred dollars."

"Define 'mild'."

"Slaps on the ass. Reddening's okay, bruising not so much. I'm not into pain."

"Fair enough." The amused look he'd sported since the conversation began was morphing into desire. She was turning him on. Yes!

His gaze dipped to her lips. "What else?"

She leaned forward a bit more, glancing down briefly to make sure her breasts hadn't fully emerged from her clothing. They hadn't, but another half inch or so and there would be nipples visible. Perhaps she should stop there before she made a complete fool of herself.

Oh, what the hell. She was supposed to be a prostitute, after all. "Oh, there are a variety of other options available. Massage, two hundred dollars. Dressing up, two hundred. Sex toys, five hundred. And..." Her voice tailed off, vanquished by his smoldering eyes.

"And..." he prompted.

She moistened her lips. "Anal sex will cost you another thousand." They'd indulged on their second-to-last night in Fiji. Clearly, he was remembering the moment, judging by the way his pupils had dilated. It had been her first time, and the experience had blown her away. He'd been commanding, but so gentle, and it had been lying there afterward in the circle of his arms that she'd realized she didn't want to lose him.

She dropped her lashes. She didn't want to think about how they'd ended. This wasn't about relationships or accusations or recriminations. This was about two people enjoying each other's bodies, about sex, nothing more.

His hand slid under her chin and lifted it. She looked into his dark eyes. They held something she couldn't quite fathom. Pity? Understanding?

Then she caught her breath as he leaned forward across the table and kissed her.

His lips were warm and firm, and he slid his hand to the back of her neck and held her in place as he moved his lips across hers.

When he finally pulled back, she pressed her lips together, enjoying the rapid thump of her heart, but sent him a remonstrative look, pretending to be shocked. "You're not supposed to sample the goods before you've paid."

He grinned. "Put it on my tab."

"So you'd like to purchase?"

In answer, he reached into his back pocket and brought out a pen and his wallet. Opening it, smirking at her, he removed a folded-up blank check and unfurled it.

"Wait," she said. "I haven't finished."

"Oh?"

Time to enter the realms of fantasy and get him really steamed up. "Don't you want to hear about the other services I offer?"

He twirled the pen in his fingers, studying her with an amused smile. "Sure."

"Alternative locations for sex, a sliding scale depending on how likely we are to be seen. For example, back seat of the car in the middle of the forest, a hundred dollars. Photo booth in the middle of the chemist, five hundred dollars."

He chuckled. "Cheap at twice the price."

"What about other people?" She leaned forward again, propping up her bosom.

"Other people?"

"Per person watching, a hundred dollars." She licked her lips. "Per person taking part, five hundred dollars."

His gaze dropped to her mouth again. "Male or female?"

"Either. I'm easy."

His lips twitched. "I guess that comes with the job."

They both laughed. She kicked off her sandal and ran her foot up his leg. "If you want to film it, that would be extra."

"Naturally." His eyes widened as she slipped her bare foot between his thighs and rubbed it between his legs. "I thought it was me who should be checking out the goods before I buy."

"Consider this a free sample." She winked, pleased to find him already firm under her toes.

He let her play, lips curving, his gaze growing more exasperated as she giggled when he grew harder. "Anything else I should know?"

She thought about it as she finished off her wine. "Well, we have a variety of packages incorporating a range of those services." Careful.

She hadn't drunk for a very long time, and she was getting naughty. She couldn't help it, though. The intense look in his eyes was driving her wild. She wanted him desperately.

"Like…"

"Well, I'll describe the gold package for you. It's very exclusive. It involves three other people—you can choose, men or women, or we'll find willing strangers to take part." She was getting in the swing of it now. "The men can take turns with me, one after the other, until I'm all hot and sticky, and then you can watch me play with the girl— or you could join in, if you like."

She leaned her head on her hand dreamily as she continued stroking him with her foot. "I could lie there and let her climb on top. While I kissed her and played with her breasts, you could get behind and slip…"

She trailed off as his eyes went glassy. "Oops. Too much?" It didn't feel like too much, judging by what was happening beneath her toes, but the look on his face gave her pause.

He cleared his throat, moved back away from her foot, and adjusted his jeans before picking up the pen again. "You have no idea," he said gruffly, writing out the check. He was a lefty, she realized with surprise. Why would that surprise her? Only because he was Charlie's father, and yet she didn't really know anything about him except what kind of cocktails he liked and the fact that he looked damned good in a pair of swimming trunks.

He finished writing and passed her the check.

She looked at the amount. "Fucking hell." Was that *four* noughts?

Smiling, he slipped the pen back into his pocket. "Hopefully that will cover everything."

"What the fuck do you want to do tonight?"

He laughed. She flushed. It wasn't for real. It might as well have been a million dollars. He was only playing the game.

Still, it gave her goose bumps to wonder exactly what he expected for his money.

She folded up the check and slipped it into her bra, making him smile. Then she pulled her sandal back on, rose and took his outstretched hand, and let him lead her out of the bar, trying not to notice the smirk on the barman's face.

"Do you know him?" she whispered as the door swung shut behind him.

"Oh yeah. We went to school together."

"Oh Christ, I'm sorry. Have I caused a local incident?"

"Let's just say my street cred's gone up a few hundred percent." He walked over to his car and pressed the button to unlock it. "Every guy in that bar wanted to take you home tonight, and I get to be the one lucky dude who achieves it."

She opened the door, slid in beside him, and reached up to get her seat belt. "That's a nice thing to say." She clipped it in, only to look up and find him staring at her.

"I wasn't just being nice. I was telling the truth. From the moment you walked into the bar, every man in the room couldn't take his eyes off you."

Her cheeks burned. "Don't talk rubbish."

He slid the key into the ignition and started the car. "And the eyes of several of them nearly fell out of their heads when they saw what you were doing with your foot."

Her cheeks burned hotter. "Shit. People saw?"

He laughed as he pulled away. "Of course people saw. I assumed you knew that, being in a public place and all."

She was mortified. "I didn't think anyone would take notice of us sitting in the corner."

"You're kidding me, right?" He glanced over at her and obviously realized from the color in her cheeks that she wasn't. "You really think you can walk into a public place wearing a dress like that and not cause every guy's tongue to roll onto the floor?"

She looked down at herself. "I know it's tight. It's just... I didn't think anyone would find me appealing. I've had a baby. I have bumps and bulges where I didn't have them before."

He heaved a sigh. "Girl, you desperately need showing how attractive you are."

"I'm not going to argue with that." She knew she was being pathetic, but couldn't help asking. "You still find me attractive then?"

"Couldn't you tell with your foot?"

She chuckled and looked out of the window at the lush greenery of the Northland. Charlie had never seen so many palm trees before he came to Kerikeri. He'd told her on the way to Faith's house that it looked like Jurassic Park.

Thinking of Charlie made her wonder how he was doing with Faith, alone with two strangers in a strange house. He'd hardly looked up as she left, entranced by Rusty lying on the bed with him reading Thomas Tank stories, but maybe he'd noticed she'd gone and was playing up?

She glanced at Toby. "You haven't had any calls on your mobile?"

"No." His dark eyes considered her for a moment before returning to the road.

She'd spoken without thinking—had she ruined the moment? She was supposed to be a slinky call girl, not a mum worrying about her two-year-old. Was he annoyed because she'd raised the subject? She'd tried not to think about Charlie while they were in the bar, and it had worked, but now…

"I'm sorry," she began, but stopped as he reached into his jeans pocket and pulled out his mobile.

He flipped it open, checked the screen and pressed a few buttons, then handed it to her. "That's Faith's number."

She could have kicked herself. "It's okay, I can go out for an hour without having to call, I'm not an over-protective mother or anything…"

"Esther, are you under the impression I'm mad at you? I'd been thinking the same thing myself, wondering if he was okay. Go on, double check. If he's upset, I'll take you to Faith's. If he's fine, well then, we can relax, can't we?"

Her throat tightened. He understood. He was Charlie's father, and he felt the same way about their son as she did.

High-class hookers didn't burst into tears when they were shown a bit of kindness. Nevertheless, she had to bite her lip hard as she pressed the button to ring.

Chapter Seventeen

Esther cleared her throat as Faith answered the phone. "Hey, Faith, it's Esther."

"Hey, Esther. You okay?"

"Yeah, good. I just thought I'd check that Charlie isn't driving you insane."

"Nah, he's cool. Rusty's captivating him with a story about King Arthur and the Knights of the Round Table. Don't worry, he'll be asleep soon. Charlie, I meant, not Rusty. Although possibly Rusty as well."

Relief swept over her. "Oh, that's good. I thought I'd better check."

"Yeah, no worries. You two having a good time?"

"Yes, thanks."

"Still at the bar?"

"No… We're heading back to his place." Her cheeks burned.

Faith laughed. "I'll see you in ten minutes then."

Esther giggled. Toby glanced over at her and raised an eyebrow. Esther repeated her words, and he grinned. "Make it fifteen," he said, raising his voice, "and we'll have time for a pizza afterward."

The girls laughed and said goodbye, and Esther closed the phone. "Thank you," she said, handing it back to him.

"No worries." He tucked it back in his jeans.

"Sorry about laughing at her comment."

"Meh. Don't worry about it. I'm used to it."

She looked at him curiously. "Why do you let them tease you like that? Doesn't it upset you? You're hardly bad in the bedroom—don't you feel insulted sometimes?"

He shrugged. "I think they forget we've all grown up." He sighed. "I guess you should know—Eve and I slept together once."

"Eve, the bride-to-be?" Jealousy stabbed through her.

"Yeah. It was eons ago. I was twenty-one, she was…eighteen, I think. Maybe seventeen. We were both pretty drunk. She'd broken up with a boyfriend and wanted consoling, and one thing led to another. Well, I hadn't been with a girl for months and it didn't take very long. My technique wasn't as improved then as it is now." He smiled at her before returning his gaze to the road. "And now my skill in the bedroom—or lack of it—is a standing joke."

"It was only the once?"

"Yeah. It wasn't great for either of us, and we decided to just forget about it."

"Was it awkward?" She was curious whether it was possible to stay friends after breaking up with someone. After all, she was going to have to learn how to do it when she went back to Christchurch, if Toby wanted to continue to play a part in Charlie's life.

He shrugged. "It didn't mean anything. It was just consolation sex."

She nodded and looked out of the window. That was what she had to learn. Sex didn't always involve the heart. And that was what tonight was about, wasn't it? Disassociating her heart from the rest of her body. She wanted Toby desperately—wanted to kiss him, hold him, welcome him inside her. But it was a purely physical need—that was why she'd suggested the Naughty Nights as a tool to remind her.

He turned into the driveway and pulled up in front of his house. The sun had set, and the lemon and mandarin trees cast shadows across the gravel road. It was warm and humid, and a trickle of sweat ran between her breasts.

He turned off the engine, unclipped his seatbelt, and turned to face her. They studied each other in the fading light, the only sound the chirping of cicadas in the trees.

"Have I put my foot in it?" he said. "Mentioning Eve. I thought it best to tell you in case one of the others said something."

"It doesn't matter."

"She's marrying Dan," he said. "They're crazy about each other."

She smiled. "Toby, seriously, don't worry about it. It's none of my business who you've slept with in the past, or who you sleep with in the future."

"I guess. But I don't want you to think badly of me."

She frowned. His face was open and honest, earnest even. It mattered to him. That warmed her. Sex might just be sex, but he did care for her.

"I forgot to ask you," he said softly. "What's your name?"

She blinked and then realized he was referring to the role-play they were supposed to be doing. "Roxie Glitterhorn," she said. "Pleased to meet you."

He burst out laughing. "What a great name. A stage name, I'm presuming?"

She put on an affronted look. "How rude. My mother gave me that name."

"Little did she know how well it would suit you." He smiled. "You want to come in?"

She nodded.

"You're sure?" He seemed hesitant. He must be worried he was pushing her to do something she didn't really want to do.

She unclipped her belt and turned to face him. Raising a hand, she brushed his cheek and his long dark sideburns, and slipped her fingers into his thick, curly hair. Then she leaned forward and pressed her lips to his.

He inhaled, and then he lowered his arm around her and held her as they kissed. His lips were firm and warm, and when she opened her mouth, he stroked his tongue inside. She murmured her pleasure, and his arm tightened as he deepened the kiss, causing her heart to hammer as her breathing quickened.

When they finally pulled back, she pressed her lips together, shocked at how much she hungered for him.

He cleared his throat. "I'll take that as a yes."

She followed him as he got out of the car and walked across to the house.

He opened the front door and they went inside, and he switched on a lamp in the corner, casting the room in a warm glow. He was such a big man, tall, broad-shouldered, heavily built and well muscled. Although he had the reputation of being clumsy, and frequently knocked over vases and lamps and walked into doorframes, he moved gracefully, his body toned and flexible. He obviously worked out, she thought, noting the way the shirt stretched over his biceps as he reached across to throw his keys onto the coffee table. He was a fine figure of a man.

Suddenly nervous, she walked through to the dining and kitchen area and perched on a stool by the breakfast bar as he followed her in.

"Glass of wine?" he asked, going over to the fridge.

"Please." She shouldn't drink any more—she'd have a hangover the size of Australia the next morning, but it would give her something to do with her hands, which shook a little with nerves.

He retrieved a bottle of white wine from the fridge, poured her a glass and slid it across to her, and got himself a Coke. As she sipped the wine, he went over to his iPad, selected a playlist, and pressed Play. The warm sounds of some folksy jazz filled the room, and he turned down the volume so it played in the background.

He perched opposite her on a stool, his long legs brushing against hers. "Hey," he said, smiling.

She smiled back, aware of her heart pounding, the adrenalin rushing through her veins. "Hey."

He reached out a hand and took hers, lacing their fingers together. "Don't be nervous."

Was she that transparent? She couldn't deny it. "Sorry."

He brushed her knuckles with his thumb. "It's okay. It's been a while for me too, you know."

She nodded, not knowing how to explain it wasn't just the fact that she hadn't slept with anyone for years. How could she tell him it was the closeness of him that was making her mouth dry—that the sight of him in a smart shirt with his gorgeous dark curly hair and tight jeans made her shiver?

"We don't have to do anything tonight if you don't want." He raised her hand and kissed her fingers. "We could just sit on the sofa and chat, if you like. I don't mind."

Chapter Eighteen

Well, that just made her melt. She took a final mouthful of wine for Dutch courage and then put the glass down, slipped off the stool, and moved closer to him between his legs. She slid her arms around his neck, and he moved his around her waist. Where he was sitting, it made them the same height, and she brushed her lips against his.

"But you've already paid," she said huskily.

"True," he said.

"So if I don't come across, I could be arrested under the Trade Descriptions Act."

He chuckled. "We wouldn't want that."

She batted her eyelashes coquettishly. "Unless you've changed your mind. Would you like me to leave?"

In answer, he pulled her hard against him and crushed his mouth to hers. The full force of his passion washed over her, and she gasped. He took the opportunity of her open mouth to deepen the kiss, and she sighed as his tongue stroked hers, warm and inviting. He slid his hands up her ribcage over the tight dress, brushing her breasts, and then pulled back.

"I'm sure you look delightful in this pretty bra," he murmured. "But I'd rather feel the real you. Can you do that miraculous trick girls do and take it off under your dress?"

"Are you sure?" Nerves filtered through her again. "It kind of props up everything that's beginning to head south." He just raised an eyebrow, however, and she cursed beneath her breath, trying to remind herself that she was supposed to be a slinky call girl. Slinky call girls didn't talk about baby tummies and sagging breasts. "Sorry."

First, she took out the check he'd given her from her bra and popped it into the purse she'd left on the table. "Don't want to lose that." She reached behind and unclipped the bra, drew the straps down her arms beneath the sleeves of the dress, then pulled the garment out and tossed it onto the table. She glanced down. The dress was really more of a long, tight tube with small sleeves, and it clung to every part of her body, leaving absolutely nothing to the imagination. Her nipples stood out like buttons through the fabric, and her breasts looked huge.

"Wow." Toby's eyes gleamed. "You have an absolutely fantastic figure."

Warmth spread through her at his admiration. "Thank you."

"You've lost some weight."

"Breastfeeding did that." The words were out before she could stop them, and she bit her lip. Could she think of any more ways to turn him off?

But he didn't look turned off. He ran his hands up her body to cup her breasts. "You're so soft."

"You're not," she said breathlessly as he pulled her to him, his erection obvious even through the jeans.

"Is that any surprise while you're in my arms, so sensual and womanly?" He moved his large, warm hands over her, making her quiver as he ran his fingers up her back, then brought them around to cup her breasts again. He brushed his thumbs over her nipples, murmuring his approval as her eyes fluttered shut. "You smell fantastic," he said. He nuzzled her neck and ear, and she shivered.

She kissed him again, holding his face with both hands as she delved her tongue hungrily into his mouth. He tasted divine. It had been so long since she'd kissed anyone—since she'd kissed him, in fact. How had she lived without this for so long?

He was coaxing her body awake, stirring long-forgotten sensations, and an ache grew between her thighs. Her nipples tightened in response to his touch, and she arched her back to push them into his gentle hands. He groaned.

Her fingers itched to touch his skin, so she began to undo the buttons of his shirt, gradually revealing his wide, bronzed chest, shaped with firm muscles. He went to slip the shirt off, but she shook her head. "No," she whispered, "keep your fuck-me shirt on."

His eyes widened with amusement. "My what?"

"You heard me. That shirt wants only one thing. You look so damn sexy dressed like that."

He grinned. "Fine." He held the bottom of her dress. "But I want you naked."

Instinctively, she grasped his wrists, stopping him. A skintight dress was one thing. Being completely naked and not in utter darkness was another.

He wrested his hands free, and gently but firmly moved hers away. "My check is now in your purse," he reminded her. "I seem to remember offering you an amount that would cover pretty much whatever I wanted." He let go of her hands and held the hem of the dress again. "Arms up." His voice was firm.

Her cheeks grew warm at the desire in his eyes. Closing her own, she lifted her arms.

He peeled the dress up her body and over her head. The fabric whispered to the floor. Fighting the urge to cover herself, she stood for a moment biting her lip. Even though her eyes were shut, she was sure she could feel his gaze burning through her.

Then his hand cupped her cheek, and she opened her eyes to see him smiling. "Hey, beautiful," he said.

She looked down at herself, finding it difficult to see anything but the stretch marks and the way her muscles had loosened since childbirth. "You want your money back?"

In reply, he kissed her, drawing her to him. He wrapped her in his arms tightly, one hand slipping down to squeeze her butt and pull her against him, the other cupping her head so she couldn't escape. Not that she wanted to. Her body was on fire, aching for him, even though the thought that she was standing in his kitchen stark naked made her hands itch to cover her breasts.

He lifted his head and studied her, obviously seeing her red face, her nervousness. Smiling, he kissed first one hot cheek, then the other, and then proceeded to kiss down her throat, touching his tongue to her skin, tasting as he went. He cupped her breasts, and then his mouth was on her nipple, and she gasped as he sucked, her body filling with erotic tingles as he stroked the sensitive skin with his tongue.

He did the same to her other breast, giving the other nipple the same attention while she sank her hands into his hair. When his hand trailed down her body to between her legs, she closed her eyes, tipping back her head when he slid his fingers into her. "God, Toby..." She clutched her fingers in his hair as he began to stroke her. "Oh..."

He aroused her slowly, moving his fingers through her so easily she knew she must be slippery with desire. He lifted his head and kissed her hard, desire making him rough and demanding. "I want to taste you," he told her, standing for a moment to tower over her, and her heart pounded at his height and strength.

"Oh, no, I—"

He kissed her on the mouth, cutting off her words as he pushed her back against the dining table. Then he trailed his lips down her neck and lower, dropping to his knees in front of her.

Here? In the middle of the dining room? She placed her hands on his shoulders, ready to push him away. "Toby…"

He ignored her and placed his hands on her butt, holding her tightly as he buried his mouth in her and slid his tongue into her folds.

"Oh… Fuck," she said vehemently. And then she lost all power of speech as he sucked right where heaven was located.

He'd taken minutes to make her come the first time he went down on her in Fiji, and it was going to be no different tonight. She'd been close to an orgasm anyway just from the stroke of his skillful fingers and the touch of his mouth on her breast—the warmth and softness of his tongue on her clit was too much for her to hold back for long.

Everything tightened, and as she clenched her hands into fists on his shoulders, he slid his fingers deep inside her and sucked firmly. She came hard, unable to stop herself crying out with the joy of it, pulsing around his fingers for what seemed like forever.

Finally, she finally pushed him away, exhausted and shaking from the strength of the sensations.

He stood, and before she could say or do anything, picked her up and wrapped her legs around his waist the way he had done all those years ago. She put her arms around his neck and kissed him, tasting her arousal on his lips and sighing while he carried her through into the bedroom.

"Sorry that was so quick," he said, walking to the bed. "I meant to make it last, but you took me by surprise." He smiled and kissed her.

Gosh, he was so sweet. She wanted to eat him up. "Jeez, don't apologize. I'm sorry I couldn't hold on, but it was too goddamn wonderful."

"I'm glad." He switched on the lamp, climbed onto the bed, and lay back with her on top.

She sat astride him and moved her hips, enjoying his hard length against the part of her that was now all soft and swollen, thanks to him. "Mm… Orgasms should be made one of the Seven Wonders of the World."

He stretched out, pulling a pillow behind his head, and drew her into his arms. "Better than the Pyramids," he agreed. "Fuck, you feel good." He ran his hands up her body and cupped her breasts.

She sighed and kissed him again, sliding her hands beneath his shirt to feel his warm skin. "You have such a fantastic body." She ran her fingers over his muscles. "Like a Greek god."

He stroked her breasts. "And you're like Aphrodite. Made for love."

"Well, that is kind of my job." Desire for this gorgeous man overwhelmed her, banishing her nerves, and she pushed herself upright and started unbuttoning his jeans.

He lay back with his hands behind his head and let her, grinning as she struggled with the button. "Come on, wench, I expect better service than this."

She tried to pop it through the buttonhole and failed. "It's too hard."

"That's not a complaint I've had before."

Giggling, she finally managed it and pulled down the zipper to reveal the erection that strained against the silky fabric of his boxers. Meeting his hot gaze, she moved up a little until the silky hardness pressed against her soft, damp skin. Moving her hips up and down, she coated him with her moisture, enjoying the way his eyelids slid to half mast as she aroused herself on him.

"Remember, it's been a while for me too," he told her huskily, holding her by the upper arms to still her movement. "I'm only human, sweetheart."

Thrilled that she was obviously turning him on, she lifted herself off so he could remove his clothes. Standing, he slipped off his shirt, laughing as she tutted with disappointment.

He removed his jeans and boxers, and she watched wide eyed, unable to believe her luck. He was toned all over from his bulging biceps to his muscular thighs and tight butt, like a male model for some famous underwear company. His erection was beautifully impressive. How had she managed to score with such a magnificent specimen of the male species? She wasn't sure, but she wasn't going to pass up on the chance to make the most of him while she had him.

He retrieved a condom from the bedside table and lay back down. "For all the fucking good they do," he mumbled as he went to tear the packet open.

"My thoughts exactly." She put a hand over his, stopping him. "Which is why I'm on the pill, if you want to leave it." The doctor had placed her on it to regulate her cycle after Charlie was weaned. She hadn't argued—she didn't know if she'd ever trust condoms again.

He met her gaze thoughtfully. "Aren't you worried about disease in your line of work?"

Her lips curved, but she knew what he was saying. "Do you usually wear a condom?"

"Never had sex without one."

"I thought as much. Me neither. So I guess we're both clean."

He looked at the packet for a moment and then threw it onto the table. "Can't say I hold much faith in them now either. Not that I'm complaining." He touched her cheek. "Charlie is the best mistake I've ever made."

As seemed to keep happening over the past few days, his words made both pleasure and wariness rise inside her. The thought that he wasn't angry at what had happened made her so relieved she could cry.

Equally, at that moment she didn't want to think about what had happened after their holiday, about their past and Charlie and where they were going. That wasn't what this was about. She'd suggested the Naughty Nights because she hadn't had sex for three years, and because he was gorgeous and fantastic in bed. Not because of Charlie, or anything to do with what had happened before. This was purely physical.

She raised herself up and straddled him, easing down until the tip of his erection pressed against her. Then she bent over him, brushing his lips with hers. "I want to give you good value for your money," she whispered. "What would you like, sir?"

Chapter Nineteen

"You're already worth every cent," he said huskily. He held her hips and pushed up, sliding into her in one smooth movement.

"Oh!" She closed her eyes, gasping at the feeling of him inside her, thick and hard, all the way. Sitting up, she tipped back her head, spread her thighs, and let him push deeper. "Oh Jesus..."

She'd been worried it might feel different after childbirth. That maybe she'd have lost sensation, or the inevitable loosening of her muscles would mean it wouldn't be as pleasurable for the guy. Judging by Toby's groan of approval, though, not a lot had changed.

Dropping her head to look at him, she rocked her hips and let him slide in and out. His hands fell to her hips, and he held her tightly as he pushed up into her. "God, that feels good," he said, fanning his hands across her ribs before returning them to her breasts.

"Oh yeah." How had she gone so long without this? For months after having Charlie, she'd been too tired to even think about sex. When he finally began to sleep through the night in his own room, she'd resorted to pleasuring herself if she felt the physical need. But nothing compared to this feeling of having a man inside, of having his hands on her, warming her skin.

She moved on top of him slowly, wanting the time to last. He'd forgotten to put the air conditioning on, and it was deliciously hot in the bedroom. Just as in Fiji, their skin grew warm and glistened with sweat, and when she bent and touched her tongue to the pulse in his neck, he tasted of salty sweetness. She grazed her teeth on him and sucked there, and he slipped his hand into her hair and pulled her head up to kiss her.

He plunged his tongue into her mouth, and she began to spiral out of control again as if he was weaving a spell around her, separating them from reality. Hot skin slid over hot skin, and his gentle fingers played with her nipples until she teetered on the edge of bliss.

At that moment, he surprised her by rolling her over so she lay under him, his weight pinning her down into the bed.

"Ooh," she said, impressed by the expert move. "That'll be another hundred dollars."

He chuckled and kissed her. "You can itemize the bill later."

She wrapped her legs around him as he moved inside her. "Jeez, I'm melting. You forgot to put on the air con."

"Didn't forget." He bent his head and licked between her breasts. "Wanted you like this."

"Gross, Wilkinson. I forgot how disgusting you are."

He laughed and pushed himself up so he could look down at her, continuing to thrust deeply inside her. "Good sex isn't about being clean and tidy. It's about being hot and sweaty and sticking to each other."

"This must be very good sex then," she said, breathless, her skin peeling away from his as he moved. She knew she was pushing for a compliment. How many women had he had since Fiji? Faith had said he liked big boobs and a pretty face. Well, she had the former, even if they had dropped a few inches. A pretty face not so much.

He caught her hands in his and pinned them above her head. "This is excellent sex." He met her gaze and his eyes gleamed. "I like having my own personal whore."

In spite of how hot she was, her cheeks grew warm. "Toby!"

He moved inside her, his lips brushing hers. "Slut, then."

"I'm not a slut," she protested, but was unable to stop herself writhing in ecstasy beneath him as he ground against her, arousing her clit.

"Could have fooled me." He thrust harder, even as he bent to nibble her earlobe. "You were a slut three years ago, and you're even more of a slut now."

"You're so rude."

"You betcha."

"Nobody's ever called me a slut before."

He gave a sexy laugh. "Ah, but I know the real you." Pinning both of her hands with one of his, he rolled a nipple between thumb and finger. "Come for me. I want to watch you."

She was inches away from an orgasm, but his intense, amused gaze made her try to hold back. "I can't while you're watching. Kiss me."

He kissed her and then raised his head again, sliding in and out of her. "Now, Roxie."

She gave a little laugh at his use of her made-up name, but shook her head. "Please, Toby…"

"I'm waiting." He ran his tongue lightly along her bottom lip.

"Turn off the lamp," she demanded.

"No." He shifted and changed angle, pushing up her knees and tilting up her hips, and she gasped as he sank deeper inside her.

"Oh God." She was losing it.

His bright eyes wouldn't release her. Intense and unrelenting, they held her captive, until her whole world consisted of this room, the rumpled bed, his hot skin sticking to hers.

"I told you I'd fuck you senseless," he murmured. "You're going to come for me now."

She shivered at his demanding tone and the thought of climaxing in front of him again, this man who was somehow both a stranger and comfortingly familiar. "No…" But they both knew she was lying. There was no way she could resist the sensations he was arousing in her.

She closed her eyes as the ecstatic feeling began low in her belly and thighs, long and drawn out. She gave repeated, *oh, oh, ohs*, the pleasure focusing on the pulses that seemed to go on forever and left her exhausted and limp in his arms. Only as she opened her eyes did he shudder and come, spilling inside her. She clutched her fingers in his hair and brought his head down to capture his groans, loving the way his whole body tightened, his muscular arms taut where he'd braced himself over her.

The blissful feeling died away gradually, like the last remnants of a storm. He rested his head on her shoulder, and she reveled in his heavy weight and the way his skin gleamed damply in the moonlight that fell across the bed.

Eventually, he raised his head and studied her with a smile. "Am I squishing you?"

"Yes, but I like it."

He chuckled and withdrew, lifting off her to the side, but immediately pulled her into his arms.

"It's so hot in here," she protested, resting her head on his shoulder.

"That's your fault." He kissed her hair. "You're hotter than nuclear fission. If scientists could harness the heat you produce, they'd be able to run a small country for a fortnight."

She pushed herself up to look at him, puzzled by his words. "It's a lovely thing to say, but I don't get it. You've had so many women, and I'm so inexperienced, I know it can't be true."

He looked affronted. "Well, firstly, I haven't had that many women. You're the hooker, remember?"

She smacked him on the shoulder, and he grinned.

"I think we can end that little charade," she said.

He studied her affectionately and with more than a little warmth in his gaze. "Honey, I will forever think of you as a whore in the bedroom. It doesn't matter that you haven't been with many guys. You are naturally slutty."

Her cheeks burned. "Toby!"

"I meant that in a nice way."

She sat up, hugging her knees to her chest, and studied him with a frown. "Why do you like shocking me so much?"

He rolled onto his side to face her, propping his head on a hand. "Dunno."

"You admit you do, though?"

"Oh yeah." He laughed at her glare. "You're fun to tease. You blush so easily. It's fascinating. I like to make you blush. It amuses me."

"I'm glad I can be such a great source of entertainment for you."

He smiled and reached out a hand, tracing a finger up her arm. "Thank you for today. It was great fun."

She met his brown eyes, her indignation melting at his gentle appreciation. "Yes, it was."

Her heart began to beat faster at the heat in his eyes, and she moved her gaze to the window. Outside, cicadas sang loudly in the bush. Moths fluttered at the window, attracted by the lamplight, and a morepork gave a low, mournful hoot.

"I wonder if Charlie's asleep yet," he said.

She looked back at him, touched that his thoughts had turned to their son. "I expect so. He usually crashes by seven and it's nearly nine thirty now. It was good of Faith and Rusty to have him tonight."

"Do them good," he grunted. "Make them realize even perfect people can't control a two-year-old."

She rested her cheek on her knees, studying him. "'Perfect people'? Why did you say that? Is that how they make you feel?"

He sighed and lowered his gaze, brushing at a mark on the duvet cover. "No, not really. That was unfair. I mean, now they seem like the perfect married couple, but they had a hard time of it at the beginning. Rusty didn't want to settle down—he thought the alcoholism that runs in his family meant he was a bastard deep down, even though it's like he was adopted at birth, you know? He's completely different from his brother. But he thought it ran in the blood, and he didn't want to pass it on to his kids. He seems to have gotten over that."

"I guess being in love means you're more able to cope with problems."

He raised his gaze back to hers. "I suppose. I've never been in love, so I don't know."

"Never?" She found that difficult to believe. "Not even with your hundred-and-one girlfriends?"

He gave her an exasperated look. "I'm not even close to a quarter of that figure. And no. I've never been in love with any of them. You?"

She picked at her fingernails. He hadn't asked about her previous sexual experience while on holiday in Fiji, but she'd told him anyway. He'd nodded, but she knew he had no idea just how different an experience it had been going to bed with him compared to having sex with the others. They had been like having ice cream for dessert. Nice enough, and she wasn't going to turn it down, but not exactly haute cuisine. Sex with Toby, however, had been like a beautiful sundae, full of different flavors of expensive ice cream, exotic fruits, liqueurs, chocolate sauce, and marshmallows. He'd be top of anyone's menu.

It wasn't surprising she'd fallen for him within days—no, probably hours—of meeting him. He was so full of life, enthusiastic, vibrant, fun. He'd taken her to dizzy heights of pleasure she'd never known existed.

No wonder the fall had been so hard.

"No," she said. "Never been in love."

Their gazes met, and they studied each other for a long, long time.

She turned and got up. "Better get going," she said. "Are you okay to drop me back?"

"Of course."

Suddenly it was all very formal. She went into the kitchen and found her clothes, squeezed herself into the skimpy dress, and slipped on her sandals. He came out in shorts and a black T-shirt, looking just as gorgeous as he had in the dress shirt.

"After you." He held open the door, and followed her out to the car.

They didn't say much as he drove her the short distance to Faith's house. When they arrived, he accompanied her to the front door.

"Well," he said as she turned to face him. "Thanks for a lovely evening."

"You're very welcome." She hesitated. He'd shoved his hands in the pocket of his shorts and looked suddenly young and uncertain. Her heart went out to him. He hadn't asked for any of this. For all his experience, he was no more skilled in relationships than she was. She smiled. "Want to come in and see Charlie?"

His face brightened. "Sure."

She opened the door with the key Faith had given her and they went in. Faith and Rusty were in the living room, curled up together on the sofa watching something on Netflix, but they paused it as Esther and Toby entered.

"Hey, you two." Faith grinned at them. "Had a nice evening?"

"Yes," Toby said, "we've had sex. Stop smirking."

Faith and Rusty laughed. "Good to hear," Faith said. "I expect a report shortly." Her eyes twinkled. "Although of course, the more data I have, the better."

Esther's cheeks burned. Faith was implying they should give the game another go. But that would be a big mistake. She could convince herself once was a blip. More than once was a pattern, and that wouldn't end well.

Toby gave Faith the sort of look Esther imagined she'd given Charlie when he'd told the kindergarten teacher that his mummy had dropped a plate on the floor and said "Fuck". Faith pulled an oops face and then winced as Rusty gave her a surreptitious kick.

That made Esther laugh. "Don't worry about it," she said, turning to leave the room. "It was a one-off, Faith, but I'm glad you gave Toby the game."

She walked along the corridor to the spare room and paused in the doorway. Charlie lay in bed on his stomach, covers rumpled around him, cheeks rosy from the warmth of the summer evening. He looked so beautiful that she caught her breath.

"Wow." Toby stood behind her. He didn't touch her, but the heat from his body radiated through her. "I can't believe we made him."

"I know. Me neither."

"You are so clever."

She said nothing but couldn't stop a smile creeping onto her lips.

They stood there for a moment, afraid to break the perfect moment. Her son content, quiet, dreaming of Thomas Tank and Lego and the swings, and Toby standing with her, such an example of strength and masculinity that she ached.

And suddenly she was glad they'd slept together for the last time. Because she could very easily fall for him all over again. And she didn't know if her heart would survive another break.

Chapter Twenty

"Wow," Dan said as Charlie tripped over his feet and sprawled onto the grass. "He's so like his father." The others laughed.

Toby smiled good-naturedly. It was Sunday evening, and at six o'clock he'd picked up Esther and Charlie, along with Rusty and Faith, and driven to Paihia, where they'd met Dan and Eve at The Seagull for dinner. The weather was gloriously warm, so they'd taken a seat in the garden overlooking the beach, the bay glittering enticingly in the background.

His gaze slid across to Esther as the others continued to talk. She'd smiled at Dan's joke, but it looked more like a smile of politeness than genuine amusement at his gag. Was something bothering her? She'd seemed happy enough when he picked her up. In the morning, he'd taken her and Charlie into Kerikeri to explore the shops, and then Faith and Rusty had joined them for a snack lunch in McDonald's. Charlie had wolfed down a six pack of chicken nuggets and then spent a pleasant half hour playing on the slides in the indoor playground while they chatted about this and that.

He sensed that Esther liked Faith, and also that she was unused to the sort of friendship Faith was offering her. She must lead a very lonely life in Christchurch. What a shame they had to live on different islands. Things might have been very different if they'd discovered in Fiji that they came from the same town, or at least the same area. Perhaps he would have made more of an effort to continue the relationship. Although would he have been ready to be a father? He was hardly ready now, but he'd grown up a lot over the last couple of years. Maybe the time just hadn't been right then.

She met his eyes, and a flush spread slowly over her cheeks before she tore her gaze away. He smiled, amused at how easily she blushed. It was difficult to stop his mind flicking through scenes of the previous night. Her beautiful, soft body molding and opening to his, her delicious gasps of pleasure that had turned him on so much, her wide green eyes, intense and hot with desire. In spite of her reticence and obvious worry about how her body had changed, and being nervous about stripping in front of him, she'd loved him with an abandonment that had blown him away.

She wasn't the most sexually aware girl he'd slept with. And yet she was the sexiest by far, although he couldn't put his finger on why. But she did something to his inner thermostat and sent it rocketing every time she lost her shyness and gave him one of those looks that made his blood boil.

She was also the cleverest girl he'd been with. He liked that she was smarter than him. Her brain was sexy, and he loved the way she seemed to enjoy listening to his opinions and encouraged him to speak the kind of thoughts he'd never have voiced to anyone else for fear of being laughed at.

"Toby!"

He jumped, only then realizing the others were all looking at him, waiting for him to answer a question. "What?"

Rusty smirked. "Mind elsewhere, was it?"

Eve sighed. "You're such a Neanderthal, Toby. Don't you ever think of anything else?"

For once, he didn't return with a wisecrack. He couldn't remember the last time he'd gotten embarrassed. As he was so clumsy and walked into doors and knocked vases over three or four times a day, he was used to looking an idiot. He was also used to the others teasing him. But for some reason Eve's comment stung.

Maybe it was because Esther was listening, and he didn't want her to think badly of him. Or maybe it was because that was what he had been thinking, but it hadn't been lewd or base as Eve had suggested. He hadn't just been thinking about sex. He'd been thinking about sex with Esther. That was something entirely different, and not something he wanted made fun of.

At that moment, Charlie fell over again, and this time he must have bumped himself because he wailed. Esther put down her knife and fork, but Toby had already finished his fish and chips, so he pushed himself to his feet. "I'll get him."

He ignored the looks they exchanged, picked up Bear, and walked across the grass to where Charlie sat, tears running down his chubby cheeks. Toby dropped to his haunches beside him and handed him Bear. "Hey, fella. What did you do?"

"Hurt my hand." Charlie clutched Bear to him and showed Toby the hand that bore the minutest of grazes. "Kiss it better," he demanded. Toby did so. Charlie stretched his arms to be picked up.

A lump formed in Toby's throat, and he slotted his hands under the boy's armpits and stood, bringing Charlie with him and balancing him on his hip. Charlie cuddled up to him and rested his head on Toby's shoulder as he sucked his thumb.

"It's okay," Toby murmured, turning to face the sea. "All better now."

Charlie took his thumb out of his mouth. "Because Daddy kissed it." The thumb went back in.

Toby said nothing, resting his lips on the top of Charlie's curls. This was his son. And his son didn't think he was an idiot. Charlie thought he was a superhero. He'd never felt so humble or so proud.

"Hey."

He turned to see Esther smiling up at him. "Hey," he said. "You want to take him?"

"No, no. He looks quite comfortable there." She stroked Charlie's hair. "You all right, baby?"

Charlie nodded, but didn't raise his head. His eyelids drooped.

"We'll get going soon," Toby promised. "Past your naptime, eh fella?" He kissed Charlie's forehead, then looked across at Esther. She had a strange look on her face. "What?"

"Nothing." She glanced back at the others and dropped her gaze to her feet.

He studied her, puzzled. "Are you enjoying yourself? You getting on okay with the others?"

"They're great. I don't like how they put you down, though."

He shrugged. "Don't worry about it. They're usually right."

"No they're not," she replied hotly, "and you shouldn't let them get away with it. I know they're fond of you, but that doesn't give them the right to treat you as if you're an idiot."

"I am an idiot."

"Not all the time." Her lips curved.

Warmth spread through him at the way she felt the need to defend him. Nobody had ever stood up for him before, not even his mother. Martha usually joined in when his father and brothers teased him—he'd grown to accept that he always bore the brunt of the family jokes. It was refreshing to have someone on his side for once.

"Thanks for last night," she said.

"You're very welcome." He smiled at the flush that appeared on her cheeks.

She looked out to sea. "I guess you can help Faith with her research now."

"Yeah." He knew Faith was itching to quiz him on the Naughty Nights game.

"I suppose you have to give the game back," she added.

"I should, yes."

She moistened her lips with her tongue. "Unless..."

He stared at her. Was she suggesting what he thought she was suggesting? "Unless..."

She sighed. "Oh, I'm not going to tiptoe around this. I'm here for a week. We're both single. I haven't had..." She glanced at Charlie. "The 'S' word for a very long time. And you're very good at it." Her eyes twinkled. "Want to do it again?"

He burst out laughing. "You like to say what you're thinking, don't you?"

"I don't see the point in being subtle."

"Clearly." This was probably a very bad idea. But he didn't care if it meant getting her into bed. "I'd very much like to do it again."

"There are some conditions, though," she said solemnly. "It's purely physical."

"Oh, absolutely."

"I mean it, Toby. We both have to understand that. I don't want to get tangled up in something that won't end well when I still live at the opposite end of the country."

"I understand." And he did. She didn't want anything more. He was surprised at the twinge of disappointment deep inside him. But he said nothing. If she only wanted sex, he'd take it. He just wanted to be with her.

She bit her lip. "Is it a bad idea? I shouldn't have said anything. It's just... You look so gorgeous, holding Charlie."

He'd been thinking the same thing—her dark hair, for once released from its clip, lifted in the late evening breeze, and she looked curvaceous and tempting in the bright orange sundress.

His lips curved. Keeping a tight hold on Charlie, who'd fallen asleep, he slid a hand into her hair and pulled her closer for a kiss.

When he finally released her, he said, "I don't see what's wrong in indulging in a bit of hot sex for a week. We find each other attractive—what's wrong with that? We're both grown-ups. I think we know the score." He ran his hands down her back. "Anyway, I'm willing if you are."

Her gaze rested on his lips. "Okay. So it's just hot sex then."

"Just hot sex." He hardened at the thought.

"When shall we pick another scenario?"

"Actually my parents have asked if they can have Charlie for the afternoon tomorrow. We can have a few hours to ourselves."

"Sounds good."

He glanced across at the table. The others were pretending not to look, but he knew they'd seen him kiss Esther. He sighed. "Come on. Let's finish up our drink and we can get going."

Chapter Twenty-One

Esther walked back to the table. Toby sat carefully, making sure he didn't disturb his son. Excitement bubbled inside her at the thought of having sex with him again. She hadn't been able to help herself. Standing there, his son cradled in his arms, his curly hair moving in the breeze, he'd looked so gorgeous that she'd not been able to resist the desire flooding through her.

"You okay?" Eve said to Toby. "I'm sorry, I hope I didn't upset you."

"Nah." He finished off his Coke. "You were right, anyhow. I was thinking about sex."

"No surprises there," Dan said. "You were awake."

Esther was unable to suppress a giggle, and Toby gave her a mock glare as everyone else laughed. "Don't you start. You're supposed to be on my side."

"I am," she said. "I'm being polite and laughing at the groom-to-be's jokes."

"Yeah, yeah." He grinned. She could tell from the intensity of his eyes that he was thinking about their next Naughty Night.

Flustered, she turned her attention to Dan. "Are you looking forward to the big day?"

"I'm terrified," he said.

"He's not joking," Eve added. "I might have to sedate him to get him down the aisle."

Toby smiled. "We'll make sure he's there."

"Yeah," Rusty said. "I've got a taser somewhere—I knew it would come in handy some day."

Dan glared as they all laughed. "Sure, have a joke at my expense."

"What are you worried about?" Esther was curious.

"Yeah," Eve said. "Have you gone off me?"

In answer, he reached out and took a strand of her long blonde hair between his fingers. He wrapped it around his hand slowly until she had to move closer to avoid losing half her scalp.

"Ow," she said, but her eyes lit up as she looked at her fiancé.

"Never," he murmured and captured her lips in a long, slow kiss.

Faith rolled her eyes and changed the subject, but Esther found it difficult to look away from their embrace. Obviously, Dan was nervous about the big day, but he was clearly devoted to his fiancée. He kissed around to Eve's ear before whispering something to her that made her giggle. It was strange to think Eve had slept with Toby. She glanced at him, wondering whether he was also watching them and if there would be envy on his face, but his gaze was fixed on his son, who was now curled up on his lap sound asleep.

He brushed a strand of hair from Charlie's face, and she caught her breath at the obvious affection on his features. He loved the boy—that much was clear. The thought that Charlie now had a father to look out for him thrilled her and made her nervous at the same time. What would happen when she flew back to Christchurch? Charlie was going to be asking a hundred questions: Where's Daddy? Why's he not coming home with us? When will I see him again? Most of which she wouldn't know the answer to.

It was great that the two of them seem to have connected so well. But had she just made things harder for herself?

*

The following day, Martha and Graham Wilkinson arrived at Faith and Rusty's house to pick Charlie up at eleven thirty.

"Hello, young man." Martha swept Charlie up in her arms and gave him a big kiss. "How do you fancy coming to the beach with me and Grandpa today?"

Charlie looked across at his mum. Esther smiled. "Maybe Grandpa will help you build a sandcastle."

"A huge one," Graham said. "As tall as you."

Charlie's eyes lit up. "With flags?"

Martha kissed him again. "Of course with flags. Can't have a sandcastle without flags. And a moat so deep you can swim in it."

Esther laughed and handed Graham Charlie's bag, complete with sippy cup, Bear, and the hundred other things a two-year-old boy couldn't do without for the day. "You have a friend for life now."

"I hope so." Martha smiled, her eyes meeting Esther's over the top of Charlie's head. They were warm, but there was also a hint of caution in them. Esther was pretty sure she knew what Martha was thinking. She wanted to get to know her grandson, but she was afraid of loving him too much because she knew Esther was going to take him away, and she wasn't sure whether she'd see him again.

Esther dropped her gaze as Graham shouldered the bag and headed for the door. At some point, she and Toby were going to have to sit down and talk properly about the future and how this was going to work. But not yet, she thought. They had a whole week to sort things out. Today, the weather was hot and sultry, and Toby was coming over to take her out and then hopefully they'd have some really raunchy sex. She wasn't going to think about the future today.

She kissed Charlie goodbye, and he went with his grandparents happily enough with the promise of an ice cream and a paddle in the sea. When they'd left, she closed the door and wandered through the house to her room. Rusty was teaching at the high school, and Faith had left early to go to the nearest big town, Whangarei, for a meeting with the editors of the magazine she wrote for, so Esther had the house to herself.

In the bedroom, she opened the sliding doors to allow the breeze from the garden to blow into the room and closed her eyes when the humid warmth flowed over her. It was the end of February, and in Christchurch the leaves would already be turning, but here autumn seemed a long way away. In fact, her whole world seemed a long way away. This was like a time out of time, as if she'd suspended reality for seven days. She'd seen the news on the TV, watched the rescue teams working to find the missing people in the crumbling city, and she'd been relieved not to be in the heart of it all.

And now she had a date. Her heart lifting, she turned and opened the wardrobe to reveal her meager rack of clothing. The insurance company would pay out once they'd assessed the damage done to her apartment, but for the moment she was limited to what she'd allowed herself to buy with Toby's credit card in Christchurch and the couple of items she'd purchased since she got access to her bank account again.

She lifted out a thin sundress. It was just a cheap cotton slip really, with a halter neck, the hem reaching to a few inches above the knee, but the light green color matched her eyes, and it would be cool and easy to wear on this late-summer day. She took off her jeans and T-shirt and pulled the dress on, not bothering with a bra, then smoothed it down her body. Soon Toby's hands would be doing the same thing. Her heart pounded at the thought.

She'd dreamed about him the night before and had woken breathless and aching with need. It had been a long morning. Walking back into the living room, she checked her watch. How long before he arrived? He'd said he'd come around for her at midday, and it was eleven forty-five.

She paced the room for ten minutes, applied lipgloss, thought about changing, decided not to, wiped off the lipgloss, put another shade on, and frankly by the time the knock came at the door at five past twelve, it made her jump out of her skin.

She opened the door, heart pounding when she saw it was him. "Hey."

"Hiya." He leaned against the doorpost. "Wow, you look good."

"Thank you. So do you." It was the truth—he wore a pair of cream chinos and a short-sleeved checked shirt, and he looked all scrubbed and clean. She backed away and let him in, staring in surprise as he produced a small bunch of flowers from behind his back.

"I'm sorry I'm a little late," he said. "I stopped to get these. I wasn't sure whether to. I walked in and out of the shop about five times."

She smiled and took them from him. "They're lovely, thank you."

He shoved his hands in his pockets. "I know this isn't a date as such. I just wanted to get you something, to say..." He thought about it. "I dunno. Thanks, I guess."

Her smile spread. He was so sweet. And he looked so gorgeous she wanted to eat him up.

Giving the flowers one last sniff, she placed them on the breakfast bar. Then, leaning against the bar, she pulled him toward her. "Hey, you."

His lips curved, and he took his hands out of his pockets and slid them around her waist. "Hey."

She moved her hands up his shirt and leaned closer to nuzzle his neck. "You smell amazing."

He shivered but joked, "I can honestly say that's the first time any girl has ever said that to me before."

"I can't believe that." She touched her tongue to where his pulse beat beneath his warm skin. "You smell of aftershave and summer and hot man."

"Yuck."

"It's not yuck, as you pointed out to me recently. It's heavenly." There was something wrong with her. Someone must have slipped her a lust potion, because all she could think about was kissing him, tasting him, having him inside her.

His hands began to wander over her body, and she kissed down his jaw to his mouth, capturing his lips with her own. He groaned and pressed her up against the worktop, and to her pleasure she felt him hard against the flat of her stomach.

"I've been in the door two minutes," he protested as she started to unbutton his shirt.

"Is that a complaint?" She reached the last button and pushed his shirt aside to reveal his tanned chest.

"It might be. Are you using me for sex?"

"Yes." She slipped her hands around him and scored her nails lightly down his back.

He shuddered. "Fair enough." Without warning, he lifted her up onto the bar, and she squealed. Pushing her legs apart, he moved between them. He pulled her tight against him and crushed her lips to his, cradling the back of her head with a hand as he explored her mouth with his tongue. Her senses spun, and she returned the kiss passionately, sighing as he cupped her breast with his other hand. "God, you're so soft," he mumbled as he ran his hands over her body. "You're so feminine, Esther. Every inch a woman."

It was possibly the nicest thing anyone had ever said to her. She bit her lip for a moment as emotion overwhelmed her. Damn the man. Why did he have this effect on her?

She knew she should pull away from him and tell him they should wait until later, but he slipped his hand between her thighs and started to arouse her through her panties, and all her willpower fled. She hitched up her dress and wriggled out of her underwear while he unbuttoned his pants and freed his erection, then pulled him back to her, and within seconds he'd parted her folds and pushed into her.

"Jesus," he mumbled. He kissed her hard and she wrapped her legs around him, welcoming him deeper in. It was heavenly, with the warm breeze blowing in through the sliding doors, him hot and hard inside her, his strong arms around her. He moved his hands over her body, clearly enjoying the lack of a bra underneath the soft cotton dress, and she leaned back on her elbows as he settled into a regular rhythm. She closed her eyes and tipped her head back, and he covered her nipple with his mouth through the cloth.

"Oh God…" She wasn't going to last much longer. How embarrassing. But she couldn't help it. It was just too wonderful.

She came in a rush of tight muscles and blissful pulses, exclaiming out loud as he continued to thrust hard. When his climax began, she opened her eyes and watched him, thinking how beautiful he was, and that she wished she could capture a picture of him like this, brow furrowed and eyes hot with desire, to keep for when she returned home.

Chapter Twenty-Two

He rested his forehead against hers while their breathing calmed down. Then they started to laugh.

"Fucking hell," he said.

"Sorry." The temperature in the room must have been in the high eighties, but she still managed to blush.

"Jeez, don't apologize." He kissed her and then withdrew with a groan. "I did not expect that. What a nice way to start the afternoon."

She reached for a piece of kitchen towel while he zipped himself up, then let him help her down from the worktop. "I'll second that."

He pulled her into his arms and kissed her. "Thank you, Esther Tyler, for making my day."

"And we haven't even done the Naughty Nights game yet," she said lightly.

"No." He laughed and kissed her on the nose. "It's in the car. You want me to go and get it?"

"Sure." He kissed her again and then sighed and walked over to the front door, disappearing outside.

She slipped on her panties, went over to the sofa on shaky legs, and sank onto the soft leather. Was she mad? They were supposed to be exploring the Naughty Nights slowly, leisurely, not tearing each other's clothes off in a mad display of wanton desire. Still, she couldn't feel too regretful. It wasn't exactly as if he'd turned her down. He'd taken only seconds longer than she had to come.

Still... She groaned and covered her face with a cushion as she thought of how forward she'd been. What ever happened to self-control? Honestly. What must he think of her?

The door shut again and then his footsteps came across the floor to the sofa. Keeping her face covered, she waited for him to sit beside her before removing the cushion.

He was grinning. "Feeling better now?"

"Sorry," she said again.

"I said, don't apologize. Do you hear me complaining? There are far worse things to do on a summer's afternoon than have sex with a horny girl."

"Toby!" Her cheeks burned.

He laughed and pulled her toward him for a kiss. "What? Nothing wrong with being horny. It's my default setting. It's great to meet someone else who occasionally feels the same."

She huffed a sigh but didn't bother to hide her smile.

He put the Naughty Nights box on his lap. "You want to pick the next one?"

"It's your turn. You have to choose from the black ones—they're for guys."

"I'll do it randomly. Then you'll know I haven't cheated." He winked at her and made a pretense of looking the other way while he picked a card.

He pulled one out, turned it over, and read it. His gaze flicked up at her and then back at the card. He read it again.

She tapped her foot. "What does it say?"

He turned the card over and inserted it back into the box. His eyes were alight with mischief. "Can't tell you. It's a surprise."

She stared at him with alarm. "I don't like surprises."

"Tough."

"What's it about?"

He gave her an impatient look as he put the lid back on the box. "I told you—it's a secret."

"Give me a clue."

Laughing, he kissed her forehead and then got up. "No. Now come on. I'm taking you out to lunch."

*

She pestered him for a while, but the only thing he'd tell her was that she was going to have to wait until the evening. When he clearly wasn't going to reveal any more details, she sighed and stopped asking, but remained in a perpetual state of apprehension about what was on the card. Over the next few hours, while they had lunch and then afterward when they went for a walk down by the inlet, every time he looked at her with desire in his eyes she knew he was thinking about the Naughty Nights, and her heart beat a little faster.

Around three o'clock, he asked if she'd liked to go to the cinema. She accepted with enthusiasm. It had been ages since she'd seen a movie on the big screen—since before Charlie was born, in fact. It turned out Kerikeri had its own three-screen cinema, and when she saw the latest Bourne thriller was on, her excitement doubled.

"I thought you would have wanted to see a chick flick," he commented with amusement as he paid for their tickets and popcorn.

"Give me an action movie any time. Although I do like period dramas."

"So do I." He raised an eyebrow at her look of astonishment. "What? Ladies in corsets and duels and soirees. What's not to like?"

"You constantly surprise me, Toby Wilkinson." She smiled and linked her fingers with his while they walked to the cinema. This wasn't a real date. But it had been ages since she'd walked hand-in-hand with a guy. It was nice to pretend for a while.

The movie had been out for a few weeks and so was showing on one of the smaller screens. When they entered the theatre, she saw there were only a few other people there and the movie was about to start.

"It's two p.m. on a school day," he said. "Everyone's at work or busy."

"I'm not complaining." She followed him up the steps. "I hate it when people talk through the movie." He smiled and led her to the top. She raised an eyebrow at him. "The back row? You're kidding me."

He shrugged and grinned. "I haven't sat in the back row for years. Might as well make the most of having a pretty girl with me."

She nudged him but smiled shyly as she sat next to him. They'd just got comfortable when the theatre went dark and the adverts began.

She'd forgotten how magical it was at the cinema. To be engulfed by the story, with the surround sound making her feel as if she were really there... She sat with eyes wide as the action played out before her.

Toby seemed to be enjoying it as much as she was. He held her hand for the first half, and when he rested his hand on her knee, she didn't object. He began drawing small circles on her skin, which she was quite happy with, and even when his hand moved higher and traced light patterns on her inner thighs, she didn't complain.

Only when he got out of his seat and moved quickly between her legs did she jump and give a startled, "Toby!"

"Shh." He pushed her back in her seat and held her there for a moment while he kissed her, hard. Her heart pounded as he thrust his tongue into her mouth. Could anyone see them?

When he eventually lifted his head, she demanded in a furious whisper, "What are you doing?"

He ignored her and kissed around to her ear, then down her throat, and finally closed his mouth over a nipple.

She gasped and scanned the others in the audience quickly to see if they were watching. The four other customers at the front had their attention fixed on the action occurring on the screen, however, and nobody paid any notice to what was going on in the back row.

Now she knew why he'd wanted to sit up the back. The instructions on his Naughty Nights card must have directed him to pleasure her in public. Her cheeks burned. The sneaky bastard. "You'll have to wait until the evening" indeed. She couldn't let him go through with it. What if the ticket girl came in to check on the audience? What if someone looked around? She'd die a thousand deaths.

She struggled against him, but he just chuckled. "Sit still," he instructed.

"No!" She glanced hurriedly around the cinema, but at the moment she spoke a truck exploded in a fiery ball and the noise drowned out her exclamation.

He held her hands and kissed down to her stomach. In one smooth move, he pushed up her dress and, catching his finger in the elastic of her panties, pulled them to the side and lowered his mouth. She panicked and tried to push him away, but it was like trying to push a brick wall, and she couldn't stop his warm tongue sinking into her.

She closed her eyes and tried to catch her breath. He brushed all the way up her with one long lick, the sensation so beautifully blissful that she stopped moving and let him hold her tightly as he did it again. Her face must have been scarlet judging by the heat it radiated at the thought of someone seeing them. However, the seats in front of them hid him from the rest of the cinema, and someone would have to be looking pretty darned hard to see what he was doing.

He curved his arms around her thighs and rested his hands on them, pulling her legs farther apart so he could gain better access to her clit. She moaned and slid farther down in the seat while he teased the spot with flicks of his tongue. The wickedness of being so naughty in public only added to her excitement. She'd never considered herself an exhibitionist, but the thought that at any time someone could look over and catch them only turned her on more.

He moved his hands up to her breasts and stroked her nipples, and she sighed. The action on the big screen was being carried out at nighttime, and darkness shrouded the cinema. Nobody could see them, and the noisy action scene masked her soft murmurs of approval. They were in their own hot, sensual world, and as he continued to lick and suck and tweak, she finally relaxed enough to let him move one hand down, open her legs even wider, and bury two fingers inside her. His other hand continued to play with her nipple, and she slid her fingers into his hair and clenched them as he aroused her relentlessly.

Before long, a warm feeling began deep in her abdomen, and she gasped at the thought of climaxing right there in the cinema. He murmured his approval, though, obviously sensing her pleasure, and she gave in and let everything tighten as she came around his fingers. Her muscles squeezed in exquisite, wonderful pulses, and she had to bite her lip to stop herself from crying out and alerting the other viewers.

When she'd finished, he withdrew his fingers and moved up to kiss her. She gave him a helpless, frustrated look, and he chuckled, pressing his lips to hers.

"Yuck," she whispered. "I can smell myself."

"Yum," he replied and ran his tongue along her lips.

She pushed him away. "You are positively evil, Toby Wilkinson."

"Mwahaha." He moved back into his seat but put his arm around her so she could snuggle up against him. "Was that nice?"

"No."

He chuckled quietly. "It looked as if you hated it."

"I did. Every moment. I faked it to make you stop."

"Yeah. I thought as much."

She glanced up and met his warm gaze. "I can't believe you just did that. I'm guessing that was the Naughty Night? What on earth made you choose the cinema?"

"Actually, I swear I wasn't going to. I was going to wait until later—sneak you off into a public toilet or something. But it seemed like the perfect opportunity."

"We've missed half the film now," she complained.

"Worth every minute." He kissed her hair.

She couldn't argue with him there.

Glancing down at his jeans, she decided he hadn't been lying when he claimed to have enjoyed the experience. Naughtiness surged through her. It would be a shame to let him go unsatisfied.

In a sudden, smooth movement, she dropped to her knees and slipped between his legs. Alarm lit his face. "Oh no," he said in a low voice, gripping her upper arms. "The card only stated that you had to be pleasured."

"Fuck the card," she whispered, her heart rate speeding up again at the thrill that widened his eyes.

"You don't have to." His protest was half-hearted.

"I want to." She unpopped the button at the top of his chinos and undid the zipper. "More than anything."

"Wouldn't want to disappoint a lady," he said faintly, sliding down in the seat.

She grinned and moved her hand along the silky boxers, stroking the iron-hard length that strained toward her. "Good boy." Pulling the elastic carefully down, she revealed his glorious erection. "Wow."

He gave a half laugh that rapidly turned into a groan as she explored the ridges and veins of the underside with her tongue. When she finally covered the plump tip with her mouth, he exhaled in a rush. "Esther! Fuck." Luckily Bourne crashed through a window at that point, covering his words.

"Mm." She sucked and took as much of him in as she could manage, tasting him on the back of her throat, enjoying the hiss of approval that escaped his lips. He threaded his hand into her hair, and as she continued to arouse him, he appeared unable to stop his hips thrusting gently, forcing himself deeper into her mouth. She welcomed it, however, loving being able to do this for him. Even though her cheeks grew warm when he pulled the hair back from her face so he could watch her, she looked up at him coyly, licking her lips before sliding them back down his length.

Before long, he tightened his fingers and his breathing grew erratic, and she moaned with pleasure when he went still before erupting into her mouth. She swallowed him down, milking him with her tongue, until he gasped and tugged her hair, too sensitive to bear any more of her administrations.

Wiping from the corners of her mouth to the center, she pushed herself up and into her seat. He tucked himself back into his pants, casting her an amused, exasperated look.

"What?" she asked innocently as she turned her attention back to the movie. "Didn't you see that on the menu beneath the popcorn?"

Chapter Twenty-Three

After the movie finished, Toby drove them back to the inlet and bought them a drink and a plate of fries in the nearby bar. They sat outside on the grassy bank overlooking the water and watched the ducks paddling amongst the rocks and tourists wandering in the gardens around Kemp House. He felt surprisingly content as they sat and talked, warm in the afternoon sunshine, Esther relaxed and blushing every time he looked at her.

It amused him that she was still so naïve, in spite of the fact that three years had passed since their holiday, and she'd had a child in the meantime. But then again maybe it wasn't so shocking considering she'd not dated anyone else since. Even though he didn't like to think of her being lonely, he was glad he'd been her last partner. His reason for being glad puzzled him. Best not to analyze that too hard when they were only supposed to be having sex.

"So, what are we up to tomorrow?" Her green eyes lit with fun.

He put on an innocent look. "My brothers want to meet you. They've invited us around for tea."

Her lips curved. "I meant with the Naughty Nights."

"Ah." He'd guessed, but he liked to tease her. "So you want to give it another go?"

"If you do."

"Absolutely." He finished off his beer. "You ready to go? The box is in the car—we can choose our next scenario."

"Ooh yes." She knocked back the rest of her glass of wine and stood up hurriedly. He laughed, pleased at her eagerness, and they walked out to the car.

Once inside, he took the lid off the box and offered it to her. She rummaged through the cards, eyes sparkling. "Randomly?"

"Up to you."

"Can I veto?"

He raised an eyebrow. "Why would you? There can't be a lot left we haven't done."

Her fingers stopped going through the cards and a blush lit her cheeks. Clearly she was thinking about the things they'd done back in Fiji too.

"You love to embarrass me," she whispered. "Don't you? Why?"

He studied her, amused. "Because I love the light in your eyes when I shock you." He tipped his head, dropping his gaze to her mouth. "Because I know you like being shocked."

"I do not." She moistened her lips, and his erection sprang miraculously to life.

He moved closer to her, slipped a hand to the back of her head and pulled her closer. Letting his lips hover over hers, he said, "Liar."

She gave a tiny shake of her head. "I don't. You... you corrupt me. You lead me astray."

He chuckled and brushed her lips with his. "And you love it."

"You're an old-fashioned knave. A rogue. You've practically stepped out of a Regency romance."

He bit her bottom lip gently and sucked. "Maybe. But you're no angel, Esther. Deep down, you're as wicked as I am."

She stiffened with indignation and went to move away from him, but he tightened his grip on her and refused to let her go. Placing her hands on his chest, she pushed, but he clamped his mouth on hers and kissed her deeply, sweeping his tongue into her mouth. She gave in almost immediately, melting against him and sliding her arms around his neck, and let him press her back into the seat.

He sat back after a few moments, breathless and uncomfortable as his erection strained against his pants. "Jeez," he said, adjusting himself. "Thirty seconds more of that and we'd be in the back like a pair of teenagers."

She grinned and picked out one of the cards. "Let's see if I can make it worse." She read the card. "Oh... Yes. I like this one." Her eyes danced.

Wariness flooded him. "Uh-oh."

She read it out. "'You are the princess in a faraway Arabian city. You have a harem of slaves at your beck and call, ready to service you.' I like the sound of that." She giggled at his expression. "It's okay, it's not directing me to invite someone else into the bedroom."

He shivered at the thought. In reality, he'd kill any guy who came near her. But the fantasy was another matter. "Jeez, Esther."

She dropped her gaze to the card. "'Choose one slave to do your bidding. He is yours for the day, and must do whatever you bid. And when you're ready, take him into the bedroom and instruct him to pleasure you in whatever way you choose.'" She looked up at him.

"Does this mean you're going to ask me to do the dishes and make you cups of coffee all day?" he said.

She smiled. "Absolutely."

He kissed her forehead. "Then I think it's more than you deserve. Come on, I bet our boy is wondering where you are. Let's go and find out if my parents have gotten him wired on ice cream and burnt to a crisp in the sun."

They hadn't, of course. They had smothered the poor lad in about two inches of sun cream, a T-shirt, and a hat, and sat him under an umbrella most of the day. But Charlie proudly showed them the photos of the sandcastle he'd helped to build, and when they went to leave, he gave his grandmother a big hug, which brought tears to her eyes.

"Glad you had a nice day," Toby said with a smile. He picked Charlie up. "And now bath for you, boyo. You're slippery as an eel."

"Yuck!" Charlie said.

"Yes, uber-yuck. We need paint stripper to get that sun cream off."

"Better than burning," Martha said as they walked out.

"Thank you for looking after him." Esther hovered awkwardly.

"You're very welcome, dear." Martha grabbed her and kissed her on the cheek. "You've done a wonderful job bringing him up, love. He's a delightful boy—polite, charming, and funny. Like his dad."

"Yes." Esther's gaze flicked to Toby, but he couldn't read what she was thinking.

He drove them back to Faith's house and carried Charlie in. For a moment, he considered asking Esther to dinner, but she looked tired, and he'd seen from his sister-in-law how tiring the bath time/bedtime routine could get. Faith went off to run the bath, and Esther accepted his kiss on the cheek and followed her. Soon the happy sounds of splashes and squeals echoed from the bathroom.

Toby and Rusty exchanged wry grins.

"Thanks for this, mate," Toby said as Rusty accompanied him out to his car. "I appreciate you having Esther here—it can't be easy."

Rusty waved a hand. "The boy's lovely. And Faith's in seventh heaven. She's treating it like a dry run of the real thing."

"How's the pregnancy going?"

"Better now she's stopped feeling sick, I think." Rusty looked off into the distance. "Weird process, isn't it? Someone's growing inside her. I can't quite get my head around that."

"I know what you mean. I still have trouble comprehending the fact that Esther and I made Charlie."

Rusty smiled. His gaze came back to Toby. "Yeah, interesting that."

"What do you mean?"

"You and Esther. She's not your usual type."

Toby scuffed the gravel with his toe. "Maybe."

"I hate to ask this, mate, but are you sure Charlie's yours?"

Toby's gaze snapped back up to Rusty's. "What do you mean?"

Rusty's green eyes were firm. "Are you sure she's not using you? She's single, no family, nobody to lean on. She saw you in the supermarket, and it must have been like a lifeline. Can you be a hundred percent certain you're the father?"

Indignation made him bristle, but he kept his voice calm. "Are you a hundred percent certain Faith's carrying your baby?"

Rusty's lips twisted. "That's a bit different."

"A bit. But it's the same premise."

"Well, we didn't use any protection. I'm assuming you did?"

Toby gritted his teeth, uncomfortable at the fact that he'd also wondered how she'd got pregnant when they'd used a condom. "No method is foolproof."

"Even so. Don't you want to be certain? You could have a DNA test carried out."

Toby's stomach churned. "That would imply I don't trust her."

"Do you trust her?"

"Yes," he said without pausing.

"Why? You've been apart for three years. You knew her for a fortnight. How do you know she didn't sleep with a dozen other guys when she got back from Fiji?"

"I think you should stop there." He had to fight to keep the nausea down.

Rusty frowned. "I'm only thinking of you, mate. You're soft-hearted and the nicest guy I know. I wouldn't want you to have the wool pulled over your eyes."

"I'm not. Charlie's mine. Everyone says we look alike."

"They would say that, wouldn't they? It's the sort of thing you say. 'Wow, he looks just like you.'"

Toby clenched his fists, and kept control over his voice with difficulty. "I trust Esther. I may not have seen her for a long time, but I know her, and I believe her. She's the most honest person I know. She wouldn't do something like that. You don't understand." It felt as if someone had tied his trachea in a knot, and he stopped, almost close to tears, which was really embarrassing.

Rusty held up his hands. "Easy, tiger." He studied his friend thoughtfully. "I didn't realize you…" His voice trailed off.

"What?"

Rusty didn't finish the sentence. He put his hands in the pockets of his jeans. "Just be careful. Do you remember when we first jumped off the waterfall in Whangarei when we were sixteen?"

Toby frowned. What the hell did that have to do with anything? "Yes, why?"

"We all stood there for ages trying to pluck up the guts to leap off, but you jumped straight in."

"Yeah, so what?"

Rusty smiled then. "Doesn't matter."

Huffing a sigh, Toby opened the car door. "I know what you're saying, and I don't want to hear it. I like her. I don't see why that's such a problem."

"The problem is that she lives in Christchurch and you live here."

"It's only sex," Toby stated firmly.

"Yeah, that's what I said." Rusty gestured with his head toward the house. "Look where it got me."

"I hurt her too badly after Fiji." Toby spoke softly. The regret that tinged his voice surprised him. "She likes me, but there's no future in it. She doesn't want anything more."

But you do. Rusty didn't say it, but Toby heard the words in his head.

He cleared his throat. "I'm off. The rugby's on in ten."

Rusty nodded, as if accepting that was the end of the matter. "Dan Carter's injured, you know."

"Yeah, I heard." That made Toby think of Charlie, which in turn made him first smile, then feel sad. He sighed. "See you tomorrow."

"Yeah." Rusty walked inside.

Toby drove off. He tried to think about the match, but his mind kept returning to Esther and Charlie. He imagined them snuggled up in bed, Charlie smelling of baby shampoo and warm milk, Esther's face filled with the tender look that appeared after the madness of the day had settled and they were curled up together. A sharp pang cut through him, and he took a deep breath to get rid of it.

How had he gotten himself into this ridiculous situation? He pounded the steering wheel to vent his frustration, glad the country road was quiet when the car almost veered into the ditch. He hadn't wanted a child, and it wasn't as if he'd been irresponsible and forgotten about contraception. "Fucking condoms!" he yelled. Knowing they could fail had put him off sex for life.

Okay, maybe not entirely put him off, but he'd never be able to have sex using one again without worrying it wouldn't work. Frustration filled him. He liked sex. He didn't want to think about children popping up all over the place every time he got his end away. Damn Esther. Why did she have to go and have a baby?

His hands tightened on the steering wheel. It wasn't her fault. And yet it was, partly. If he'd known he'd gotten her pregnant, they could have talked about whether they wanted the baby or not. He might have been able to convince her not to have it.

He went cold, stopped the car in the middle of the road, and put his forehead on the steering wheel. Shit. He didn't mean that. Charlie was the best thing that had ever happened to him. The way the kid looked at him, as if he was Indiana Jones, James Bond, and Dan Carter all rolled into one… Every man should have a son to look at him like that. There was nothing like it. He wouldn't want to be without the boy.

But he did wish he could have seen him as a baby. Been there at the birth and held her hand, and seen him emerge from her, squawking and red-faced. Held him in his arms and watched Esther breastfeed him late at night. Painted the nursery yellow and bought Pooh Bear stickers to put on the walls. He'd missed out on all that. It made him ache.

But it wasn't her fault. He lifted his head and started the car moving again, relieved at the lack of traffic. She'd tried to contact him—what more could he have expected from her? He was the one who'd walked away. She'd wanted to see him again, and he'd turned her down. He deserved everything he'd got.

Putting her to the back of his mind, he drove home and watched the rugby, had a couple of beers, and finished off with a few whiskies until his mind quieted and sleep overcame him.

But the knot in his stomach refused to go away.

Chapter Twenty-Four

Esther had most of Tuesday to herself. Toby was out with the building firm he worked for discussing jobs for the following week, Faith had another meeting in Whangarei, and Rusty was at school. Toby was going to pick her up around four o'clock to take her and Charlie to meet his brothers for tea, but until then her time was her own.

She spent most of the morning on the telephone with her landlord and the insurance company, trying to work out if any of her belongings were salvageable and whether there would be a place for her to stay when she went back. There wouldn't, it seemed—her block of apartments was going to be demolished, so she spent another hour or so ringing around trying to find another rental. Everywhere was full of re-housed people or builders and such who'd moved into the area to help out with the earthquake damage. In the end, she found a small apartment that was a bit out of town and more than she'd been paying, but at least they'd have somewhere to stay.

Slightly despondent, she played with Charlie for an hour, making Lego and watching children's programs on TV. All the while she mused on returning to Christchurch. How long would it be before the university opened again?

Maybe it was time to move on from the city. Although she loved it there, she had no family, no ties. It would probably mean she'd have to return to teaching in a high school, but she wasn't bothered about that.

Leaving Charlie playing with the Thomas train Toby had bought him, she went over to Faith's computer. Faith had told her to go on whenever she wanted, so she switched it on and started up the Internet browser. Pulling up the Education Gazette, she typed in her parameters and clicked search.

There were a handful of jobs around the country teaching English and literature. It wasn't a good time to be looking for a position.

There were a few secondary schools advertising for English teachers—a couple in Auckland, one in Wellington, one on the west coast of the South Island in a tiny school, which she didn't fancy much.

Then her gaze fell on an advert for an English professor in Otago University in Dunedin, a city at the bottom of the South Island. She scanned the details, then went onto the Otago University site and checked out the department. Their syllabus was similar to that which she'd been teaching at Canterbury Uni, and she'd have no trouble with the other texts they were currently studying. Most importantly, Dunedin wasn't on the fault line. No more earthquakes.

Her heart lifting for the first time in weeks, she rang the university and spoke to the secretary of the head of the department. The closing date was Friday, but the secretary said they were desperate to find a replacement for the professor who was retiring, and they'd be happy to accept a CV and letter from her rather than the traditional application form.

Buoyed up, she made lunch for her and Charlie, played a couple of games with him, then sat him back in front of the TV and wrote her CV and letter on the computer. She read them over several times and emailed them off to Otago.

Done.

She sat back in the chair, relieved to at last have something solid to look forward to. She'd probably have to fly down to Dunedin to interview. Maybe Toby would look after Charlie while she did that? She wondered what he was going to say about the possibility of her moving farther away. Surely it didn't matter where she was in the country if they were going to have to fly to see each other? It only added another hour to the flight from the Northland.

Anyway, she couldn't base her future on what Toby was or wasn't going to do. Although she hoped he'd play a part in Charlie's life, she'd learned long ago that she had to make her own plans without relying on anyone else.

She glanced at the clock to see it was three p.m., so she took Charlie into the bedroom and gave him a magazine to read while she got changed. What should she wear? It would be a family dinner, so nothing sultry or revealing. But she probably wouldn't have time to change later before she went back to Toby's place for their role-play game.

Even though February had now morphed into March, the afternoons were still warm and sultry. In the end, she chose a floor-length, multi-colored skirt she'd bought in Christchurch that Toby hadn't yet seen, and a light green vest a shade lighter than her eyes.

She changed Charlie too, putting him into a pair of soft denim shorts and a T-shirt that said Daddy's Boy on it. Hopefully Toby would consider it a nice touch considering they were going to see his family.

By the time Toby knocked on the door at four o'clock, Charlie was dressed, had had his hair brushed—amidst much complaining—and the rim of chocolate around his mouth had been removed.

Toby swung him up into his arms and exclaimed with delight at his T-shirt. "'Daddy's Boy'! You're not a Daddy's Boy, are you?"

"Yes!" Charlie squealed as his father blew a raspberry on his neck. "Get off, Daddy!"

The two of them scuffled and growled at each other, and Esther rolled her eyes and went to get her handbag. How odd for Charlie to have a male presence around. She didn't do the rough-and-tumble thing very well, and although he wasn't even three, Charlie sometimes overwhelmed her with his energy and boisterousness. But Toby dealt with his enthusiasm with a firm hand, countering any rough play with similarly aggressive physical contact, reminding her of a lion and his cubs. He was wonderful with the boy.

Why did that make her want him so badly? She collected her bag and walked back to the living room, shivering as she watched him manhandle Charlie easily. Toby held him squawking under one arm while he playfully smacked his butt. Was it due to some deep, prehistoric hormonal urge to have an alpha male to dominate the pack? Or was it just because he looked so damned sexy in his tight jeans and blue shirt?

Toby put him on the floor and made a show of trying to walk with Charlie clinging to his leg. "Esther, help! I've got a limpet stuck to me."

"I'm Daddy's limpey," Charlie said, arms wrapped tight around his father's thigh.

She tried to peel him away. "Let go or you'll cut off his blood flow."

"We wouldn't want that," Toby said. "Blood flow to the crown jewels area is mega-important, boyo."

She smothered a laugh as she lifted Charlie off. "There. Nicely now." She held him tightly until he stopped struggling and then put him down.

"You're so patient," Toby said. "And you look gorgeous in that top."

"Thank you." She straightened and looked into his warm eyes. "You too."

He held her gaze. Then, clearly liking what he saw, he slipped a hand to the back of her neck and held her there while he kissed her.

She stiffened, taken aback, but his mouth was soft, the kiss gentle, and he tasted of mint. So she closed her eyes and enjoyed it, pressing her hands against his chest.

"Yuck," Charlie said.

Toby pulled back, gave her a wry look, and turned to his son. "It's not yuck. I'll show you. Come here—give me a kiss."

"No!" Charlie belted away from him, and Toby chased him around the room.

Esther sighed and led the way to the front door. She was tempted to let them go through and then shut the door behind them. Especially because she was also nervous about meeting Toby's brothers. But as she reached the door, Toby skidded up to her on the wooden floor and put his hand on the handle.

"Let me, ma'am." He opened the door with a flourish and winked at her.

She remembered the role-play they'd chosen and excitement shimmered through her.

"Had you forgotten?" His eyes twinkled. "I'm your slave for the afternoon."

"I hadn't forgotten. I fully intend to make the most of it."

"Ooh, promises, promises."

"You'll regret that by the end of the day when I've made you sweep the floor and do all the washing."

"Nothing is too much trouble for my fair lady." Still, alarm lit his eyes, and she giggled.

"I'm joking." She picked up Charlie and walked to the door, finishing with a brief, mischievous glance at Toby over her shoulder. "I won't make you do all the washing. Just my lacy underwear." She left him standing open mouthed, and walked out to the car with a smirk. That would teach him to tease her—two could play at that game.

Chapter Twenty-Five

Esther was nervous about meeting Toby's brothers, although she had to admit, she was also curious. As an only child, sibling relationships had always intrigued her, and she'd wondered how alike he and his brothers were. She'd not yet been able to put her finger on why Toby fascinated her so much, but she wondered whether the other two men would hold the same attraction for her.

Matt Wilkinson was thirty-one and married to Cath with two young children. Shorter than Toby, but with the same dark curly hair and a goatee, he was a doctor, cool, shrewd and possessing a sharp manner she hadn't seen in Toby in even the minutest amount. He was nice enough to her, welcoming and friendly, but he mocked Toby relentlessly, and she detected a vein of superiority toward his brother that put her back up from the beginning.

Felix, on the other hand, she liked immediately. As tall as Toby, and a couple of years older, he was a little more slender and slightly less rugged, and she could easily imagine him in the courtroom, slick in a suit, winning over the jury. But even though he was a lawyer, and once again seemed more cool and calculating than the affable Toby, he had a naughty twinkle in his eye that reminded her of Toby's teasing manner. He clearly made a fortune judging by his expensive watch and the sleek car he'd parked outside Matt's house, and yet he was still single, although she knew he must have women falling over themselves to win him over.

To her surprise, however, neither of them made her heart beat faster the way Toby's did when he caught her gaze with his lovely brown eyes. Why was that? She puzzled the issue as they had tea— pizza for the kids, barbecued chicken and potato salad for the adults, with a huge Greek salad complete with olives and feta cheese.

What was it about Toby that rang her bell more than any other guy? There must be something, one character trait or physical characteristic he possessed that the others didn't, which caused her pulse to race every few minutes as she thought about what they were going to get up to later that evening. If only she could isolate that one trait, she'd know what to look for in future partners.

But she couldn't put her finger on it. He was gorgeous, but so were both of his brothers, especially Felix. Toby was the most muscular of them all, probably due to his manual job, but both brothers obviously worked out, and there wasn't much in it. He was funny, but both Matt and Felix were probably wittier, on the whole. He wasn't the cleverest, nor was he the richest.

And yet when he looked across the table at her and gave her that secret smile that told her he was thinking about what he was going to do to her that night, a thrill went through her, and she had to lower her eyes, a warm flush spreading through her cheeks.

Maybe it was his gentleness that attracted her—the very fact that he wasn't sharp or cruel. Even when he'd left her at the airport, he hadn't been cold. With hindsight, she could see he'd just been young, impatient, and irritated—he'd had feelings for her, and those feelings had scared him, plus he couldn't think of a way to make it work, so he'd refused to face up to how he felt, and had walked away. She knew he'd regretted that decision, because he'd tried to contact her. No, he wasn't cruel, or hard.

Still, he had made the decision to leave her. She mustn't forget that. How much could a person change? Clearly the fact that he'd walked away, and that he was still single, meant he had trouble committing. She had to keep reminding herself this was just sex, a distraction while she was on holiday. Nothing serious could come out of it. That was why she'd applied for the job in Dunedin.

Charlie played on the grass with Sasha and Jayden, Matt and Cath's children. Sasha was a typical six-year-old girl and bossed the two boys around with great delight. Jayden ignored her most of the time, but Charlie watched her with wide eyes and did whatever she told him to do, right up to jumping off a box into the paddling pool, where he promptly slipped over and fell on his butt.

Both she and Toby twitched, about to leap to their feet, but Charlie jumped up and down when Sasha squealed with delight at his antics, enjoying every minute of playing the fool.

"So like his father," Matt said.

"Falling on his ass?" Felix remarked.

Matt grinned. "I meant showing off for the girls, but yeah, now you come to mention it."

Toby smiled affably as everyone laughed, but Esther wondered whether their comments stung. Did he mind being the butt of everyone's jokes? Or did it rile him as it riled her? She'd ask him about it later.

Meanwhile, she determined to cheer him up. She caught his eye and waved her glass at him. "Could you get me another drink of lemonade please?" Making sure nobody was looking, she finished by mouthing the word *Slave*.

His lips curved slowly. "Of course." He took the glass, refilled it, and handed it back to her. "There you go." *Mistress*. He mouthed the word.

"Thank you." She sipped it and winked at him. His hot gaze told her he was thinking about what she might order him to do later that evening.

As the afternoon wore on, she enjoyed herself by continuing to ask him to do things for her. Fetch her cardigan from the car when a light breeze lowered the temperature. Cut her another piece of cake. Sort Charlie out when he needed the bathroom. Carry the dishes in while she stretched out on the lounger. The funny thing was, none of the others mentioned it. Was this what it was like for ordinary couples? She'd never had anyone to ask before to fetch her drinks or do things for her. She decided she could rather grow to like it.

While Matt and Felix played football with the kids and Cath snoozed in the late sun, Esther placed her feet on Toby's lap and wiggled her toes.

"My feet ache," she said quietly, so only he could hear her. "Could you massage them please, slave?"

"As my lady demands." He took them in his big hands and pressed his thumbs into her soles, brushing down to her toes with sensual strokes that soon made her realize her plan was backfiring.

"Mm." She shifted in the chair, growing aroused at his gentle, sure touch. "Stop."

He tightened his grip on her ankles, however, refusing to let her go, and she sat still and glared at him. She couldn't escape without making a fuss and alerting everyone to what they were doing. He stroked up the arches of her feet, slipped his fingers between her toes, stroked up her instep, and circled her ankle bone until she shivered all over.

"Toby…"

"What?" He continued to play with her, sending delicious sensations right through her body. She hadn't realized her feet were so sensitive. Or maybe it was just the thought of how it would feel to have those same hands on her body, arousing her slowly until she thrummed like a guitar string, singing the special song she sang only for him.

The sun came out from behind the clouds and warmed her through, and she closed her eyes and tipped up her face to capture its rays and give herself over to his light, gentle touch. She sank into a kind of sexual trance, and it was only when Matt and Felix walked up to them that she shook herself out of it and pulled her legs away.

Her face flushed. Had they seen her and Toby? Matt went over to his wife and woke her with a kiss, but she could tell from the smile on Felix's face that he'd observed what they were doing.

He sat opposite them, took a swig from his beer and said, "So, are you two an item?"

"No," they said together.

"Huh." His eyes danced, but he didn't say anything.

Esther's cheeks burned even more when he exchanged an amused smile with Toby. She stood and asked Matt, "Can I use your bathroom, please?"

"Sure." He gave her directions to it, and she walked into the house. Why did she get embarrassed so often? She was a grown-up, and what she and Toby chose to do in their own time was nobody else's business. So why did his teasing smile make her feel like a sixteen-year-old on her first date?

*

Toby propped his feet on the small wall running around the decking and lowered his sunglasses. Unfortunately, he could still see his brother's grin.

"Not involved?" Felix said. "Yeah, right."

"You don't have to be involved to have sex," Toby said.

Felix raised his eyebrows. "Oh?"

"It's a mutual arrangement while she's here in the Northland. It's not a thing."

Felix pointed his beer bottle at him. "It's totally a thing, and you're kidding yourself if you think it's not."

"Bollocks," Toby said, getting annoyed. "It doesn't mean anything."

"To you maybe. She's got stars in her eyes when she looks at you."

Toby opened his mouth and then shut it again. Esther had feelings for him? He knew how he felt about her, but it was always so difficult to gauge someone else's reaction. She liked him, and of course she fancied him. But she'd made it quite clear their current arrangement was purely about sex. She hadn't had sex for three years—it made sense to him that she'd take the opportunity to sleep with him when they'd had such a great time in bed before. He wasn't insulted by that fact. He liked to think he was good in bed, and he'd done the same thing himself before when sex was being offered.

But still, Felix was implying there was more to it than sexual gratification, and that unnerved him.

"Ah," Felix said.

"Ah what?" Now he was growing irritable, and he shifted in his seat as Matt and Cath sat back up at the table and listened to the conversation.

Felix's eyes gleamed. "You've got feelings for her too."

They all stared at him. Toby tipped back his head with a sigh and stared up at the sky for a few moments before returning his gaze to them with exasperation. "She's the mother of my son. Of course I have feelings for her. I like her. She's gorgeous. I want to have sex with her. That doesn't mean it has to be deep and meaningful."

"Of course it doesn't," Matt said. "You don't do deep and meaningful."

Toby said nothing as the others laughed. Once, he would have agreed with them. Now, he wasn't so sure.

Chapter Twenty-Six

"What's the joke?" Esther rejoined them at the table.

"We were just saying how Toby doesn't do deep and meaningful," Cath said.

She met Toby's gaze. "Oh, I think there's more to him than meets the eye." She smiled.

"Nah," Matt said. "When he was asked in an exam at school 'Where was the Treaty of Waitangi signed?' he wrote 'At the bottom'."

Felix and Cath burst out laughing. Toby sighed and nodded his assent, seemingly unembarrassed by the admission.

"That doesn't mean he's shallow," Esther protested, wondering why she felt the need to defend him repeatedly. "He's actually very thoughtful and insightful."

Felix raised an eyebrow. "Are we talking about the same brother here?"

She glared at him, annoyed that she was annoyed. He held her gaze, clearly interested in the relationship between her and his brother.

He said something, and she blinked because he'd said it in Latin. Of course, he was a lawyer—he'd be familiar with the basic structure of the language.

It had been a while since she'd studied it, and it took her a moment to translate the words.

"Do you love him?" he'd asked. Toby stared at him, then at her, but she didn't look at him.

She scowled at Felix, but he refused to be stared down. "He is a good man," she replied carefully, also in Latin.

"He loves you," he replied.

Her eyes widened. "Bollocks," she said in English before she could think better of it.

Matt glanced at Felix with amusement. "There's your answer." Of course, the damn doctor had also understood what they were saying.

"I'm sitting right here," Toby said mildly. "I'm guessing the three of you know how incredibly rude you've just been?"

The guys just smiled, but Esther looked down as the conversation continued, knowing he was right. Her stomach tightened in a knot. Damn Felix and his penetrating gaze. He didn't know what he was talking about. He'd implied there was some kind of romantic involvement going on between her and Toby, and he was completely wide of the mark. Of course she was fond of Toby—he was the father of her child, for heaven's sake. And she fancied him rotten. That didn't mean she loved him. She wasn't going to let herself love him.

For years, she'd studied novels where the heroine swooned every time the hero passed by, unable to control her passionate feelings for him. Much as she loved classical literature, it was all romantic nonsense. A person absolutely could control their feelings for another person. Or at least, that person could control the way they reacted to those feelings. Although she was sympathetic toward women who'd been mistreated by men, deep down she couldn't understand a woman who stayed in a destructive relationship. "But I love him" was not an excuse that passed muster for her.

Love wasn't an airy-fairy thing that could be caught like the common cold. Love started with plain, old-fashioned lust, a surge of hormones caused by a prehistoric urge to copulate and reproduce. Attraction was a physical, chemical thing—everyone knew men liked women with big breasts and shapely butts because on some subconscious level it meant they would be suitable to bear their children. And lust developed into love over time, maturing like expensive whisky, born out of trust and comfort and feeling safe and secure with your mate. A person couldn't "fall in love". Lust, yes. Love, no. She'd never been in love, and she had no intention of succumbing to it, either. She'd assuage her physical need and Cupid could bugger off and shoot someone else.

She looked at Toby, not overly surprised to find him studying her thoughtfully. She smiled, but he didn't return it. A frown hovered on his brow. He was upset. Why? What had annoyed him?

"Okay." He pushed his chair back. "I think Esther and I will make a move, if that's all right. Are you sure about looking after Charlie, Cath?"

"Of course." The plump, amenable Cath smiled. "Where are you off to—the cinema?"

"Yeah. One of the Bourne films." Toby's gaze met Esther's. "We're really looking forward to seeing it, aren't we?"

Well, she could hardly contradict him now. "Mm," she said in a non-committal voice.

He held a hand out to her. "Come on. Don't want to miss the exciting opening scenes, eh?"

She took his hand and smiled at Cath. "Thank you for looking after Charlie. If he gives you any hassle, just call Toby's mobile."

"No worries. We'll have an ice cream sundae in a minute and he can choose what toppings he wants—kids love doing that. Then he can have a bath with Jayden. That'll keep them both amused for a while."

"Thank you." Esther couldn't get rid of her shyness at the thought that these strangers were happy to look after her son. But Matt and Felix were Charlie's uncles, and Sasha and Jayden were his cousins. They were his family. And even though they were practically strangers, blood had an odd effect on people. When she was younger, her father had taken her to the Crusaders rugby matches in Christchurch, and there had always been a kind of tribal atmosphere as they'd walked to the ground wearing the team jersey. This felt similar, the same kind of affinity with total strangers because they were your family, your kin.

Matt and Felix stood as they went to leave, and Matt came forward to kiss her on the cheek. "Sorry if we embarrassed you," he murmured. His eyes were gentle. "We're so used to teasing each other we forget some people don't like it."

"I'm an only child," she admitted. "I'm just not used to it, that's all."

"Just tell us to fuck off if we go too far." Felix also kissed her on the cheek. "We won't be offended."

She laughed. "I couldn't possibly do that. But thanks."

Toby tugged her hand. "Come on." He nodded to his brothers. "We'll see you later." He walked around the house to the front where they'd parked the car, bringing Esther with him.

She frowned at him as he unlocked the car and got in. His jaw looked knotted as if he was clenching his teeth. She opened the door, slid into the passenger seat, and clipped herself in before turning to him. "What's up?"

He glanced at her as he clipped in his seatbelt, and then turned his attention back to the car, slotting in the key and starting the engine. "Nothing." He pulled away smoothly and guided the car onto the main road toward his house.

She studied him, puzzled. It was the first time since she'd met him that he'd seemed preoccupied. Tentatively, she laid a hand on his arm. "What is it?"

He said nothing for a moment, taking the time to negotiate a junction. She rubbed his arm, thinking that if she had to guess she would have said he seemed slightly depressed.

"Come on," she said, "you can tell me."

He sighed and leaned his right elbow on the windowsill, his fingers brushing his lips. "Nothing deep and meaningful."

She recognized the phrase and frowned. "Is this to do with your brothers?"

He shrugged.

Continuing to rub his arm gently, she said, "What did they say that bothered you?"

"It wasn't what they said." He glanced at her and then looked away.

So it was something they'd done. She thought furiously about what could possibly have upset him. He'd been fine until they'd got up to go. Then Matt and Felix had kissed her goodbye and... Oh.

Her lips began to curve. "Toby Wilkinson, are you jealous?"

He glared at her. "Of course not."

"You are. Because they kissed me goodbye?"

He said nothing, staring moodily at the road.

"No," she said softly. "Not just that. Because you think I like them."

"Why wouldn't you? They're smarter, richer, funnier than me. Why the fuck would anyone pick me out of the three of us?" He moved away from her, and her hand fell into her lap.

She said nothing more as he drove the short distance to his house. He wasn't just jealous, she thought. It went deeper than irritation. He was angry, and he was hurt. All his life, his brothers had mocked him, and now he thought they'd charmed the woman he'd been sure would be loyal to him because he was the father of her child. How odd that so many feelings people experienced started at the prehistoric level. *Woman mine*. He obviously wanted to yell it from the rooftops, but he couldn't because they weren't dating, and he knew he had no right to claim any possession over her.

He pulled up outside his house but left the car engine running. Without looking at her, both hands on the steering wheel, he said, "Perhaps I should take you back to Faith's house." He rubbed at a mark on the wheel with his thumb. "I don't know that I'm in the mood for any Naughty Nights."

She bit her lip. If she came on to him, would he turn her down? Could she bear the humiliation? And yet he was hurting, and she wanted to ease that hurt. More than anything, at that moment, she wanted to make him feel better.

She'd take the chance. If he turned her down again, that would be it.

Chapter Twenty-Seven

She unclipped her seatbelt. "I don't want to go Faith's house. Come inside."

He didn't move. His gaze remained fixed on the steering wheel.

"You may not be wearing a loincloth," she said softly, "but I seem to recall you're my personal slave. And at the moment, you don't seem to be doing what you're told."

His lips curved at that, but as he glanced across at her, she could see he was going to turn her down. "Esther…"

"Toby, if I had to choose, I'd choose you every time," she said hurriedly. Oh God, please don't let him turn her down. "Matt and Felix are both nice, but they're not you. Why won't you believe me when I tell you how special you are?"

"I'm not special," he said, a little sadly. "I'm just me."

"And I'm just me. You make me feel special—why can't I do the same for you?" Tears pricked her eyelids. Why didn't he believe her?

He stared out of the car for a moment, and then finally relaxed his grip on the steering wheel. He sighed and looked across at her. "Felix liked you," he said.

"I get the impression Felix likes most members of the female sex."

His lips twisted. "That's probably true. But he knows we're not an item—that you're fair game. He won't hesitate to make a move on you."

Indignation made her sit up straight and frown. "Well, first, even if he did, that doesn't mean I'd say yes. And second, I don't believe he'd make a move on me right in front of you. He's your brother, for Christ's sake."

"You don't think propositioning you in a language I don't understand counts?"

Oh… He was upset because he didn't know what they'd talked about. That was fair.

She sighed. "He wasn't propositioning me. What he said in Latin... He asked me how I feel about you." It was only a little lie.

That obviously surprised him. "What did you say?"

She smiled. "I said I liked you."

"Did you now?"

"I did." She lifted herself up in the seat, leaned over, and hovered her lips above his. "I refrained from pointing out we had an arrangement, but I think he got the general idea."

He brought his hand up and slipped it into her hair, brushing her cheek with his thumb. "I'm sorry," he said huskily. "I'm not normally the jealous type, and I know I have no right to be. But watching them talk to you, kiss you, even on the cheek... It did something to me inside."

She understood. She'd had the same feeling when she'd wondered who he'd slept with since Fiji. Was he not normally jealous? If not, why was he jealous where she was concerned? What were they getting themselves into?

"Don't think about it now," she murmured, brushing her lips against his. "It's just me and you here. And right now, you're all I need. All I want."

She kissed him, relieved when he responded with a heartfelt and passionate embrace. He still wanted her, still desired her. She kissed around his jaw, up to his cheekbone, touched her lips to his closed eyes and forehead, then back to his mouth.

He sighed deeply when she lifted her head, and she looked into his eyes. "Better?" she asked.

He smiled. "Yes."

"Then why don't we go inside? I've been looking forward to this all day."

"Ordering me about?"

"Yeah." She moistened her lips with the tip of her tongue and said huskily, "I'm going to make you kiss me all over." She met his gaze boldly. "And then I'm going to ask you to fuck me into next week."

He blinked, pupils dilating. "Wow. Way to give a guy an instant erection."

She giggled. "Come on then."

They got out of the car, Toby rising so hurriedly he bumped his head. He grabbed her hand and led her toward the house, his fast stride making her laugh. He let them in, and she threw her handbag on the table, then led him to the sofa, switching on a lamp in the corner. The light was fading outside, and the lamp made the room glow.

He glanced at the kitchen. "Don't you want a drink?"

She shook her head, breathless with anticipation. "No. I want you."

He moved closer to her, his hands on her hips. "I'm all yours." He touched his lips to hers. "Tell me what you'd like me to do."

She stepped back from him. "First, slave, I'd like you naked. Strip."

He put his hands on his hips. "Strip?"

"Strip. Remove your clothes. Disrobe. Get your kit off."

"I get the idea," he said wryly. "Do I have to do it to music?"

"Great idea." She went over to his iPad, pulled up YouTube and selected a song. Then she pressed Play. Joe Cocker's husky voice started singing 'You Can Leave Your Hat On'."

"Jeez." He rolled his eyes. She giggled and took a seat on the sofa in front of him.

"Come on." She motioned with her hand. "Show me that manly body of yours." She sat back, making herself comfortable. "I should have bought some popcorn."

With a sigh of resignation, he began to unbutton his shirt. She drew up her knees and wrapped her arms around them, enjoying every moment of the role-play. What was not to like? He had natural rhythm, and even though he'd made a show of being exasperated at her instructions, within minutes he was strutting his stuff and performing, to her delight.

Starting at the top of the shirt, he worked his way down, sliding his finger between each button. He held her gaze as he did so, moving his hips to the music, and her face began to grow warm at his sexy grin.

When he reached the bottom, he opened one side of the shirt and then closed it and opened the other, teasing her. She fanned herself, and he laughed and let the shirt fall from his back, catching it in a hand. He threw it at her, and it landed on her head. She crumpled it into a ball and buried her face in it. The warmed cloth brought out the subtle smell of his aftershave, and her pheromones stirred, yawned, stretched, and looked around with interest.

"Yum," she said, her gaze wandering over his torso. Wow, what a body.

He turned so his back was to her and continued to dance, rolling his shoulders, and she admired the way his muscles moved beneath his tanned skin, imagining them underneath her fingers, solid and warm.

"Does my lady like what she sees?" He turned back and posed.

"She'd like it even more if you got your pants off."

"What's the rush?" He hooked his thumbs in the waistband of his jeans and ran them around to his hips, then back again. "Waiting increases the anticipation."

"Just as long as you don't mind drowning in a sea of drool."

He chuckled. "That's gross, but it's possibly the nicest thing anyone's ever said to me."

She smiled and kept her nose buried in his shirt as he started to unbutton his pants. Did he have any idea how gorgeous he was? She suspected not. He carried himself with the ease of a man who worked hard to keep fit but didn't spend every five minutes looking in a mirror. Not that she would have blamed him if he did. She could easily stare at that body all day, from the toned abs to the defined stomach muscles to the wonderful line of hair that trailed enticingly into his jeans.

He moved his fingers to the zipper and pulled it down. Then he turned his back to her again and wiggled his hips.

She groaned. "Tease."

He stuck his thumbs in the waistband and gave her a glimpse of his boxers. Still moving to the music, he lowered the jeans and slid them down his legs.

She sighed and studied his tight butt encased beautifully in the silky fabric of his underwear. "That should be framed and put in the Auckland Art Gallery."

He laughed and kicked off the jeans. "I feel so sorry for you. Obviously, you have so little sexual experience you find the most meager male body exciting."

"Sweetheart," she said, breathless with desire, "the very last thing you are is meager. Your body is…" Her voice trailed off as he turned around and the evidence of his desire strained toward her through the boxers. "Ooh. Sublime."

He ran a finger along his erection and raised an eyebrow. "Does it meet the lady's requirements?"

"Um... hmm... I'll let you know at the end of the evening." She pointed to his underwear. "Take them off."

First, he walked over to the iPad and selected an album of some slow, sexy music and pressed Play. Then he came back to stand before her. He lifted the elastic over his erection and lowered the boxers. Giving her a taunting smile, he walked forward to stand in front of her, completely naked, hands on hips. "I'm all yours, my lady. Ready to service your needs, whatever they are."

She licked her lips. The swollen tip was inches from her mouth. Naughtiness flooded her. He was hers for the evening—she could make him do anything she wanted. "Show me how you touch yourself."

He didn't look the tiniest bit shocked. Obediently, fixing his hot gaze on her, he grasped his shaft in his left hand and started to stroke himself.

She inhaled, so turned on at the sight that her mouth watered. He kept his right hand on his hip, closed his eyes and tilted his head back as he continued to arouse himself. Speechless with desire, she watched for about twenty seconds before she couldn't stand it any longer.

Pushing herself to her feet, she stood before him. "Undress me," she commanded huskily.

He opened his eyes and went to kiss her, but she put a hand on his chest. "Undress me," she said again, more firmly.

Eyes half-lidded with desire, he pretended to doff his cap. "Yes, ma'am."

He stood a few inches away from her and held the bottom of her vest. She lifted her arms, and he drew the vest up and over her head, letting it drop to the floor.

The heat of his eyes burned into her naked skin like the rays of the sun.

"No bra," he murmured. "Nice." He lifted a hand to cup her breast, but she stopped him.

"No touching."

His lips curved and he dropped his hand. "Yes, ma'am. Okay. You tell me exactly what you want me to do."

She couldn't believe she was being so bold. "Finish undressing me."

He tugged at her skirt, and the elasticized waist expanded to slide down her hips. She held her breath as the skirt dropped with a rustle to the floor. She'd gone commando, and she would have laughed at the look on his face if she hadn't been so turned on.

His hands twitched as if he wanted to touch her, but he remained still, instead caressing her with his gaze.

Slowly, she lowered herself back onto the sofa. "Kneel between my legs," she instructed him.

He did so, moving forward so his hips brushed the inside of her thighs. He rested his hands on the top of her legs, but couldn't seem to stop the instinctive brush of his thumbs against her skin. "What now, my lady?" he asked.

She fixed him with her gaze, letting all her desire show in her eyes. "Kiss me."

Chapter Twenty-Eight

He leaned forward and covered her mouth with his. The tentative, playful kisses vanished—instead his red-hot embrace scorched through her, setting light to all her nerve endings. She moaned as he plunged his tongue inside her mouth and threaded her hands into his hair, holding him as they kissed. But when he placed a hand on her breast, she smacked it playfully.

"Mouth only," she said, breathless.

He nodded, smirking. "What do you want me to do with it?"

"Kiss my neck."

He touched his lips compliantly to the spot behind her ear and kissed down the sensitive skin of her neck.

"Slowly," she commanded, in a hazy, sensual dream.

So he took his time, tracing his tongue on her skin, tasting her, and when he closed his mouth over where her pulse beat and sucked gently, she groaned. She ran her fingers up his arms and across his shoulders. He was so much bigger than her, all height and breadth and muscle—she'd never been so conscious of the difference between the sexes.

"You get to touch and I don't?" he said, lips hovering over hers. "Unfair."

"Who's the boss here?"

He brushed his lips against hers. "You."

Except it didn't feel like it. She was supposed to be in charge, but, as always, he played her body like a harp.

He ran his tongue along her bottom lip. "What now?"

She swallowed. "My breasts."

"Absolutely. Thought you'd never ask."

Once again, he kissed her neck, but this time he continued down and placed light kisses on the swell of her breasts. She leaned back on her elbows so he could get comfortable. Her nipples throbbed with the expectation of his mouth closing on them, but he kissed around them, and his warm tongue remained clear of the most sensitive skin.

"Stop teasing me," she begged eventually.

He lifted his head and raised an eyebrow. "What do you mean? I'm only doing what you told me."

He was going to make her spell out every little thing she wanted done and play her at her own game. But she couldn't describe every part of the lovemaking process—she'd die of embarrassment. Surely, he'd finally take the initiative and do what he knew drove her crazy?

She squirmed beneath his continued ministrations, but when he showed no sign of moving his lips where she wanted them, she gave in. "My nipples," she begged. "Kiss them."

He smiled and did so, placing his warm lips on the soft skin, but even though she arched her back toward him, he still didn't do it the way she wanted it. She closed her eyes. "Use your tongue," she whispered.

He murmured a triumphant "Yes." Before she could steel herself, he brushed his warm tongue over her right nipple.

"Oh…" The swollen skin tightened, and she tipped her head back. After all the anticipation, the sensation rippled through her exquisitely.

He did the same to her other nipple, blowing on it, and she gasped when it also peaked. "Suck them," she pleaded. "Please."

He covered one with his hot mouth and sucked, and she moaned at the answering tremors deep inside her. "Don't stop," she murmured and slipped a hand back into his hair, enjoying the feel of the silky curls in her fingers as he continued to arouse her.

She instructed him to move from one to the other and he did so, until she knew if he carried on she was going to come. And she didn't want to come—not yet. She was enjoying herself too much.

"Stop," she said huskily, and he raised his head. His pupils had dilated, and his eyelids had lowered to half-mast. He moved forward, and his erection pressed between her legs. When he rocked his hips, the solid length slid through her folds, pressing on her clit.

She gasped and pushed him away. "Kiss the rest of me," she demanded, "toes up."

Laughing, he did so. He began with her toes, taking each one into his mouth and sucking. He flicked his tongue in between them and then trailed it along her instep and circled her ankle bone. Then he worked his way up each leg, nibbling and kissing, until eventually he reached the apex of her thighs, where he stopped and raised his head.

160

"Tell me what you want," he said, his low voice sending shivers through her.

She'd lost all her inhibitions by that point. "Make me come with your mouth," she ordered, loving the way he smiled sexily at her words.

"You'll have to give me better directions than that." He gestured at the sofa. "First, move up."

She did so, shifting her butt further to the back of the sofa. He put his hands on her knees and spread them, pushing them up until her heels rested on the edge of the sofa cushions. He surveyed her with approval, and he reached out and brushed his thumb through her core, spreading her moisture across her folds. "Nice." He looked up at her. "You smell wonderful."

"Oh man, you're disgusting."

He grinned. "Tell me what you want me to do."

"Use your tongue," she said faintly. "Lick me."

He ran his tongue very lightly up her center and then stopped.

"Oh…" She nearly passed out with pleasure and anticipation. "Again."

He repeated the movement.

"Harder," she said, closing her eyes as he did it more firmly. "Oh yes, that's right. Again. Keep going."

She enjoyed the long, slow licks for a while, but eventually he lifted his head and demanded, "What else? Tell me, Esther. Tell me what you like." He pushed her legs. Dear God, he wanted her to open them even wider. She surrendered to the pressure and dropped her knees open, exposing herself completely to him.

"I want your tongue inside me," she said without opening her eyes.

First, she felt his hot breath on her, and then the warm softness of his tongue as he slid it into her opening, as deep as he could go. He licked and sucked at her, and before long she could take no more.

She lowered her fingers and circled them around her clit. "Here," she moaned. "Suck me here."

He did so, and the beautiful tightening began in her abdomen and thighs, gradually focusing deep inside her. "Put your fingers in me," she managed to say. He slid two into her and sucked hard, and she came around them in an intense clench and burn of muscle.

When the orgasm finally subsided, she pushed him away and collapsed, limp and exhausted. "Wow."

He leaned over her, supporting himself on his powerful arms, and pressed his erection against her hot, sensitive flesh. "What now, my lady? Are you done?"

"God, no." She arched her back blissfully as he stroked along her. "I want that inside me." She opened her eyes and met his gaze.

He was breathing heavily, but his lips curved as he said, "How do you want me?"

"I don't mind," she said dreamily. "I give you permission to use your initiative."

She thought he'd just push straight into her. Instead, to her shock he moved her left leg over her right and rolled her onto her front, and she squealed loudly. Without hesitating, he tugged her hips back so her knees fell to the floor either side of his. He knelt between her legs, and as he widened his knees, they forced hers apart.

"Hey." She rose up in indignation at his roughness. "I'm a lady. You're supposed to be doing what you're told."

"You told me to use my initiative." He spoke into her ear and put his arms around her. Cupping her breasts, he squeezed her nipples. "So I did."

"Ooh. I didn't mean—"

"I don't care. You gave me permission." He pushed her forward onto the sofa, held her there with a hand between her shoulder blades, and dipped the other underneath her to slide into her warm folds. "I know what you want better than you do."

She inhaled, outraged, as he slid his fingers deep inside her. "You do not! Let me go."

"No." He started to arouse her again, massaging her already sensitive skin.

"Some slave you are," she complained, trying to push his arm away, but it was like trying to move an iron bar. "You should be whipped."

He chuckled. "Promises, promises." He raised his hand to tug her nipples again.

"Ow," she protested, although desire shot through her, and her internal muscles clenched. She struggled against him, but he just widened her legs even farther.

"Fight me all you like," he said, "you're not going anywhere." He moved his erection beneath her.

He'd taken her from behind before, but she'd forgotten the animal nature of it and what a dominant position it gave him. How demeaning. She didn't want to be dominated.

Her excited, pounding heart had other ideas.

She tried to ignore it. Leaning on one elbow, she reached around and pushed him. "Let me go!"

He caught her hand and held it behind her back, linking their fingers. Leaning close, he said with amusement, "You wanted me to fuck you into next week. I'm only obeying orders. *My lady.*"

"Yes, but—" Her power of speech evaporated as he thrust forward without any further warning and slid into her, hot and hard, all the way up.

"Fuck!" she yelled. He'd penetrated deeply, filling her to the brim, her body stretching to accommodate.

"Whatever the lady desires." He pulled his hips back and thrust forward firmly.

Esther gasped and tried to yank her hand free, but his iron grip refused to release her. Unable to move, she could only lie there as he pounded into her, his body meeting hers with a sharp smack each time he thrust. With every movement, he slid deeper inside her, and she shuddered as his not-inconsiderable erection stretched her until she didn't think she had anything left to give.

She wanted to hate him for it, for his strength and supremacy over her. But as he pushed her forward with each thrust, her breasts swung and her nipples grazed the abrasive sofa cushion. Soon she was writhing beneath him, incredibly turned on by his forcefulness and the base, feral nature of the position, as if she were a mare being mounted by a stallion in the field.

"Jesus, you're an animal." She exhaled with a rush at each thrust.

Her accusation didn't seem to bother him. "Yes, my lady." His hips slapped against hers. "You want me to stop?"

"Yes." She had to accept the protest didn't sound very convincing. "Slave," she added, to tell him she was still playing.

"Tough." He thrust harder and, without warning, smacked her butt.

She tightened instinctively around him. "Ouch. Shit."

He gave a throaty growl of approval. "Oh yeah. Do it again."

He smacked her once more, harder this time, and it stung so much, she squealed. But he just laughed and thrust harder.

"Toby!" Squirming, she tried to push herself up, but he put his free hand back between her shoulder blades and held her there. She must look a right sight, she thought, breasts bouncing all over the place. It would have been humiliating if it weren't so incredibly sexy. She was totally conquered and at his mercy, like an Anglo-Saxon wench taken by a lusting Norman knight.

"You wait," she told him through gritted teeth, knowing he'd won this time. "I'll make you pay for what you're doing. I'll have you whipped!"

"Oh… you know how to turn a guy on, don't you?"

She rolled her eyes, unable to believe how completely immoral he was. "You're going to hell for this, you realize."

"If I am, you'll be right behind me." He stroked her rump fondly as he spoke.

She tried to stop her head banging against the back of the sofa and failed. "I'm a lady! You can't talk to me like this."

Still holding her hand, he moved his other beneath her to feel her swinging breasts. "Christ, Esther, your body's fucking amazing. I wish I could screw you like this all night."

All night. Dear Lord. She shuddered with desire at the thought.

He licked his fingers and brushed one nipple after the other, transferring the moisture to her soft skin. Lessening his thrusts slightly, he pulled her hips to his rhythmically instead, increasing her movement and the drag of her breasts over the rough fabric. Wet and swollen, they turned extra sensitive as the material teased them. When she groaned, he chuckled. He obviously knew exactly what he was doing to her.

She implored between thrusts, "Oh—God—Toby—please."

"Please what?" His hand tightened on hers where he held it behind her back, but he stroked her palm with his thumb, a strangely tender gesture in the middle of his lustful authority.

"Let… me… oh…" Her plump nipples dragged up the cushion, and the muscles deep inside her clenched.

"Let you what?" His fierceness surprised her, his voice as insistent as his body. And the realization came to her. This was to do with how his brothers had made him feel. He needed to prove she desired him—that she wasn't thinking of anyone else while he took her at his will.

In spite of his forcefulness, he wasn't doing anything she didn't absolutely adore deep down. He'd never hurt her—she knew that instinctively. He was perfectly aware how much she was enjoying herself even though she protested otherwise. Still playing the game, he wanted her to beg, to convince him he was everything to her at that moment. And she'd been there—she'd had that desperate need to feel wanted. She knew that pain. And she was happy to play the submissive if it made him feel better.

Chapter Twenty-Nine

She moaned softly. "Let me come, slave, please." She didn't have to completely fake the plea. Her clit throbbed and her nipples burned from the coarse material, but her release remained out of reach all the time he refused to let her touch herself.

"You want to come?" he murmured.

At last... "Oh God, yes."

"Well, you'll have to wait until I'm ready." His voice was firm, although his harsh breathing told her she wouldn't have to wait long.

She pushed back against him, trying to grind herself on him as he moved. "Touch me, please..."

He leaned her on her to stop her moving. "Not yet."

"Toby, you're driving me crazy..."

"When—I'm—ready, m'lady." His voice was a growl, low in his throat, as he thrust hard. "You can—fucking—wait."

Lust shot through her. Did he know his filthy language drove her wild?

He leaned over her, clamped his mouth in the crook of her neck and sucked hard. She squealed. "You'll give me a hickey!"

"Yep." The word held more than a hint of satisfaction as he inspected the bruise. "Now everyone will know you're mine."

She tried to fight him and wrench her arm free again. "Don't talk to me like that. I'm your mistress. You belong to me."

His hand tightened on hers at her continuation of their role-play. "And this is what you've wanted, isn't it, all this time? To be screwed from behind by one of your slaves."

"No, of course not. I'm a lady. I'll have you punished for this." Her breasts bounced, nipples grating on the prickly cushions. She'd pay for that the next day, but at that moment it was driving her wild.

"Yeah right." He knotted his hands in her hair and pulled her head up. "You love it."

She looked over her shoulder and met his hot gaze. "How dare you treat me like this?"

"Just watch me." His hips slapped loudly on her butt as he pumped in and out of her. Her muscles burned and moisture ran down the inside of her thighs. She let her head drop, where it bumped regularly against the back cushion. God, she was so close to coming. She didn't have to fake the begging anymore. "Do whatever you want to me, just let me come…"

He swore under his breath. Running a hand over her butt, he pulled out of her for a second and laughed as she complained. "Just wait." He dipped a thumb inside her and collected the wetness that pooled there. Then he filled her again quickly with his iron-hard length, and she gasped. Without stopping his punishing rhythm, he stroked up between her butt cheeks. "See if this helps." He slid his thumb into her tight muscle.

She jerked at the unfamiliar sensation, her body tightening erotically, and groaned. "Oh… Oh my God."

"Yeah." He moved his thumb in and out, matching the pace of his thrusts. "How does that feel? I seem to recall you like being touched here."

"Oh…" Her cheeks flamed. She couldn't believe he'd brought that up. "You're… You're…" Her words trailed off, and she nearly cried with the intensity of the pleasure.

"I'm what? Tell me." His breath was warm on the back of her neck, his voice silkily smug. The damn bastard was so sure of himself. How did he know the way to control her so competently? He continued to torture her with his thumb, teasing the muscle.

"Evil. I hate you." She spoiled the curse with an erotic groan.

He gave a deep, sexy laugh. "Yeah, it looks like it."

"Oh, Toby, please." She wailed mournfully.

He leaned forward. "Yes," he growled, "beg for me, baby. Tell me you want me."

"I want you." She tried to pull her arm away again and groaned as he refused to let go. His hand tightened on hers, almost hurting. He thrust hard, and she bit her lip, desperate for release, suddenly realizing that even if she wanted to, she couldn't break free from him—she really was at his mercy. When had this stopped being a game?

He slid his thumb out and slapped her butt again.

"Ouch."

He did it again, and again, and the final time it stung and she cried out. In answer, he slid his thumb back into her, plunging it in and out more roughly. He wanted to punish her with pleasure—why? For talking to Matt and Felix in Latin? For liking Felix? Not letting her move, he forced her to take what he was willing to give. She protested, so he slid his thumb in farther, groaning his pleasure as she squealed.

"Tell me again," he demanded.

"I want you, God, can't you tell?"

Her muscle burned, and she squirmed at the exquisite torture, her knees automatically widening until she'd opened right up to him, sprawled on the sofa, devoid of resistance. Jesus, could she be any more submissive? At some point, she'd stopped playing an active role in this sex game. He could do whatever he wished to her and she'd be powerless to stop him.

Hell, if that wasn't the most erotic thing she'd ever experienced.

"When you're with me, you won't ever look at another man," he said fiercely, pumping so hard she thought he might drill her into the sofa.

"I won't, I swear." She was panting now.

"You're mine. Say it," he snapped.

"I'm yours." A tear ran down her face and her heart ached at the reality of the words. This so wasn't a game. "I've only ever been yours." Her nipples were so sensitive she could have screamed, and her whole body throbbed hungrily, desperate for release.

His thrusts grew gentler, as if he could sense her heartfelt emotion, and he squeezed his fingers where they linked with hers. "Okay, baby, here it comes. Get ready." He released her hand, whacked her butt hard, and then slipped his fingers beneath her to press on her clit.

She clenched as her skin stung from the spank, and came immediately, and he exclaimed out loud as he erupted into her at the same time. She squealed, shocked at the intensity of the orgasm, squashed beneath him as he pushed her down hard into the cushions and continued to thrust until he'd completely emptied into her.

Her muscles pulsed and pulsed, and when she'd finally finished she lay there in an exhausted heap until he lifted himself off and collapsed onto the sofa beside her.

He pulled her into his arms. "Fucking hell." His glazed eyes studied her with awe. "You are incredible, Esther Tyler."

She buried her face in his neck. "Oh God, don't." How embarrassing. She'd completely unraveled in his arms. She was the world's biggest whore.

He kissed her hair. "Look at me."

"No." She'd rather die.

He forced her chin up. His warm eyes caressed her. "You're fantastic, you know that?"

"You too." Her cheeks burned, and he smiled and kissed them.

Then he stretched out, and she curled up against him, comforted by the tightness of his arm around her.

Outside, a kiwi called in the bush as their breathing slowed and the sweat cooled on their skin. Her thoughts drifted hazily—brief replays of the sights and sensations she'd just experienced mingled with the thoughts and emotions spiraling through her. *I'm yours*, she'd said, and the truth had brought tears to her eyes. But she'd only said it in the passion of the moment. It was all part of the role she'd been playing. Wasn't it?

After a while, he shifted onto his side, propping his head on a hand so he could study her.

"Hey," he said, smiling.

"Hey." She couldn't stop the shy blush that crept over her cheeks. "You'd make a terrible slave."

He chuckled. "Is that a complaint? Did you not enjoy it?"

She shrugged but couldn't stop her mouth curving in a smile.

He kissed her. "I didn't hurt you?" Worry flickered across his face.

"No, of course not." She loved his rough play, but she also adored how he could be so gentle sometimes. Then she rubbed her butt. "My ass is sore though." He pulled her forward to look at it, and she frowned at his wince. "What?"

"There may be a handprint on it."

"Jeez," she said. He pulled an *eek* face and she rolled her eyes. "A bit late for guilt now."

"Sorry, honey. You do strange things to me. You make me all…" He shifted uncomfortably.

"Horny?"

"Hah. That too. But I was going to say 'forceful'. I don't know why. I'm not like that normally." His lips twisted wryly.

"Funny, because I don't think I'm submissive outside the bedroom either."

He snorted. "No. Definitely not." He smiled and kissed her. "I guess that makes us pretty well matched between the sheets."

She wasn't going to think about that. Reaching up a hand, she scraped the pads of her fingers along his bristles, pondering on how he'd nearly had a change of heart. "Are you glad you didn't take me back now?"

He sighed and ran a hand through his hair.

"What?" She was surprised to see the sad look return to his face.

"I'm sorry." His brown eyes looked troubled.

"What about?" she said, genuinely puzzled.

"I know I have no right to be possessive. I shouldn't have said that to you about not looking at another man. I know I'm being an idiot." He was clearly uncomfortable with the way he'd acted.

"It's okay," she said lightly, determined not to make it into an issue. "We were role-playing. We all say things we don't mean in the heat of passion."

"I guess." He kissed her fingers. He didn't sound convinced, but she understood how he felt. She was the mother of his child, and even though they weren't involved as such, he wouldn't necessarily want her going off with other guys under his nose. Yes, it might be a bit dog-in-the-manger, but she could understand it. She wouldn't want him dating other girls in front of her either.

Although, of course, he would date again, and soon probably. Next time she saw him, whether he came down to Christchurch or Dunedin or wherever she ended up going, he'd probably have a partner. Perhaps he'd bring her with him to meet his son. This girlfriend would want to please Toby, so she'd probably fuss over Charlie and spoil him rotten. And he'd put his arm around her and be all pleased and kiss her, and then...

Esther blinked at the disturbing images. There was no point in worrying about the future. So much could happen in the meantime. Maybe she'd meet someone else too, and then when Toby visited with his girlfriend, the four of them could go out together.

Depression settled over her, and her shoulders slumped. Way to go, Esther. Thinking about meeting the next guy when she was still in bed with the present one. What a ho. And anyway, she didn't want to meet anyone else. The thought of another man touching her repulsed her.

She caught her breath. The statement may have been true, but the notion shocked her. So what was she saying—she wanted to remain single for the rest of her life? Didn't she ever want to settle down, get married? Provide Charlie with a father who could be around all the time?

Her chest tightened at the thought. Toby was Charlie's father. She didn't ever want another man claiming that relationship, and neither, she suspected, would Toby.

"What?" A frown appeared between his eyes as her body tensed.

"Nothing." She pushed herself up off the sofa. "Come on, we'd better get going and pick up Charlie. He's probably driving poor Cath around the bend."

He caught her wrist as she went to stand and pulled her toward him. She fell onto his chest, her hair tumbling around him.

"Hey," she protested.

He looked deeply into her eyes. "What's the matter?"

"Nothing." She tried to push herself up again.

"Esther…"

"Let me go." She whacked him, irritated at her feelings. "I don't have to explain every little thought that goes through my head."

"True." He released her and watched her collect her clothes and walk through to the bedroom.

She dressed quickly in the jeans and T-shirt she'd arrived in, fighting back tears, then grabbed his comb from the table and tugged it through her hair. This was stupid. They were supposed to be having fun—there was no point in going on with the Naughty Nights game if she was going to get all deep and meaningful every time they had sex.

She slipped on her sandals and turned, catching her breath automatically at the sight of him leaning against the doorjamb. She pressed a hand to her chest. "You made me jump."

He said nothing. He'd dressed and looked hot and sexy with his ruffled, fucked-you-five-minutes-ago hair. His intense gaze made her heart continue to pound at the thought of how commanding he'd been, and how easily he'd controlled her desire, arousing her at his own pace. Against her will, muscles deep inside her clenched.

She walked toward him crossly, intending to slip past him.

He put an arm up onto the other side of the doorway as she reached him, forcing her to stop. His other hand slid to her hip, and he pushed her against the wall, towering over her, intimidating with his superior height and the breadth of his shoulders.

"It's time to go," she said, and swallowed.

"Don't over-think it," he murmured as if he hadn't heard her. "It's just sex."

Something in his slightly distant gaze made her think he wasn't talking to her. Was he trying to convince himself?

He lowered his head and kissed her, a sweet, lingering, gentle kiss that nevertheless made her heart pound and her knees weak as she wondered if he was going to start all over again. But he lifted his head and gave her a slight, sad smile before turning and taking her hand to lead her to the front door. "Come on," he said, squeezing her hand. "Let's go and get our son."

Chapter Thirty

"No," Faith said for the eleventh time. "Still not right."

Esther gritted her teeth and stared at her reflection in the shop mirror. "What's wrong with this one? I like the color."

"Yeah, the green's nice, but it's just not…I don't know. What do you think?" Faith quirked a brow at Eve.

The two girls were sitting on a bench in the women's changing rooms, assessing Esther's choice of dress every time she came out of the cubicle.

"No," Eve agreed. "It's not The One."

"I want to wear it, not marry it," Esther grumbled as she returned to the changing room. It had been a tiring, frustrating afternoon. The two friends had taken her to Whangarei, a small city an hour from Kerikeri with a couple of department stores and lots of boutique dress shops, to look for an outfit for Esther to wear to the wedding on Saturday. So far, however, they'd disagreed with everything she'd tried on, and her patience was wearing thin. Shopping was not her favorite activity.

"What's next?" Faith called.

"I'm through this lot. I might have one more look on the racks," Esther called back. She slipped on her jeans and vest, glad she hadn't worn anything thicker. It was even more humid than usual, in spite of the fact that March would have its autumnal claws on the country farther south.

She came out carrying the half a dozen items she'd already tried, and the two girls took them from her. "We'll hang these back up," Eve said. "You go see if there's anything else out there that takes your fancy."

"I feel guilty doing this," Esther protested, not for the first time. "I should be helping you shop, not the other way around."

"I told you—I have everything I need for the big day," Eve said. "Besides, I want to see Toby's eyes light up when you walk through the door in the right outfit."

Faith gave Eve a sharp nudge in the ribs and she winced. Esther looked away. As much as she kept trying to tell herself she wasn't dressing up for Toby, she couldn't deny that every time she put on a dress, her first thought was "Will he like it?" It made her both excited and sad at the same time.

She wandered into the shop, disconsolate, not wanting to think about the future. The purpose of this expedition was to buy an outfit for a wedding, and she wouldn't think any further than that.

Browsing slowly, she tried to think about nothing except the clothes and what might look good on her figure. The trouble was that she hated dressing up and felt uncomfortable in anything too fancy. Faith and Eve had got her to try on all manner of flouncy gowns, but nothing had fitted right. But what else could she wear to a wedding? She wanted something special—something she felt at ease in.

She picked up a cream two-piece that had a nice shimmer to it, and a short black dress that was a little staid but had some pretty shaping around the collar, as well as a burgundy-colored longer dress that had a rather boring top but a pretty flowing skirt. She couldn't imagine either of the two girls would approve of any of them, but she was getting tired and didn't have the stamina for many more shops.

And then her gaze fell on a dress at the back of a rack. There was only one, but she pulled it out and saw it happened to be in her size. What luck! She held it up and caught her breath. It had a halter neck, a mermaid-style flare at mid-thigh, and reached to a few inches below her knees. The label declared the color as "hunter", a deep turquoise, slightly more green than blue. The label also told her it was made of "elastic woven satin", and she could see it would cling to her curves, leaving little to the imagination. She wouldn't be able to wear a stitch under it.

Toby would love it.

She bit her lip and her hand hovered over the rack, ready to put it back. It wasn't her at all. She shouldn't choose something just because Toby would like it.

But Eve's words rang in her ears: *I want to see Toby's eyes light up when you walk through the door in the right outfit.* She wanted to see that too, hating herself for thinking it, but honest enough with herself to admit it. And anyway, what was wrong with it really? Perhaps he'd realize what he'd turned his back on all those years ago. Stubbornness surged through her, and she folded the dress over her arm. Maybe he'd have to accept he'd done the wrong thing in deciding not to see her again. That would serve him right.

Faith and Eve were sitting on the bench when she returned to the changing rooms. She locked the cubicle and tried the cream two-piece on first, bursting into giggles as she realized she couldn't get the buttons done up over her boobs. She came out to show the others and they all giggled when Eve said, "Yeah, that'll get him going!"

She went back into the cubicle, removed the cream suit, and took the turquoise dress off the hanger. She hesitated for a moment, then removed her bra before slipping the dress over her head. It fell past her knees in a rustle of satin, cool on her skin as she zipped up the back. She smoothed her hands down it, liking the sensual feel of the material. She could imagine the way Toby's eyes would widen when he realized she wasn't wearing anything underneath. How his eyes would darken when he pulled her to him and ran his hands over her butt...

"Come on," Faith said impatiently. "Don't be a chicken—show us."

Esther opened the door hesitantly, hoping the two girls wouldn't pull a face and declare she'd made a mistake again. To her delight, approval lit their faces immediately.

"Wow!" Eve jumped up and came over to her. "Oh my God, Esther, that looks fabulous."

"You think?" Esther twirled in front of the mirror, and the mermaid skirt fanned out.

"Absolutely," Faith grinned. "The best yet. Jeez, you have a fantastic figure—that fabric really shows it off."

"And the color's perfect," Eve added.

Esther smiled shyly. She opened her mouth to ask whether they thought Toby would like it, but stopped herself at the last minute. She didn't want them to know how much she longed for his approval and admiration.

As Eve carried the unused items back to the rails, however, Faith leaned forward and whispered, "He'll love it, no question, Esther. Great choice."

Esther's cheeks grew warm, and she dropped her gaze as she slipped back into the cubicle to change. But she couldn't deny the glow of pleasure that spread through her at Faith's words.

Their purchases complete, the girls made their way to a nearby coffee shop and treated themselves to a latte and a muffin to keep their strength up.

"I'm going to get big as an elephant," Faith muttered as she tucked in to hers. "Rusty says we must be having sextuplets because I'm eating enough for seven."

Esther pulled a face. "Make the most of it—it's the only time you can have a really good excuse for eating."

Faith sighed and put down the muffin. "And now I need to pee. The delights of being pregnant. 'Scuse." She shuffled out of her seat and nipped down to the Ladies'.

Esther exchanged a polite, somewhat awkward smile with Eve as they sipped their coffee. Eve lowered her lashes, examining the chocolate muffin on her plate, and Esther decided to put her out of her misery. "Toby told me about you two," she said.

Eve blushed to the roots of her blonde hair. "Oh crap. I'm sorry."

Immediately Esther regretted mentioning it. "Oh God, don't worry about it. I probably shouldn't have said anything—I just thought it was bothering you."

"Not in the way you might think." Eve drew in the foam of her latte with a spoon. "It was so long ago, Esther, I was only eighteen. And I was pretty drunk. I don't remember much. He was... convenient, and that's a terrible thing to say and not fair on him at all. I just needed comfort, and he happened to be there."

Jealousy surged through her Esther, and she bit her lip. "I understand."

Eve's frowned. "I'm not sure you do. It didn't mean anything, and I know he feels the same. At the time, we all joked about it, but we've never mentioned it since to each other. I thought you may have heard and, well, I'd hate you to think I was jealous or something, because really, I'm not. I'm marrying Dan, and I'm crazy about him. Toby and I are just friends." She spoke earnestly.

Esther softened. "I do understand. You and Dan are obviously perfect for each other. I could see at one glance that he loves you very much."

Eve smiled. "Thank you. The thing is... I've known Toby a long time. Charlie's captivated him—I've never seen him so proud of anything."

Now it was Esther's turn to blush. "Oh, that's a nice thing to say."

"But that's not all. He's clearly mad about you too."

Esther's smile faded. She glanced over as Faith walked toward them, and lowered her gaze at the other girl's searching look.

"What's going on?" Faith demanded, sitting and stirring her latte before taking a sip.

Eve scowled. She'd clearly been warned not to talk about Toby to Esther. "Nothing."

Faith glared at her. "What have you said?"

"Only that Toby's bonkers about her."

Faith rolled her eyes. "Eve, what did I say?"

Esther cleared her throat. "It's okay. It's very nice of you to say such a thing, but the point is, whether you're right or not, it doesn't really matter. We're having great fun at the moment, but on Sunday I'm probably heading back down to Christchurch, and that's going to be that."

"There's no hope at all you two could make a go of it?" Faith's voice held more than a hint of hope.

Esther shook her head firmly. "He's going to university. It's a single man's life—you both know that."

"Would you want a relationship, if he was interested?" Faith's brown eyes were curious, and a little bit demanding.

Esther thought how devastated she'd been when he'd walked away from her. She couldn't go through that again, if at any point he decided he'd had enough. And besides, he still didn't know about the messages she'd torn up. As soon as he knew the truth, it would be over between them. And she couldn't live with a lie—she'd have to tell him. She thought of the disappointment that would appear on his face. She couldn't do that to him. No, things were good the way they were—a bit of lighthearted sex before they moved on with their own lives.

She shook her head and smiled brightly, maybe a little too brightly, judging by Faith's frown and the pitying look in Eve's eyes. "No, it's done. But that's fine—I'm okay with that. Now come on, I want you to tell me all about the hen night on Friday. Where are we going, and how drunk is Dan going to be the following morning?"

Chapter Thirty-One

"Okay," Toby said, "tell me about the dress."

"No." She grinned impishly. "You'll have to wait and see."

"Tease." But he couldn't complain overmuch. She was clearly excited at the prospect of wearing her new outfit, and he liked to see her eyes light up and her face glow.

The clock on the dash read five past eight, and he was in the process of driving them to his house. They'd settled Charlie and had a quick drink with Faith and Rusty, and then sneaked out once Charlie's eyes had closed.

Toby glanced across at the woman sitting next to him. She had one elbow on the windowsill, and her fingers played across her lips while she stared unseeing at the lights of the town as they passed by. In spite of her obvious excitement about her dress, she'd been very quiet, and he wondered what had transpired over the time she'd been with Faith and Eve.

"You're very secretive today," he said. "You still haven't told me what your Naughty Night instructions are."

She glanced back at him then. "No, I haven't." Her eyes twinkled.

He smiled and reached out to take her hand. The memory of the night before and how awkward things had been after they'd had sex in the living room still lingered in his head.

The sex had been fantastic. The best ever, possibly. Esther was hotter than lava, and she'd thrown herself into the role-play with joyful abandon. She'd blown him away, but afterward he'd been very aware of something going on in her head.

Not that it had surprised him. Because his brain had been buzzing too. He could have kicked himself for the way he'd demanded she never look at another man. Why had he forced her to make such a declaration? It was unfair and selfish, even though afterward they'd both kidded themselves it had all been part of the role-play. It hadn't, and he knew it. He didn't want any other man touching her. When he'd watched Felix flirting with her, it had taken an immense amount of self-control not to lean over and punch his brother's lights out.

And how unfair was that when they were only supposed to be having a fling? He sighed, tightening his hand on hers. This was getting horribly complicated. As he'd told her afterward, they had to be careful not to over-think things. They were having sex. Period. He mustn't think any deeper than that.

He drew up outside his house, applied the handbrake, and switched off the engine. Then he turned to her. "Are you okay? Are you sure you want to go ahead with this tonight?" He wouldn't be shocked if she said no. His heart begged her to say yes, though. She wore a simple blue cotton dress that came halfway down her thighs, and he was sure she wasn't wearing anything underneath it. His fingers itched to slide down her body and test out his theory.

To his relief, she grinned and said, "You betcha. I've been waiting for this all day. Come on." And she scrambled out of the car and positively skipped toward the front door.

Lips twisting wryly, he followed her. His erection sprang to life even as he walked up the path. Down boy, he thought with amused irritation. He should wait and see what she had planned first. Maybe it was something he wouldn't like.

That made him smile. He couldn't imagine Esther coming up with anything in the bedroom that he wouldn't enjoy doing to her, or having done to him.

He unlocked the front door and let them inside. He'd left a lamp on in the corner, and it filled the living room with a warm glow.

"Glass of wine?" he asked, throwing his keys on the table by the door.

Her eyes were dark and full of promise, but she just smiled and said, "Sure."

His heart rate beginning to speed up, he walked through to the kitchen, poured them both a glass of wine, and brought them back to the living room. She sat on the sofa, and he sat beside her, turning slightly toward her so their knees touched. He gave her one of the glasses.

"What shall we drink to?" she whispered.

He tipped his head, studying her as he swallowed the first cool mouthful of wine. "To sexual anticipation." He held his glass toward her.

She giggled and touched hers carefully against his with a ring of crystal. "To sexual anticipation."

"Which I've been feeling all day," he added truthfully.

She sipped the wine, her eyes dancing over the rim. "Been on tenterhooks, have we?"

"Just a bit." That did not come close to describing how he'd spent all day picturing various sexual scenarios.

"Good." She rubbed her knee against his, and he almost groaned. He was so hard now he'd be lucky if the stitching didn't give way on his shorts. She winked. "I suppose I can finally reveal what was on my card."

"It would be a good idea, before I die of curiosity."

She laughed. "It's really not that big a deal. Well, it won't be to you, I'm sure." She fished the card out of her bag. "This one was quite short. All it says is, 'Tonight, treat yourself to a sexual position you've never indulged in before. Something you've always wanted to try.'"

He raised his eyebrows. "Oh. Nice."

"Very nice."

"So what have you decided on?"

She nibbled her bottom lip and deep red seeped into her cheekbones.

Affection swept over him, and he picked up her hand and laced his fingers through hers. "Hey, don't be embarrassed. How can you be embarrassed after what we've done?"

"I know, it's silly." Her green eyes met his, cool and clear, and for a moment he could see all the vulnerability and wariness inside her through those glassy windows.

"It's not silly," he said. "It's endearing. Just something else about you that drives me crazy."

She smiled shyly and lowered her eyes to their hands, rubbing her thumb across his knuckles.

"So give me a clue," he said. "I'll try to guess." What position would she be unlikely to have done? He didn't want to think about her previous partners and what they might have gotten up to, but they'd managed a fair few themselves in Fiji.

She remained quiet for a moment. And then she raised her eyes to his. "It's a number."

He stared at her. Then amusement flooded him. "You little minx."

She blushed again and pushed him. "Don't embarrass me."

He put his arm around her, careful not to spill his wine, pulled her to him and nuzzled her ear. "Hey, I'm thrilled. I can't think of anything more enjoyable than engaging in a sixty-nine with the hottest girl in New Zealand."

She shivered as he touched his lips to her throat. "Really?"

"Really," he murmured, kissing around her jaw to her lips. He touched his nose to hers. "Can't you tell?" He moved their linked hands onto his lap, and her eyes widened as her hand rested on his erection.

"Ooh." She licked her lips and whispered, "I can't wait to get that in my mouth."

He gave a short laugh. Placing their glasses on the table, he pulled her onto his lap. "You are the sexiest girl who ever lived, you know that?" He slid his hand into her hair and pulled her lips to his.

She opened her mouth willingly, and her tongue tangled with his in a sizzling hot embrace. For the first time that night, he laid his hands on her body, and he wasn't surprised to find her soft and yielding beneath his touch, absent of any form of underwear. He murmured his approval as he stroked up from her waist to her full breasts and cupped one in his hand. It sat heavy in his palm, the nipple tantalizingly soft between his fingers. He squeezed it gently, and groaned when she arched into his touch with a sigh.

"Bed?" he murmured, kissing down to her throat.

She pushed back, breathless and flushed. "No, not yet." He must have look disappointed, because she chuckled. "Shower first. I... um... did some research, and they suggest it's a good idea before oral sex to make sure everything's... um... well, you know."

"Rubbish," he said, nibbling her ear. "I love the taste of you hot and sweaty."

"Oh, stop it." She levered herself off his lap. "Come on. We've got all evening—there's no need to rush things."

He sighed, but couldn't find it in himself to protest overmuch when the notion of Esther wet and slippery in his hands was on offer. Accepting her hand, he followed her along the corridor to the bathroom and began to unbutton his shirt while she switched on the shower.

She soon stopped him, however, placing a hand over his on his shirt. "That's my job," she said.

"Absolutely." He wasn't going to object when it involved the removal of clothes.

She smirked and slowly popped the buttons through the holes until she reached the bottom. He put his hands on her hips and watched her reaction when she pushed his shirt to the side and smoothed her hands up over his ribcage to his shoulders. "You have such a fantastic body." Admiration was written all over her face.

"Thank you," he said, genuinely touched by her praise.

"I mean it, Toby. You're a fine specimen of a man." She ran light fingers over his pecs and the muscles in his abdomen, then brushed his nipples. "You're like a model you'd see in GQ or a Levi ad. You have the build of a rugby player—better than Dan Carter."

"The ultimate compliment. Now stop or I'll blush."

"I just don't understand, that's all." She swallowed, uncertainty crossing her features. She lowered her eyes to his chest, tracing fingers around his ribs. "You're like a god, Apollo or Hercules. The Greeks would have made statues of you. What do you want with me? I'm ordinary and dull and have a baby tummy. What could you possibly find interesting about me?"

He stared at her, shocked by her statement. Was she searching for compliments? But the hesitation remained behind her eyes. She truly believed what she'd said.

Okay, he thought. He'd played her game long enough. Yes, they were only having sex, and no, they weren't going to get involved. But it was time to tell her the truth, and show her how he truly felt about her.

Chapter Thirty-Two

He held the clip at the back of her hair and squeezed the sides together, releasing her hair so it fell in dark brown curls. He placed the clip on the shelf and slid his hands into the strands, loosening them around her shoulders.

"First," he said, sliding his fingers through the curls, "I love your hair. I don't know what conditioner you use, but it's so soft and silky, it feels like ribbons in my fingers." He moved closer and nuzzled, not missing her answering shiver. "And it smells of strawberries and summer. It makes my mouth water."

He moved back and cupped her face. Were there tears glistening in her eyes? He studied them for a moment, losing himself in the dark green depths, noting how they carried gold flecks near to the pupils. She blinked a couple of times. Yes, they were definitely shining. She probably didn't get many compliments—she had no father to praise her up, not even a brother to tease her and look out for her.

He didn't mention it, though. Instead he brushed her cheeks with his thumbs and smiled. "I love the freckles on your cheeks and nose. There aren't many, just a scattering, but they're gorgeous." He kissed them and ran the tip of his tongue lightly across her skin, and she giggled. "Stand still," he reprimanded her. "I haven't finished with you yet."

She rolled her eyes. "You don't have to do this, you know."

"Yes, I do. I want to. Now shush." He was enjoying himself and liked the way she blushed shyly every time he said something nice.

He traced his thumbs over her eyebrows. "I love your eyes. They're very expressive. Now don't get me wrong—I love your ass and your tits are magnificent, but if pushed I might have to say your eyes are your best feature."

Her mouth fell open in amused shock and she smacked his arm. "You're incorrigible."

"Yeah, yeah. You love it." He moved his hands to her shoulders and slid them down her arms to take her hands. "Now this may sound weird, but you have very pretty hands."

"Pretty?"

"Yes. You'd be surprised how many women have unattractive hands. Wrinkled, or with bitten fingernails, or podgy fingers. But yours are elegant. Long fingers, pale smooth skin, nails just long enough to be feminine, but not horrible talons. I can't stand those."

She raised an eyebrow. "But women in porn movies always have long, painted false nails. I thought men liked them."

"Other men might. I don't. I'd much rather have these closing around me." He brought her fingers to his lips and kissed them, smiling as the blush reappeared in her cheeks.

"Now," he continued. "On to your body."

"Oh dear."

"Yes. This may take us a while. There's a lot to comment on." He stepped back, holding her hands, and studied her feet. "I'll start by saying I don't particularly have a foot fetish. I'm not one of those guys who gets off on sucking toes. However." He moved her so she leaned her butt against the basin, then knelt and lifted one of her feet onto his lap. "Your feet are divine."

"Jeez, Toby. Major hyperbole alert."

"I'm not exaggerating. You know what you said about the Greeks carving statues—well your feet could have come from the Venus de Milo."

"The one without any arms?"

He sent her a wry look. "I'm trying to pay you a compliment." He ran a finger along her instep, then smoothed up over the top. Her unblemished skin held a light tan. Her nails were short and tidy, painted a pretty red. He bent his head and kissed them. "I've never been turned on by feet before, but there's something about these that sends my thermostat shooting up."

She giggled, and for the first time her shoulders relaxed and her frown lines disappeared. "Okay, how else am I beautiful?"

"Oh, where to start," he sighed, thrilled that she was enjoying herself. "What about your calves?" He cupped her heel and then slid his hand up her leg to the back of her knee. "They're just right—toned without being muscular, and so soft..." He ran his fingers up her shinbone. "How the hell do you get your skin so silky?"

"Waxing and lots of cream." She closed her eyes as he drew circles on the sensitive skin behind her knee. "Oh."

"You like that?" He slid his other hand up to the back of the opposite knee and did the same, brushing the skin with gentle strokes.

She tipped her head back, and her mouth fell open. She moistened her lips with her tongue. "Mm."

He made a mental note of that. Continuing with the movement, he said, "Now, your knees…"

"Surely there can't be anything sexy about knees," she said faintly, lowering her head and opening her eyes. They looked dazed and slightly out of focus.

"Ah, that's where you're wrong." He moved his hands around to the front of her legs and drew his warm palms over them. "Some knees are bony and stick out, but yours are set deep into the muscle. Do you run?"

"I used to, before I had Charlie."

"They're beautiful." He traced the muscles from her knees up her lower thigh. "Strong and supple. I can just imagine them wrapped around me."

This time she didn't protest, just sighed as he brushed her thighs lightly. "What else?"

"For the rest I need you naked." He stood. The room had started to fill with steam, and he was growing warm.

He slipped off his shirt, then hooked his thumbs in his shorts and pulled them off. He kicked them away and rested his hands on her hips, noting the way her pupils dilated as she observed his very eager erection.

"I love what you do to me," he said, moving closer so he could press his erection into her soft mound. "I only have to think about your body and I'm harder than Chinese algebra."

"Is that harder than ordinary algebra?" Her voice was little more than a whisper as she clasped her fingers around him.

"Much," he murmured, lowering his lips to hers for the briefest of kisses. "Now I'm feeling distinctly underdressed here. Time for you to catch up." He grasped the hem of her dress. "Arms up."

She did so, closing her eyes, and he drew the cotton shift up her body and over her head, letting it drop to the floor. He'd guessed right—she was naked beneath it, her skin warm and with a slight sheen from the heat of the room.

"My, my," he whispered. "Aren't you an absolute picture?"

"You like?" She opened her eyes and met his, bold for once.

"Mm." He fanned out his hands on her stomach. "I don't know why you think your body isn't attractive because you've had a child."

"It's flabby."

"It's really not, Esther. It's softer, yes. But I like that. I like you being soft." He smoothed his hands around her waist. "I wish I could have seen you pregnant."

Lines of regret shadowed her face and she bit her lip.

"No," he said quickly. "No accusations, no regret, not now. I'm just saying. I'd like to have seen your body change. Watched it swell as our lad grew inside you. It's amazing, what you went through for him."

She shook her head. "It was nothing women all over the world haven't done for millions of years."

"That doesn't make it any less marvelous. You grew a person inside you, Esther. A tiny person—you cherished him, nourished him with your body, and made him into what he is. How can I put into words how that makes me feel? You amaze me. I worship the ground you walk on because of what you did for me, for Charlie."

A tear ran down her cheek. "Don't."

He leaned forward and kissed it away. "Cry all you like. I'm not going to stop. You're fucking amazing. I'm in awe of your body. As if these weren't amazing enough—" he cupped her breasts, "—you nurtured our son with them. I wish I could have seen that. Watched you nurse him in the middle of the night."

"Yeah right," she said weakly, sniffing. "You'd have turned over and started snoring."

"I wouldn't. I'd have brought him into our bed and watched you feed him. And then when he was done, I'd have taken him back to his cot and climbed back in beside you." His blood surged around his body as if he had a fever. He moved closer to her and licked away the tears that continued to fall down her cheeks. "Then I'd have tasted them myself, suckled some of that life-giving milk."

"Oh jeez, you're disgusting." But she shivered, her nipples peaking in his hands.

"Oh yeah." He brushed his tongue into her mouth, loving the way she moaned at the deep kiss. He lifted his head. "And then I'd have stroked you slowly and gently." He moved a hand to the hair at the top of her legs and slid his fingers down through her moist skin. She was already swollen, and her juices coated his fingers when he slipped them inside her. "Oh, Esther, always so ready for me."

He drew his fingers back up and caressed her clit. "I would've loved to have aroused you in the darkness, our son content and asleep, and given you pleasure as a reward for your generous selflessness. I'd have made you come on my hand, or on my mouth, whatever you wanted, and then I'd have wrapped my arms around you and let you fall asleep all safe and secure."

Her bottom lip trembled. "Stop. Please."

He hesitated. He'd gone too far. She'd had to live through those difficult early months alone—had even had to cope with the death of her father. She didn't need to be reminded of how hard it must have been, or how he could have helped her through it.

He enfolded her in his arms and kissed her hair. In spite of his words, regret surged through him. He should have been there to look after her and support her. But he'd abandoned her and made it twice as hard for her to cope. He'd never forgive himself for that.

There was no point in beating himself up about it now, though. Better to try and show her how sorry he was.

"Come on," he said gently.

He drew her into the shower and directed her beneath the spray. The water soaked her dark curls, turning them to glistening mahogany strands in his fingers. He squeezed shampoo onto his hand, massaged it into her hair carefully and rinsed it clean. Then he poured some coconut-scented shower gel onto his hands and smoothed it over her body.

She'd stopped crying, but her eyes were wide and glistening as she leaned against the wall and let him wash her. He kissed her cheeks, her eyelids, her nose, her lips, while he trailed fingers across her silky skin, cleansing her, trying to say he was sorry without having to say the words. Don't be angry, he thought, staring intently into her eyes before kissing her again. He hadn't meant to upset her, only to explain that he understood what she'd had to go through without him.

When he'd done, she did the same to him, and her gentle touch as she washed his hair and then his body showed him she wasn't angry with him, just sad, maybe, that things had worked out the way they had.

When they were finished, he turned off the shower and stepped out of the cubicle. Taking a towel from the rail, he dried her slowly, then let her do the same to him. Her hair fell around her shoulders in a tangle of brown curls, but he left it, liking the wildness of it.

He took her through to the bedroom and kissed her again, deeply. Then, eventually, he raised his head. "Are you ready, sweetheart?"

She chewed her bottom lip, and her eyes lit with excitement. To his surprise, she took his face in her hands and said fiercely, "I want you, Toby. Don't doubt that. Whatever's happened, whatever's going to happen, here, now, I want you more than anything in the world."

Chapter Thirty-Three

He nodded and swallowed down the lump that appeared in his throat. "Come on." He pulled her over to the bed and they climbed on.

He lay back, and she knelt by his side. She blushed. "Um... How do we start?"

Smiling, he twirled a finger to encourage her to turn around. He had to lighten the atmosphere a little. It was his fault they'd got all deep and meaningful, and he wanted her to enjoy her Naughty Night.

She turned her back to him. He maneuvered the pillows into a comfortable position and then smacked her butt.

"Ow!" She looked over her shoulder at him with an amused glare.

He winked. "I bet I can make you come before you do the same to me."

Her mouth fell open, and then her lips curved. "You are absolutely on with that bet, mister." She giggled as he gestured for her to climb on top of him and lifted herself over his chest to straddle his shoulders. She waggled her backside at him. "What do I get if I win?"

"My undying gratitude?" he said faintly, eyes boggling at the stupendous view.

"Winner gets to choose the next card?" she suggested.

"Deal," he said. But in his head he thought, *Fuck*. He was going to have trouble winning that bet. She smelled wonderful. The musky scent of her arousal stirred his pheromones, and every single red blood cell in his body flooded to his groin.

She positioned herself in front of his face. As she lowered herself down, her soft breasts pressed against his chest. Her knees rested either side of his head, and her hot, moist sex opened to his gaze.

He groaned. Her pink skin glistened with moisture. He couldn't resist running his tongue up the center of the swollen, luscious folds.

She jumped and exclaimed, "Hey, unfair. You can't have a head start."

He chuckled and then caught his breath as she closed her hand around his erection. He was so hard now it almost hurt. She touched her tongue to the bead of moisture on the end of the swollen tip, and he groaned again. "Game on," she said, and then she closed her mouth over him, enclosing him in wet heat.

He nearly came on the spot and had to use every single ounce of self-control he possessed to keep it together. He had some pride after all—jeez, he had to last longer than ten seconds at least. *Focus, Toby.* He forced himself to concentrate on the moist, soft flesh by his mouth.

All the skin around her sex was soft and smooth. He ran his tongue up the center of her again. She shivered, and he stroked his hands along her sides and back down her spine to knead the cheeks of her ass. He nudged her legs farther apart, and she relaxed into him, opening up for him.

In spite of the bet, he knew she was as keen as he was to make the moment last. He'd never been so turned on, and judging by the amount of moisture she was producing, neither had she. He lapped it up slowly, dipping his tongue inside her before sliding it between her folds to reveal the small bead that would be her undoing. He licked it gently, flicking it with the end of his tongue, and she rewarded him with another flood of moisture and an erotic sigh. The hairs on the back of his neck stood on end, and he groaned.

She explored him at the same time, brushing the warm pad of her tongue across the swollen head of his erection. But when she took him into her mouth and leaned forward to slide her lips down his shaft, he nearly lost the plot. He tightened his fingers on her ass and she lifted her head and let him relax. She blew gently on his hot skin and giggled. "That was nearly one-nil," she said.

"Right." He brushed his tongue through her, determined she wouldn't win so easily. She moaned, and he slipped his hand underneath her, using his fingers to probe gently. He slid them in and out of her as he continued to lick and suck.

"That's cheating," she mumbled before closing her mouth over him again.

He gave a short laugh and then groaned as she sucked hard. Pressing the swollen skin on either side to reveal her clit again, he flicked it with his tongue.

She spread her legs wider, taking him deeper in her mouth at the same time.

He sucked, his hips automatically pushing up as she squeezed him with her hand.

She slid her lips down his shaft, taking him so deep inside her mouth he nearly passed out.

His heart hammered, and the fingers of his other hand sank into her hip as they tightened automatically.

He wanted her to feel what he was feeling. Was she close to climaxing? He pushed his fingers into her and sucked hard as her clit hardened. Moisture coated his tongue, and for a brief second she raised her head to moan deeply. Yep. She was nearly there.

He curved his fingers inside her to find the swelling on the front wall of her vagina and stroked firmly. She caught her breath and triumph flooded through him. He was going to win.

Clearly, however, she had other ideas. She closed her lips around him and moved them along his shaft. To his amazement, she took him even deeper into the warm cavern of her mouth, so deep he touched the back of her throat.

There was no coming back from that. His balls tightened, and heat spread through his lower stomach, thighs and groin as hot fluid rushed through him into her waiting mouth.

Luckily, her own climax overwhelmed her at the same time. He wrapped an arm over her and held her tightly as she shuddered, her internal muscles squeezing his fingers, and he pressed his tongue against her firmly as she tensed in regular, rhythmic pulses.

It was the most incredible sensation he'd ever had—her warm and wet on his mouth, him swollen and throbbing in hers, and by the time they'd both finished, she'd reduced him to a limp ragdoll of a man, unable to do anything but lie there and sigh as she rolled off him and collapsed onto the bed.

"Fuck," she said to the room.

He didn't have the energy to do anything more than chuckle. "Yeah."

Her hand found his on the duvet and she linked their fingers together. He stared up at the ceiling, his heart rate gradually slowing, sated and content like a just-fed cat.

She sat up and shifted so she could rest her head on her chest.

"Thank you," she whispered.

"Sweetheart, thank *you* for coming up with that brilliant idea."

She giggled. "I've always wanted to try it."

"Honey, if you come up with any other hypothesis you'd like to test, I'm always happy to oblige."

She smiled, but she also lowered her gaze, and he cursed himself silently. Why did he keep putting his foot in it? Today was Wednesday—he had her for Thursday, Friday and maybe Saturday. Sunday she'd probably be gone. What was the point in talking about "always"?

She curled up next to him, and he rested a hand on her hip, stroking up her back. His heart went out to her. She was made of granite on the outside, but soft as cotton wool on the inside. He could see it now. She'd been different back in Fiji—hopeful, excited, completely open emotionally. She'd believed in them, thought they'd had a future. And what had he done? Taken her vulnerable heart and stomped on it.

And yet she'd still taken him into her bed again. He couldn't believe that.

He stroked up her side, and she wriggled when he touched the sensitive skin beneath her arms. Raising himself up, he rolled her onto her back and looked down at her. Cupping her face, he ran his thumb across her lips. She kissed it, and he smiled. He couldn't think what to say, so he just lowered his lips to hers, kissing her leisurely until she opened her mouth and welcomed his tongue inside.

He deepened the kiss until she was breathless, stroking her soft, damp skin and sliding his fingers into the heart of her. She didn't protest, her cool green eyes watching him as he aroused her. He kissed down her neck to her breasts, took her velvety nipples in his mouth and teased them to hard peaks, fierce joy flooding him as she writhed and moaned. This time he wanted to watch her come apart, knowing he was the cause.

He moved on top of her, and she welcomed him inside eagerly. His erection slid easily into her moist, swollen flesh, and they both groaned. He began to thrust slowly, kissing her all the while, drinking in every erotic sigh she gave. Arousing her was like fine tuning an instrument, he thought in a delirious haze, knowing where to touch, to lick, to squeeze with his fingers to take her that step closer to fulfilment.

It wasn't long before she bit her lip and her breathing grew irregular, and he lifted his head and watched the orgasm overtake her like a surfer tumbled by a powerful wave. He kissed the frown lines that appeared between her eyes and captured her cries with his mouth, at that moment so satisfied and complete that not even the arrival of his own climax could top his contentedness.

He'd given her pleasure. Nobody else.

He couldn't think of a better way to say he was sorry.

Chapter Thirty-Four

It was with some nervousness that Esther walked into Rusty's high school at lunchtime the following day.

She signed in at the office, and the receptionist directed her to his classroom at the bottom end of the social sciences building. Luckily, she didn't have to walk all the way through the school—she found him outside the staffroom, talking to a group of students.

She stopped and waited for him to finish. They spotted her before he did and lost no time in pointing out he had a visitor. He looked over his shoulder at her, then sent the group of giggling girls on their way.

Esther smiled wryly. It didn't surprise her that he should be one of the most popular teachers in the school. Tall, slender, and with a casual sexiness he carried with ease, Rusty drew the eye of most of the senior girls he passed as he came over to her.

Much of her nervousness was due to meeting him. She couldn't quite put her finger on why. It might be the vague sense of disapproval she'd sensed in him from the moment she landed at the airport. Why would he disapprove of her? Usually, she would have asked a person outright if she thought they had a problem with her, but something about him made her nibble a fingernail as he came toward her.

"Hey." He smiled warmly, though.

"Hiya." She smiled back. She was imagining it, she tried to convince herself. He didn't dislike her.

He indicated a package he held under his arm, wrapped in a carrier bag. "All done."

She had the grace to blush. Before she'd left Toby's house the previous evening, they'd drawn the next Naughty Nights card together, and he'd read it out to her.

"'It's Schoolgirls' Night at the local nightclub. All the women there are dressed up in schoolgirl uniform. Pick one who takes your fancy, and spirit her off to your place. You can then give her extra tuition—and be as strict as you please!'"

"Where am I going to get a school uniform?" she'd asked him.

"Rusty'll be able to buy a second-hand one in the school's uniform shop," Toby had told her.

She'd stared, horrified. "I can't ask him!"

"I'll do it then."

And he had. So here she was, standing before the history teacher with cheeks burning at his obvious amusement.

She held out her hand. "Stop smirking."

"I'm not smirking." He grinned. "Okay, maybe I am."

She flicked her fingers. "Come on, hand them over."

He put his hands in his pockets, the parcel still under his arm. "Not yet. Come for a walk with me."

Exasperated and embarrassed, aware she couldn't just tussle with him and wrestle the parcel away, she fell into step beside him as he walked along the boulevard toward the field. Younger kids tore around them yelling and throwing rugby balls, but Rusty seemed oblivious to the mania, like a pop star walking through the crowd to the stage.

What did he want? And why did he make her feel so awkward?

"I should get going," she protested. "Faith has Charlie, and she's got a meeting at two."

"We won't be long." He remained unperturbed by her nerves.

They exited the buildings and walked onto the fields. The warm March sun beat down on the students playing rugby and football, or lazing at the edges, talking. Clouds bunched along the horizon, and it had turned humid, promising rain.

He stopped and turned to her, and she fidgeted under his calm gaze.

"For God's sake," she snapped. "Stop acting like I'm one of your naughty schoolkids."

"Sorry." His lips curved. "I'll leave that role for Toby."

"Rusty!" She frowned, too irritated now to hold back. "What do you want? Is this about the uniform? If you didn't want to do it, you should have said no to Toby."

He laughed and handed her the package. "I couldn't care less about the uniform."

"So what's up?" She tucked the bag under her arm and forced herself to meet his gaze. "I know you disapprove of me. You might as well come out and say it."

A frown flickered on his brow, and his expression turned to sympathy. "Oh, Esther, I don't disapprove of you—far from it."

Her jaw dropped. "Oh."

"Is that what you thought? I'm sorry. No, it's just..." He sighed and looked across the fields, eyes distant for a moment. "I've been there. I can see what you're getting into." His gaze came back to her. "And I wanted to warn you—you're making it terribly hard for yourself."

"We're only having sex," she said boldly, trying brush aside the niggling concern. His question stirred the worry that had coiled in her stomach for a while.

He said nothing, but his eyes—green like her own—studied hers challengingly, and she dropped her gaze.

"Yeah," he said. "I thought as much. I told you—I've been there."

"Yes," she protested, "but you and Faith were already good friends. It would have been impossible to stop seeing each other romantically when you were together all the time. It's different for me and Toby. Soon I'll be going back to Christchurch. Actually, maybe even Dunedin. So we won't be able to stay together."

"Dunedin?"

"My university will be shut for a while, and I've had my fill of earthquakes. I've applied for a job in Dunedin."

"Does Toby know this?"

She flushed. "No."

"So there's no chance of the two of you getting back together again?"

"No. We are attracted to each other, but there's too much water under the bridge. He didn't want me, Rusty. He walked away from me. And he'll never be able to forgive me for not telling him about Charlie."

He smiled. "Oh, I don't know. Toby has a pretty big heart."

She didn't return the smile. The urge to confide overwhelmed her. Rusty had been through a hard time—maybe he would understand. "He doesn't know the whole story. He thinks I tried to find him when I found out I was pregnant, but I didn't. And the messages he left me at the university—I did get them. I threw them away."

"Ah." He studied her for a moment.

"Now you disapprove of me," she whispered.

"Not at all. We all have our reasons for doing the things we do. I'm can hardly lecture on How Not to Make a Mistake in a Relationship." His lips twisted wryly.

Curiosity made her ask, "Was it easy—the decision to marry Faith after the problems you had?"

"Yes…and no. Yes because, well, she's everything," he said simply. "She filled a hole in my life I hadn't even realized was there. But no, it hasn't been plain sailing. Sometimes, when I'm grumpy or being an ass, I want to yell at her for marrying me, because I don't want the responsibility of having to be a good husband, and I don't want to feel crap when I'm not. I have to fight the feeling that she deserves better than me—that I don't deserve her."

Compassion flooded her. "Aw Rusty, you're so sweet. How can you possibly think you don't deserve her?"

He shrugged, smiling. "Low self-esteem, I suppose."

She would never have guessed he suffered from low self-esteem. He acted so confident, and he was such a clever, handsome man. Why would someone like him have low self-confidence?

"So I know where you're coming from," he said. "And it's a shame you think you don't deserve him, because he's clearly crazy about you."

She opened her mouth to contradict him. But the words didn't come. Did Rusty speak the truth? Was the main problem that because of what she'd done in keeping Charlie a secret, she thought she didn't deserve to end up with Toby?

He's clearly crazy about you. Eve had told her a similar thing. Was it true, then? Toby fancied the pants off her, and he hadn't passed up on the chance of some free, no-strings-attached sex, but what red-blooded male would have?

However, it wasn't all about sex. The memory of the way he'd worshipped her body the night before, spending ages telling her exactly what he loved about each part of her… It had excited and saddened her in equal measure. It was as if she were a diabetic and someone had taken the time to make a delicious cake in front of her, filled with jam and icing that she couldn't possibly eat.

Despair swept over her. Oh jeez. What were they both getting into?

*

She thought about it all the way back to Faith's house, the parcel growing warm under her arm. Palm trees and rustling lush greenery filled the gardens on either side of the pavement, making her think of Charlie's observation of it being like Jurassic Park. Her lips twisted wryly. The only monster threatening to overwhelm her at the moment was the fear that Rusty had conjured up.

As she walked, she attempted to keep the tide of panic from washing over her. What the hell did Rusty know? Toby had told her enough about Rusty's relationship with Faith for her to understand that he was hardly an expert on emotional matters. He'd nearly screwed up his own future with Faith. She couldn't rely on him to know Toby's state of mind.

And anyway, so what if he was crazy about her? She was crazy about him too. He was gorgeous, and she loved his boyish vulnerability. She was enjoying spending time with him. He was great in bed. Why wouldn't she be crazy about him? And when it came to an end, she'd be sad. But after Fiji, she'd learned a lot about expectations. And basically, she didn't have any now.

At the weekend, or at least very soon after if her interview came through for Dunedin, she'd be flying back. Maybe in retrospect, it hadn't been the greatest idea to indulge in the Naughty Nights. Yes, it was going to make it harder. But not impossible. She wouldn't be lying there the nights leading up to leaving wondering if he would ask her to stay. There wouldn't be that desperate hopefulness, followed by the mind-numbing, heart-wrenching, painful disappointment when he said no. She wouldn't ever put herself through that again.

It would only ever be Charlie and her. All the time she could keep that in her mind, this current affair would be easy to manage.

Rain started to spot on the pavement, and she increased her pace. She'd come to realize that in the Northland it would be hammering down within minutes.

She thought of what the parcel held and sighed as her heart rate increased. Yeah, yeah. You're totally in control, Esther Tyler. No worries at all.

Chapter Thirty-Five

Toby lay on the sofa, eyes closed. Outside, heavy sub-tropical rain hammered on the decking and streamed down the windows, almost drowning out the music playing in the background. The temperature had risen by a few degrees, and his shirt stuck to his skin. He was used to the Northland weather, but it had been refreshingly dry in Christchurch even though it had been the height of summer, and he'd enjoyed the crisp mornings and scorching afternoons.

Esther was in the bedroom, singing along to the music as she got changed. He covered his eyes with an arm. Hopelessness settled over him like a blanket. He'd said yes to Esther's suggestion of exploring the Naughty Nights game because he liked her, he hadn't had sex in a while, and he hadn't seen the harm in it. How stupid was he? Why on earth had he thought he could have some free sex and not get his heart involved?

But he knew the answer. Because he'd done it so often before. How many times had he slept with a girl for fun, without worrying about where it would lead? And after a few dates when he'd got bored, he'd brushed them off and moved on without a second thought. He'd even done it to Esther in Fiji, although he'd cursed that decision ever since. But he thought he'd got over her, and he'd been certain their dalliance would just be a fun way to pass a few days while he got to know his son.

Fucking idiot. He groaned. How could he have thought he'd got over her? Why didn't he realize he'd be thinking about her twenty-four/seven once they went to bed again? For God's sake, last time she'd haunted him for years after only two weeks in her presence, and this time he was emotionally invested from the start. She was the mother of his child.

He was in love with her.

The thought shocked him so much, he sat up. His heart pounded. "Fuck," he said out loud.

"Yeah, all right," Esther said from behind him. "Give me a minute. Whatever happened to foreplay?"

He turned and nearly fell off the sofa at the sight of her. She stood with one hand on her hip, posing like a teen with attitude, clearly enjoying his reaction. The navy skirt reached barely halfway down her thighs, and the white shirt stretched tight across her breasts. She couldn't get the blazer done up, but the way it hugged her was hardly a turnoff. The tie hung in a loose knot. She even wore long white socks with gym shoes, and she'd braided her hair into two pigtails.

She sucked the lollipop in her right hand and pointed it at him. "What's up mister? Never seen a schoolgirl before?"

His heart—still racing from his eureka moment a few moments before—increased its pace. "Not like this, no. Wow."

She sauntered forward, stood before him, and slid the lollipop in and out of her mouth, eyes fixed on his. "Everything all right, sir? You look kind of... shocked."

No way would he admit to her what he'd been thinking. He had to do some serious damage control here. This was physical, he told himself firmly. This was all about sex. That was the reason why he couldn't get her out of his head. She was a good fuck, nothing more.

The thought made him wince, and he apologized in his head. *Shit. Sorry.*

She pulled the lollipop out of her mouth and surveyed him with a curious smile. "Are you sure you're okay? You look weird."

"I didn't mean it," he said.

"Didn't mean what?"

He stared at her helplessly. "Um... I meant..."

She toed off her shoes, came forward and climbed on top of him. She straddled him and sat on his lap, then offered him the lollipop. He closed his mouth around it, tasting cherry, and then she removed it and placed it back in her mouth again, grinning. He hardened beneath her. Why was that so sexy?

She moved a little closer, opening her thighs so she could slide toward him. "I'm guessing you like the outfit?" The stick moved from side to side as she turned the lollipop in her mouth. He couldn't take his eyes off it.

"It's very... ah... entertaining."

She chuckled. "I'd never understood the male fetish for the schoolgirl look before, but I have to admit there's something sexy about it. I guess it's the innocence thing. The chance to corrupt and degrade." Her eyes gleamed.

"Yeah." His voice was little more than a squeak.

"Do you like the white cotton panties I'm wearing?" She hitched up her skirt to show him she spoke the truth.

He groaned as she moved her hips from side to side and rubbed her soft mound against the rock-hard length in his pants. "Oh jeez."

"The thing is, sir. . I've been very bad." She batted her eyelashes, playing the naïve girl, even as she continued to arouse herself on him.

"You have?" His voice came out weak. He felt completely out of control, physically and emotionally.

"Mm. The principal caught me behind the bike sheds doing something very naughty." She ran the lollipop over her lips, coating them with red gloss. "And he told me you were going to have to chastise me."

Various scenarios ran through his head of how to discipline her until she begged for his forgiveness, and a deep, warm feeling of contentment crept over him at how much he was enjoying their game. But that was accompanied by a sharp sadness at the knowledge that it all had to end. He gave a long, resigned sigh, unable to think what to say.

She lowered the lollipop and studied him. "Are you sure you're okay? You have a very strange look on your face."

He nodded feebly. What the hell was he doing? Why did he get himself into such impossible situations?

She gave him a sympathetic, amused look, wrapped the lolly back in its wrapper, and placed it on the table. Moving even closer to him, she wriggled until her breasts brushed his chest. Fixing him with a gentle smile, she cupped his face in her hands. And then she lowered her lips to his.

Chapter Thirty-Six

Esther kissed him, enjoying the warmth of his body against hers. But even as she pressed her lips against his, she pondered on his strange expression. What was bothering him? Why had he stared at her with that odd mixture of helplessness and desire, as if he couldn't make up his mind?

Usually his hands would have been wandering all over her by now, but this time he'd linked them loosely behind her back. Not that he didn't seem to be enjoying the kiss. As she moved her hips, he was hard against her, and he returned the kiss happily enough, eyes closed as his tongue played with her own.

He's clearly crazy about you. Rusty's words rang through her, clear as someone tapping on crystal. She lifted her head. Toby opened his eyes and looked into hers. On the one hand, his shone like discs of polished oak, reflecting all her emotions back at her. Yes, of course he had feelings for her. He adored the mother of his child. She had no question about that.

Equally, although she studied him carefully, his expression remained unfathomable. Was he just thinking about how sad he'd be when she took Charlie with her—this new, ready-made family she'd sprung on him? Or was it more than that?

She brushed his stubble with her thumbs. Did he love her?

That thought made her blink. What? Why had that popped into her head? This was nothing to do with love. It couldn't be. All the time they were just having sex, the problems that lay between them like a minefield didn't matter—they could step around them and concentrate on having a good time. But falling in love would be a disaster, because to have a relationship they'd have to face up to their past and address the issues that both of them were managing to ignore. It wouldn't work—it couldn't. It would be too hard, too painful to sift through the whys and wherefores of Fiji and Charlie and why she hadn't contacted him.

Shame flooded her, the same way it always did when she thought about bringing Charlie up on her own, and she lowered her eyes and let her hands slide down his chest. Any feelings he'd developed for her would dissolve like salt in warm water once he found out she'd got the messages he'd left for her. Maybe she should tell him now and get it over with.

But he put a finger under her chin and lifted it so he could look into her eyes, and his were filled with such warmth and gentleness that she couldn't bring herself to say the words. He slid his hand into her hair, brought her head down and kissed her, and this time the usual heat that simmered between them flamed and engulfed her.

He wrapped his other arm around her and pulled her tight against him. She sighed and opened her mouth to his searching tongue. He slid the hand resting on her back around to her breast, and she arched against him as he squeezed the nipple through the lace.

Tears pricked her eyelids, and she squeezed her eyes shut tight, determined not to let them fall as he kissed down her neck. For crying out loud, this was supposed to be fun. The last thing he'd want was her collapsing into a sniveling heap. Desperation rising inside her, she grabbed his hair and pulled his head back so she could kiss him again. She plunged her tongue into his mouth and ground her hips against his, wanting to fire both of them up until the sexual daze overtook them and forced these uneasy thoughts from her head.

He seemed happy to go along with that plan and groaned at her insistence, his hands becoming rougher as they wandered over her body. He moved one between them and hooked it around the leg of her panties. His fingers glided through her folds so easily she could tell she was already slippery with desire for him.

"Fuck, Esther." He slid two fingers deep inside her. "You're so wet." He curved his fingers and searched until he found the spot he was looking for.

She gasped at his words, as well as his actions. "And you're so rude!"

"Because I tell the truth?" The mischievous glint in his eye was back, thank goodness, replacing the tenderness that had nearly been her undoing. He stroked firmly, and she knotted her hand in his hair as her internal muscles rippled with pleasure. "There," he said in a contented voice. "Good girl."

She tipped her head back blissfully. "I know why you like the schoolgirl thing. You love the thought of corrupting me, don't you?"

"Yep. I like doing and saying things that make that look appear on your face."

"What look?" She dropped her head to give him an indignant glare. "You're making it up."

"No, I'm not." He continued to stroke her. "You want a mirror so you can see it?"

"There's... no... 'look'." She was having trouble stringing a sentence together.

"Absolutely there's a look." His eyes gleamed. "It's about to appear now, when I tell you I'm going to get my cock out in a minute and fuck you hard with it." She inhaled and whacked him on the arm, and he laughed. "There you go."

She lifted herself off him and mumbled to herself as she removed her panties. "You should be ashamed of yourself. Leading an innocent girl astray." She slipped off the tight jacket, waiting until he'd unzipped his jeans and freed his erection from his boxers before she climbed back onto him. "It's shocking."

"One does one's best." He put his hands on her hips and moved her on top of him until his swollen tip parted her equally swollen lips. "It's a practiced art," he said, finishing with a groan as she gyrated her hips and rubbed herself along him.

"Hmm." She met his gaze. "I think it's more of a natural skill where you're concerned."

"Maybe."

They both smiled, then inhaled jointly with a gasp as she relaxed and let him slide inside her.

He pulled her toward him, burying himself within her deeply, and tightened his arms around her. "Damn, you feel good."

"Oh, you too." She loved the way she could feel him all the way up inside her as her muscles clenched around his thick, hard length.

He caught one of her braids and tugged it to bring her head down for a kiss, curling the dark plait around his fingers. "You look so young with these," he murmured when she lifted her head.

"That was kind of the idea." She began to move on top of him, rocking her hips so he slid in and out of her. "Too much though? Want me to undo them?"

He shook his head and cupped her cheek in his big hand. "I wish I could have been your first."

That puzzled her. "Why?"

"I don't like to think of another man touching you."

A shiver went through her. That was dangerously close to possessiveness again, something they couldn't afford to indulge in.

She decided to go down the playful route. "Not even if you were watching?"

His eyes held a warning glare. "Esther…"

She nibbled his earlobe as she continued to move her hips. "How about if both of you had me?" She kissed around his jaw to his lips. "At the same time?" She lifted herself up until she just teased the tip of him repeatedly. "You'd be in charge, of course. We'd tell him what to do."

He closed his eyes, his breathing harsh. "Esther…"

She sucked his bottom lip. "I could slide onto you like this, while he watched. And then he could kneel behind me and push his cock into my—"

Suddenly he lifted her, cutting off her words. She squealed. He moved forward onto the soft rug without withdrawing. Lying on her back, she looked up at him with startled eyes. "What was that for?"

He didn't say anything. He braced his hands either side of her and studied her for a moment, unsmiling. She held her breath. What had she said? Why was he in such a strange mood? She'd only been playing, trying to turn him on.

He knelt up, still inside her, grasped both sides of her shirt in his hands and pulled it apart. Buttons popped and flew across the carpet, and she squealed. "Toby!" She tried to push him away, but he ignored her feeble swats and bent and covered her nipple with his mouth through the white lace. She gasped as he sucked hard. "What… what did I say?"

He kissed up her neck to her mouth and delved his tongue inside. He began to move his hips, and she exclaimed as he thrust hard repeatedly.

His eyes held a dangerous glitter. She blinked at them, unsure what to say or do, knowing she'd somehow upset him. "Toby…"

"You're mine," he said fiercely. "No other guy's going to get his hands on you."

"Jeez—I—was—only—playing." The words came out staccato as he continued to thrust.

"Well, don't." He pressed his hips down, pushing against her as he thrust, arousing her in spite of her growing annoyance.

Indignation spread through her. They were supposed to be role-playing, weren't they? It was all a game. And even if they weren't, he had no right to be so jealous. "I don't belong to anyone," she snapped.

"At this moment, you do." He caught her face in his fingers and kissed her, hard.

She wriggled with irritation. "I don't 'belong' to you. Why do you have to make me so mad every time we have sex?"

He laughed. "Yeah right. I'm the one at fault here. I'm supposed to be disciplining you, remember?" He thrust hard, then paused, pushing forward, stretching and expanding her and making her groan with pleasure.

So now he was pretending it was all a game? She couldn't bring herself to smile—he'd gone too far with his possessiveness and exasperated her. She didn't want to have to deal with his jealousy. This was a mutual sexual arrangement, nothing more. "I'm the one who should be putting you over my knee," she complained.

He pretended to look shocked. Before she could say anything more, he captured both her hands and pinned them above her head with one of his, holding her easily even though she wriggled and swore at him. He pushed his other hand up her thigh, raising her skirt and baring her bottom. He gave it a sound whack. "Bad girl."

She jumped. "Argh. Toby!"

He chuckled. "Serves you right." He kissed her, plunging his tongue into her mouth.

She bit his lip, infuriated that she was turned on by his forcefulness again. "Get off me."

"No." He bent and sucked a nipple through the lace.

"Stop it. I mean it." Her protest was half-hearted, her body arching into him even as the words came out of her mouth.

He smacked her again. "Stop talking and keep quiet while you get what you deserve."

It stung deliciously, and she clenched around him, making them both groan. Unbidden, however, tears came into her eyes. She didn't want to be turned on when she was so annoyed with him. She shouldn't have gone to his place. She'd already been emotional before they'd started. This was all a huge mistake.

He raised his head and froze as a tear welled and slid down her cheek. Immediately he released her hands. She rested them on his chest, and he waited, presumably to see whether she'd push him away.

She hesitated, too confused and emotional to know what she wanted.

He pressed his nose to hers. The naughty glint had disappeared from his eyes. The tender look was back. "I know," he murmured.

Another tear escaped and she bit her lip. He understood what she was feeling, because he felt the same. Rusty had been right.

He kissed the second tear away, touching his tongue to her skin, and then kissed the rest of her face, her cheeks, nose, closed eyelids, then finally her mouth. He lingered there, brushing her lips with his, then teasing them open with his tongue and tasting her gently. Her resistance melted.

Yes, this was just sex, but even "just sex" involved emotions. Of course he'd feel possessive while he was lying on top of her, inside her. Why wouldn't he? And the aggressive, demanding role he took on had always been part of their sex play. She enjoyed it—enjoyed fighting him and being dominated. It was the only place she'd let anyone dominate her, and having to give in to him, letting his sheer strength win her over, turned her on. He knew that—he was playing the game. Could she damn him for that?

She relaxed into the rug, raising her arms around his neck, and he sighed and began to move again. He continued to kiss her though, delving his tongue into her mouth, and she gave herself over to him, letting him take charge.

So he did. He aroused her gradually, and by the time her muscles started to tighten, she was panting with desire and desperate for release. Sweat covered both of them, skin gliding and sticking to skin, and his harsh, heavy breathing sounded like music to her ears.

"Oh..." She arched against him, closing her eyes as all her attention focused between her legs.

He smacked her butt lightly, though, saying, "Open."

She opened her eyes with surprise to see him watching her, and now his eyes were hot again, demanding, wanting to feast on her arousal as she came apart in his arms. He liked to watch her come.

She flushed, but was unable to stop the orgasm spreading through, and climaxed under his warm brown gaze. He stilled, his muscles going rigid beneath her fingertips, and she sighed as he spilled inside her, his hips jerking and his breathing ragged as he gave in to his release.

He rested his nose against hers again and kissed her, his pulse still beating rapidly in his throat. "I'm sorry."

"For what?" She frowned at the regret in his eyes. Sorry they'd had sex? Or sorry she'd cried? He didn't answer her, so she closed her eyes, enjoying her heightened senses—the softness of the fur rug under her back, the bulge and dips of his arm muscles beneath her fingers, the smell of their arousal, the taste of their sweat on her tongue.

He withdrew, and she mumbled a complaint, but he scooped her up into his arms and pulled her tight to him as he rolled into his back. She nestled against him, suddenly shy, and buried her face in his neck. This man would be her undoing. He seemed to know exactly the way to unspool her in his arms. No matter how much she tried to keep up a strong front, in bed—or on the floor, or wherever else they happened to be—he dismantled her defenses brick by brick.

He kissed her hair. "Sorry," he said again.

She raised herself onto her elbow and looked down at him. "For what?"

Still he didn't reply. He looked up at the ceiling, although he didn't loosen his grip around her.

"Sorry you had sex with me?" She couldn't help the way her voice came out small.

He grinned. "Of course not. I'd never be sorry for that."

She leaned on his chest and rested her chin on her arm. "So what are you apologizing for?"

"For making you cry."

"You didn't make me cry. I made me cry."

He stroked her hair. "I'm still sorry." He was—she could see it in his eyes.

She lowered her gaze and trailed her fingers through the hair on his chest. "Why did you say 'I know'?"

He stroked his fingers up and down her back. "I felt..." His words tapered off. He tipped his head. "I thought... maybe you felt the same way I did." He didn't elaborate.

She swallowed and rested her lips on his chest for a moment. She did, but she couldn't confirm it. There was no point in them indulging in declarations of affection. This was going to hurt enough when the time came to part.

She raised her head. "There's something you should know."

"Oh?"

"I've applied for a job in Dunedin."

Immediately his eyes cooled and his smile disappeared. "Dunedin?"

"I don't have ties to Christchurch anymore, and who knows how long the university will be closed? And it's perfect for me. Pretty much the same stuff I'm teaching now. And it's a great university."

"Sounds fantastic." But his voice was as cool as his eyes.

"Are you angry?"

His brow furrowed at that. "Angry? No. Why would I be angry?"

She swallowed. "It's farther for you to travel to see Charlie. If you want to see him…"

He sat up, forcing her up too. "Of course I want to see him. Did you think I wouldn't?"

Her pulse sped up. "No. But nothing's changed since Fiji. We're still islands apart." How ironic, she thought. That statement could apply physically and metaphorically.

"Something's changed," he said. "Now we have a son." He glared at her. "You thought I'd turn my back on him the moment you flew south?"

"I didn't know how you'd feel," she said, turning defensive at his accusing gaze. "You've been great with Charlie. But soon you'll be moving on. You'll be going to university. I've been there—I know how all-consuming that life is. You're young enough to be able to make the most of that life. You'll get a girlfriend and a life of your own." She ignored the stab of pain in her gut as she said those words. "I'm being practical, that's all. I have to look after myself and Charlie. There's no point me getting all romantic about us playing happy families when we'll be living at opposite ends of the country."

He moved so he sat back against the sofa. Legs stretched out, ankles crossed, he appeared remarkably unaffected by the fact that he was completely naked. In contrast, feeling vulnerable, she drew her knees up and wrapped her arms around them.

She waited for him to talk, but he didn't say anything. He surveyed her calmly, arms along the sofa cushions.

Unable to stand the silence any longer, she said, "We shouldn't have had sex, Toby. It's just made things harder."

His lips twitched. "That's generally a good thing."

She rolled her eyes. "You know what I mean."

He smiled and looked out at the rain.

They sat quietly for a while. She rested her cheek on her knee and studied his profile. Gosh, he really was gorgeous. His hair had grown long and curled around his neck and ears, and his sideburns needed trimming, but she liked the ruffled, carefree look it gave him. His smile had faded, however, and he looked sad. In another world, another dimension, would the two of them have worked? Could they have been happy?

He looked back at her. His brown-eyed gaze roamed down her to her feet, then slowly back up. By the time it reached her face again, he looked different—his eyes had taken on a determined, steely glint. What was he thinking?

"You want to stop now?" he said. "Because I don't want to be a mistake."

"You're not a mistake," she murmured. "I didn't mean it like that."

"Didn't you?"

Her cheeks grew warm. "It wasn't like I was drunk or anything when I came up here. I knew what would happen. And I don't regret it. I didn't mean that when I said we shouldn't have had sex. It's been great fun."

"So what did you mean?"

Suddenly she realized what was shimmering in his eyes—not anger, but hurt. She couldn't help but soften. "As I said, it's been great, but it means it'll be more difficult to leave. I enjoy being with you. It's a shame it has to come to an end."

"Does it have to?"

Her throat tightened. Was he asking her to stay?

She couldn't think about it. She couldn't tell him about those messages she'd destroyed. Not now, not after what they'd just done.

To her surprise, he reached forward and pulled her into his arms. "Tomorrow's the stag night," he said as if he hadn't just asked her not to leave. "And then of course Saturday's the wedding. But I have a suggestion. Mum and Dad have said they'll be happy to have Charlie in their room for the night so we can... get some sleep. Or not." He winked at her. "You want to have one last Naughty Night before you go?"

Tears welled in her eyes and she bit her lip. He'd read her reluctance, and he wasn't going to push it anymore. He'd taken her answer as yes, it did have to end. But in his usual warm-hearted way, he wasn't going to get angry at her answer. Instead he was offering her one last night of passion before she left.

Did she want a last night? Well, honestly, yes. It was already going to be difficult to leave him. She might as well enjoy the short time they had together.

They both started to smile as the moment drew out.

"Okay..." she admitted eventually. "But we do need to talk about how it's going to work when I leave."

"I know." His gentle voice soothed her worried nerves. "But not yet, eh? We have a few days left. I don't want to talk about you going away until I have to."

"We can't ignore it," she said softly.

"I know."

He tightened his arms around her, and she rested her head on his chest.

Chapter Thirty-Seven

Esther wasn't drunk. She was tipsy, she decided. Merry. Well, after several years of not drinking a single drop, two glasses of white wine and two single malts were going to go to a girl's head.

Luckily, she was in good company. Eve was decidedly giggly, even though she'd told everyone she wasn't going to drink too much because she didn't want a hangover on her wedding day. Most of the other seven girls in the group were comfortably hazy. Only Faith remained sober, but Esther suspected from the way she constantly rested a hand on her tiny bump that the baby more than made up for her inability to consume alcohol.

They'd had a meal at the Italian restaurant, and by the time they got to dessert, the owner himself came out to investigate the raucous goings-on at table nine. He ended up having his photo taken with a flushed and giggling Eve, and gave the girls a free bottle of champagne to end their meal on, for which he received a round of applause and cheers.

By the time they left the restaurant, Esther had warmed to the occasion, and the nerves that had flared earlier on had dissipated. She still couldn't believe Eve had been kind enough to invite her on her hen night. The other girls were either Eve's close friends or relatives, but when Esther had announced that she was quite happy to stay at home alone, Eve wouldn't hear of it.

She'd spent the first hour a little intimidated by the other girls. She also missed Charlie. Toby's parents had offered to have him for the night again. Esther had accepted gratefully, pleased that her son was happy to go to them and relieved on the surface to have more time to herself. But it was strange spending so much time away from him. It had been the two of them for so long, she felt as if half of her was missing.

As the Sauvignon took hold, however, and the other women welcomed her into their conversation, she gradually relaxed and joined in the fun. She even accepted the tiara and veil Faith had made for them all to wear. She caught her breath when Faith showed her the photo she'd taken of her on her phone. The white lace framed her flushed cheeks, and her green eyes sparkled. It wasn't only the wine that had given her the glow, however. At that moment, Faith had said, "Smile for Toby, Esther," and just the mention of his name had brought heat to her face.

She'd put him to the back of her mind, though. She didn't want to start thinking about Toby Wilkinson while under the influence of alcohol or she'd end up either depressed or randy, and neither of those options was likely to have a happy ending.

Full with pasta and tiramisu, the girls wandered down the high street toward the wine bar. Faith and Rusty had planned a route for the two pre-wedding parties so they wouldn't meet, to keep the tradition of the bride and groom not seeing each other the night before. The guys were going to an Indian restaurant for a curry before making their way to the sports bar.

Esther walked in a hazy dream, thinking how exotic the palm trees looked outside the shops, and how lovely and warm it was, even at ten o'clock at night.

She rounded the corner, slightly ahead of the other girls, and stopped in her tracks at the sight of the guys milling about close to the wine bar.

She squealed and several of them turned, so she walked backward, bumping into Faith. "Groom alert!" she said hastily.

Faith woman-handled Eve into an alleyway. "What are they doing here?" she snapped. "I mapped out the route for Rusty, for God's sake."

"I'll go see." Esther, along with a couple of the other girls, walked unsteadily toward the men. One of them whistled, and several others cheered. The other girls giggled. Esther's amusement fled at the thought of seeing Toby and her heart pounded. Where was he? She couldn't see him.

She approached Dan, who grinned. His brown hair was ruffled, his eyes at half-mast, and he'd clearly had more than a few beers.

"What are you doing here?" she scolded him. "You're supposed to be at the sports bar."

"We had a detour," he said, speaking very carefully as if he was worried he wouldn't be able to pronounce the words. "How is my lovely wife-to-be?" He stared hopefully up the road.

"You're not allowed to see her, Dan. It's unlucky."

"I miss her." He looked forlorn.

She laughed and rubbed his arm. "Only a few more hours, then you'll be stuck with her for life. Don't stress."

Rusty pushed through the guys and came up to her. "Hey, Esther."

"Faith's pissed with you," she said. "You weren't supposed to come this way."

"We'll be off in a minute. One of the guys needed some cash from the cashpoint." Like Dan, his hair was ruffled and his eyes slightly feverish.

"Are you drunk?" she asked suspiciously, trying not to slur her words while accusing him. "I didn't think you liked alcohol."

"It seemed rude to let him drink on his own." He blinked slowly.

"You're with about ten other guys, Rusty."

"Oh yeah." He rubbed his nose. "I've only had a couple. Mind you, it only takes a couple for my hamster to break loose."

She narrowed her eyes. "Is that prison slang? For God's sake, don't get your 'hamster' out in public or Faith'll never hear the end of it."

Behind her, someone snorted with laughter, and then a pair of warm arms slid around her and a nose bumped the back of her head. "Hello sweetheart."

She turned with surprise, warmth stealing up through her body and into her face as she realized it was Toby. "Hello. I'm guessing you're pretty plastered too."

"Not at all. I'm the only sober one here." He planted a kiss noisily on her cheek.

"Hmm." She eyed him suspiciously.

He raised an eyebrow. "Hey. She who wears tiara and veil in public should not throw stones." She'd forgotten about the veil. She snatched it off her head hurriedly, and he grinned. He pulled out his phone. "Don't worry, I have a beautiful picture to remind me." He clicked a few buttons and then turned it to show her the photo Faith had taken.

"She sent it to you?" Her voice rang with indignation.

"Yup." He kissed the screen. "You look gorgeous."

She couldn't stop her lips curving. "Dear, oh dear. You are drunk. Lord, you're clumsy enough when you're sober."

His eyes met hers. He slid his phone into his pocket, put his arms around her and pulled her up against him. "Not that drunk."

"Toby…"

He took the tiara out of her hand and placed it back on her hair, then adjusted the veil around her face. "It suits you," he mumbled when she protested. He studied her for a moment, face serious, his eyes clear.

Then he kissed her.

A series of wolf whistles arose from the men, along with cheers from the girls who'd spotted what they were up to.

"Put him down," Rusty said. "You don't know where he's been."

Her cheeks burned, but Toby tightened his arms around her, and in the end she gave in and kissed him back. She closed her eyes, wrapped her arms around his neck and opened her mouth to his tongue as he kissed her deeply.

"Great." Dan said to one side. "Now Toby's getting some and I've got to sleep on my own tonight. How's that fair?"

"It's your last night alone," came Rusty's voice. "Think of it as a farewell party for your right hand."

Esther couldn't stifle a giggle and Toby pulled back, chuckling. "Sorry," he whispered. "But you look so lovely." He brushed her cheek with the back of his fingers.

She shook her head, embarrassed, flustered and a tiny bit pleased. "For goodness' sake. Now go on, all of you, off to the sports bar. The girls want a drink!"

Laughing, the guys headed off down the road, sending final catcalls along to the girls. Esther watched them go, lips curving. She touched the veil where it lay on her neck, the cheap lace stiff between her fingers. Would she ever get to wear one for real? She'd never thought about getting hitched before.

For a brief moment, she entertained the notion that it was she who was getting married the next day, and it was her hen party they were out on. How exciting would that be? To know the she'd be going to the church to declare her intention to love her man forever. For richer, for poorer. In sickness and in health. Her husband would be at her side every day. Every night. To support her and Charlie, to look after and love them both.

She bit her lip. It was a fine fantasy. Too bad fairy godmothers didn't exist in real life.

Chapter Thirty-Eight

Toby arrived at Rusty's house at eleven the next morning to pick him up distinctly the worse for wear.

A bleary-eyed Rusty opened the door, confirming that Toby hadn't been the only one to lose track of the number of whisky glasses on the table the night before.

Rusty winced as Charlie hollered from the bedroom. "I wish kids came with a mute button." He stepped back to let Toby enter.

"You think this is bad?" Faith gave him a dark look as she passed with a basketful of washing. She wore a bathrobe and her hair was wrapped in a towel. "Wait until it's an octave higher and twice the volume at two a.m."

Rusty watched her disappear along the corridor and smiled sheepishly. "She's mad at me."

"Why? You throw up on the sofa or something?" Esther must be with Charlie in the bedroom, Toby thought.

"On the duvet. She had to change the entire bed at three in the morning. She wasn't a happy bunny."

Toby pulled a face and then smiled brightly as Faith came back along the corridor. "Morning."

She glowered at him. "Don't you start."

"Me? I haven't done anything."

She stopped and stared at him. A thoughtful expression settled on her face. "Hmm."

"What?" Unease settled over him. "What did I do?"

Her lips twitched and she shook her head. "I'll tell Esther you're here." She went along to the bedroom, knocked, and slipped inside.

Toby met Rusty's bloodshot eyes. Rusty shrugged.

"Did I do something last night?" Panic rose inside Toby. "Shit, I can't remember."

"I have no idea. I can barely remember making it home."

"We got Dan back to the house though, didn't we?"

"Far as I remember."

They both fell quiet for a moment.

"I seem to recall stopping by Eve's parents' house," Toby said after a while.

"Yeah. Why did we do that again?"

"Dan wanted to see Eve."

Rusty frowned. "Did her Dad come out and yell at us?"

"Um, yeah, for trampling his begonias."

Toby scratched the back of his head. Rusty cleared his throat.

Toby sighed. His stomach roiled uneasily. "Oh well, I guess we'll find out what else we did soon enough."

"Hmm."

They both watched warily as Faith came out of the bedroom, followed by Esther. Toby's heart swelled. She wore trackpants and a T-shirt. Her hair hung damply about her face, and she'd yet to put on her makeup.

She looked fresh as a glass of cold water, and he could have done her right there.

His head throbbed. Okay, maybe not. But she was beautiful. And he had to fight not to fold her in his arms.

He met her gaze warily, however, conscious that she'd carefully arranged her features into a blank, quizzical stare. "Morning," she said. She folded her arms, her whole body tense.

"Morning." He smiled hopefully. Her lips twitched but didn't curve into the reciprocal smile he wanted. "Everything okay?" What the fuck had he done? He remembered meeting the girls outside the bank and kissing her. Had that pissed her off?

She exchanged a glance with Faith, who raised an eyebrow and shrugged as if to say, "Told you." Her gaze slid back to him and she exhaled slowly, her mouth now curving into a welcoming, if rueful, smile.

"Daddy, Daddy!" Naked as the day he was born, Charlie shot out of the bedroom and ran like a bullet to wrap his arms around his father's knees. "I'm going to a wedding."

"Hey, buster." Toby bent and lifted his son into his arms. "Are you going to church like this?"

Charlie giggled. "No, Daddy. I've got to get dressed."

"Well, thank goodness. You'll frighten all the bridesmaids."

Esther rolled her eyes. "He's pretty excited. I've been trying to get him into his clothes for the last half an hour."

"I've got a tow bar," Charlie said.

Esther laughed. "He means a bow tie."

"Have you got one?" Charlie asked his dad.

"No—I've got an ordinary tie. A shiny silver one."

"Where is it?"

"At Dan's house. Rusty and I are going there to get dressed."

"Can I come wiv you?"

Esther smiled and stroked his hair. "No, sweetie. Daddy has a special job to do, remember?"

"Yes." Charlie beamed. "You're going to be the brest man."

They all burst out laughing at the look on Toby's face. "How does he know?" he said.

"Why's everybody laughing?" Charlie protested.

"It's *best* man," Esther told him, highly amused.

Toby grinned. At least she was smiling. "Okay. We'd better be off and make sure Dan's up."

Faith led Rusty off to give him instructions for the day. Toby put down the wriggling Charlie and watched, smiling, as his son ran down the corridor. Then he turned his attention to Esther.

Her eyes looked sad. Why was she sad? He cupped her face. "Are you okay?"

"Yeah." She stood woodenly for a moment, and then visibly softened and nestled her cheek into his palm.

He leaned forward and kissed her. He'd only meant to make it a quick kiss, but his lips lingered, entranced by the softness of hers. In response, she slipped her arms around him and molded her body to his. He sighed inwardly and threaded his hand through her damp hair, holding her as he deepened the kiss. She tasted of chocolate, and her skin smelled fresh, of oranges and strawberries.

When he lifted his head, she was smiling.

He brushed her lips with his thumb. "Still on for tonight?"

"Sure. Have you drawn the card?"

"Oh yes." Desire curled through him at the thought of what awaited them that night. He glanced over his shoulder. Faith and Rusty had disappeared into the kitchen. He could hear her chewing him out again, poor guy. "You want to read it?" he asked, pulling the card out of his pocket.

She took it and read it quickly. He grinned as twin spots of color appeared on her cheeks. Previously, they'd picked their cards at random, but he'd taken his time choosing their last Naughty Night. He could remember the wording. *It's the twenty-fourth century and the galaxy is in turmoil. Mutinous workers are threatening to overthrow the state. You've captured a protestor, and you've been instructed by your superiors to interrogate her for information. Feel free to restrain her, and use every skill at your disposal to extract the secrets she knows...*

She raised her gaze to his. "Tying me up, huh?"

He pulled her closer and nuzzled her ear, breathing in the strawberry scent of her hair. "Any objections?"

"No," she said, breathless. She played with his shirt. "I've got something to tell you."

"Oh?" He pulled back.

"I've got an interview in Dunedin."

His heart bumped unnaturally and then sank into his boots. But he forced a smile onto his face. "That's great news. I'm really pleased for you."

Her shoulders lost some of their tension and the frown between her eyes disappeared. "Oh, thanks. Yes, it is good news."

"When is it?"

"Soon as I can make it. I was thinking maybe about flying down Monday, if you wouldn't mind looking after Charlie? I know you've got to get back to work though."

"I can take one more day. Of course I'll look after him."

She nodded. Their gazes locked for a moment, a thousand things unspoken. He was going to lose her, he thought miserably.

"Until later, then," he said eventually.

She nodded. "Good luck."

"Hopefully I won't need it, but thanks." He released her, his hand lingering on her hip as if it couldn't bear to lose contact with her.

Rusty and Faith came out of the kitchen. Rusty looked smug and Faith's cheeks were pink, so Toby guessed they'd made up. "Ready?"

"Yep." Rusty lifted his suit from the hanger and grabbed his bag. He kissed Faith. "See you later, sexy."

"Don't push your luck." But she smiled.

They headed out to the car, and waved to the girls as they drove away.

"You made up then?" Toby queried.

"Yeah. I groveled. And made a few promises for later." Rusty grinned.

"Faith being pregnant hasn't damaged your sex life then," Toby said, amused.

"Quite the opposite. She's insatiable." Rusty rolled his eyes. "I'm exhausted."

"You're really complaining about your wife's increased sex drive? Dude, what's wrong with you?"

Rusty laughed. "Point taken. I'm guessing there won't be so much of it when the baby's born, so I suppose I should make the most of it." He sighed.

"Yeah, but the baby won't stay a baby forever," Toby said. "And you've got the rest of your life together."

"True." Rusty smiled.

Toby concentrated on the road. Rusty had a hell of a year ahead of him. All the troubles and worries of Faith's pregnancy, the stress of the birth and getting screamed at in the delivery room, the sleepless night, the dirty nappies, and vomit everywhere.

And Toby was green with envy. He should have had all that. It churned him up inside that he'd missed out on it. He hadn't even seen any pictures of his son at birth, and probably never would, as Esther had told him her photos had been lost in the damage from the earthquake. He'd never get that time back again—those precious memories of Charlie having his first chocolate bar, saying his first word, sitting on a swing for the first time.

"Dude," Rusty said. "You okay?"

Toby followed his gaze to see his hands gripping the steering wheel, knuckles white. He forced himself to loosen his grip and sighed. "Yeah."

"You thinking about Esther?"

"How did you guess?" He smiled wryly.

"Been there, done that."

"Yeah, I'd forgotten."

It had been a peculiar couple of months when Rusty and Faith had gotten together, supposedly under the excuse of doing research for some articles Faith was writing, even though Toby knew Rusty had wanted to get her into bed for years. They'd not told anyone they were hooking up, but he'd known something was going on. There'd been an odd atmosphere in the group, and Rusty had been preoccupied and moody toward the end, although Toby had not been able to put his finger on why.

"What made you decide?" he asked.

"Decide what?"

"That you wanted to stay with her," he said. Rusty had always been determined to stay single due to the severe alcoholism that the men in his family suffered from.

"I missed her," Rusty said. "When I wasn't with her. I couldn't think about anything else." He studied Toby thoughtfully. "Is that how you feel about Esther?"

Toby said nothing.

"Ah."

Toby sighed. "It doesn't matter. Even if she does feel the same way about me, she's off to Christchurch soon, or maybe even Dunedin—she's got an interview Monday. It wouldn't make any difference what we feel. She'll never forgive me for leaving her in Fiji."

"Are you sure about that?"

He glanced at Rusty. "What do you mean?"

"I mean she's crazy about you, man. It's written all over her."

He looked back at the road. "She thinks I'm all right in bed, if that's what you mean."

"That's not what I mean. She watches you all the time, when she thinks you aren't looking."

A shiver descended from the roots of his hair across his shoulders and down his spine. "Stop shitting me."

"I'm not shitting you. I swear. She's nuts about you. God knows why. And maybe you should take the time to talk to her about the future, rather than assume you know what she's thinking all the time."

That made him think. Was there any possibility of a future for the two of them together? It was difficult to convince himself there was. Because her being crazy about him was one thing.

Her forgiving him for walking away from her was another.

Chapter Thirty-Nine

They arrived at Dan's house, half-expecting to find him still in bed, but to their surprise he was up, showered, and fresh as a daisy. The room smelled of bacon and eggs, and Toby's stomach rumbled.

"Last chance," Rusty said as they followed Dan into the house. "If you want to escape to Antarctica or something, now's the perfect opportunity."

Dan laughed as he walked into the kitchen. "Nah, I'm good. I'm looking forward to it. It's not every day you get to promise the woman of your dreams you'll love her forever in front of all her friends and family." He stopped then. "Crap, now I'm nervous."

"You'll cope." Rusty gestured at the frying pan on the hob. "Feeding the five thousand, are we?"

"I figured you'd both be hungover, and I don't want you throwing up over the altar or something. Get the toast." He started sharing the bacon and eggs between three plates.

"Why do you never have a hangover?" Toby complained. He seated himself at the breakfast bar and buttered the toast.

"Skill and an excellent constitution. Oh, and about three pints of orange juice before I went to bed."

Rusty grabbed the ketchup from the fridge. "I'll never forget that first night you both got me drunk. I couldn't believe how awful I felt. I swear I threw up three times the quantity I actually consumed."

"Yeah, but you proposed to Faith, so at least something good came out of it." Dan grinned and pushed their plates over.

"Just you left now," Rusty said, pointing a fork at Toby before tucking in.

"Yeah." Toby concentrated on cutting up his bacon. He didn't want to discuss what was going to happen after the wedding when he wasn't even sure himself.

They ate their breakfast and then got dressed. All three of them had hired traditional wedding suits with morning coats, pinstripe trousers and wing-collar shirts. Toby's and Rusty's waistcoats and ties were silver paisley, while Dan had chosen a burgundy one with a silver swirl.

They'd just finished dressing when Toby's parents turned up to check on them. Martha fiddled with their ties to get them right, and then Graham took a photo of the three of them in the garden. Finally, they left the guys alone to go to Faith's house, as they were taking Esther and Charlie to the wedding.

Rusty switched on the TV, and they sat and watched the highlights of a recent All Blacks rugby game. Dan started to get twitchy, though, and got up and paced the floor, straightening photographs on the table and checking his tie repeatedly in the mirror.

They sat him down and played X-Box instead, letting him beat them at *Halo*. It worked for a while, although eventually he declared he couldn't concentrate anymore and turned the machine off.

Both Toby and Rusty made a few phone calls to the wedding organizer and her helpers to check on the progress of events, but everything was going smoothly. The organizer told them Eve had finished getting dressed, the photographer was there taking photos of her in her parents' garden, and the bridesmaids had turned up at the house. The flowers had arrived, and the afternoon wedding meal was progressing according to plan. There was nothing left to do except make sure Dan made it to the church on time.

Luckily, it wasn't long before the car turned up. There was a last-minute flurry of activity as they made sure he had his bag packed for the honeymoon, and that he knew where the flight tickets were and had his passport.

"Got the rings?" Toby asked Rusty for the hundredth time.

Rusty patted his breast pocket. "Stop panicking. Do you want to look after them?"

"God no. I know I'd lose them. I can't believe I agreed to do this again—I'm terrified." He checked his suit in the mirror again and ran his hands through his hair.

"I'd never have guessed," Rusty said wryly.

"Why aren't you nervous?"

"I've been the groom. Nothing beats that for nerves. This is a cinch."

Dan came out of the bathroom looking as white as his shirt.

"You all right?" Rusty asked, half-amused, half-concerned.

"I threw up. God, what am I doing? Why am I putting myself through this? We should have eloped."

The three of them stood in the living room, looking at each other.

Rusty smiled. "You'll be all right when you get there and see her."

"Nothing's going to go wrong," Toby reassured him. "Look at us. We're too gorgeous."

Dan laughed and brushed down his jacket. "Do I look okay?"

"You look great," Toby said. "Your mum would have cried if she could see you."

"I'll take that as a compliment," Dan mumbled. He breathed deeply and let it out slowly, giving a shaky smile. Toby's heart filled with sudden affection for him. They'd all been through a lot together. They'd known each other for eleven years now, and he was as close to them as he was to his brothers.

"Come here," he said, and he gave Dan a manly hug. "You're going to knock Eve's socks off. Imagine her face when she sees you."

He released him, and Rusty took his place, hugging him tightly. "Being married is the best thing in the world," Rusty said. "It's worth all this, believe me."

Dan stepped back and straightened his coat. "Thanks, guys. I'm glad you're here. You know how I feel about you. Insert some incredibly girlie declaration of affection here." He cleared his throat. "I'm going to the car."

He walked out.

Toby met Rusty's gaze, and they both laughed.

"Want a hug?" Toby said.

"Nah, I'm good." Rusty gave him a wry look. "But thanks. I'm glad we're both here for him. It makes all the difference on the day, knowing your mates are looking out for you." He headed out.

Smiling, Toby locked up the house and followed.

They slid in the car, trying to make sure they didn't catch their coattails in the doors. Toby's heart increased its pace even more. And he wasn't even the one getting married.

He'd felt the same at Rusty's wedding, which had been slightly more eventful leading up to the ceremony. Rusty's brother had gotten into a fight on the stag night and sported a beautiful black eye the following morning, causing them both to have a blazing row when Cole turned up at the house. Rusty had lost his tie and spent a frantic half hour looking for it before remembering he'd put it in a drawer for safekeeping. Then he'd gone into a complete panic when Dan had phoned Faith's house only to discover she'd gone out for a walk, without her phone. In spite of their attempts to console Rusty, he'd convinced himself she'd got cold feet, and when Eve eventually rang back to say she'd turned up happy as Larry wondering what all the fuss was about, he'd had to have a glass of brandy and then lie down with a cold flannel on his face for half an hour.

Rusty had thrown up three times before he got to the church. But Toby and Dan had been at his side the whole time supporting him, and it had been worth it to see the look on Rusty's face when Faith had appeared in the aisle, resplendent in her simple white gown, her dark hair curled and tumbling around her bare, pale shoulders. Toby could still remember that look now—the sheer wonder that not only had she turned up, but she was marrying him, Rusty—she'd chosen him above all others. From that moment on, Rusty had relaxed and thoroughly enjoyed himself, and the rest of the day had gone without a hitch.

What would it be like to know you were about to commit yourself to one woman for the rest of your life? Toby had never given much thought to the prospect before. Monogamy had always been a laughable proposition. Why tie yourself to one girl when there were so many out there to have fun with? Moving in together, marriage, children, and forever were concepts he'd never explored.

But now... His mind wandered, and he pictured Esther getting dressed in a wedding gown, Faith and Eve titivating with her veil. Charlie in a pageboy's suit, running around getting under everyone's feet. Would he be nervous? Would he be panicking at the thought of being tied to one person for the rest of his life? Or would he be excited, filled with wonder that she loved him enough to make such a commitment?

"We're here." He was distracted from his musings by an agitated Dan, who practically leaped out of the car before it had stopped moving.

The next forty minutes passed in a blur of meeting guests, helping the ushers to organize seating in the church, and trying to keep Dan calm.

Toby kept one eye on the door, waiting for Esther to appear. At twenty to two, his parents entered the church, and right behind them, Esther, holding Charlie's hand.

Toby stared at her. He knew she'd bought a dress when she'd gone shopping with Faith and Eve, but she'd refused to tell him anything about it. He'd imagined some smart suit or fancy outfit, but his heart nearly stopped at the sight of her in the dark green, slinky dress. It was another warm day, and sweat trickled down his back beneath the shirt and coat, but Esther looked cool and fresh, her brown hair pulled back on one side with a matching green flowery, feathery thing. She also wore the highest heels he'd ever seen her in, and she looked slim and elegant.

She took his breath away.

Charlie ran up to him, and Toby bent to admire his white shirt and tiny bow tie. "Well, don't you look the bee's knees," he said, ruffling his curls, and swelling with pride.

Charlie's eyes widened. "Daddy, you look beauty-ful."

Esther laughed as she walked up behind them. "We don't say men look beautiful," she corrected him. "Daddy looks very handsome." Her eyes met Toby's, warm with approval.

He stood, then bent and kissed her on the cheek. "You look stunning."

"You like?" She smiled and reached up on her toes to whisper in his ear. "I'm not wearing any underwear."

He sighed, his hands itching to run down her back and confirm her words. "Great. There's me thinking the worst I'd have to worry about was tripping over the pews. Now I have to stand in front of a hundred people trying to hide a hard-on."

She giggled and stroked his arm. "Your suit suits you." She fingered his tie, then ran a hand down his shiny waistcoat. "Very nice."

"Thank you." Warmth threaded through him at the obvious desire in her eyes. He took her hand and led her along the aisle to a pew near the front. "Here you go." He picked up Charlie and lifted him onto the seat beside her. "Now you be good during the wedding, won't you? No running around or shouting or anything."

"Yes, Daddy."

"I'll try to keep him quiet," she said nervously.

Toby smiled. "Don't worry too much. Dan and Eve are fairly relaxed about this sort of thing. Just take him outside if he gets too twitchy."

"Okay." She looked over her shoulder. "Is Eve here yet?"

"Not yet. I'd best go check on Dan."

"Good luck."

He squeezed her hand and then walked over to the side door.

Rusty was waiting for him in the doorway. "Any sign of Eve?" he murmured.

"No."

"I think I'll give Faith a ring." Smiling and nodding to everyone, Rusty walked down the aisle and outside the church to check what was happening.

Toby slipped through the door into the antechamber.

Dan stood in the center of the room, looking surprisingly young and nervous.

Toby smiled, went over, and pinned his carnation to his coat for him. "Are you going to throw up again?" he asked, seeing how white Dan was. "Only it would probably be better to do it in here rather than in the font or something."

"Nope." Dan swallowed and met his gaze. "I don't think so. What do I do if she doesn't turn up?"

Toby grinned. "She will."

"But what if she doesn't?" Panic filled Dan's eyes. "I don't know what I'll do without her. What if she's having second thoughts?"

Toby smoothed down the carnation, then rested his hands on Dan's upper arms. "She'll be here," he said firmly. He'd never been more sure of anything. "Mate, she's crazy about you. You're everything to her. She's just a few minutes late, that's all. Bride's prerogative. It's to keep you on your toes." He grinned and released him. "You can punish her for it tonight."

Dan's lips twisted wryly and he went to reply, but the door opened and Rusty slipped through.

He closed the door behind him and surveyed them both seriously. Fuck, Toby thought. Surely not. She loves Dan. Please, please don't let her have gotten cold feet.

Dan swallowed again. "What's going on?"

For a moment, Rusty said nothing, drawing out the moment. Then, slowly, his lips curved into a smile. "Your blushing bride's just turned up, and she looks absolutely breathtaking."

"Bastard," Toby said with relief. Dan looked like he might cry, so Toby clapped him on the arm. "She's here. Told you! Are you ready to get hitched, mate?"

Dan nodded, took a deep breath, and gave the first genuine smile of the day. "Let's do it."

They went out and stood at the front of the church. Toby's gaze drifted to Esther, waiting in the pews with Charlie. To his surprise, she was looking at her phone.

He frowned as something twinged in his memory. Phone. Text message. Hold on.

He thought furiously, forcing his brain to try and remember the night before. He'd done something. In the midst of his drunken state, he'd sent Esther a message.

Toby caught a flash of a bridesmaid's dress in the doorway and knew they must be arranging Eve's gown and veil before she walked down the aisle. He only had a few seconds.

He pulled his phone out. Quickly, he brought up his messages and checked his sent folder. Yep, there was one to Esther, sent the night before. He pulled it up and read it.

"Holy fucking hell."

He only realized he'd spoken out loud when Rusty elbowed him and Dan sent him an exasperated look. One of the maiden aunts in the front pews was glaring at him. He'd forgotten he was in church. He sent an apologetic glance to her, and then one up to the heavens. *Sorry.*

"What?" Rusty said.

Toby's heart hammered. "I sent Esther a text last night."

"So?" Dan's gaze was fixed on the doorway. Rusty frowned.

Toby swallowed. "Apparently I asked her to marry me."

Chapter Forty

The ceremony passed in a blur. Toby was vaguely aware of Eve arriving at the altar, glowing with happiness in her frothy white gown. He watched them exchange vows, and he sang along lustily with the hymns. But all the while, his mind was working furiously.

He'd proposed to Esther. Fucking hell, why had he done that? What on earth had possessed him to do it—and to do it over the phone, for God's sake? He could vaguely remember having a conversation with Rusty and Dan as the three of them had walked Dan back to his house. Something about them teasing him that he was the last bachelor and that nobody would ever love him because he was a Neanderthal. Esther didn't think he was a Neanderthal, he'd thought, and a surge of affection for her had prompted him to take out the phone and send her a message.

But had he said, Hey Esther, how are you doing, did you have a nice evening?

No, he'd simply texted, *Hey E. Miss you! Will u marry me? :-)*

Christ, he'd even finished with a fucking smiley face. What a dork.

He hadn't even bothered to type out her whole name. No wonder she'd looked so weird when he'd walked in that morning.

Throughout the ceremony, he'd managed to avoid looking at her. He knew if he did, he'd shrivel inside with mortification. At that moment, however, there was a scuffle in the pew, and he glanced over. Esther was speaking furiously to Charlie, who wriggled in her arms. As he watched, Charlie wrested free of her grip, slipped off the seat, and darted along the aisle toward him.

Esther turned crimson and sent Toby a horrified, apologetic look as she jumped to her feet, but Toby just smiled and held up his hand, and she sank back into the pew. He walked forward as Charlie climbed the steps, and lifted his son into his arms.

"Sorry," he said, aware the vicar had paused halfway through the vows.

Dan smiled and said, "No worries," and Eve grinned at him.

He walked away with Charlie into the south transept where it was cooler and quieter as the vicar continued to speak.

"Quiet now," he whispered to his son.

"What are they doing?" Charlie said in an amusingly fierce whisper.

"They're saying they love each other, and they're promising everyone in the church, and God, that they'll look after each other forever and ever." A tingle descended his spine.

"Oh," Charlie said. He rested his head on Toby's shoulder.

Toby kissed his curls, and against his will his gaze strayed across the aisle to where Esther sat. She'd been watching him, but dropped her gaze as he looked at her, cheeks flushing. He wondered if the butterflies dancing in his stomach were something to do with the hangover or whether they were connected to the text he'd sent.

How could he have been so stupid? Even if he'd meant it, he couldn't think of a less romantic way to ask a woman to marry him than to text it to her.

Had he meant it?

He listened to Dan's low voice as he proclaimed his intentions to Eve. "To love and to cherish as long as we both shall live. This is my solemn vow and promise."

Could he see himself doing the same with Esther? Telling her, telling everyone, including God, that he'd look after her, stay with her, love her forever?

Charlie nestled against him, and Toby tightened his arms around him. He had to think carefully about this. He mustn't mistake an overwhelming love for his son and a desire to protect him for love for Esther. Gone were the days when a couple had to get married because they had a child. Esther wouldn't want that, and neither did he. If he ever got married, he wanted to do it out of love and affection for his wife, not guilt or responsibility.

She looked up then, her gaze meeting his. She didn't smile. Eve was saying her vows now. Was Esther thinking the same as him? Wondering if it was something she would ever want to do?

She must have told Faith, judging by Faith's comment earlier that morning. Faith had realized he didn't remember sending the text, and she'd gone into the bedroom to tell Esther. And Esther hadn't mentioned it. Why would she? She would have known he was drunk when he sent it. Now she'd be waiting to see if he'd say it when he was sober. Was she hoping he'd ask her? Or dreading having to turn him down?

She'd already booked her flight to Dunedin for her interview. She hadn't discussed that at all with him. They hadn't yet had a conversation about the future and his role in Charlie's life, and she was already off planning her own life.

He couldn't blame her—she'd had a rough deal of it so far, had had to cope on her own for so long that she was used to looking out for herself. It made sense that she'd want to provide for herself and Charlie, and ensure she had a good job. It wasn't her fault Christchurch had had an earthquake and the university had closed for a while.

And, let's face it, at no point had she insinuated that she was looking for anything further from him. She'd made it quite clear at the start that they were just having sex, and she wasn't expecting anything more. Just because they were great in bed didn't mean she wanted to spend the rest of her life with him. How many times had he slept with women purely to satisfy a physical need?

In the corner of the church, the organist began playing, and the strains of "All Things Bright and Beautiful" filtered down the nave. It had been Dan and Faith's mother's favorite hymn, and Eve had been happy to have it for their last song.

Toby sang along to the words, aware that Charlie's thumb had crept into his mouth where he snuggled against his chest. The boy was probably exhausted from the excitement of the morning. He sang softly to him for a while, and then as the boy drowsed, said in his ear, "I'm going to take you back to Mummy now, okay?"

Charlie nodded sleepily, and Toby walked quietly back along the aisle to where Esther sat and handed his son over as the last strains of the song echoed through the church.

"Sorry," she whispered, her green eyes wide and apologetic.

"Don't worry. It was nice to have a cuddle." He smiled and kissed her forehead, then slipped back into place beside Rusty as the vicar asked for the rings.

Dan placed the ring on Eve's finger. "I, Daniel, give you, Eve, this ring as an eternal symbol of my love and commitment to you." She did the same to him, repeating the words and changing the names around.

Toby touched his thumb to his ring finger. How would it feel to wear that solid gold band, a visual reminder to everyone that he belonged to one woman, and she belonged to him? His gaze crept back to Esther, who crooned quietly to Charlie. How would he feel if she promised to love him forever?

The bright autumn sun shone through the stained glass, casting colored fragments of light like jewels onto the flagstones.

Toby's lips curved slowly into a smile.

The vicar gave his closing prayer, and then suddenly it was all over. Dan kissed Eve, and then they walked along the aisle to the smiles and cheers of their family and friends.

Rusty took the hand of Eve's sister, Carla, who was the other adult bridesmaid, and Toby held his arm up to Faith. She looked gorgeous in her slender blue dress, her bump only just visible.

She took his arm, and they followed Rusty and Carla down the aisle.

"That was nice," he said. He winked at Esther as they passed her in the pew.

"Lovely," Faith said. "I'm sorry we were late. Eve couldn't find the locket her grandmother gave her and she really wanted to wear it—it was her 'something old'. She found it in a drawer at the last minute. Was Dan panicking?"

"Yeah. He thought she'd got cold feet."

Faith laughed. "I guess everyone worries their partner won't turn up."

"Did you?" he asked, smiling and nodding at friends in the congregation.

"Of course. This is Rusty we're talking about. I expected all along that he would change his mind. I was more shocked that he *hadn't* vanished." For the first time in ages, she looked very young and unsure of herself.

Toby's heart went out to her. They'd known each other a long time, and he was very fond of her. "He never mentioned it once, Faith. He was nervous about the ceremony—which is crazy considering he stands up in front of his class twenty times a week—and he worried that you'd suddenly realize what a mistake you'd made, but he never, ever mentioned not turning up. And you should have seen his face when you appeared in the doorway in that dress. He could have lit the whole of Eden Park."

Faith bit her lip and to his surprise, her eyes filled with tears.

"Hey." He put his arm around her. They'd stopped walking while the photographer took photos of Dan and Eve in the doorway of the church. "What's this about?"

"Pregnancy hormones," she sniffed. "And weddings." She smiled brightly. "It's just… I wish Mum could be here and see how happy I am, and how happy Dan is."

Toby's throat tightened, and he hugged her. He kissed the top of her head. "I asked Esther to marry me," he mumbled.

She chuckled. "I know." She pushed herself back. "By text? So romantic, Toby."

Shame washed over him. Yet again he'd proved to his friends he was an idiot. "Was she embarrassed when the text came through?"

Faith studied him thoughtfully. "That's not quite the word I'd use, no."

"What—" But the photographer had finished, and they all moved out into the sunshine to have their photograph taken.

There was no time to speak to Faith alone again. For the next half hour, they were in and out of shots as the guests spilled onto the gardens overlooking the beautiful Kerikeri inlet. The sun beamed down on the water, and the kids played under the trees. It couldn't have been a more beautiful day.

And all the while, Toby's gaze strayed repeatedly to Esther as a plan formed slowly in his head.

Chapter Forty-One

Martha and Graham had bought some natural petal confetti, and they gave Esther a box while Rusty and Toby asked the guests to form a line to the waiting car.

"What's this?" Charlie asked when she took a handful out of the box.

"Confetti." She offered the box to him, and he plunged his tiny hand in it and opened and closed his fingers on the petals. "We throw it over Dan and Eve when they go past."

"Why?"

"Because it looks pretty. It's a tradition. It's been done at weddings for hundreds of years."

She smiled as Dan and Eve began to walk between the two lines of guests, Eve squealing when Carla managed to shove a handful of confetti down the front of her gown. It had been a relaxed and informal wedding, thank God, considering that Charlie had refused to sit still. And yet it had also been somehow strangely beautiful and ethereal with the bright Northland sun crowning the bride and groom with gold where they'd stood at the altar.

Or maybe it was just her mood. As the week had passed, her emotions had intensified, like a camera lens gradually bringing the moment into focus. For the last three years, she'd managed to convince herself she'd been mistaken about the powerful feelings she had for Toby. She'd blamed them on the holiday, because didn't holiday romances always end in disaster? And she'd told herself she couldn't possibly love him.

But once again, after only a week in his company, the tiny seed of affection had grown and bloomed, until all she could see and hear and think about was him, and how it felt when she was in his arms.

She'd nearly passed out when she walked into the church and saw him standing there, dressed in his best man's outfit. All men looked good in suits, she'd told herself desperately, but it didn't change the fact that she couldn't take her eyes off his broad shoulders in the long black coat. The silver waistcoat and tie emphasized his healthy tan and gave him an exotic, Mediterranean look, as if he were some kind of Greek or Italian prince. Her fingers itched to slip beneath the white shirt and touch the firm muscles she knew lay underneath. He looked like a movie star, and he'd drawn the eyes of every girl in the church. She couldn't believe she'd been to bed with him.

As Dan and Eve neared, she felt a pressure at her shoulder and turned to see Toby by her side. He reached across her for some confetti, saying mischievously, "Mind if I dip my fingers in your box?"

"Subtle," she said as he grinned, but she couldn't stop the smile creeping onto her lips. "Help yourself."

"I intend to," he murmured into her ear, stepping back as the bride and groom neared. She tried to ignore the answering shiver that trickled down her spine, and threw the confetti up over Dan, who stopped and bent his head so Charlie could add his small, sticky handful to the layer coating Dan's hair. Charlie squealed in delight, and Dan laughed and ruffled his hair.

They were such nice people, Toby's friends and family. She bit her lip and squeezed Charlie to her as the bride and groom had more photos taken by the car before sliding inside. It had been nice to have a brief glimpse of how things could have been in an alternative world, with a network of people around her rather than it just being her and Charlie. But she had to remember it wasn't her world. She was just window shopping—that was all.

*

She tried to remind herself of that fact repeatedly as the day wore on, but it was difficult when all around her everyone was so friendly and welcoming, including her in their social circle as if she'd always been around.

She returned with Martha and Graham to the hotel where the happy couple were holding the reception, and sat with them during the wedding meal. She enjoyed Toby's and Rusty's witty speeches when they teased Dan and Eve and told bawdy jokes. She made the most of the beautiful menu crafted by Eve's chef cousin, Fox, inspired by Kiwi "fusion" cuisine—dishes from across the world incorporating New Zealand ingredients.

When the dancing started, Esther watched Toby have the first dance with Faith while Rusty danced with Carla. She wasn't jealous at the sight of another woman in Toby's arms because it was so glaringly obvious how much in love Faith was with her husband. Sure enough, after the first song finished, Rusty was quick to pass Carla onto her boyfriend so he could get his hands on his wife.

Esther watched them dance to a slow, romantic number, her throat tightening as Rusty nuzzled Faith's ear and she giggled in response, pressing up against him. Faith's tiny bump was barely visible beneath her slinky dress, but nobody could be in any doubt as to her condition if they watched the way her husband fussed over her. He wouldn't let her lift anything heavier than a glass, fetched her a chair to put her feet up on when she finally sat down for a few minutes, brought her a plate of nibbles from the running buffet, and generally acted as though she was the center of his world—which indeed she seemed to be.

How would it have felt to have Toby there with her when she was pregnant with Charlie? She could remember struggling to load her shopping from the trolley into her car at the supermarket. Having to walk miles to her apartment when her car broke down because she couldn't afford to get it fixed. Spending long, lonely hours in the hospital when the baby was due because she couldn't think of a single person she could call to be with her. At the time, she'd reveled in her loneliness, using it as a shield to protect herself, grateful that she didn't have anyone to think about except herself.

For the first time, however, sitting there watching Rusty and Faith, Esther finally acknowledged what a farce it had all been. She hadn't been single out of choice—it hadn't been a noble decision as an independent, modern woman to have her child alone. She'd been forced into the predicament, and she'd made the best of it she could.

But she would have killed to be in Faith's position—treasured, treated as if she were the most precious thing in the whole world because she was having her husband's baby.

Her breath caught in her throat, and she took a sip of wine, forcing herself to swallow it down. It was too late for self-pity. She'd lasted this long on her own—she could make it a few more years. Maybe when Charlie was older and a bit more self-reliant, she'd meet someone and allow herself to fall in love again.

A shadow fell over her, and she looked up to see Toby standing there, hand extended toward her. "Like to dance?" he said, smiling.

She glanced across at Charlie, but he was occupied with some of the other children, joining them in skidding across the wooden dance floor in his socks. Ten-to-one he'd fall over and start wailing before the hour was out, but for the moment he was happy, following one of Eve's nephews around. The boy was a few years older than Charlie and happy to boss the youngsters into playing his game.

Toby had taken off the black coat and rolled up the sleeves of his white shirt, but he still wore the silver waistcoat and tie. His eyes were gentle, as if he'd seen the sad thoughts passing through her mind. He looked strong and healthy and dazzling—if the archangel Michael had been best man at Gabriel's wedding, he might have looked something like this.

And that's when she knew. She'd fallen in love with him—again. Or maybe she'd never stopped. Like falling into a deep well, plunging far to the bottom until the light of freedom was a tiny speck way off in the distance. How was she going to climb back out this time?

He reached down and picked up her hand, and then bent and kissed her fingers. "Come on. Dance with me."

She stood obediently and followed him onto the dance floor, but all the while her mind worked furiously. How could she have been so stupid? How many times had she told herself this was supposed to be just a physical arrangement? She should have kept herself distant and her heart intact. But maybe it was foolish to have ever thought that was going to happen. She'd fallen for the man in a fortnight when he was a stranger—what hope had she had once his child had grown inside her?

He led her to the middle of the floor, and even though it wasn't a particularly slow song, he turned her to face him and brought her close. Her right hand nestled in his left, and he put his right hand around her waist as he began to move her to the music.

"This is hardly a smoochy song," she complained to take her mind off the gentle affection in his eyes. The heavy bass tried to persuade them to move faster.

"Don't care," he said. He pulled her even closer. "I want you in my arms, even if they're playing Iron Maiden."

Where had her breath gone? He'd somehow stolen it from her. He was so tall and broad—he oozed masculinity, with his five o'clock shadow on his tanned skin, his unruly black curls, and his sexy smile. She wanted to get him into bed.

She wanted to cry.

A puzzled frown marred his forehead. "You look sad."

"Weddings always make me sad."

"Why?"

Because statistics said many marriages ended unhappily and deep down, she was an old romantic. Because she knew many of the people present there that evening, and their generosity and affection had touched her more than she'd thought possible.

Because she would probably never have a happy ever after like this.

She looked away and forced a smile on her face. "Look at him. Little maniac."

Toby followed her gaze and laughed at the sight of Charlie dancing, encouraged by one of the little girls, who'd taken him under her wing. "He'll sleep well tonight." His gaze moved back to her. "Which will please my parents. Unless you'd rather keep Charlie in your room." He brushed the back of his fingers against her cheek. "It's up to you."

She swallowed, suddenly uncertain. Maybe he'd changed his mind. "Do you still want me?"

He studied her. "Do I still want you?" Impatience lit his eyes. "You really have to ask me that? Standing there wearing not a stitch of underwear beneath that slinky dress?"

She couldn't stop the smile stealing onto her lips. "I take that as a yes."

"Yes, Esther Tyler." He touched his lips to her temple. "Yes, whether you're wearing slinky dresses or jeans and a T-shirt or nothing at all, I'll always want you."

She closed her eyes. It was just a figure of speech.

"Besides," he murmured, his breath now warm on her ear. "We have our Naughty Night role-play to carry out."

"Mm." She was getting distracted. His hand had slid onto her butt. And in spite of her wish to stay distant, her nipples had hardened where they brushed against his chest.

"Guess what I brought with me," he asked softly.

"I've no idea…" She shivered as he nibbled her earlobe.

"Silk scarves," he whispered. "To tie you up while I torture you for information."

Her eyes flew open. "Toby!"

"What?" He gave her a wide-eyed, innocent look. "Don't you like that idea?"

Her heart pounded at the thought of being completely at his mercy. "Um…"

He kissed her. "I want you," he murmured. "Stay with me tonight." He kissed her again, his warm lips lingering on hers. "Let me pleasure you."

She was going to melt into a puddle at his feet if she didn't stop this soon. It was all about sex, she told herself. And that she could cope with.

"Okay, Mr. Seductive." She slid her hand into his hair and kissed him back. There was never any question of her refusing him. Although she hated herself for it, she'd always take what he was willing to offer of himself until he decided it was time to move on. And once she accepted that, maybe things would go a little smoother.

Chapter Forty-Two

The rest of the evening passed in a blur with the promise of what was to come hovering over her. When Charlie finally crashed, she went up to Martha and Graham's room with them to settle him. They decided to retire themselves and took him into bed with them, turning the TV on and cuddling up together to watch *The Simpsons*. Charlie cuddled Bear and waved goodbye to Esther, and she left with a smile, touched that he felt so comfortable with his grandparents, and that they seemed to love him so unconditionally.

She returned to the hall and rejoined the party, and spent a pleasant couple of hours with the others, dancing and eating and drinking until the hour grew late.

Gradually people started to make their way to their rooms, and the party began to wind down. Dan and Eve weren't leaving for Rarotonga until the next morning, so they stayed until the end, saying goodbye to their guests. Faith went up a bit earlier, worn out and with aching legs, but Rusty remained to make sure everything was in order and those guests who weren't staying had successfully found themselves taxis.

Esther stood in the foyer and removed her shoes, flexing her aching feet as she waited for the others to say goodbye to Eve's old grandparents. Her body ached a little and the alcohol was beginning to have an effect on her, but the thought of going to bed with Toby kept the adrenalin pumping.

He joined the others at the doorway, and she leaned her head on the doorpost and watched him fondly, wondering if Charlie would grow up to look like him. How often would she get to see him once he started university? Obviously only during the holidays, and he'd have to split those between time with her and the rest of his family up in the bay.

The group of them at the door finished saying goodbye to the guests and came into the foyer.

"Oh well, I guess that's it," Eve said sadly. "My special day's finally over."

"We still have breakfast with our guests tomorrow," Dan reminded her as he put his arms around her. "And besides, the evening's not over yet." He whispered something in her ear and squeezed her butt, and she giggled.

The rest of them laughed. "Come on," Rusty said, "let's go up to our rooms. I want to check on Faith."

Toby and Esther crowded into the elevator with the rest of them—Dan and Eve, Rusty, Carla and her partner, and a couple of others including Toby's brother Felix, who'd turned up for the reception. Rusty pressed the button for the floor where they were all staying. Toby leaned against the wall and pulled Esther to him, her back to his chest. He wrapped his arms around her, and she relaxed contentedly while the elevator ascended. If she didn't think about it too much, she could almost imagine they were a married couple, and that she belonged here, with his friends.

It was a nice fantasy.

The elevator dinged, and they spilled out into the corridor. Dan bent and lifted Eve into his arms, a pile of white lace and satin, and she squealed. "Dan!"

"I'm going to carry you over the threshold," he explained. "Behave."

Everyone else led the way to their suite, laughing, and Toby swiped their keycard and opened the door for them. Dan carried her in—just missing hitting her head on the post by an inch—and then he stopped and they both stared at the confetti-strewn duvet littered with pillows in the shape of love hearts, cuddly toys with "Happily Married Couple" embroidered on their clothing, and balloons tied to the end of the bed.

"Enjoy," Toby said, smiling.

"Don't do anything we wouldn't do." Rusty winked as Dan smiled wryly, and he closed the door on them.

"Did you two do that?" Esther asked them.

"Some of it. We—" Toby stopped as, from behind the door, Eve gave a huge squeal and yelled "We're married!" and they all burst out laughing.

"I'm off to find my wife," Rusty said. "I miss her."

"Yeah, you've been apart all of fifteen minutes." Toby grinned and held out his hand. "I enjoyed today. Glad you were there."

"Me too." They shook hands. Esther swallowed, touched at how close they were.

Rusty waved to the others. "Good night."

Carly took her partner's hand and said goodnight too. Felix sighed. "Well, I guess I'm off to bed. Alone again, naturally. I thought there'd be a bridesmaid to cop off with, but no luck. They're all taken." He raised an eyebrow at Esther. "What are you up to? Need someone to scrub your back in the shower?"

Esther giggled as Toby glowered at him, and she patted Felix's arm. "Don't worry, there's someone out there for you."

"Yeah, some girl who's escaped from a mental institution," Toby grumbled.

Felix gave him the finger and walked off, muttering to himself. Toby laughed, grabbed Esther's hand, and pulled her toward their room.

"Poor Felix," Esther said. "He's a nice guy—he deserves a nice girl."

"He's very rarely short of company," Toby said, swiping his keycard. "Don't feel sorry for him. Besides which, he has a practiced right hand, don't worry."

"Toby!"

He chuckled and opened the door. "After you."

She went into the room and he followed her. The door shut behind them with a soft snick.

Immediately, her heart began to hammer, but she kept her cool and tried not to act nervous. She placed her shoes by the bag she'd brought up earlier and turned on the soft lighting over the bed. Toby went over to the fridge and extracted a bottle of wine. He poured two glasses and brought them over to where she stood with hands folded in an attempt to stop them shaking.

She took the glass and sipped the cold Sauvignon, hoping the alcohol would help her to relax a little. The several glasses she'd had during the course of the evening didn't seem to have affected her at all, and she could really do with some Dutch courage.

Toby stood before her, hand in his pocket, and took a swallow of his wine. He was so much taller than her when she took her shoes off. She looked up at him to see him surveying her. He'd hung his jacket over the chair, and her fingers itched to touch his silver waistcoat, then slide underneath and feel his muscles through the white shirt. His dark hair was ruffled, and his eyes had the sultry look of a man who'd drunk enough glasses of whisky to let the naughty side of him out.

"Stop smirking," she said uncomfortably.

"I'm not smirking. I'm amused."

"At what?"

"You. You look nervous."

"I am nervous," she said nervously. "You make me nervous."

"Even after all we've done?"

"Maybe because of that." She took another hasty swallow of wine and licked her lips, not missing the way his gaze fell to them. "And because you keep doing that."

"What?"

"Looking at me like you're lost in the desert and I'm an oasis."

He chuckled, finished off his wine and placed his glass on the table. Then he bent to place his lips against her throat. "I can see your pulse racing." He touched his tongue to her skin, and she shivered. "Mm," he said. "Do that again."

"I thought you were supposed to be interrogating me."

"Oh, I will." He kissed up to her jaw, then along to her lips. Sliding his right hand into her hair, he cupped her head. "But I've been waiting all night to kiss you properly."

"Oh…" That was the last word she could utter, as then his lips were on hers and all thoughts fled her mind. He wrapped his arms around her, pulling her tightly to him, and kissed her. First his lips were gentle, placing light butterfly kisses on her lips and cheeks. She let him, trying not to sigh, enjoying the way he overwhelmed her with his masculinity, from the brush of bristles against her cheek, to the taste of whisky in his mouth, to the firmness of his muscles beneath her free hand where she pressed it to his chest.

And then, when he brushed his tongue across her lips, she opened them to welcome it inside. And it seemed to fire something up between them, causing his fingers to tighten on her butt and knot in her hair as he plunged his tongue into her mouth. They both groaned, and Esther couldn't stop herself pushing up against the hard length that pressed on her stomach. She needed him inside her.

There was no point in denying it. Whatever he wanted, she'd comply, like a remote-controlled toy to which he possessed the controls.

He lifted his head, eyes gleaming in the dull light. "God, you're sexy," he murmured, running his hands down her body. "All night I've thought about the fact that you're not wearing any underwear beneath this. It's been driving me crazy."

"I'm glad," she said, breathless. "Because the sight of you in that suit has driven me nuts."

He chuckled and pulled back. "So we're even." He cupped her cheek, and bent and kissed her lips lightly. "Maybe I should keep the suit."

Bitterness made her clench her hand on his chest. What was the point when she was going away? She lowered her gaze to her fist and forced herself to relax, smoothing her palm against the silky waistcoat. She had to concentrate on tonight, nothing more.

"So," she said lightly. "Where do we start?"

Chapter Forty-Three

Her heart increased its rate again as the heat level rose in Toby's eyes.

"Hmm," he said. He walked over to his bag and rummaged around, then withdrew an item and turned to show it to her. It was a weird hat, like an army officer's peaked cap but made out of a shiny silver fabric. It looked like something Peter Cushing might have worn in *Star Wars*.

He pulled it on, raised an eyebrow and waited for her reaction.

She giggled. "Where did you get that?"

"Rusty got it from the drama department at his school." He pulled the peak down a little. "Now, Miss Tyler, I understand you know the secret code to the rebel forces' hidden base." Clearly, he'd also thought that the hat looked like something George Lucas might have designed. She had to bite her lip to stop the giggles.

Tossing back her hair, she gave him her best rebellious stare. "Yes, and we're going to destroy the Empire's Death Star. What are you going to do about it?"

Warmth spread through her as he smiled. Or was it the alcohol finally beginning to have an effect? No, it was definitely the look in his eyes.

He ran his gaze down her, lingering insolently on her breasts before returning to her face. She'd thought the hat looked funny at first, but oddly, as he continued to study her and a look of determination replaced his smile, she didn't have much trouble imagining what he would have looked like as a real bad guy. Her amusement fled as she began to wonder how he was going to torture her.

She swallowed the remainder of her wine, and he took the glass and put it on the table next to his own. He moved away, leaving her standing there, put his hands behind his back and surveyed her silently.

She fidgeted, picking at her fingernails, uncertain what he wanted her to do.

"Stand still," he said.

Her heart slammed against her ribs at his soft but authoritative tone. She dropped her hands, and he nodded with approval.

"I'm glad to see you're going to be cooperative." He walked slowly around her. "My superiors assure me you know the secret code. You are going to tell me that code."

"I won't tell you anything," she said rebelliously.

He stopped walking and bent to whisper in her ear, "Oh, yes you will."

Every single piece of her stood on end in heightened awareness of him. The Naughty Nights card had included an added instruction for the woman involved in this role-play. She had to think of a piece of information he didn't know about her, and try to keep it from him as he tortured her. It hadn't been difficult to come up with a secret. But she was determined not to tell him. Surely she could hold out against whatever he did to her?

He walked to his bag again and extracted something else—a silk scarf—then brought it over to her. "Temporarily," he said, his eyes warm. He folded it into a narrow band and placed it around her eyes, tying it at the back of her head. "And so it begins," he murmured in her ear.

"Toby..." She swallowed. Her mouth had gone dry. Her world was now dark, and all her other senses strained toward him.

"You can call me 'sir'," he instructed. His deep voice reverberated through her, while the scent of him—whisky, warm male, and aftershave—filled her nostrils.

"Yes, sir," she whispered.

Fingers brushed up her arms, arousing goose bumps on her skin. "Much as I adore this slinky dress," he said, "it's time to see that beautiful body of yours." He moved behind her and unzipped the garment. "Raise your arms."

She did so, aware of him grasping the hem. The cool material slid up her thighs, rustled over her hips and skated across her breasts as he lifted it over her head. It dropped to the floor in a sigh of satin, and her nipples tightened instinctively at the sensation of standing naked in front of him.

He walked around her, his feet almost silent on the carpet, and stopped. She waited, heart thumping. She wasn't quite sure where he was, and automatically crossed her arms over her breasts.

"Now, now," he said from just in front of her. "I told you to stand still. If you don't cooperate, I will have to punish you." He sounded amused.

She shivered and dropped her arms to her sides. He moved away and she heard him rummaging in his bag. There were various rustling noises, and at one point footsteps sounded behind her as he walked to the bed. She remained standing, vulnerable and exposed, but forced herself not to move. He was trying to unnerve her, and she was determined not to make it easy for him.

He came back to her, took her hand and, to her surprise, turned her in a circle a few times.

"Are we playing Blind Man's Bluff?" she asked, puzzled.

He chuckled. "Just trying to disorient you."

It worked—she had no idea which way she was facing. He led her forward a few steps, then turned her around again.

He was behind her now, and the bed squeaked as he sat.

"Move back," he said. "Carefully."

She did so until the mattress bumped against her legs.

"Sit," he said. He placed his hands on her hips and guided her down.

She realized she was between his legs, and as she sat, her butt nestled between his thighs on the bed. The mattress met the back of her knees. He was still dressed—the buttons of his shirt touched her skin between her shoulder blades and his erection pressed against her through the fabric of his pants.

She felt slightly less vulnerable within the circle of his arms, however, safe and protected by his strong, broad frame. He placed a kiss on her shoulder. "You really are very beautiful," he said, his voice husky.

"You're going to have to work harder than that to get me to divulge information," she replied, although inside she glowed at his compliment.

He chuckled. "I'm working on it." He shifted, and then his arms came around her. Something slid beneath her right leg, soft and silky. Another scarf. What was he doing? His hands moved deftly, and the material tightened on her leg, although not uncomfortably. He did the same thing to her left leg, sliding a piece of material beneath it, tying it on the other side. The inside of his thighs pressed against the outside of hers, warm even through the material of his pants.

Next he took one of her wrists and looped yet another scarf around it, tying it securely. Her heart began to pound again. Now what?

"I hope you got a discount on all those scarves," she said, nerves making her flippant.

He kissed her shoulder again, but didn't answer her this time. He tied the other end of the scarf around her left wrist. She moved them—they were about eight inches apart.

"Lift your arms," he said.

She raised them in front of her. He took her wrists and moved them up over her head and then over his hair until the scarf rested on the back of his neck. The position forced her to arch her back as she stretched out along him, and she gasped as he slid his arms around her waist and stroked up her ribcage. Her breasts lay exposed and open to his touch, and her nipples tightened again as he brushed around them with light fingers.

For a moment, she thought she couldn't have been more vulnerable. But she'd forgotten about the scarves tied around her thighs. Behind her, he opened his legs, and with shock she realized he'd tied their thighs together, so she had to widen her knees to follow him. She lay open to him, defenceless and stripped bare of her decency as well as her clothes.

"Toby!" Her breasts heaved, and she tried to calm her rapid breathing.

In answer, he ran his fingers up the inside of her thighs, stopping just before he reached her most sensitive parts. "What did I say you should call me?" he demanded.

"Sorry... sir." She bit her lip. At least she was facing away from him. Yes, this was a little undignified and humiliating with everything on show, but there was something incredibly erotic about being in his control like this, too.

"Good." He stroked up her sides, circled her breasts, and continued to graze up her ribcage and under her arms. She squirmed against him, and he grunted when she pressed back against his erection. "Sit still."

"I can't. You're tickling me."

"I have to torture you. It's in the rules. Mwahaha."

She wriggled again as he stroked downward this time, his fingers so light on the sensitive skin of her upper arms that shivers ran all the way through her. "Ooh. Stop it."

He brushed his palms more firmly back down to her waist. Then he brought his hands up to cup her breasts. "Is this better?"

She said nothing, automatically holding her breath. His hands were warm as he squeezed and lifted her breasts, weighing them in his palms. He ran his thumbs over her nipples, and she shuddered. *Uh-oh.*

"Uh-oh what?"

She hadn't realized she'd said it out loud. "N-nothing."

"Come now, Miss Tyler. You know you want to tell me your secret." He flicked her nipples with his thumbs.

"I won't," she whispered. "You can't make me talk."

"We'll see."

He took her nipples between his thumbs and forefingers and pulled them gently, stretching them until she gave a shocked "Oh!" and arched her back with a groan.

"What?" His voice was all innocence. "Sorry, Miss Tyler. Do you not like that?"

She was in serious trouble. He'd only just started, and she was so turned on, she was close to telling him every secret she'd ever known in her entire life. How embarrassing—she had to last ten minutes at least, or she'd never hear the end of it.

Besides which, she didn't want to tell him her secret. She'd have to make something up if she came close to giving in, because she couldn't possibly divulge the piece of information she'd been thinking of.

He plucked her nipples again. "Talk to me, Miss Tyler."

"Oh... what... what do you want me to say?"

"Tell me your secret."

"N-no."

He kissed her neck, then fastened his mouth where it joined her shoulder and sucked, hard.

"Ouch! Oh jeez, another hickey."

He licked the place where he'd bitten, his tongue warm and wet. "Tell me."

"No. God, please."

He chuckled. "He's not coming to help you." He pulled and stretched her nipples again, almost to the point of pain, and she was just about to cry out when he released them.

"Oh... oh no..."

Something brushed her lips—his thumb. She shook her head, keeping her mouth shut tight. In reply, he pinched her nipple and she gasped, and he slid his thumb between her lips.

She moaned as he swept the digit across her tongue, unable to stop herself sucking it, and he gave an answering growl before taking it out. He slid his other thumb between her lips. This time she didn't try to stop him but welcomed the invasion, sucking fiercely and moaning again as she clenched deep inside.

He removed it and brushed both of them across her nipples, deploying the wetness there. She caught her breath, knowing how sensitive it was going to make the delicate skin. Sure enough, this time when he rolled them with his fingers, the answering shockwave rippled right through her, and she arched her back again, pushing her breasts into his hands.

"Ready to talk yet?" he murmured, stretching and plucking at her nipples.

"No... oh, stop..."

He didn't, though, continuing his relentless torture until she writhed against him, aching inside.

Then he lifted his hands. She almost sobbed, partly from relief, partly from disappointment. But this time, his fingers brushed down her body to her knees. Then, slowly, they travelled back up her inner thighs.

"Look at you," he said softly, drawing light circles on her skin. "All open and swollen, ready for me."

Fingers brushed her pubic hair and she jumped.

"Sit still," he demanded.

"Sorry, sir." She was nearly panting now.

He brushed her hair again. Then his warm fingers slid down into the heart of her. They moved easily, so she knew she was slick with desire, and he groaned as he slipped them deep inside her.

"You're so wet," he said, kissing her neck, nibbling her ear. "Who'd have thought being tortured would turn you on so much?"

"Don't embarrass me," she said, cheeks burning. "You're so rude."

He chuckled. "Tell me the secret and I'll stop."

"No."

"Fair enough." He slid his fingers out of her and his arm moved. Then there was the distinct sound of him sucking.

"Toby!" She squirmed against him, clenching her fingers in his hair. "God, you're so wicked."

"Not half as wicked as I'm going to be." He slid his fingers back inside her, then brought them up again. "If you're not going to call me sir, I'm going to punish you. Open your mouth."

She pressed back against him, away from his hand. "No…"

But he was already slipping his fingers between her lips and when she opened them, he brushed them inside, filling her mouth with the salty, musky taste of her own arousal. Everything inside her clenched, and she moaned, growing desperate for release.

He removed his fingers and lifted his hands to the back of her head. "Time for this to come off, I think." He untied the scarf around her head and let it fall to the bed.

Chapter Forty-Four

She opened her eyes and blinked, then stared, shocked. They were sitting on the side of the bed, facing the built-in closets. What she hadn't realized was that the doors were mirrors, and they were only six feet away. Where she sat stretched out against him, she was totally exposed to his gaze, her breasts full and high with the rosy nipples wet and puckered, the area between her legs glistening with her moisture. Her nakedness seemed all the more evident because he was fully clothed, having removed only his shoes and tie. He still wore the hat, and his eyes glittered in the shadows cast by the peak.

She stared with horror, her face growing scarlet. "You've been watching me all this time."

He met her eyes in the mirror. "Oh yes. And I'm so turned on now that when we're done here, I'm going to fuck you five ways till Friday, so you'd better be prepared."

She shivered, her nipples tightening again, and tried to close her legs, but it was like trying to move two tree trunks. He chuckled. "Not a chance, sweetheart. I'm enjoying the view. And now I have something else to try on you."

He reached behind him and brought an item back. It was an electric toothbrush.

She blinked. "Are you going to give me a dental hygiene lesson now?"

He grinned. "Not quite, no. I don't have a vibrator, so I'm improvising." He held the toothbrush up and pressed the button, and it started buzzing. He met her gaze, his eyes gleaming.

"No," she said firmly.

He raised an eyebrow. "Going to tell me your secret?"

"Um, no."

"Well then." He lowered the body of the toothbrush onto her nipple.

She squealed and wriggled against him, but he tightened his other arm around her, and eventually she gave in. She obviously wasn't going anywhere. Closing her eyes, she bit her lip and tried to think about something else, but it was no good, the sensations were too intense. She dug her fingers into his hair and moaned as he transferred the toothbrush to the other nipple for a while, then back again.

"Nice?" he murmured, kissing her neck.

"No."

"Liar." He dropped his other hand between her legs and slid his fingers into her. "You're so wet, baby, you can't lie to me."

She cursed and tried to close her legs again, to no avail. "This is so humiliating."

"I hope so. The best sex always is." He bit her ear and she squealed. "Watch," he instructed.

She opened her eyes. He moved her forward a little so he could widen his legs farther, stretching hers apart until there was nothing left to hide. He'd been circling his fingers at the top of her legs, but when he saw her eyes open, he lowered his fingers down into her, and she groaned as he moved them in and out. God, that was sexy, watching him fuck her with his fingers, slow and rhythmically. Every now and again he slid them deep inside her, stroking the front wall of her vagina, and she squirmed and moaned. His hand glistened, coated with her moisture. When he finally raised it, she almost exclaimed a protest.

He slid the handle of the toothbrush down her stomach to between her legs.

The vibrations sent tremors all the way through her, little ripples of ecstasy, and she cried out with pleasure. He circled it slowly on her clit, which throbbed in response, and she panted as everything started to tighten.

He lifted the handle. "Steady now. We're not ready yet."

"Fuck you," she snapped, frustrated.

"Later, sweetheart." He lowered the handle again. "Now, what about this secret?"

"Get lost."

He pushed the handle lower, right into her soft folds, and she moaned. "Toby…"

"Sir," he corrected. "Bad girl." He plucked at her nipple with his other hand, squeezing and stretching it so she squirmed in his arms.

Yet again, though, as she began to clench inside, he lifted his hands and waited until the quivers inside her died away.

She leaned her head back against his shoulder and groaned deeply. "I hate you."

He chuckled in her ear, flicking the toothbrush over her nipples. "Mm. I know."

She sank her hands into his hair. If she wanted, she could easily lift the scarf over his head and untie the ones around her legs. She wasn't really a prisoner here. But the sensations were exquisite, and she didn't really want to move.

He dipped the handle below again to tease her, alternating between that and her nipples, light, tantalizing touches, lifting his hands away each time her breathing grew irregular and her thighs tightened.

Eventually he turned off the toothbrush and dropped it behind him. He smoothed his hands over her body as if he were honing wood, brushing down her ribs, over her hips, along her legs.

"Your body's fucking fantastic," he murmured, stroking between her legs while he flicked her nipples. "It's taking all my self-control not to throw you on the bed and take you."

"Do it," she begged, aching and throbbing, desperate to have him inside her.

"Oh no." He lifted a hand to turn her face toward him. Touching his lips to hers, he said, "You still haven't told me your secret."

"No, don't make me," she begged.

"Tell me." He played with her nipples, rolling them, tugging and pulling them, and she clenched deep inside. But release remained out of reach all the time he refused to touch between her legs. Or did it? She thought she might come anyway, even though he wasn't touching her. She was so close.

He rested his hands on her waist. "If you come without telling me your secret, I'll just start all over again."

"Toby…"

"What did I tell you about calling me sir?" He pinched her nipples, stretching them until she cried out. She knew nothing about the boundaries between pleasure and pain, had never guessed such torture could be so pleasurable.

"Fuck." She panted, her mind spinning in a sexual haze. She hardly recognized the writhing, flushed creature in the mirror. "Please... sir... Let me come."

"No." He stroked her body, then plucked her nipples again, twisting them gently. "Tell me."

"I... I can't..."

He stroked feather-light between her legs, avoiding her swollen clit, then slid his fingers inside her, but didn't move them. She tried to grind herself against them, but he withdrew them again and sucked casually on them as he met her gaze in the mirror, smirking. Her cheeks burned. The kinky bastard really wasn't going to let her come until she confided her secret.

She nearly cried. It was time to make up a code word to tell him, a rude word or something. But as she turned her head to look up at him, his eyes were alight with desire and affection, and the truth slipped out before she could stop it.

"I love you."

His eyes widened. For a brief moment, he just stared at her, clearly astonished. He obviously hadn't expected that.

Then one side of his mouth quirked up. "The torture works," he said, adjusting the hat. He kissed her cheek, then her mouth. "Come on baby. Come for me."

He stroked between her legs while playing with her nipple with his other hand. Her orgasm hit, and he slid his fingers deep inside her, pressing on her clit with his thumb. Her muscles pulsed in slow, exquisite waves, and she arched against him, crying out, knowing he was watching her in the mirror, but unable to do anything about it.

Eventually the pulses died away, and he withdrew his fingers and deftly untied the scarves around her thighs and behind her head. She relaxed limply, and he stroked her arms and planted soft kisses on her shoulder and up to her ear as her heart rate gradually slowed.

She closed her eyes, unable to believe she'd told him. But the fact was that she could easily have admitted something else, some personal piece of information that didn't involve telling him her deepest feelings for him. Deep down, she'd wanted him to know how she felt about him. Because this beautiful night was going to come to an end, and then it would be too late. He had to know, before he found out the even bigger secret she'd kept from him, the one that would destroy any feelings he'd ever had for her.

She nestled against him, content and warm in his arms. His erection continued to press, long and firm, against her lower back, but he made no move on her, bless him, content to wait until she was ready.

She licked her lips and met his gaze in the mirror. Now she'd told him how she felt, it was as if a weight had lifted from her heart. She'd opened fully to him, physically and emotionally, and there was nothing else she could do.

"Right," she said, wiggling her hips and pressing back. "What did you say about fucking me into Friday?"

Chapter Forty-Five

Toby smiled wryly as Esther squirmed against his erection. He'd had a hard-on for what seemed like hours, and he was desperate to plunge into her. She was incredibly swollen and wet, and he knew it was going to feel like heaven when he eventually slid inside her. But he'd enjoyed teasing her, taking her to the brink.

Her revelation had stunned him, though. He'd thought she was going to tell him some jest about her favorite form of chocolate or something. Instead she'd rocked his world with her declaration, three little words he'd never expected her to say.

In truth, he didn't know what to make of them. He knew she wanted him, that she desired him, that she enjoyed being with him. But that she loved him? What did it mean? Did she want to stay with him? Be a part of his life? And how did he feel about that?

It wasn't the right time to talk or even think about it, but he filed it away in his head for later. Now, he just wanted to fill his senses with her—touch, taste, smell her.

He lifted the cap off his head and put it on her. "You're in charge," he said. "What do you want me to do?"

She lifted a hand to touch his cheek and kissed him. "You can just sit there."

He started to unbutton his shirt, but she shook her head and pushed herself to her feet. "Leave it on," she said, looking adorable where she stood with hands on hips, wearing only the officer's cap. He was warm in his clothes, but happy to follow her instructions if it turned her on.

She climbed onto the bed and smiled mischievously. Then she sat astride him—facing away.

His kissed her shoulder as she began to unbutton his pants. "Reverse cowgirl, Miss Tyler?"

"Is that what it's called?" She giggled and unzipped his fly. Then she pushed down his boxers and freed his erection.

She gave him a long, slow stroke, and he groaned and flopped back on the bed. He held her hips as she lifted up, positioned herself above him, then sank slowly down, letting him slide deep within her.

He closed his eyes. "Fuck."

She chuckled and rocked her hips. "Is that nice, sweetheart?"

He lifted his arms over his head on the bed, enjoying the feeling of being encased in her wet warmth. "It's fucking unbelievable."

"Your language is shocking." She continued to rock her hips, driving him in and out. "I should punish you for that." She lifted up, letting him slide almost out of her, and teased the tip of him for a moment.

He groaned and shifted on the bed, turning slightly so he could see their reflection. She had a blissful look on her face, her eyes closed, and as he watched she tipped back her head and her hair tumbled between her shoulders.

He let her ride him for a while, enjoying the view, especially when she began to play with her nipples, but it wasn't enough—he wanted to drive into her.

Holding her by the hips, he lifted her up off him, making her squeal, then sat up and grabbed her by the waist. He turned her effortlessly onto her hands and knees on the bed, stood and stripped, then knelt behind her.

She cast him a remonstrative look over her shoulder. "I thought I was in charge." She'd knocked the hat, and it sat askew on her dark hair.

"Sorry, ma'am." He guided himself into her. "I lied." He thrust forward, burying himself deep inside her, and she gasped and clenched around him.

"I'm—wearing—the hat," she said in between thrusts. "I thought—it gave me—the power."

"You'll always have power over me." He leaned forward and fondled her breasts while he thrust.

"That's—not what—I meant," she complained, widening her knees so he could thrust deeper. "Oh…"

"Are you complaining?" He smacked her rump.

"Ouch!"

He laughed and pulled out of her, then got to his feet and drew her up with him. He moved her over to the wall, pushing her up against it with a bump, then took her face in his hands. "You are just sublime, you know that?"

She flushed prettily. "And you're insatiable tonight."

"I told you, five ways till Friday." He put his hands under her butt and lifted her, and before she could say anything, he slid inside her up to the hilt. "That's position three."

"Oh my God, Toby Wilkinson, you'll be the death of me." She grasped his shoulders as he began to thrust. "Oh dear Lord."

He kissed her. "You want me to stop?"

"Oh fuck no."

He laughed and plunged into her, so thoroughly enjoying himself that he didn't want to stop ever. They were both covered in sweat, and her breathing, like his, was beginning to grow ragged.

He slowed his pace, not wanting them to come just yet. Lifting her off the wall, he carried her over to the bed and lowered her down, still inside her. The hat fell off but she left it, her hair sticking damply to her forehead.

He began to move more leisurely, taking the time to enjoy the sensations of her around him. He tasted the sweat between her breasts and kissed her deeply, his tongue playing with hers until her sighs turned to moans and she began to meet him thrust for thrust.

He lifted his head. "Four," he said.

Her glazed eyes studied him. "And number five?"

"You choose." He kissed her nose.

"From behind," she whispered. "Lying down."

He withdrew and turned her over, tucked a pillow under her hips and pushed up her knee. She pulled another pillow down to hug as he slid inside her. They both sighed. Facing the mirror, they had a perfect view, and she turned her head to watch him move behind her.

"You like it this way?" he murmured, nuzzling her neck as he thrust.

"Mmm." Her eyelids fluttered shut briefly. "I like feeling…"

Her words trailed off and she opened her eyes, meeting his gaze in the mirror.

"Feeling…" he prompted, moving inside her leisurely.

She turned her face into the pillow. "Nothing."

"Don't make me torture you again." He kissed her ear, tucking his hand underneath her and beginning to stroke her again. "Tell me."

"Controlled," she whispered. "I don't like it outside the bedroom, but here..."

"You like me taking charge." He parted his fingers, feeling himself sliding in and out of her. Fuck, that was erotic.

"Mmm." She rested her cheek on the pillow, watching him in the mirror. "Like this it feels so... um... feral."

"I suppose there's a reason they call all fours 'doggy style'," he said, amused.

"I guess." She ran a hand up his thigh. "But it's more than that, it's... I don't know. Primeval. I can forget who I am, what I'm supposed to be, when I'm like this with you."

He kissed her neck and up her throat, turning her face to his so he could plunge his tongue into her mouth briefly before releasing her. "I know what you mean. Modern women are supposed to be in control and independent, and men are supposed to be gentle and considerate." He stroked her hip and bottom as he moved. "But sometimes, you just want to get rid of all that and fuck like rabbits."

She exhaled and sent him a wry look. "That wasn't what I meant at all."

"Wasn't it?" Desire and lust were overtaking his attempts to be gentle and considerate. He pushed himself up on his hands. "So you don't want it rough, then?" He thrust hard inside her, pushing in deeply.

She groaned and lifted her hips. "Oh God..."

"Just say the word and I'll stop." He thrust again, his hips meeting hers with a sharp smack.

She spread her legs, burying her face in the pillow again. "Oh no..."

He couldn't hold back any longer. "Grab onto something, honey, because this is going to be hard and fast."

She exclaimed loudly as he began to pound into her, her hands reaching out to grasp the slats of the headboard. Encouraged by her lack of complaint, he gave into his urge to be forceful, thrusting hard until he could think of nothing else but the sensation of being inside her, of claiming her in the most basic way a man could claim a woman. It was aggressive and rough, and to his delight, he could tell she was loving every minute of it.

At one point, he was vaguely aware of her climaxing beneath him with a squeal, but his body was on autopilot, and he continued to thrust until the heat rushed up from his balls into his groin, and he spilled inside her with a triumphant roar. He clutched hold of her, burying himself inside her, wishing he could hold onto the moment, both the exquisite physical ecstasy of coming, as well as the emotional satisfaction of a job well done.

But the seconds ticked by, and he came back to earth gradually. Esther lay limp beneath him, strands of hair sticking to her face with sweat. He rested his forehead on her shoulder for a moment until his breathing regulated, then gently slid out of her. She shuddered, but didn't move, so he curled around her and pulled her back against his chest.

He kissed her cheek. "Are you okay?"

"Mmm." She nestled back into him. "Exhausted. I think you finally wore me out."

"Sorry about that." He was already regretting being so rough. "Did I hurt you?"

"I may never be able to get my knees together again." She glanced over her shoulder at him, and smiled. "But no. You didn't hurt me." She yawned. "Having to walk like John Wayne when he gets off his horse is a small price to pay for such a good time."

He chuckled and kissed her ear. He was tired too, and he pulled a couple of pillows down to make himself more comfortable. She felt good in his arms. He didn't want to let her go.

And maybe he didn't have to. Hadn't she told him she loved him?

Warmth spread through him at the memory. She loved him. She'd had his baby. Surely that must mean there was a future for the two of them? It was too late to talk about it now, but he'd raise the subject in the morning.

"Good night," he whispered. "Thank you."

"You're welcome."

"I enjoyed our Naughty Night."

She giggled. "Yes. The cap was a very good idea!"

He laughed. "I thought so too."

She snuggled in his arms. Warmth and contentment flooded him. He'd never felt like this before, never had this sense that everything was right in the world—that this was where he was supposed to be. He wanted to stay there forever.

Her body was warm, soft and silky. He nuzzled her neck. Tomorrow he'd talk to her about it. Now he just wanted to sleep.

Chapter Forty-Six

Toby stirred and opened his eyes. Light filtered through the curtains, which had been dark the last time he'd roused to visit the bathroom some time around three a.m.

Esther stood by the mirror, tying her hair into a ponytail. As he moved, she glanced over and smiled. "Morning, sleepy."

He blinked, sat up and rubbed his eyes. "What time is it?"

"Nearly seven thirty. We're supposed to be having breakfast at eight. I was about to wake you."

His arms around his knees, he clasped his hands together loosely and sat watching her as she finished dressing. He'd slept soundly all night apart from the bathroom visit, no doubt due to the exercise he'd indulged in beforehand.

He noticed that her hair was damp around the nape of her neck. "Have you had a shower already?"

"I've been up for ages."

He frowned. "I was hoping to share the shower with you." He'd dreamed about soaping her slippery body.

She flashed him a smile. "Sorry." The smile was a fraction too bright.

Hmm. "How are you feeling?" he asked.

She smiled wryly and stretched up her arms. "Achy and a bit sore."

He winced. "Sorry."

"It was worth it." She began to pack her case. Her movements were brisk and efficient.

Puzzled, he got up, went over to her, and put his arms around her from behind, still naked. "Hey, you." He nuzzled her neck.

"Hey." For a brief moment, she relaxed into his embrace. Then she cleared her throat and leaned forward to do up the zipper on the bag.

He caught her arm and turned her around. "Half an hour to go yet." He cupped her face and moved closer. "I can think of a few things we can do in thirty minutes."

"You need to get ready," she scolded, taking his hands, and moving them away from her face. She left him and walked over to where she'd put her makeup bag and brought it back to stuff it in the end compartment of her bag.

Something was definitely up. "We need to talk," he said.

She glanced over her shoulder.

"Shower and dress first. Talk later," she directed. "We don't want to keep everyone waiting.

He frowned, but went into the bathroom and switched on the shower.

Part of him hoped she'd join him, but she didn't.

Within five minutes he was out, and he dressed quickly in jeans and a T-shirt, same as her, and hung his suit up. His bag packed and zipped, he caught her hand. "Now," he said. "We need to talk."

She turned to face him. Her face was blank, cold even. "Do we have to do this now?"

"Yes." He cupped her face. Where had the hot little sex kitten that had been in his bed disappeared to? "Yesterday you told me you loved me."

Her lips curved a little. "You were torturing me at the time."

"Even so," he said, heart thumping, "does that make it untrue?" Was she going to deny it?

She looked up, her green eyes large and filled with uncertainty. "No," she whispered. "I do love you."

Pleasure flooded him, and he smiled with relief. "Then I think it's time to talk about our future."

She cleared her throat and moved away. "We don't have a future, Toby. Not in the way you mean."

What the fuck? He gripped her upper arm firmly and forced her to face him. "I don't get it. We're meant to be together. I've never felt like this with anyone else. I've never said this to anyone else."

"That's only because..." she gulped, "...you don't know everything."

"What are you talking about?"

"I don't..." She shook her head. "I don't want to talk about it now." Her chin lifted stubbornly.

He was too angry to let it go, though. "What's going on? What do you mean, I don't know everything?" He glared at her. "I'm not letting you out of this room until you tell me what you meant."

"We'll be late for breakfast."

"Fuck breakfast. I'm not hungry. Talk to me."

Her chest heaved. She stepped back and massaged her arm where he must have gripped her too tight, but she didn't turn away.

"Okay." Her eyes sparked as if she'd accepted a challenge. "You know you left messages for me at the university after Fiji?"

He frowned, surprised at her choice of topic. "Yes."

"I told you I never got them."

"Yes…" He didn't like the sound of where this was going.

"Well, I did." She met his gaze, her eyes cool. "I threw them away."

He stared at her. His heart pounded in his ears. "I don't understand."

"I knew where you were, Toby. I knew you wanted to contact me. But I chose not to let you know where I was. I chose to keep Charlie a secret from you." She didn't look regretful or guilty. Her expression said *Fuck you. What are you going to do about it?*

Disbelief made him dizzy. She'd refused to tell him about Charlie on purpose? Not because she couldn't find him, but because she didn't want him involved in Charlie's life?

"Now do you see why we're not going to work?" she said flatly.

"Why?" An incredible wave of hurt washed over him. "Why would you do a thing like that?"

"Because you abandoned me." Her eyes blazed. "I begged you to stay in touch with me—I gave you everything during our time in Fiji. I opened up to you like I'd never opened up to anyone before. And what did you do with my heart? You crushed it! Like a fucking snail beneath your foot."

Guilt rose in his throat like bile. "I know. But Christ, did that justify being cut out of my son's life?"

"You didn't deserve him," she snapped. "Why should I have come to find you when you'd already turned me down? How did I know you wouldn't do it again?"

"This was different. This was about denying a child his father." He stomped on the guilt and let his anger override it. "Esther, I haven't said anything to you about the fact that you kept me out of your life, mainly because I didn't realize it was by choice. But knowing that you did it on purpose… It was an incredibly cruel thing to do, both to me and to Charlie."

"Don't you dare start telling me what's best for my son!"

"He's my son too," he pointed out.

"You left me," she whispered. "And now you're going to university. There'll be thousands of young women there. Do you really think you'd be able to stay faithful?"

Coldness settled in his stomach. What a pathetic excuse for not wanting a relationship. Because he might cheat on her. "I've never cheated on any girl I've been with."

"That's because you've never dated anyone longer than about two weeks."

"You don't know a thing about me." He glared at her. "You have no idea what relationships I've had—we've never talked about it. You've never asked, and I've never told you. You're just striking out because you're afraid, and I understand that, but it's not pleasant being your punching bag, Esther."

There was a knock at the door, and they both jumped. Toby opened his mouth to tell her to leave it, but before he could say anything she marched over and opened it.

Rusty and Faith stood there, smiling. "Coming down?" Rusty asked.

"Sure," Esther said, grabbing her purse. She walked out past them without another look at Toby.

He followed her out and along the corridor to the elevators, gritting his teeth. He couldn't believe her revelation. Had she really not told him about Charlie on purpose? Anger and resentment entwined with hurt and sickness inside him. The last thing he wanted was breakfast.

"Sleep well?" Rusty asked.

"Fine," Toby said. He glanced at Faith, who was as white as if she'd been drained by a vampire. "Are you okay? Morning sickness striking again?"

"Particularly virulently." She smiled weakly. "I just hope they don't shove eggs and bacon under my nose. I won't be held responsible for my actions."

The elevator pinged and they went inside. Toby pressed the button for the ground floor.

They stood silently. Rusty and Faith glanced at Esther, who stood looking at her fingernails sullenly. Rusty met Toby's gaze and raised his eyebrows. Toby gave a slight shake of his head and glared back. He didn't want to talk about it.

"I wonder how Charlie slept with his grandparents," Faith said lightly.

Esther gave a shadow of a smile. "I hope they don't mind playing trucks at five a.m."

"See what we have to look forward to?" Faith said jovially. Rusty smiled, but they fell silent again, and Toby cursed Esther for spoiling the moment. Why couldn't she have awoken in his bed with him? They could have made love, showered together, made love again. Then he could have brought up the fact that he'd asked her to marry him by text. And the fact that she'd told him she loved him. They would have laughed about it, told each other how they felt, and decided to sail off into the sunset with Charlie close behind.

Instead, they had this awkward, painful silence that was tying his stomach in knots, and the memory of her words, *I chose to keep Charlie a secret from you*, bouncing around inside his head like a ball in a squash court. His head ached. That could be a hangover though. He desperately needed a coffee.

The elevator pinged again, and the doors opened. They walked out together and crossed the foyer to the restaurant. A couple of long tables had been set up for the guests who had stayed the night. Dan and Eve were already seated, sipping orange juice and coffee, talking to Felix, Carla, and some of the others who'd managed to make it down. Toby's parents were there with Charlie, who ran up to them as he saw them.

"Daddy!" Charlie exclaimed, running past Esther and up to him.

Esther sent him a look that would have frozen lava, but he ignored her and picked Charlie up. The boy wrapped his arms around his neck, and he caught his breath with sudden emotion. This was his son. What right did she have to deny him access for all that time?

"Hey, buster. How are you this morning?"

"Fine, Daddy. Look at my new car." Charlie showed him the toy his grandparents had bought him. "It's a Porsch-a."

"It is a Porsche," he said, smiling. "A shiny red one." He kissed Charlie's curls. Suddenly he didn't want to put him down. Esther could pick him up and walk out of the hotel, and he might never see her again. She was going to Dunedin for the interview. What if she got the job? What would happen to his relationship with Charlie then?

Charlie struggled to get down, though, and ran over to Esther. "Look, Mummy."

"It's beautiful." She lifted him into the chair next to Martha and sat beside him. "How was he?" she asked his grandparents.

"Energetic," Graham said, but he grinned, showing he didn't mind that much.

"Would you like a cup of tea or coffee?" Toby asked her politely.

She looked up and met his gaze briefly, then looked away. "Coffee would be nice, thank you."

He nodded, walked over to the table and poured them both a cup, taking the opportunity to try and calm himself down. He shouldn't get angry, however annoyed and upset he was at what she'd done. Nothing would be solved by anger. It was difficult not to though. Her betrayal bubbled inside him. Could he forgive her for such a cruel act?

Chapter Forty-Seven

Esther's heart rate had been going at pretty much double speed since she'd first admitted to Toby that she'd purposefully kept Charlie's presence from him, and it showed no signs of slowing down. She took the cup of coffee he offered her and glanced up at his face, wondering if he was angry, hurt, upset or a combination of all three. He sat opposite her, but his expression was carefully blank, and she couldn't tell what he was thinking.

She sipped the coffee and broke a croissant into pieces for Charlie, half-listening to the conversation around the table. This was a nightmare. She wanted to grab her things and run. She'd told him now—what else was there to hang around for?

The conversation bubbled along, and nobody except perhaps Faith and Rusty seemed aware of anything amiss between the two of them. She concentrated on helping Charlie with his breakfast. No way would she be able to force any food past her own lips.

She'd been aggressive when she told Toby, but now she regretted her attitude. He probably thought she didn't have any remorse for what she'd done, and she did in droves. It was guilt that had forced her to be so confrontational, when in fact she should probably have apologized profusely and begged his forgiveness. Would he have forgiven her? Or was the deed itself too terrible for him to ever excuse what she'd done?

Tears pricked her eyelids. She'd been selfish in keeping Charlie to herself. Toby was right—his actions in Fiji, terrible though they had been, hadn't justified what she'd done.

She took a swallow of the coffee, which was so hot she burned her mouth. Great. Now she had a blister to add to the rest of her pain.

"I'm so excited!" Eve was practically dancing in her seat. "Rarotonga, here we come!"

Everyone laughed. She looked so pretty, thought Esther, glowing with newlywed bliss. As did Faith, who'd regained a little color after nibbling some toast. Rusty put his arm around her and whispered something in her ear. It must have been rude because she blushed and pushed him, giggling. Esther dropped her gaze again, loneliness sweeping through her. Why had she come here?

"You'll have to take loads of photos," Faith said, sipping her orange juice. "I've never been to the Cook Islands."

"Have you been?" Rusty asked Toby.

"No." Toby buttered some toast. "I'd thought about saving up for a holiday but I doubt I'll have the money now I'm going to uni."

"When does your course start?" Dan asked, leaning back as a waiter placed a plate of bacon and eggs in front of him.

"I applied too late for this year, but next semester I'm doing some correspondence courses to give me some background into the subject."

"You do know it means you actually have to write things down," Dan said with a grin, and everyone laughed.

"Really?" Toby raised his eyebrows. "Damn."

Esther gritted her teeth. She hated how he let the others put him down like that.

"And you have to sit still for more than five minutes in seminars," Eve said. "Do you think you'll be able to manage that?"

"I'll do my best." He smiled, but Esther could see the hurt shining behind his eyes. Why didn't they realise how their comments made him feel?

"He'll be all right if he has to count up to twenty providing he can take his socks off," Rusty said.

Esther slammed her cup down with a crash into the saucer. "Stop it!" she yelled.

Everyone stared at her. "Esther…" Toby said cautiously.

Nausea rose inside her, but she wasn't going to keep quiet. She'd probably never see them again anyway—what did it matter if she upset them all?

"No," she said, "I'm fed up with everyone talking to you like this." She glared at Rusty and Dan in turn. "You always put him down and talk to him like he's an idiot. He has feelings, you know."

"It's all right, Esther," Rusty said calmly in what she assumed was his best teacher's voice. "He knows we don't mean it."

"Does he?" She met his green gaze boldly. "Did you all know that he's only taking this degree for you?"

Everyone around the table stared at her. Toby stood, his face thunderous. "Come with me."

"No." She stayed sitting.

Martha frowned. "What do you mean?"

"He loves his job. He's a fantastic carpenter—he's got a natural talent for it. So he's not an academic—that doesn't mean he's inferior to the rest of you."

"We've never said that," Dan told her, his eyes cool.

"Maybe not, but you imply it every time you call him a Neanderthal or a caveman." She'd hit home—they all looked guiltily at each other. "He's more intuitive and thoughtful than the rest of you put together. He's only doing this course because he thinks he has to, to get your approval."

"Esther!" Toby's face flushed. She'd embarrassed him.

"But I'm right, aren't I?" She stood, burning with her intense need to make them all understand. "You don't really want to do this. You're not interested in architecture, not in this way. You're amazingly skilled, Toby—I've never met anyone with your talent. You're going to be wasted sitting behind a drawing board. What's the point, when all you want to do is get out there and deal with the buildings themselves?"

He fixed her with a steely gaze. "You're spoiling everyone's breakfast. Outside, now." It was the tone he used on her in the bedroom. The "do as you're told" tone.

Silence descended on the table. Her bottom lip trembled, so she bit it. Martha stood, pity on her face, and held out a hand toward her, but she ignored it and bent and picked up a quiet Charlie out of his seat.

"Sorry," she said quietly. "I didn't mean to ruin breakfast."

She turned and walked out.

Toby caught up with her in the foyer. He grabbed her arm and forced her to turn around. "Where are you going?" he snapped.

"I'm getting my bag, and then I'll call a taxi to the airport."

He stared at her. "But your flight's not until Monday."

"There are always free seats. I'll wait until one becomes available."

His eyes blazed. "So you're running away?"

"What's the point in staying?" Misery made her angry. She hefted Charlie onto her hip, and he sucked his thumb, curling up against her. "We're over, Toby. We were never going to be anything more than just sex. We both knew that. How could we be, after what we've done to each other?"

"I love you," he said simply.

She caught her breath. It was the first time he'd said it.

"I love you too." She swallowed. "But it's not enough. We've hurt each other too badly."

"Bullshit." For the first time he looked really angry, clenching his hands as he glared at her. "I asked you to marry me."

Indignation made her raise her voice. "By text! When you were drunk!"

His jaw bunched as if he was gritting his teeth. "Even so. There's more at stake here than me and you. There's Charlie, and we have to talk about him."

"We will. I'll call... or something. But now, I just want to go."

He stepped in front of her as she went to walk away. "Well, I want to talk. For God's sake, we have a son. Surely it's worth us at least trying to discuss having a future."

"You really think we could be happy?" she snapped. "Knowing what we've done? How could we be sure the hurt we feel would ever go away?"

"We can't. But that doesn't mean we shouldn't try. Sweetheart, relationships don't come with a guarantee. That's what makes them exciting. Two people have to spend time together to explore whether they're right for each other. Sometimes it doesn't work out."

"Or ever, in your case," she said spitefully.

"Or yours," he snapped.

She looked away. A tear ran down her cheek.

In her arms, Charlie started crying. She kissed his curls, aching inside.

"I've got to go," she said to Toby.

"Don't do this." Toby caught Charlie's fingers in his own. "Don't take him away from me."

"I'll be in touch." Tears poured down her face. "I'm sorry. I know I'm a coward."

"We can sort something out..."

She disengaged his fingers from Charlie's. The pain on Toby's face made her curl up inside. But she had to get away before she collapsed into a sobbing ball. "I'll call you."

"Daddy!" Charlie screamed as she turned.

That made her pause. A long-term relationship with Toby would never work, and breaking his heart—and her own—was an inevitability she had to deal with.

But breaking her son's heart was something else.

She should stay and plan the future, work out a way for Toby to play a part in his son's upbringing and reassure Charlie he wasn't losing Toby forever.

But at that moment, she knew that if she stayed she would totally break down, and she needed to be as strong as she could for Charlie.

Tears pouring down her face, she walked away.

Chapter Forty-Eight

When Esther left, the summer seemed to leave with her. The weather turned cold, and it rained continually, dense, heavy subtropical rain that pooled on the drive and made the water tanks overflow.

Toby lay on the sofa, thinking that he should really get up on a stepladder and pull out the plants he'd seen peeking over the edge of the guttering. But he didn't move, too listless to motivate himself to do anything but lie there and listen to the music playing on his iPad.

He did rouse himself when a knock came at the door, even though his heart sank at the thought of seeing his mother's worried face again. His fridge was full with pasta bakes and shepherd's pies as she tried to encourage him to eat, but his appetite had completely vanished after Esther left.

He opened the door, surprised to find not his mother's worried face but instead two other equally worried faces.

"Hey," Rusty said. "Can we come in?"

"Please?" Faith begged.

Toby looked at his feet for a moment. Rusty had rung repeatedly for the past two weeks, asking him to come out, and they'd even come around a few times, but each time he'd turned them away, insisting he was fine and just needed some time to himself.

This time, however, he couldn't resist the tears that glistened in Faith's eyes. "Sure." He walked into the living room, leaving them to close the door. Hands in the pockets of his jeans, he turned as they stood awkwardly before him. "Want a drink?"

To his surprise, Faith walked up to him and slid her arms around his waist, resting her cheek on his chest. Startled, he took his hands out of his pockets and put his arms around her, looking at Rusty over the top of her head. Rusty just gave a rueful smile.

"Hey, you. Everything okay? Is the baby all right?" Concern swept over him, and he pulled back and looked at her waistline.

"The baby's fine," she said huskily, resting her hand on the growing bump.

"Good—come and sit down though." He led her to the sofa where she sat next to Rusty and took the chair opposite them. "What's up?"

Faith glanced at Rusty, and they exchanged a look. "We're worried about you," she said.

He leaned back and scratched at a mark on his jeans. "I'm all right."

"You look better than I thought you would," Rusty said. "I thought we'd find you surrounded by empty whisky bottles, unshaven and staring at Esther's picture."

Toby gave a ghost of a smile. "Well, as you can see, I'm completely sober, beardless, and there's not a picture in sight." Mainly because he only had the one picture of her on his phone. And none of Charlie. His son.

He hadn't drunk a drop of alcohol since she'd gone.

He was kind of worried that if he started, he wouldn't be able to stop.

"Actually that's even more scary," Faith said softly. "Have you heard from her?"

He looked out at the rain. "She rang a few days ago from Christchurch. She got the job in Dunedin. They're moving down on Friday."

Faith frowned. "Did you talk to her?"

"I just said—"

"No, I mean talk *to* her? Or did you both talk *at* each other?"

He said nothing. They'd hardly talked at all, to tell the truth. A few brief, clipped sentences. Both of them defensive, waiting for the other to warm. Both of them cold and refusing to give in.

He sighed, wishing he'd told Faith and Rusty to go away. "Forget it, Faith. It's all done and dusted. I wish it had turned out differently, but it's too late now."

"It's never too late," she said.

"I wish I could believe that, but things are too far gone to mend." Sadness overwhelmed him. He'd be damned if he was going to cry in front of them though.

"It's never too late when there are those three little words left to say," Faith said.

He heaved a sigh. "I told her I loved her. She said she loved me too, but that it wasn't enough."

"Not those three little words," Faith said impatiently. "The other three."

There were another three little words? Puzzled, he glanced at Rusty, who pulled a 'no idea' face and shrugged.

Faith rolled her eyes. "Jeez, you two are hopeless. I. Am. Sorry?"

"Oh…"

She smiled. "It's amazing how far that sentiment can take you, sweetie. I have to ask you something. Did you ever apologize for walking out on her in Fiji?"

He opened his mouth to tell her yes, of course he had. Then he closed it slowly.

Had he? He must have, when he met her in Christchurch during the earthquake. He tried to think. He couldn't actually remember saying it. After they'd first made love? Surely he had, somewhere along the line. "Um…"

Rusty looked exasperated. "Dude…"

"Yeah," Faith said to him, "you're skating on thin ice, Thorne."

"What have I done?" he said indignantly. "I apologized. On numerous occasions."

"Eventually." She relented and leaned over to kiss him on the cheek before turning back to Toby, who sat there with his head spinning. "The thing is," she continued, "and I know you know this—you hurt her dreadfully when you walked away from her in Fiji. You broke her heart. She is absolutely crazy about you, honey. Yes, she should have tried to find you and tell you about Charlie. That was dumb, and spiteful, and hurtful. But she knows that, and she regrets it every day." Faith sighed. "She did it out of self-preservation. She was terrified that if she came to find you, you'd just turn your back on her again. For God's sake, you rejected her after a holiday romance. Why would she think you'd be interested in happy ever after?"

He ran a hand through his hair. "How can we ever get past what we've done to each other? She'll never be able to forgive me for walking away, and I don't know that I can ever forgive her for not telling me about Charlie."

"The thing about forgiveness is that it's not about forgetting. It's not about pretending it didn't happen. It's about accepting that someone made a mistake. That they did something because they were hurt, or angry. And it's about acknowledging that although it's not okay, providing they show remorse, it is possible to move on. You have to accept the other person isn't perfect. Loving someone—real love, not hearts and flowers stuff—is about recognizing their faults and saying it's okay, I'm going to love you in spite of them."

"She knows what she's talking about," Rusty said. "Hell knows she's had enough to forgive where I'm concerned."

"Hey, we've all done things we regret," she said. "We're only human."

Toby thought about her words. Hope simmered somewhere inside him. Was it possible they could grow to forgive each other? Enough to move on and work toward a future, anyway?

"The thing is," he said, "when I spoke to her, she said nothing about putting things right. I don't think she wants to work it out."

"She's racked with guilt, Toby. She knows damn well what she did to you, and to Charlie, and she'll never be able to forgive herself for that. She doesn't think you want a future either."

He stared at Faith. "You've spoken to her."

She scratched her nose. "Maybe."

"When?"

"Most days, since she left."

He couldn't think straight. Why would Esther be speaking to Faith and not to him? "I don't understand."

Her expression softened. "She loves you, honey. You should have seen her face when she got that text from you—the one where you proposed. She lit up like a firework display."

"But…" His heart banged away at the notion that she'd been excited at his proposal. "She thought I was an idiot, texting when I was drunk."

"Well, you were. It doesn't change the fact that you did it."

They fell quiet for a moment. He was surprised they couldn't hear his heart, it was so loud in his ears.

"How's the project coming along?" Rusty asked.

Toby smiled slowly. "Pretty good."

"Can I see it?" Faith said eagerly.

He stood and walked over to the corner, where an item stood draped in a cloth. He lifted the cloth off.

"Oh my God." Faith covered her mouth with a hand and went over to examine it. "Oh, Toby, it's beautiful."

He ran a hand along the wood. "Do you think he'll like it?"

"He'll love it."

"It's fantastic," Rusty said. "Esther was right—you *are* talented."

Toby shrugged, but their words pleased him, even though he was conscious part of the reason they were praising him was due to their guilt after Esther's accusation at the breakfast table. They'd all apologized to him afterward, which had embarrassed him immensely. Dan had even rung him from Rarotonga to chat over the phone and say he was sorry, followed by Eve, who had cried when she said how bad she felt. He'd brushed them all off, but deep down he had appreciated it.

"When are you going to send it?" Rusty asked.

"I'll finish it over the next couple of days and get it couriered down." He covered the item with the cloth.

"Okay," Faith said. "We'd better go. But look, think about what I said, won't you?"

"Yeah." He kissed her on the cheek and shook Rusty's hand. "Thank you for coming around."

"No worries." Rusty steered his wife toward the door, a hand in the small of her back. "Let us know if you need anything."

Toby waved them goodbye, then shut the door and went back to the sofa.

Outside, the rain hammered against the window. It made him think of the day Esther had dressed up like a schoolgirl. Against his will, his lips curved.

He thought about what Faith had said. Those three little words.

Esther hadn't said she was sorry for not telling him about Charlie either. That rankled. Why should he be the one to apologize?

But then maybe she felt if he wasn't going to apologize, why should she?

For the first time, maybe, since he walked away from her in Fiji, he made himself really think about what he'd done. Yes, he'd regretted it, but he'd only really been thinking of himself when he'd tried to contact her at the university. He'd wanted to see her again. He hadn't contacted her to say sorry. Maybe that was why she'd thrown the notes away.

He forced himself to picture her in the airport, that fateful last day of their holiday. They'd been standing by the coffee bar, and she'd looked up at him with hope when she asked if they could stay in touch. He made himself remember the way the light had died in her eyes when he said no. All he'd been thinking about was how he didn't want to be tied down.

Faith said his words had broken Esther's heart.

A lump formed in his throat, and he covered his eyes with his arm, but it couldn't erase the image of her from his mind, nor the memory of her standing there in the foyer of the hotel, misery etched into the lines of her face. She loved him. He knew that, and she'd even admitted it.

She'd been cruel. But so had he.

He lifted his arm and stared out at the rain. Yes, Charlie was his son, but he'd always be Charlie's father. The question wasn't really did he want them in his life.

The question was: Could he live without Esther?

And he realized he'd always known the answer to that.

Chapter Forty-Nine

"You're snoring," Charlie said, shaking his mother's arm. "Wake up."

Esther opened her eyes and sighed. She'd been having a lovely dream. She'd been lying on a desert island somewhere in the Pacific, the ocean lapping at the sand while seagulls cried overhead. The sun had warmed her skin, and she'd even been able to taste the salt in the air.

Toby had been leaning over her, trailing a finger along her arm. She could still see his smile, and the way the sun had highlighted the coppery tones in his hair. If she closed her eyes, she could even feel his gentle touch...

She opened her eyes again. Charlie was drawing on her arm with a ballpoint pen.

"Charlie!" She sat up, exasperated. Uneven blue lines covered the slowly fading tan.

Her son stuck out his bottom lip. "You were snoring," he repeated. "I wanted you to wake up."

"You could have just said, 'Wake up, Mummy'." She sighed and picked him up, taking the pen out of his hand. "Come on, let's get something to eat, shall we?" Food invariably distracted him.

He'd needed a lot of distracting lately.

She took him into the kitchen, sat him on the work surface, and opened the pantry.

She brought out a box. "Want some cereal?"

"Plizz."

She gave him the box while she retrieved a bowl and the carton of the milk from the fridge. When she turned back to him, he was examining the photograph on the back of the box. "Dan Carter!" he said triumphantly.

"Yes, it is," she said, a lump in her throat.

"Daddy's superhero," Charlie said.

"Yes." She bent forward and kissed his head, her lips lingering on his curls.

When they'd first left, Charlie had surprised her by not mentioning Toby at all. He'd not spoken about him on the plane back to Christchurch, nor at all during the first few days in their old city. That had made her both sad and thankful. He'd obviously picked up on her distress and knew better than to question when they were going to see Toby again.

Since then, he'd mentioned him a couple of times in passing, but she hadn't had any of the expected "Where's Daddy?" questions she'd expected to have to field.

Now, however, he studied her thoughtfully. "Daddy smelled nice," he said unexpectedly.

Her lips curved. "Yes, he did."

"Why?"

"Because he used nice aftershave."

"What's that?"

"It's like perfume a man puts on after he shaves his face."

"Daddy shaves his face?"

"Yes," she said, thinking about the way his bristles had given her a rash all over her breasts.

"Why?"

"Because men have hair on their face."

Charlie crunched a piece of cereal as he thought about that fascinating fact. "Will Charlie have hair on his face when he growed up?"

She heaved a sigh. It had been nice for a few days for Charlie to be able to ask Toby these sorts of questions. She'd thought she could be everything to her baby boy, but she was beginning to realize he needed more than just answers to his questions. He needed a role model—he needed to see with his own eyes the way other men behaved and acted.

He needed his father.

Too bad she'd ruined that for him.

She opened her mouth to say something, but at that moment there was a knock at the door. She lifted Charlie down, and they walked over together to answer it.

A courier delivery person stood there, a huge box at his feet. "Ms. Tyler?" he asked hopefully.

SERENITY WOODS

"Yes." She stared at the box. "What's this? I haven't ordered anything."

He checked his notes. "It's definitely for you. From the Bay of Islands?"

She felt as if he'd punched her in the ribs. "Oh. Yes. Thank you." He held out the form and she signed it, then stood back so he could lift the box into her apartment.

"What is it?" Charlie asked.

She closed the door and dragged the box into the living room. It was heavy. "I've no idea, sweetie." She grabbed a pair of scissors and ran the blade across the tape. The box was full of polystyrene pieces, and the package in the middle was wrapped securely in bubble wrap.

She lay the box on its side and drew the package out carefully, not caring that the floor was soon covered in polystyrene beans that had Charlie squealing with joy as he threw them up in the air like snowflakes.

Even before she'd begun to strip the bubble wrap off, she could see the item inside.

It was a rocking horse.

She turned the horse over onto the rocker and lifted off the remainder of the packaging. Charlie froze in the middle of the white beans and stared at it. "What's that?"

Esther covered her mouth with her hand. The horse was beautiful. Immediately she knew Toby had made it. Carved from native kauri wood, it wasn't constructed like the cheap horses she'd seen in the department stores, which had flat pieces of wood cut into shapes and slotted together, with manes of sheepskin. This had been hand-carved in the likeness of a real horse, the head and mane engraved into the wood, varnished so it gleamed.

"What is it, Mummy?" Charlie came over and touched the horse as if it were made of glass.

Tears ran down her face. "It's for you. Daddy made it for you."

He blinked. "For me?" His face lit up. "From Daddy?"

She bent and picked him up, placing him on the sculpted saddle, and put the leather reins in his hands. "You can ride it," she said, showing him how it rocked. "Like a real horse."

He clung hold of the mane, steadying himself as he got used to the movement, and then began to swing his legs backward and forward as he grew more confident.

She stood up, only then seeing the envelope on the floor amongst all the white pieces. Heart pounding, she picked it up and opened it.

It contained a single piece of white paper with a simple message written in Toby's loopy, untidy handwriting.

To Charlie—this is for you. I hope you like it, my lovely, lovely boy :-)

To Esther—sweetheart. I'm sorry.

He'd underlined the word "sorry" three times.

The paper crumpled in her hand.

She sat on the sofa and burst into tears.

*

Toby took a deep breath and knocked on the door.

It was dark—the only flight he could get had landed at seven thirty, and by the time his taxi had wound its way from the airport to the city center, the sun had set and the lights had come on in the parts of the city that hadn't been destroyed.

He waited nervously. It had been a huge leap of faith to come all the way to Christchurch. He hadn't spoken to Esther since he'd had the rocking horse delivered. He'd thought about taking the box on the plane and delivering it himself, but he wanted her to have a day to think about the short message he'd written before he turned up on her doorstep.

Now, though, he began to worry she'd turn him away. He didn't expect her to fall into his arms, nor even to ask him to stay, but he crossed his fingers and hoped she didn't just shut the door in his face. He hadn't meant to be presumptuous, just impulsive.

The door opened.

Esther stared at him. She wore a pair of silky pink pajamas, and her ruffled hair framed her pale face. Her mouth formed a perfect O as he waited, wondering what she was going to say.

Before any words could form, however, a tiny person pushed from behind her legs and looked up at him in delight. "Daddy!"

"Charlie boy." He bent as his son rushed out, and picked the boy up. Charlie flung his arms around his neck and gave him a death grip, and he laughed and made choking sounds. "You're strangling me!"

"I missed you." Charlie buried his face in his father's neck.

"I missed you too." He looked at Esther over the top of his son's head, hoping that this wasn't coming across as emotional blackmail. He certainly hadn't planned it.

Esther's eyes shone, but she didn't look angry. She stepped back, indicating for him to come in. "We've both missed you," she said huskily.

He walked past her into the living room and smiled as he saw the rocking horse in the center, in prime position.

"Look Daddy!" Charlie wriggled to get down and rushed over to it. "I can climb on it myself." He stuck a tiny foot in the stirrup and pulled himself up, scrabbled a bit, then hung, complaining, over the seat.

Esther giggled. "He's been doing that all day." She walked over and lifted him on. "Nearly there, honey."

Charlie hooted and rocked the horse, kicking his heels. A lump formed in Toby's throat to see his son enjoying his handiwork.

"Gently," Esther scolded. "Remember, this took Daddy ages to make."

"It's okay," Toby said, unable to stop himself beaming. "I don't care what he does with it. They're not meant to be kept pristine. I'd rather it was well-used, even if it means it gets bumped and scratched."

They stood together and watched Charlie sink slowly onto the horse's mane, his thumb in his mouth as he became distracted by the TV.

"He fell asleep on there this afternoon," Esther said. "I've hardly been able to get him off it." She smiled and walked toward the kitchen. "Want a drink?"

"Sure."

"I don't have any beer. White wine okay?"

He sighed. "That would be great."

She poured them both a glass and they sat up at the breakfast bar sipping it, watching Charlie.

"You'll have to put pillows around him," Toby said, "in case he falls asleep and slips off."

She smiled. "Yeah." She looked up and met his gaze. "Thank you for the horse, Toby. It was a lovely gift—you've worked really hard."

He shrugged, although her comment pleased him. "I enjoyed it." He cleared his throat. "I thought a lot about what you said, about the fact that I'm only going to university because I want approval from everyone else."

She reddened. "Oh jeez, I'm so sorry about that, I shouldn't—"

He held up a hand. "You were right. My heart's not in it. My talent lies with working on the actual wood, with making other people's plans reality. I have to accept that's a skill in itself, and it's something to be proud of."

"It is." She looked earnest.

"Yes, I think so, and you're the one who made me see that. And with that in mind, I've decided, I'm not going to university. Instead, I'm going to work on some wooden sculpture in my spare time, and hopefully sell a few pieces, maybe even build a business." He shrugged. "I'll see where it takes me."

Her face lit up with a beautiful smile. "I think that's a wonderful idea. Imagine how many of these horses you could sell."

He glanced over at Charlie. "Nah. I'll only ever make one rocking horse." The boy's eyes were closed. He looked completely comfortable draped over the wooden toy. Toby walked over and placed some of the sofa cushions around him, just in case. If his son was anywhere near as clumsy as himself, he'd almost certainly fall off.

Esther sipped from her glass. When he looked back at her, he saw it was to cover the tears in her eyes.

"So what about you?" he said. He glanced around the room. "I thought you'd be all packed and living out of boxes."

She swallowed the wine and lifted her chin. "Actually, I've decided to stay here."

His eyes widened. "Oh?"

"I've been in touch with Canterbury University and they plan to reopen soon. And it's odd—although I have some difficult memories here, with my parents dying and everything, I feel disloyal thinking about leaving. It's not the city's fault. I want to be part of the reconstruction, and help it to go back to what it was."

He smiled. "That's great. I understand."

Their gazes met. Her green eyes were wary. He still had no idea how she felt about him. Sure, his gift to Charlie had touched her. But whether that meant she could forgive him, whether they had a future, he wasn't sure.

He took a deep breath and reached for her hand. "I'm sorry," he said.

Chapter Fifty

Esther's heart stopped. Well, it felt like it might have. Her head spun and it was difficult to breathe.

"For what?" she whispered.

"For many things. Mainly for walking away from you in Fiji." He examined her fingers. "I was young and foolish then. I'd had a lot of girlfriends, none of whom had been serious, and all my mates were single. I wasn't ready to settle down. Marriage, mortgage, children, the thought scared the crap out of me."

Her lips twisted wryly. "It didn't take a genius to guess you'd freaked out at the thought of some girl getting serious about you."

He frowned. "No, you don't quite understand. During those two weeks we spent together, I had feelings for you that I'd never had before for a girl. I fell in love with you, Esther."

Her jaw dropped. "Oh…" She'd never guessed that was the case. She'd assumed he'd panicked at the thought of a girl having serious feelings about him when he didn't reciprocate them.

"I'd never been in love before. I didn't recognize it at the time—I thought I was caught up in the excitement of the holiday. I thought what I was feeling couldn't possibly continue into real life. I assumed when you asked to see me again that it was a waste of time—not only did we live at opposite ends of the country, but we were high on summer and the sand and the sea, and we couldn't carry on like that. I didn't realize what being in love felt like."

He raised her hand and kissed the tips of her fingers. "But now I do. Now I know that what I was feeling was true, and it wasn't going to go away. As soon as I got on that plane, I knew I'd made a mistake. The moment I got home, I tried to contact you at the university. I was devastated when I couldn't find you. I didn't date again for ages. And even when I did date again, I didn't feel anything like the emotions I had while in Fiji."

She pressed her other hand to her mouth. "Oh, Toby…"

He smiled and cupped her cheek. "I'm so sorry I broke your heart. I'll never forgive myself for that. And I know I can never make it up to you. But I'd like to spend the rest of my life trying. I asked you to marry me on the night before Dan's wedding. I know I was drunk and I did it by text." He winced. "But the sentiment was true. I love you, Esther. I'd like to move to Christchurch and work here, for a while anyway, and help to rebuild the city. And I'd like to share the renewal with you."

Tears streamed down her cheeks. "But... what about the fact that I threw away your messages? That I didn't tell you about Charlie? How can you ever forgive me for that?"

He dropped his hand. "A wise woman told me that real love is about recognizing your partner's faults and saying you're going to love them in spite of them. We've both made mistakes, honey. But the important thing is that we both regret doing them. If we really regret it, then there's no reason we can't move on."

"I do regret it," she said, wiping her face and sniffling. "So many times I picked up the phone to try and find you, but I was hurting so much that every time I hung up, because I wanted to punish you for leaving me. But deep down I knew it wasn't working, because how could I be punishing you when you didn't know about Charlie? I think I was punishing myself—forcing myself to cope alone because I felt I'd been stupid to fall in love, and even more stupid to get pregnant."

He looked pained. "I'm so sorry you had to go through it all alone. And I'm so sorry about that fucking condom."

She bit her lip. "It must have been such a shock for you, finding out about Charlie after the earthquake. I can't believe how nice you were about it. You could have been so angry with me."

"Angry?" He looked puzzled. "Why would I be angry? He's an angel." His gaze drifted to his sleeping son, and his expression softened.

He really loved Charlie, she realized.

And he really loved her.

His gaze came back to her. He smiled. "Thank you for giving me my son. It's the best present I've ever had. Even better than the huge box of Lego I got on my eighth birthday."

She laughed through her tears. "I'm so glad the two of you get on well. He's missed you so. That week we spent together made me realize how important it is for a boy to have his father around. Oh, I know many women cope perfectly well as single mothers, and there's nothing wrong with that, but watching you with him made me understand how much our parents are role models for us."

"Maybe." He picked up her hand again and then, to her surprise, got off the stool and sank onto one knee. "So, what about it? Will you marry me? For real? I can't promise I'll be a perfect husband. I can't iron to save my life. And I suck at cooking anything more complicated than pasta. But I'll try." He kissed her fingers again. "I love you."

She bit her lip and nodded. "I love you too. And yes, I'll marry you."

Relief flooded his face and he stood and pulled her into his arms. "You won't regret it, I promise."

"Oh, Toby."

He lowered his lips to hers. She slid her arms around his neck and returned the kiss, wanting to cry again at the beautiful familiarity of the feel of his hair in her fingers, the slide of his tongue against hers. She loved him, and she wasn't afraid to admit it any longer. True, there were no guarantees that this would have a happy ending. But love didn't come with guarantees. Like the city in which they were going to live, they would rebuild their relationship brick by brick, stone by stone, from the foundations up.

He lifted his head and cupped her face. "I'm so happy right now."

"I have one question." She couldn't contain the happiness bubbling inside her and let it spread across her face. "Can we buy the Naughty Nights game off Faith?"

He smiled. "Absolutely." With a quick glance at Charlie, he moved closer to her and hovered his lips above hers. "When we're married, I think we should make every night a naughty night."

A shiver ran through her at the thought of being able to role-play with him for the rest of their lives. "I like that idea."

And she let him kiss her again as Charlie rocked slowly in front of The Simpsons, oblivious to the sparkling future that lay ahead.

The Heartfelt Series

Book 1: Mr. Sinful (Rusty)
Book 2: Mr. Seductive (Toby)
Book 3: Mr. Sensational (Felix)

Find out what happens next in Felix's story – Mr. Sensational.
Available from most major retailers.

Excerpt – Chapter One

"Sex," Coco said. "And lots of it."

She'd been looking out of the window as she spoke, but on glancing back at her friend, realized by Amy's startled look that she must have spoken louder than she'd meant to, and her voice had carried across the small coffee shop. The young barista foaming the milk behind the counter giggled, and the man leaning on the bar waiting for his latte looked up from his iPad and raised an eyebrow.

Coco's eyes widened with dismay. She'd spotted him as soon as she walked into *Bella's*. Although he was dressed much the same as the other early morning office workers in a dark suit and a long black coat to ward off the cool New Zealand air, something about him made him stand out from his surroundings. Maybe it was his height—he must have been at least six two. Or perhaps it was his dark hair, short and sleek at the back, longer and falling over his forehead at the front in a style that declared "I'm a naughty boy beneath this demure image—deal with it."

Yum, she'd thought as Amy had ushered her in out of the rain. Very tasty. But he hadn't looked up, busy concentrating on his Financial Times app or whatever had captured his attention so completely, and she'd torn her gaze away, her mind too full of her own busy day to dwell on the guy, however hot he might be.

Now, though, his eyes met hers and one corner of his mouth curved up.

"Classy," Amy said as they moved to the counter. She waved an apologetic hand at the man. "Sorry. I was asking her what she wanted for Christmas this year."

The man chuckled, put down his iPad, and accepted his latte from the barista. "Interesting request. Most women ask for perfume or jewelry." His deep, gravelly voice made the hairs rise on the back of Coco's neck.

She cleared her throat, mortified he'd overheard her words, and decided the only way out would be to make a joke of it. "Yes, well, that's what springs to mind when you sit on Santa's lap as a grown-up."

Amy snorted and started relating their order to the amused girl behind the counter. Coco couldn't tear her eyes away from the man's, though. Deep brown and warm with amusement, they crinkled at the edges as he smiled. He leaned forward conspiratorially and said in a low voice, "What I want to know is… have you been naughty or nice this year?"

She caught her breath. He smelled enticing, a mixture of manly body wash, hot muffins, and coffee, a mouth-wateringly morning smell. A vision shot through her head of him getting dressed, buttoning up the white shirt over tanned skin, hair ruffled from a night of passionate lovemaking…

She blinked, shocked at her train of thought. What the hell? Get a grip, Coco. His smile spread as if he'd read her mind, and she dropped her gaze, searching for something to say, a way to escape the conversation without embarrassing herself further.

Luckily, her gaze fell on his iPad, and what she saw there made her laugh out loud. Not the Financial Times, in fact not any newspaper app.

"Angry Birds?" She raised her eyes to his again. "Really?"

"What?" He gave her a mock-affronted look and tucked the iPad under his arm. "I'm up to level ten. It's addictive."

"I'm sure it is." She smiled. "Don't worry, your secret's safe with me."

He laughed and turned to go. As he passed her, he bent and whispered in her ear. "I hope Santa brings you everything you want for Christmas." His warm breath on her skin sent a shiver across her shoulder blades and down her back.

She watched him walk away, unable to stop her lips curving as he turned to push open the door and winked at her before letting it shut behind him.

"Yowza." Amy's wide eyes echoed her approval. "I wouldn't be disappointed to find one of those in my stocking."

Coco smiled wryly and accepted the cappuccino from the barista. "I wouldn't let a man like that anywhere near your stockings, Amy dear. He'd devour you in one gulp."

"One can only hope."

They both laughed and headed for the doorway.

"Shame you didn't find out where he worked," Amy said. "He was interested in you."

Coco opened the door and turned up the collar of her raincoat. It wasn't raining, but she was determined to stop the notoriously brisk Wellington wind from sliding its fingers down the neck of her shirt. She glanced up the street—he'd vanished, no doubt heading for one of the financial institutions downtown. She'd probably never see him again.

Squashing the answering ripple of disappointment, she frowned at Amy. "Don't exaggerate. I barely said two words to the man."

"Yes, but one of those words was 'sex'. His eyes lit up like the patient's nose in the game Operation."

She couldn't deny that—his eyes had definitely glimmered with interest. But it didn't make any difference. "That may be, but you know I'm not looking for anyone. Far too much on my mind at the moment."

Amy sent her a remonstrative look as they walked along the pavement. "You've always got too much on your mind. When was the last time you actually went on a date?"

"2010. But that's not the point. It's an important day today. I need to have my wits about me." *And I need to stop thinking about those brown eyes and that quirky smile.*

"True, this is probably the most important day of your life." Amy slurped her coffee. "So far, anyway. I hope you're prepared."

"Thanks. No pressure or anything." Coco's stomach continued to churn the way it had since she'd awoken that morning. Luckily, she had the coffee to settle it. *Thanks, Amy. Way to go to calm me down.*

Her best friend seemed oblivious to her nerves. "Absolutely there's pressure." She fell into step beside Coco as she started walking along Lambton Quay to their place of work. "It's not every day you get to become Queen of the Revolting Peasants at McAllister Dell."

"That's not my actual job title, you know."

"It should be. It suits you."

Coco sent her an amused look and followed it with an involuntary shiver. It was mid-December and they should really be heading toward a sultry New Zealand summer, but in Wellington, the capital city, it felt distinctly like early spring, and the fact that the sun hadn't yet woken up didn't help. The streets were shrouded in twilight, and the wet roads smelled of petrol and damp leaves. "Jeez, it's cold."

"Well, you would insist on getting to work at the crack of dawn instead of rolling in at five to nine like normal people."

"You didn't have to come in with me." Coco stepped carefully around the puddles in her high heels. The last thing she needed today was to slip, fall on her butt, and start the morning off looking like she was auditioning for *Singing in the Rain*.

"Oh, I'm not going to miss out on a chance to see Miss Stark at work. Especially when there's a new shipload of minions arriving today. I enjoy watching her cracking the whip, and I'm not going to get much chance over the next week." Amy was going on holiday the next day to visit her father up in the Bay of Islands.

"You know it freaks me out when you talk about me in the third person like that."

Amy shrugged. "Well, it's like you're two different people. I like Coco, she's warm, funny, and friendly. She's my best friend and I'd do anything for her. Veronica Stark—not so much. I'm glad I work in HR and don't have to deal with her. She scares the crap out of me."

Coco laughed and sipped her coffee. "You make her sound like a right old dragon."

"You know that's your nickname at the firm, right?"

Coco grinned. "Yeah. I kind of like it."

Amy rolled her eyes. "The crew arriving today doesn't know what's going to hit them. How many are coming again?"

"Not sure exactly. Half a dozen legal execs, several lawyers and, of course, Mr. Hotshot Fancy Pants himself."

"I hope you're not going to call him that to his face."

"Only if he annoys me." Which he had already, thought Coco, and he hadn't even set foot in the office yet.

"You should give him at least five minutes before you decide you're not going to like him," Amy scolded.

Coco said nothing. A sweep of uneasiness made her stomach flip again, and she wished she'd gone with her initial instinct and refused breakfast. But her mother had practically forced her to have a slice of toast, saying she needed to keep her strength up on such an important day.

"What's his real name again?" Amy asked.

"Felix Wilkinson. A.k.a. Fancy Pants."

Amy giggled. "What don't you like about him?"

"I've never met him. But he sounds like one of the young, flash, arrogant lawyers that are so annoying."

"Is he single?"

Coco sent her an exasperated look. Amy was desperate to get married, settle down, and have babies. Her job was just a convenient way for her to earn money to buy things to make herself prettier so she could attract a guy and achieve her dream. Coco didn't resent her for that, but a little part of her envied her best friend. What must it be like not to have the responsibilities piled on Coco's sometimes too-narrow shoulders?

She sighed, not wanting to think about the pressures and strains of life outside the office when such an important day loomed. Amy was right. She shouldn't judge Mr. Hotshot until she'd met him. But she couldn't shake the feeling that she was almost certainly going to hate his guts.

Part of it, she was sure, was the age-old competition between the Auckland and Wellington branches of McAllister Dell. The Wellington branch was the oldest and most prestigious, but for some reason Auckland had a tendency to grab the best young lawyers. Felix Wilkinson already had a reputation throughout the company of being a fantastic family lawyer, and it rankled amongst most of the Wellington partners that the Auckland branch had nabbed him. It did make sense that the person chosen to investigate the recent sexual harassment claim against one of the Wellington partners was from a different branch, but still, they could have got someone in from Christchurch or Dunedin, somewhere that didn't have the same rivalry.

But if she was honest with herself, that wasn't the main reason she was angry. The case was dredging up old memories and feelings about the accused partner—Peter Dell—she'd thought long buried. The guilt that had lain at the bottom of her stomach like sand on a riverbed was stirring up inside her, and nausea kept threatening to rise, together with uncharacteristic flutters of nerves.

She had to stomp on that before she walked through the doors. Veronica Stark did not get nervous. Veronica Stark did not have nerves. Or a heart, for that matter. She was a medical marvel. And the sooner she adopted her alter ego's persona, Coco thought as she took another swallow of coffee, the better.

"Poor Coco," Amy said, reaching out to squeeze her arm, obviously realizing Coco couldn't put her resentment into words. "It's a shame you have to deal with Mr. Hotshot on the day you take over the office."

Coco sighed. "Well I have practically been doing the job for three months, so it's no big deal really. It's kind of a relief that Mrs. Ingram's retired. At least I'll get paid for doing the job now."

"Youngest officer manager the firm has ever had," said Amy, shaking her head. "Who'd have thought it? I'm so proud of you."

"Yeah. Me too." Coco smiled.

"Why didn't they make you start on Monday?" Amy wondered.

Coco shrugged. "Something to do with the pay cycle starting on Fridays, plus yesterday was Mrs. Ingram's official last day. I wasn't going to argue—I was just pleased to be asked at all."

It was only another hundred yards or so until they reached the door to McAllister Dell, so she stopped in front of a shop window to check her appearance. There was no need to be nervous, she told herself as she took out her lipstick. This was just another day doing a job she loved. Still, her hand shook a little as she smoothed the lipstick over her lips. She always felt better once the lipstick was on.

Amy tried to coax her curly brown hair back into its clip and frowned as Coco ran a hand along the blonde locks that remained rolled into a tight bun.

"How come you don't have a hair out of place in this wind?" Amy asked resentfully.

"A shedload of hairspray."

"I know for a fact you don't use hairspray. I don't think Veronica's hair dare misbehave."

"Damn straight." Coco pulled her glasses out of her pocket and slid them onto her nose. She only needed them for reading, but she liked the professorial look they afforded her and tended to wear them most of the time in the office. "There. I hope they're ready for Miss Stark, because she's more than ready for them."

"Strength and honor," said Amy, putting her fist on her chest in a grand impersonation of Russell Crowe's Maximus.

"Don't make me laugh. You know Miss Stark doesn't smile."

"Oh yeah. I forgot."

Coco lifted her chin as they walked toward the large glass doors that marked the entrance to McAllister Dell's lobby. *I'm Veronica Stark*, she thought. She ran the office. And she wasn't going to let Peter Dell and Mr. Felix Fancy Pants ruin her special moment. No matter what the day threw at her, she'd take everything in her stride, the same as she usually did.

*

Available at most major retailers.

About The Author

Serenity Woods is a USA Today bestselling author. She lives in the sub-tropical Northland of New Zealand with her wonderful husband and gorgeous teenage son. She writes hot and sultry contemporary romances with a happy ever after, and would much rather immerse herself in reading or writing romance than do the dusting and ironing, which is why it's not a great idea to pop round if you have any allergies.

She is the author of over fifty romance novels. You can check them all out on her website.

Website: http://www.serenitywoodsromance.com
Facebook: http://www.facebook.com/serenitywoodsromance
Twitter: https://twitter.com/Serenity_Woods

Printed in Great Britain
by Amazon

38079928R00169